THE LAST BOTTLE

MARCIA BREECE

Publishing Partners
2025

Library of Congress Number: 2021930029
ISBN (print): 978-1-944887-02-6
ISBN (ebook): 978-1-944887-65-0

Contents

The meaning of life is to find your gift.
The purpose of life is to give it away.
—Pablo Picasso

Books by Marcia Breece

Finding This Place

Secrets Lost

Kala's Choice

Yutka And the Voyage of the Parita

The Last Bottle

Family Tree

Family Tree
Simone Dupré
DOB 1987
Adopted by
Audrey Dupré in 2000
Sergei Sapozhnikov
DOB 1938
Adopted at birth by
David and Adina Sapozhnikov
William Phan Gramtham
DOB 1988
Emily
DOB 2004
2 brothers
DOB 2001, 2003
Tom ?
DOB 1972
Suzie Taylor
DOB 1972
3 brothers
DOB 1973, 1974, 1979
Elliot Hart Jr.
DOB 1973
Chau Phan
DOB 1952
* Robert Grantham
DOB 1952
* Teddy Grantham
DOB 1951
Gertie Grantham
DOB 1950
George Taylor
DOB 1950
Elliot Hart Sr.
DOB 1945
Trudy Wurtzburg
DOB 1950
4 siblings
Mark DOB 1946
Walter DOB 1948
Rebecca DOB 1952
Meredith DOB 1960
Audrey Dupré
DOB December 1922
4 brothers
DOB 1908, 1910,
1911, 1912
Ted Grantham
DOB June 1924
Evelyn Reilly
DOB 1927
6 siblings
DOB 1917, 1920,
1922, 1923, 1925,
1927
Richard Wurtzburg
DOB 1921
Catherine O'Brien
DOB 1922
2 brothers
DOB 1923, 1925
Eiffel Dupré
DOB 1890
Esther Mancini
DOB 1899
Theodore Grantham III
DOB 1898
Alice Stradivari
DOB 1898
? Reilly
DOB 1905
?
DOB 1907
? Wurtzburg
DOB 1895
?
DOB 1895
Innis O'Brien
DOB 1899
Nora Gallagher
DOB 1899
indicates illegitimate
indicates no DNA relatioship
* Gertie's half brothers

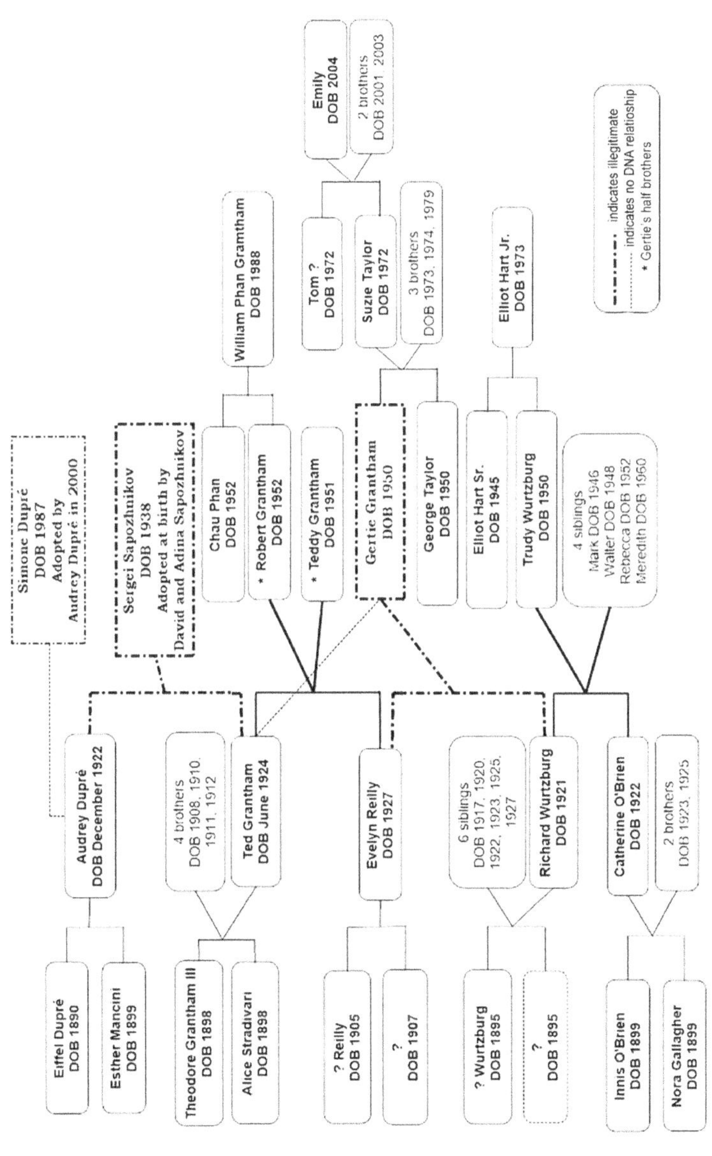

TED GRANTHAM

1938, COLUMBUS, OHIO

Ted stood at attention in the doorway of his father's study, listening to the squeak of the leather chair, the ting of ice in the crystal highball glass and the pounding of his own heart.

"At ease, son," Admiral Theodore Grantham III grumbled with a quick glance away from *The Columbus Dispatch*. "What is it? You look like you're about to face a firing squad."

"Well, sir…" Ted filled his lungs with the familiar scent of leather, whisky and cigarette smoke. He shifted on one foot, then the other, "Well sir…." His long arms and legs, awkward as always, "Ahh… well... um."

The words caught in his throat as he watched the cigarette smoke curl around the six-foot, shovel-shaped antlers of the moose head that seemed to charge through the hunter-green wall, ready to defend its territory. Flanking the formidable moose, a sweet-faced, pointy-horned gazelle and a meek-looking, ten-point white-tail buck gazed through the smoke with glassy, unblinking, eyes. A thousand-pound Blue Marlin hung with its intimidating three-foot sword-like snout pointing toward his heart. Ted's father killed them all long before Ted was born.

Behind the Admiral, shadowbox frames guarded Purple Hearts, Silver Stars, Bronze Stars, an Air Medal and a Medal of Honor, all earned by Grantham family warriors. A Military Badge of Merit from the Revolutionary War. A musket used in the Civil War by Ted's third-great grandfather. A wooden stand on the sofa table cradled a sword and scabbard once carried by his seventh-great grandfather in the Revolutionary War.

Ted and his brothers called this The War Room. They entered only by invitation or summons. Today, Ted came with neither.

The vainglorious display of hunting trophies and war memorabilia reminded Ted he would never live up to his father's expectations. His brothers had made the Admiral proud by excelling in high school sports, then enlisting in the military, but Ted, the youngest by over ten years, preferred singing and playing his violin.

"Spit it out son."

Ted swallowed. "My girlfriend is pregnant."

The Admiral slowly folded the newspaper, placed it on the ottoman and drained the last of his Glenlivet single malt scotch. "You have a girlfriend!?"

"Yes, sir, Audrey, sir."

"That pretty girl you play music with? The French scientist's daughter is your *girlfriend*?"

The Admiral let out a low whistle, took a deep drag from his Lucky Strike and exhaled out the side of his mouth. "Well, I'll be damned." He placed the highball glass on the side table. "How old is the girl?"

"She'll be sixteen in December, sir."

"You mean she'll be sixteen when the baby's born," he said, as he snuffed out his cigarette.

"Yes, sir."

"When do you leave for boot camp?" The Admiral's cold gaze finally locked onto Ted.

"In June, sir, after graduation."

"Well, that gives us time for a civil ceremony." He stood, tucking his shirt into his trousers. "Have you asked the girl to marry you?"

"No, sir. She told me about it yesterday when I walked her home from school. She wasn't in music class today."

"Have you told your mother?"

"No, Sir."

"That's good. Best not to upset her until we work this out." His hands dropped onto Ted's shoulders. "You realize you have to do the right thing here, son."

"Yes, sir," said Ted, trying to keep his voice steady.

The Admiral gave a sharp nod. "Let's go over there. Make this right."

"Yes, sir."

Ted and his father marched toward the Duprés' like a two-man infantry. Their long strides matched, their backs held straight with military precision—obviously father and son, yet miles apart in spirit.

At eighteen, Ted was lanky and long-limbed, with teeth too big for his mouth. Not the dreamboat pretty girls swooned over. His thick brown hair glistened like lacquered wood in the dappled sunlight. Next to him, Admiral Grantham's scalp glinted through his regulation buzz cut, his bearing as crisp as his reputation. With their task at hand, neither noticed the green blush of new maple leaves shading their path, or the scent of peonies, lilac and freshly mowed grass filling the warm spring air.

The Dupré residence was around the corner from Grantham's eight-bedroom brick colonial in Upper Arlington, not far from Ohio State University. Their neighbors were highly educated and successful in diverse fields: actors, sports figures and businessmen.

When they turned onto Hillside Drive, they were surprised to find a Realtor's For Sale sign and a van from Columbus Moving and Storage parked in front of the Duprés' four-bedroom stone colonial.

Across the manicured lawn, brocade chairs, antique tables and stacks of boxes sat stranded in the sunlight like guests left behind after a party. The front door gaped open. Inside, movers weaved through rooms, their voices rising above the shuffle of boxes and the scratch of tape.

A white box truck backed into the driveway with Mid-State Piano Moving and Storage painted on the side. Burly men dressed in dark blue uniforms, rolled up the gate and gathered moving blankets, straps and dollies.

Ted rang the bell. "Could I speak to Mrs. Dupré, please?" asked Ted, he knew Audrey's father was traveling. He stepped aside, allowing the piano movers to pass.

The foreman shook his head. "Ain't nobody home, kid. Family left town."

"Do you have a forwarding address?"

"Sure don't, kid." The moving foreman sponged the sweat from his brow with a red bandana and tucked the stained chambray work shirt stretching over his beer belly. "Missuz Dupré paid us ta pack up the house and put everythin' in storage. Said she'd let me know where ta send some a the books, outta the country somewheres, Paris, I think. Gave me strict orders not ta share that address with anyone."

"Thank you, sir," nodded Ted as he turned toward home.

"Didn't expect to find a moving truck," muttered the Admiral. "Do you think they left just because their daughter's knocked up?"

"I'm not surprised at all," said Ted, ignoring his father's vulgar language. His perfect posture slumped. Ted had known Mrs. Dupré since elementary school and Audrey had talked about her mother enough for Ted to know what probably happened. Mrs. Dupré would choose to leave town rather than face the disgrace of neighbors and colleagues knowing her daughter was in trouble.

They walked in silence for a stretch, the Admiral slowing to keep pace with Ted.

"I should ask you son, are you in love with this girl?"

Ted's shoulders slumped even more. He mumbled, "Yes sir."

"Is she in love with you?"

"Yes, sir. We've been—well—best friends, I guess, since I was nine and she was six." His words faded, "We were going to perform a duet at the Spring Concert tomorrow night."

The Admiral gave a huff of amusement and clapped Ted on the back. "Looks like you dodged a bullet here son. Let that be a lesson. Let's not mention this to your mother."

"Yes, sir," said Ted, trying to sound more self-assured than he felt. He didn't understand the jocularity. Ted's father seemed proud that Ted got away without marrying the pregnant girl. As they turned the corner toward home, Ted kept his face turned away to hide his feelings of sadness and loss, the hollow space where Audrey had been since childhood.

Audrey Dupré

1925, Columbus, Ohio

"**A**udrey, *ma petite chèrie*, you look like a child model on the cover of *The Saturday Evening Post*." In her heavy, French accent, *Mademoiselle* Claudette welcomed Audrey and her mother, "*Joyeux Noël!*"

Three-year-old Audrey's smooth black hair reached her earlobes and heavy bangs played across her forehead in a French bob, all the rage for little girls in 1925. *Mademoiselle* Claudette knelt to Audrey's eye level. "This is a lovely holiday outfit," said *Mademoiselle* Claudette. "What color is your dress?"

"Red and white," said Audrey, touching the wide, white satin collar on her red velvet dress. "And my shoes are black." She lifted her foot to show *Mademoiselle* Claudette her shiny black patent leather Mary Janes.

"I understand you had a birthday last week, how old are you now?"

"I am free," Audrey answered with a baby-tooth grin, holding up three fingers.

Mademoiselle Claudette noticed how effortlessly Audrey held down her little pinkie with her thumb, not a simple task for most three-year-old children. She cupped Audrey's dexterous little hand in her palms, "I'm so happy you could join your maman tonight. What books did you bring to read?"

"Peter Rabbit and Papa's book about stars," said Audrey, her voice delicate but mature for her age as she presented her books to *Mademoiselle* Claudette.

"She insisted on bringing that textbook her father wrote," laughed Audrey's mother, Esther Dupré. "She lugs that heavy old thing everywhere."

About an hour later, *Mademoiselle* Claudette noticed Audrey had left the party. "Where is our little model?"

"She's wandered off," said Esther, putting her second martini on the cocktail table next to Audrey's abandoned books.

"I will check the music room." *Mademoiselle* Claudette, a member of the Ohio State University music department faculty, walked beyond the kitchen toward the studio where her most talented college students came for private instruction. From the hallway, she heard Audrey's little voice singing "Jingle Bells" while someone tapped the tune on the piano. *Mademoiselle* Claudette quietly stepped into the room and was astonished to find Audrey accompanying herself. From the doorway, she listened to the tiny, perfectly tuned voice.

Dashing through the snow
In a one-horse open sleigh
O'er the fields we go
Laughing all the way

Slowly, *Mademoiselle* Claudette slid onto the bench next to Audrey and played a simple one-handed tune, *Ah, vous dirai-je, Maman*. "Can you play this?" asked *Mademoiselle* Claudette.

Audrey listened intently, watching *Mademoiselle* Claudette's fingers, then gently placed her tiny fingers on the keys. She played the notes she'd heard. "*Magnifique!*" said *Mademoiselle* Claudette, hugging Audrey. It was Audrey's first Mozart. Then, as Audrey played, *Mademoiselle* Claudette taught her the words of a poem set to "*Ah, vous dirai-je, Maman*", "Twinkle, Twinkle, Little Star."

When she found them, Esther scolded, "Audrey, you shouldn't be wandering around in *Mademoiselle* Claudette's house by yourself."

"*Non! C'est bon.* Watch this." *Mademoiselle* Claudette repeated the process, using both hands this time. Audrey gently placed her tiny fingers, as if not to wake the keys and again, played the notes perfectly, this time with both hands.

"Remarkable, I had no idea!" murmured Esther. "Do you know where she can begin lessons?"

"I'd recommend Miss Watkins. She teaches at the Lutheran Church and it's close enough for Audrey and her nanny to walk there," said *Mademoiselle* Claudette.

Ten months later, Esther talked to *Mademoiselle* Claudette. "Miss Watkins said Audrey has surpassed her teaching abilities. Do you have any other ideas?"

"Of course, I am not surprised," laughed *Mademoiselle* Claudette. "I'd be happy to teach little Audrey, but she needs a piano at home for daily practice."

Esther hired movers to remove all but the overstuffed chair from the light-filled parlor and bought a Blüthner grand piano for Audrey's fourth birthday.

Mademoiselle Claudette came to their parlor every week to give Audrey instruction. "I am honored to have this remarkable little prodigy as one of my students," gushed *Mademoiselle* Claudette, refusing payment.

Aimée

Audrey's parents, Eiffel and Esther, invited Eiffel's niece, Aimée, to move to Columbus, Ohio and live in the nanny's apartment above their garage. Their nanny had retired at the end of August; it seemed the perfect fit.

Aimée hadn't seen her Uncle Eiffel in many years so when he stepped away from the crowd at the train station, tears pooled in her eyes. Thick black eyebrows shaded her uncle's round tortoiseshell spectacles and a bushy mustache covered his upper lip. Too busy for frequent haircuts, his wild, wire-like black hair with silver threads waved over his ears and collar.

"*Mon Dieu.* You look so much like Papa!" cried Aimée, throwing her arms around her uncle. Aimée spoke French, German and Russian, but not English. They conversed in French.

"When we were children, people often thought your papa and I were twins," smiled Eiffel. "But he was two years younger. I'm so sorry. I'm sure you miss them terribly." He hugged his niece, then whispered, "But we are pleased to have you here with us. *Bienvenue.*"

As she leaned into his hearty hug, Aimée's mind drifted to that terrible night. She heard her mother scream, the screeching tires and the terrifying sound of twisting metal.

Aimée and her parents drove home after a hotelier's convention. During the four-hour trip from Paris to Beaune, light rain wetted the road after a long dry spell. When the Renault ahead of them spun out on the slippery surface, their car broadsided the spinning

vehicle at high speed. Sixteen-year-old Aimée was the only survivor of the crash.

For nearly a year afterward, Aimée lived in the hotel her father had managed in Beaune. The chef and Madame Laliberty, the head housekeeper, looked after her while her broken bones mended and her heart healed.

"Aimée, we'd like you to meet our daughter Audrey. Audrey, this is your cousin, Aimée," said Esther.

"*Bienvenue,*" said Audrey, her tone reeking with reluctance. Audrey made it clear she did not need a new nanny.

Sensing Audrey's hesitancy, Aimée said, "*Bonjour,* Audrey, I remember we met in Paris as children."

Even at thirteen, Audrey was as tall as Aimée. Their doe-eyes, more olive-green than brown, shone with intelligence. They both had long black hair with natural streaks of deep blue and auburn; however, Audrey's, with bangs across her forehead, hung down her back, glossy and straight like her mother's, while Aimée's curls, resembling her uncle's, escaped her chignon like twisted willow branches. Except for the texture of their hair, they looked more like sisters than most sisters.

As Aimée, Audrey and Esther entered the apartment above the garage, Aimée said, "The apartment is lovely. *Merci,*" as she traced the wood grain in the little dining table.

"We're happy to have you, Aimée. Now, I'll leave the two of you to get to know each other," said Esther, closing the apartment door behind her.

Audrey sat with her elbow on the table, supporting her chin in her palm as she gazed out the window at a robin perched in the red maple tree. Her expression and body language communicated clearly; she was reluctant to accept Aimée into her life.

"Audrey? Will you help me unpack? I brought special food from France."

Aimée had packed ingredients she might not find in Columbus, Ohio: jars of pâté, Niçoise olives, capers and Dijon mustard, tins of anchovies, *Fleur de sel* and dried herbs from Provence, rosemary, thyme, oregano, lavender and tarragon, as well as packages of Tarbais dry beans and two carefully wrapped bottles of Burgundy, one red, one white. The trunk also held an assortment of wire whisks and a heavy waxed canvas pouch containing professional chefs' knives, each wood-handled knife nestled into its own special slot.

When Aimée swung open her steamer trunk, Audrey closed her eyes as if memories filled the room along with the scent of Paris. Every summer when school was out, Audrey and her mother made the voyage to Paris to be with her father and they often walked through the market on Rue Cler, so different from the Big Bear grocery store in Columbus. She remembered the colors and sweet scent of peonies, snapdragons, lilies and of course roses in every color imaginable. The scent of cinnamon and butter wafted from the bakery. Tomatoes, onions, broccoli and peppers in every color, were stacked next to apples and peaches in the produce stalls. She remembered the taste of sweet strawberries when she sat between her parents on a park bench.

Aimée's voice jolted Audrey back to Columbus, Ohio.

"Will Aunt Esther mind my tools in her kitchen? I am happy to be cooking for you and your maman and Uncle when he is here."

"Sure. Maman will love having you in the kitchen. She doesn't cook and neither do I," said Audrey, inspecting a jar. "Why did you bring olives? You can buy a can at the grocery store."

"These are special Niçoise olives. They have a nutty—ah, what you say—*au goût amer*—bitter flavor? I doubt they are sold here. Maybe tomorrow I make *salade niçoise* for our lunch."

"And bowls? We have lots of mixing bowls."

"Yes, but do you have copper bowls?"

"No, ours are glass."

"Copper bowls are best to create some recipes. One day I show you, yes?"

Audrey realized she and Aimée needed each other. Aimée had lost her family in a terrible accident and, although Audrey no longer needed a nanny, she was far less lonely after Aimée arrived.

On a cool autumn afternoon, Audrey took Aimée on a walking tour of the community. Helping Aimée learn English, she named everything along the way: grass, tree, leaf, car, street. When Audrey introduced her cousin to the butcher's son, Roger, he gushed, "Miss Dupré, I didn't know you had such a lovely sister."

"Aimée is my cousin. She just arrived from Paris."

He cut a thin slice of honeyed ham, put in on white paper and passed it to Aimée. "Welcome Miss Aimée," he said with sparkling eyes and a crooked grin.

Back on the sidewalk, Audrey whispered in French, "He likes you!"

Aimée blushed. The butcher's son was rather homely, with too thin, too sharp features, but the sparkle in his big dark eyes had captured Aimée's attention.

That summer, Aimée threw herself into cooking and learning English while Audrey practiced classical piano and voice. Aimée felt more at home in the kitchen than any other place. Before her parents died, their family lived in the walled city of Beaune, in the Burgundy region, southeast of Paris. Her mother had worked at a vineyard for Côte d'Or, while her father had managed a boutique hotel. The kitchen staff taught Aimée to cook. She stood on a wooden milk crate, learning to whip soufflés and sauté vegetables to crispy perfection, becoming a skilled chef even before her tenth birthday. Cooking fragrances, whether frying onions, baking bread, or roasting meat, reminded her of happy times with her parents and the hotel staff she loved.

During her first month in Ohio, Aimée prepared standard French recipes: *poule au pot, coq au vin, soupe à l'oignon a*nd *salade niçoise. Salade niçoise* quickly became Audrey's favorite for lunch or dinner. She loved the rich, nutty flavor of the little black olives Aimée brought from France.

"*Laissez-moi vous montrer comment fouetter un soufflé,*" suggested Aimée.

"I'll learn to make a soufflé if you ask me in English."

"Me teach you soufflé, yes?" Aimée ventured.

Aimée realized Audrey had little interest in learning to prepare her recipes. Audrey would rather play the piano than eat, however, Aimée convinced Audrey to try.

They spent an afternoon laughing as Audrey tried to whip egg whites in spite of herself. First, she faced the challenge of separating the yolk from the white, destroying almost a dozen eggs while trying to collect six egg whites in a deep copper bowl. "When you whip egg whites in a copper bowl, the whites are glossy, firm and not over-whipped. This is why I bring copper bowls from France."

Aimée and Audrey both giggled as Audrey thrashed with the big wire whisk. Frothy egg whites splattered across the counter and what remained in the bright copper bowl never reached the desired stiff peaks. "*Pas de soucis,*" shrugged Aimée. "We 'ave omelet for dinner. Extra eggs I use for cookies."

While Audrey went back to her piano, Aimée made a batch of chocolate chunk cookies from a recipe she had created herself by adding eggs, brown sugar, leavening and a chopped bitter-sweet chocolate bar to a shortbread cookie recipe.

Spring Concert

1938, Columbus, Ohio

Ted and Audrey's music teacher had selected Rodgers and Hart tunes from the Broadway musical, *The Boys from Syracuse*. It was adapted from one of Shakespeare's early plays, *A Comedy of Errors*. "I want you to sing and play a duet at this year's Spring Concert." She handed them the sheet music for "Falling in Love with Love." The audience will think they're listening to Jeanette MacDonald and Nelson Eddy," gushed their music teacher, clasping her hands over her heart.

Ted walked Audrey home after school on that unusually warm March day. They intended to practice. He carried his violin in one hand and her books in the other. Sunlight shone through the bare maple branches along the sidewalk, dappling her pale complexion as a breeze tossed her dark ponytail and mussed the bangs across her forehead. She was tall, naturally fit and matched his stride with ease.

In the kitchen, sunlight sparkled through the window, giving her raven-black hair an auburn halo. Ted tucked a loose strand behind Audrey's ear as she opened two bottles of Coca-Cola.

As they leaned on the counter enjoying the sandwiches and chocolate chunk cookies Aimée had left for them, Audrey asked Ted, "Do you think we'll go to war? In the newspaper, I read dreadful stories about Hitler."

"I'll be a Navy aviator either way," he said, stretching even taller, lifting his chin slightly. "I'll leave for boot camp after graduation, but I won't get my orders until June, after I turn eighteen."

Walking into the parlor, Audrey turned to look at Ted, "I'll miss you," she said. "High school will be a drag without you in music class."

"I'll write as often as I can," he promised as he lifted his violin out of its worn leather case.

Instead of taking her place at the piano, ready to practice, Audrey sat on the big leather chair, "Will you play Mendelssohn for me?"

He looked into her dark eyes. "Of course," he grinned. Positioning the violin on his shoulder, he closed his eyes and began the rapid string crossings. Audrey swung her legs over the arm of the chair and threw her head back. Her ponytail slid down the side of the chair as she let the cadenza carry her away. From the haunting opening to the stormy coda, tears filled her eyes. The music felt like a special gift from Ted, a view into his soul.

"That was even more beautiful than usual. I can hardly breathe," she said with her hand on her chest. "Your talent is stunning." She smiled up at him from the comfortable chair.

Ted put the violin on the piano bench, then bent to kiss her. He burrowed next to her in the overstuffed chair and pulled her onto his lap. As they kissed, he unhooked her bra and put his hand up her skirt. When he started to unbutton his trousers, she pulled away, "Ah… we should practice," she said as she jumped to her feet, reached under her sweater to hook her bra. She handed him his violin and opened the piano bench to find the sheet music for "Falling in Love with Love."

A few days later, they enjoyed the usual after school treats Aimée had left for them, but instead of practicing for the spring concert Ted followed the scent of Audrey's hair into the parlor, leaving his precious violin on the kitchen counter next to her books.

Remembering the taste of her kisses and the shape of her breast in the palm of his hand, hormone-soaked Ted watched Audrey sit down at the gleaming grand piano and slowly lift the fallboard. "You and the piano are my only friends, really," she said, more to the keyboard than Ted.

He sat on the bench beside her, feeling the warmth of her thigh pressing against his. She limbered her fingers with a few bars from popular songs, then softly sang the lyrics:

They say it's wonderful,
To hold a girl in your arms is wonderful, wonderful,
In every way,
So they say...

As she sang, Ted leaned in, his lips brushed her ear. His whisper came out deep and slightly hoarse. "When will your mom be home?"

"Not until late. Maman's been having dinner and playing bridge with her friends every Friday since Papa left for Paris." She giggled and looked at Ted with an impish sparkle in her dark eyes. Then, slowly, she reached under her pink angora sweater-set and unhooked her bra.

Still sitting on the piano bench, a soft groan escaped his throat. Reaching beneath her soft sweater, cupping her bare breast, his lips found hers with an urgency that made them both tremble.

She tugged at his belt and slowly unbuttoned his trousers.

"What about Aimée?" he whispered, barely audible.

"Aimée's on a date with the fella from the butcher shop," she breathed. "Let's go to my room."

Leaning one hand on the white and gilded French provincial nightstand with curly drawer-pulls, Audrey tugged back the chenille bedspread that matched the pale mauve walls and floral border near the high ceiling. She dropped her skirt, pink angora sweater-set, bra and panties on the mauve carpet, then crawled between the white Turkish cotton sheets. She unclipped her barrette and let her long black hair fall like a raven's wing across the white pillow.

His breath shallow and ragged, Ted walked between the four-poster bed draped with white organza canopy and the five-foot stuffed giraffe Audrey's father brought from Africa. It stood next to the Jenny Lynd bassinet she had occupied as a newborn, now filled with well-dressed baby-dolls that never held her interest.

Ted carefully draped his shirt, trousers and underwear over the handlebars of the velocipede rocking horse Audrey's father once played with, then slid between the sheets, barely able to breath. They kissed as he ran his fingers through her silky hair. "I love your hair like this," he murmured as one hand slid around her waist and the other drew her face to his.

"Mmm, I love your kisses," she purred, nestling into him.

With his wavy, brown hair falling into his face, he hugged her tight as he rolled her onto her back.

Their kisses deepened—at first slow and uncertain, then a quiet urgency built between them, like Vivaldi's Four Seasons rising to a crescendo. Ted's hands trembled, not from fear, but from awe.

Their bodies moved with shy reverence, but there was something ageless, like the music they played from their hearts, transporting them to a deeply enchanted realm.

Their first union was tender yet passionate, a revelation to them both. It was as if the longing they'd shared in silence had finally found its private composition.

Afterward, as he held her in his arms, her head on his shoulder, he whispered, "I've loved you since the day we met in elementary school."

"I fell in love with you the first time I heard you play your violin. The look on your face, as if you had gone to another realm, took my breath. I knew we would go to that place together for the rest of our lives… You were nine and I was six."

He rolled onto his back and they made love again, this time with Audrey on top. The evening sun through the sheer curtains of the second-story window turned her skin golden. As he moved, he watched her close her eyes and toss her head back, her long black hair falling around her shoulders.

Finally, as their breathing returned to normal, they nearly fell asleep. Pushing the hair away from her face, Audrey sat up and pulled the sheet around her, "I suppose we should practice before Maman gets home. It would not be good for her to find you asleep in my bed," she laughed.

"Hmm hum," Ted murmured, his face in the down pillow.

"Where did you learn to make a bed like that?" asked Audrey as Ted tucked military corners, using the clean sheets he found in the linen closet.

"My dad's Navy and believes men should know how to take care of themselves. I've helped the housekeeper with laundry since junior high and I'm learning to cook too. Last night, Mom had her women's club, so I made spaghetti and meatballs for Dad and me."

"That's... actually very impressive," she said as she watched him tuck sharp corners. "You're going to make *someone* very lucky one day."

"I thought I already did," he grinned, his eyes sparkling.

She laughed softly, "You did. You do."

They kissed, then he continued making the bed.

"Aimée tried to teach me how to make a soufflé, but I failed miserably. We ended up with scrambled eggs for dinner and she made cookies with the rest."

"A spaghetti dinner isn't difficult. I boiled water in a big pot to cook the pasta, rolled ground beef into balls and opened a jar of tomato sauce the housekeeper canned last fall," said Ted. Then he asked Audrey, "Where should I put the soiled sheets? You don't want your mom finding them."

"Just put them in the canvas bag in the closet. Maman sends the laundry out every week." Her chest tightened with affection as he stuffed the sheets into the canvas laundry bag and put it back into the closet. He was not just a boy being helpful, he treated her space with respect, just as he treated her heart with reverence.

As they returned to the kitchen, she snickered, "I can't make soufflé, but I do know how to open a Coke." She rolled her eyes with a light musical laugh that drew Ted close for another kiss.

"Good thing you're beautiful."

Combing her hair with his fingers, he whispered, "Your hair is so sexy, you should wear it down more often." He lifted her black mane and kissed her neck. She twisted toward him. "Kiss me again."

He did. Long and slow.

Finally, she turned toward the parlor. "We really should practice."

When Audrey's mother came home, they were at the piano, practicing for the concert. Audrey played and sang while Ted played his violin, watching her lips move with each note.

Falling in Love with Love. Her mother didn't notice the twinkle in Audrey's eyes. They shared a secret, glowing between them like candlelight.

> *I weave with brightly colored strings*
> *To keep my mind off other things*
> *So, ladies, let your fingers dance*
> *And keep your hands out of romance*

Aimée's Cassoulet

Columbus, Ohio, 1938

Unaware of the impending upheaval, Aimée spent the week gathering and preparing ingredients for cassoulet, a favorite that reminded her of home. The butcher hand crafted special sausage just for her cassoulet and she had promised to bring generous helpings to him and his sons in return, an exchange of kindness that made her feel rooted, at home.

The bouquet of assorted meats, onions, garlic, thyme, bay and parsley wrapped around her like a warm, familiar quilt. She was sure the aroma would draw Esther straight to the kitchen the moment she came through the door.

Aimée was setting the table in the dining room when she heard Esther arrive, but the aroma didn't draw her to the kitchen. Aimée strained to hear Esther and Audrey talking in the foyer. She couldn't distinguish their words, but their conversation sounded tangled and urgent. One at a time, she heard them climb the stairs. First, the door to Audrey's room slammed shut, then the library door banged like a judge's mallet.

An hour later, when everything was ready, Aimée knocked on the library door, "Aunt Esther, dinner is ready."

From inside, Esther's voice sliced through the heavy door, "Audrey and I will not be eating dinner tonight."

Aimée gripped the door frame and pressed her forehead to the door. It was the end of spring quarter for Aunt Esther. Aimée thought tonight would be a celebration.

Leaning on the door, she remembered the fuss her maman and papa had made over the first cassoulet she created. Putting her hands over her face, she shook her head and pushed emotional pain back into the dark corner of her heart. Then, taking a deep breath, she slowly returned to the dining room.

Sunlight crashed through the high, stained glass transom window, the glare fracturing off the chandelier above the table, casting bright star-like shards around the room. The open bottle of wine caught the light and threw a red glow across the steaming cassoulet Aimée had spent the whole week preparing.

She served herself, gathering chunks of duck, pork and the specially made sausage, along with beans and vegetables. Slowly, she poured a glass of Pinot Noir and drifted to the kitchen to eat her banquet for one.

After savoring a small second helping, more out of resolve than hunger, she put the unused dishes back into the cupboard, transferred the remaining cassoulet into an oven-proof container, pulled a shower-cap-like elastic cover over the top and put it in the refrigerator.

As she washed her dishes, she felt disappointed, but she had learned, in this household, plans could change. She knew the cassoulet would be even better the next day.

Then she heard Audrey scoot the piano bench over the wood floor in the parlor next to the kitchen. The pounding surf of Rachmaninoff filled the kitchen. Aimée had never heard Audrey play with such force. The music rose like a storm gathering over water. She stepped toward the parlor, then stopped mid-stride as the music slowed to soft rain drops, seemingly becalmed, like a sailboat adrift, then it rose again, as if the music struggled to find its own words.

She knew whatever was happening in the household would be revealed in due course. With leftovers in the refrigerator and dishes washed and put away, she tiptoed toward her small apartment above the garage, trying not to distract Audrey.

THE ANNOUNCEMENT

Esther found Audrey waiting on the stairs when she came home. "I just turned in my students' final grades," Esther said. "Spring quarter is over; it's officially summer."

Before Esther had time to put down her satchel, Audrey blurted, "I need to tell you something…, I'm pregnant."

Esther stared at her daughter, stunned. "…How can you be sure?"

"I went to a lab at Ohio State for a pregnancy test."

"Why the OSU lab of all places?" Esther snapped.

"I remembered an article in your OSU Newsletter asking for volunteers who thought they might be pregnant."

"My God, did you give them your name?"

"Of course not mother! I used a false name and lied about my age."

"Maybe the test was wrong."

"Today, I went for a follow-up visit. They said the rabbit died. I'm due in December." She handed Esther the report.

The hand gripping Esther's satchel finally unclenched. The satchel slid from her fingers and thudded to the floor, unnoticed. With her face still bent toward the report, she murmured, "Go to your room, we'll discuss this later."

Audrey's door banged shut.

Esther climbed the stairs, tugging on the banister, her legs heavy. She stepped into the library and slammed the door behind her. Melancholy seemed to fill the stuffy room, as if it had held its breath since Eiffel left for Paris. She threw open the heavy draperies, allowing a flood of golden light to pour across Eiffel's mahogany desk. The desk chair's long shadow stretched across the Persian carpet, the same carpet that had covered the floor in her parents' library when she was a girl, the reds brilliant in the sunshine.

Her fingers danced over the vast collection of books covering every wall, nearly to the ceiling, including leather-bound first editions that once belonged to Esther's grandparents. Esther sat on a rung of the rail ladder. She blankly stared at a white alabaster lamp and black telephone on her husband's seldom-used desk.

Finally, she reached for the receiver and placed a call to him in Paris. While she waited for an international connection, her shadow moved back and forth over the bright carpet. Her mind raced, hardening into a plan. When Eiffel came on the line, she blurted, "Audrey's in trouble." Her voice cracked with anger as she forced back tears.

"I assume the father is the boy who plays the violin. They've been friends since elementary school, haven't they?" he asked, his comforting voice fractured by static on the telephone line.

"Does it matter?" She sank into his leather desk chair. "She's only fifteen; they're both too young to be parents or to get married."

He asked, "What's your plan?"

"I'm thinking, we'll leave town before anyone finds out. Today was the last day of spring quarter. I handed in final grades. I'll give the department my notice, sell the house and leave Columbus. I'll call an attorney I know of in Manhattan who can arrange an adoption. We'll stay at the Plaza Hotel until the birth. Afterward, we'll join you in Paris." Her words poured out, stiff and sharp.

"Don't you think you're taking drastic measures? You could send Audrey to live with me here in Paris until she delivers. I'm not traveling as much and I'm sure the housekeeper would love having her here."

"No, that's too obvious. Everyone here would suspect what happened and tenants in your building would know. And what would you do with the newborn? No, my plan is better."

"Are you certain you want to give up your professorship?"

She was silent for a long time, then in a faint voice she answered, "I have no choice."

"In that case, here is what I suggest. Go to New York for the birth, then we'll reevaluate coming to Paris based on the political climate. Send my professional books here and put the rest of our books and household goods in storage. Make arrangements for Merchants Bank to pay the storage facility and leave all of our important documents in the safe deposit box. Make sure both you and Audrey have the power to access the accounts and the safe deposit box. In the meantime, we'll see if the war escalates. I took a long walk yesterday and found the cafés busy and people shopping. Most Parisians I talk with say we have nothing to worry about. I hope they're right."

At the end of the call, Esther sat frozen in the desk chair, staring but not seeing the long shadows beyond the window. When Aimée knocked to say dinner was ready, Esther snapped, "Audrey and I will not be eating dinner tonight."

For over an hour, as the sunset turned a deep, bruised crimson, Esther fought her emotions, especially anger at the teenaged boy, who, no doubt, caused this debacle. He seemed so refined. So innocent. Her eyes stung, but she refused to cry.

Esther entered Audrey's room without knocking. "I discussed the situation with your father and we agree; I'm putting the house on the market and we'll leave for New York before daybreak Saturday morning. You will not leave the house until then. I have no intention of allowing your prodigious talent to be stifled by this unfortunate turn of events."

Leaving Audrey's room before Audrey could respond, Esther crossed the hall to her bedroom. Pulling her luggage from a closet, she began packing what she would need in New York. She filled a steamer trunk with winter clothes to ship to the Plaza Hotel; there would be no room in the car. She went back to the library to mark books for packing and storage and gathered a few volumes she couldn't bear to be without.

The next morning, Esther entered the kitchen and announced, in a tone suggesting this sort of thing happened often, "I am selling this house."

Aimée opened her mouth to ask questions, but Esther quickly continued.

"We will leave for New York before dawn on Saturday morning. You'll have room only for two small suitcases in the car. I plan to drive to Harrisburg Saturday night, then arrive in New York in time for you to board the *SS Normandy* leaving for France on Sunday evening. Your Uncle Eiffel will meet you in Le Havre and accompany you by train to our flat in Paris."

Esther's voice was hoarse but unwavering. "Please pack food for our road trip. I plan to stop only for gas."

Aimée handed Esther a cup of black coffee, as she did every morning. Esther faintly whispered, "Thank you," then left the kitchen without another word.

Aimée had no time to consider alternatives. She had no other family and nowhere else to go. From an immigration perspective, she was employed as Duprés' *au pair*. If they didn't need her, her work visa would be invalid. She was tied to Audrey's family like the apron strings around her waist.

While Audrey and her mother went to the bank, Aimée packed two small suitcases with her personal things for the crossing. Then she packed her steamer trunk, making several trips to the kitchen, collecting the treasured utensils she had brought from France less than three years before, including the heavy brick-colored *cassole*, her copper bowls, wire whisks and the pouch of knives Chef had given her when she left France.

In the kitchen, she readied two picnic baskets with paper plates, wooden cutlery and napkins, leaving room for leftover cassoulet, fruit, cheese and a tin of her special chocolate chunk cookies. She put three mason jars of water in the freezer that she planned to use to keep the food chilled. Two thermos bottles were ready to fill, one with black coffee for Esther, one with coffee and cream for herself and Audrey.

Audrey struggled with her conflicting emotions. She knew Ted would leave for boot camp in a few days. No matter what, she wouldn't see him for a long time, especially if Hitler's war escalated. She didn't want to become a mother or get married at fifteen. But since she was six years old and he was nine, she had assumed they would be together always, playing their music for the rest of their lives.

She thought her mother was being impetuous but wouldn't dare say so. Leaving Columbus so suddenly was unnecessary, but Audrey knew, once her mother made a decision, it was final.

She unclipped the barrette holding her ponytail, sat on her bed under the white organza canopy and brushed her long black hair. Besides Ted, she had only one friend she could turn to when her world frayed around the edges, her Blüthner grand piano.

She tiptoed past her mother's bedroom door, down the stairs and to the parlor. She began to play Rachmaninoff's Concerto No. 2—gently at first, then with a passion that grew heavier and wilder, as if the Russian chords could wring clarity from chaos.

Her long hair whipped around her face like window curtains in a storm.

I've been a good girl all my life… always focused on my music… I never drank… never smoked… never stayed out late… I try to be kind to people I meet. Now I've ruined my life… my mother's life… and… probably Aimée's.

During the night, Audrey crept into her father's library. She silently closed the door and turned on the alabaster lamp, while breathing the scent of old books and pipe tobacco. She huddled on the floor in a dim corner, her knees pulled to her chest, her back pressing against her father's books as if to be close to him.

Her mother had announced, without discussion, they were moving to New York and then to Paris… *afterward*. She would have no opportunity to say goodbye to Ted or her beloved piano teacher, *Mademoiselle* Claudette.

Esther had already taped notes to the shelves in the library, indicating which volumes to ship to Audrey's father in Paris and which to put in storage.

Audrey unfolded from the floor and circled the room, her fingers slipping from book to book like a stick on a picket fence, careful not to disturb the notes left by her mother. Although she thought of this room as her father's library, she realized many of the books were her mother's, mostly in French, some quite old.

She found the low shelf of children's books her mother had marked for storage, the ones her nanny had read to her. Audrey sat on the floor and pulled the books into her lap like old friends, including two by Beatrix Potter, one with the glassine dust jacket still perfect, the other, *The Tale of Peter Rabbit*, more worn. She opened *Peter Rabbit* and discovered the author had signed it, *For Esther, Merry Christmas, December 1902*. She'd never noticed it had been her mother's childhood book. Audrey smiled, remembering the voices her nanny had given the characters. The soft, sweet murmur of Peter rabbit's mother and gruff Mr. McGregor. She returned the books to the shelf, then pulled *The Tale of Peter Rabbit* back into her lap. Audrey felt compelled to take it with her to New York, but on that dark, lonely night, she didn't know why.

As if browsing a bookshop, Audrey spent more than an hour collecting books she wanted to read, including her father's well-worn textbook, *Les Étoiles;* she had carried the book everywhere when she was little but never read it. She added a tattered copy of *The Adventures of Tom Sawyer* by Mark Twain Papa had read as a boy. She leafed through a like-new volume of poetry, with tissue-thin gilt-edged pages filled with poems lamenting broken love affairs. She returned it to the shelf marked storage. *Lyrics of Life* by Florence Earle Coates and *Voices of the Night* by Henry Wadsworth Longfellow, joined her collection on the desk.

Early Saturday, in dark, predawn hours, Audrey loaded her heavy bags, filled with sheet music, books and very little clothing, into the car. As the Packard backed out of the driveway, Audrey's mother whispered to Aimée, "We're leaving Columbus because Audrey's in trouble. We'll join you in Paris… *afterward.*"

In the spacious back seat, as far from her mother's gaze as she could manage, Audrey considered her situation. She loved playing music with Ted but, even as a toddler, she felt more at home when her family spent the month of August and weeks at Christmas time in her father's flat in Paris.

During the chaos of their abrupt departure, she hadn't yet grasped the full weight of what was happening—she was going to have a baby. Instead, she felt as if she had contracted a despicable disease.

Avoiding any further thought, Audrey curled up with her pillows to read the copy of *The Tenant of Wildfell Hall* she'd borrowed from her parents' library. The protagonist in the story was a widowed mother who made an income selling her art. This scandalous behavior created curiosity and gossip among her neighbors. Audrey turned to the copyright page. The book was first published in 1848.

She thought, *Social norms haven't changed much in the ninety years since Anne Brontë wrote this. Women are still expected to marry, have children and depend on their husbands for support. It's appalling.*

Audrey thought her mother was overly concerned about their family's social reputation, but she also knew her mother was the exception to the norm when it came to motherhood: a mother with a career. Esther had been one of only a few female professors. She used her maiden name—Professor Mancini—the only female professor at the university with a husband and child, although the faculty and staff were unaware of her married status.

Audrey admired her mother's independence and unconventionality, but she made a quiet promise as she snuggled into her back seat nest, *I will never marry or raise children.*

Esther Dupré

1938 Road Trip

Esther Dupré kept the Packard just over the speed limit as they passed endless flat fields of ankle-high corn and dark, rich soil lined with small soybean plants.

To anyone passing by, Esther looked completely calm and composed, yet she gripped the steering wheel with such intensity that her knuckles blanched. Her fingers were numb. Trying not to think about her daughter becoming a mother, she let her mind drift to her own childhood.

1902

Three-year-old Esther crawled into the lap of the governess who supervised Esther's education and taught her the French language. She read The Tale of Peter Rabbit, *in English, then in French for the third time. Mr. McGregor's voice held the same grouchy baritone in both languages. Esther clapped, "Again, encore."*

"Sorry little one, that's the last time for today. Your maman and papa will be home soon. You must go inside now and dress for dinner."

Nanny gave Esther a bath in a big brass tub and dried her with a stiff, line-dried towel infused with sunshine and lavender. She pulled a pale-yellow dress with a wide collar and lots of lace over Esther's head then Esther sat on a little stool by the fireplace in her room while Nanny combed her thick black hair, longer and thicker than most three-year-old's hair. When it had dried sufficiently, Nanny made two long braids and tied them together at the end with a big white bow like angel wings on Esther's back.

Esther followed Nanny into the large dining room where her father sat at the head of the table with a guest, Mr. Potter, seated to his right. At the other end of the long mahogany table, her mother sat with Mrs. Potter to her right.

While Nanny waited by the kitchen door, Esther passed five empty chairs next to the long table covered with a hand embroidered linen tablecloth. "Hello little darling," her father leaned over so Esther could kiss his stubbly cheek. "Mr. Potter, this is our daughter, Esther."

Esther curtsied and said in her tiny but strong voice, "Nice to meet you Mr. Potter."

"She's lovely," said Mr. Potter, looking at Esther's father, as if Esther were a doll rather than a living, breathing child.

"Come here darling, I want you to say hello to Mrs. Potter," said Esther's mother.

Esther walked to the other end of the table and curtsied again. "Hello Esther," said Mrs. Potter. "I understand you're learning to read."

"Yes ma'am," said Esther.

"That's wonderful… Are you having dinner with us?"

"When she is older," Esther's mother interrupted. "Now Esther, give me a kiss and go have your dinner."

After Esther curtsied again, Nanny took her hand and lead her out of the lavishly appointed dining room. With a large apron covering her beautiful lacy dress, Esther ate her dinner in the kitchen with the servants. After dinner, Nanny helped her out of the fancy dress and pulled a cotton nightgown over her head. "Now climb up here and I'll tuck you in," said Nanny.

Esther fell asleep listening to her mother play the piano for their guests, like a lullaby drifting through the floorboards.

Bringing her mind back to the trip, Esther realized she was hungry and she needed to fill the gas tank. She stopped the Packard at a Sohio service station near the Pennsylvania border. While the attendant filled the tank, Audrey and Aimée opened their doors.

Esther said, "Be quick. We'll stop for lunch in just a few minutes."

As she paid for the gas, Esther asked the attendant, "Is there a place nearby where we could have a quick picnic?"

He directed them to a city park on the next block. She took a break from driving long enough to use the facilities and eat the lunch Aimée had packed. Soon they were back on the road.

That night, they stayed in a small hotel in Harrisburg, Pennsylvania and set out on their journey early Sunday morning. Esther soon realized she clutched the wheel as if it might escape her grip. Aware of her wedding ring digging into her skin, she thought about her husband, Eiffel. He was a master at helping her let go of tension.

She exhaled deeply, took a deep breath, released her firm grip and let her shoulders fall. She remembered the day they met.

1919

As the world recovered from WWI and the influenza cataclysm, Esther returned to her university studies in French literature, working toward her Ph.D.

On her first day as a French instructor, she hurried past bright orange oak trees flanking the Ohio State University Oval. She stopped for a moment by a small lake to catch her breath and calm her jitters. Sitting on a cold stone bench by the spring fed pond, hugging her stack of books, she inhaled the musky-sweet fall scent and watched the brilliant yellow ginkgo and deep red maple leaves reflecting in the glass-like surface. When a slight breeze scrambled the perfect likeness, mixing yellow and red ripples, she took a deep breath of cool air and continued to the lecture hall.

After hanging her brown wool coat on a hook and gathering all the power she could muster, twenty-year-old Esther stepped to the front of the amphitheater classroom with her chin high and her back erect. Her deep blue dress reached mid-calf, the straight, up and down style with its low, loose hanging belt did little to camouflage her hourglass figure. Her thick raven-black French braid fell over her shoulder as she put her books on the big oak table in front of thirty-some students, mostly freshman, mostly male.

"Bonjour à toute la classe," she said in strong,

confident tones and a wide, friendly smile.

From the top row, a deep voice answered loudly, "Bone jar," then snickered.

A female voice answered, "доброе утро класс." Another answered, "Good morning." The rest of the students stared like cattle in a pasture.

In English, Esther reviewed administrative matters, then began her well-organized lesson plan, thinking, This might be even more difficult than I imagined.

After class, her faculty advisor entered as the students filed out, "How was your first day?" he asked with a grin.

"The class went well, but I have my work cut out for me."

"I suspected as much. Actually, I stopped by because there's a reception for a visiting French astrophysics professor in the faculty dining hall at 4:00. I'd like you to attend. We need at least one French speaking faculty member."

"I was planning to spend the afternoon modifying my lesson plans. This class isn't exactly what I expected."

"The reception is only an hour or two. I'm sure you'll have time to prepare for tomorrow. I'll see you there."

At the reception, the intense guest scientist, Eiffel Dupré, gravitated toward Esther even before he knew she spoke French. He monopolized her time, happy to find someone in Columbus, Ohio, who spoke fluent French. Eiffel Dupré had earned a Ph.D. in both astrophysics and mathematics. He traveled the world studying the birth, life and death of stars, planets, galaxies and nebulae. He'd published a book Les Étoiles *based on his Ph.D. dissertation about spectroscopic binary stars. His enthusiasm made the unusual field of study sound exotic and exciting. Eiffel Dupré, like many brilliant professors, was charming and equally awkward and shy and yet his dry sense of humor made Esther laugh. She admired his intelligence and he made it clear, "I travel far too much to have a family."*

"I never want to marry either," offered Esther. "I'm focused on literature. Marriage and children would mean death to my studies."

Intellectual equals, Esther and Eiffel studied

together in the library. She often encouraged him to stop long enough to grab a bite to eat. As they spent more time together, he convinced her they could have an unconventional marriage. He would keep his professorship at Sorbonne Universite in Paris and continue to travel a great deal to study the cosmos, with extended trips to Africa and South America. She would teach and write and continue her work toward a Ph.D. and professorship. They would travel together when her schedule allowed.

At their wedding, while a pianist played "Clair de Lune," they gave each other wide gold bands, each engraved with their names and wedding date, Esther and Eiffel Dupré, June 26, 1920. They agreed they would never have children. Esther continued to use her maiden name, Mancini. They kept their marriage secret to protect her position at the university.

Eiffel kept his flat in Paris and she bought a cottage just off High Street near the Ohio State campus.

In spring of 1922, when she realized she was with child, Eiffel had just left for South Africa to establish an observatory. Although it was not obvious, she was four months along when he returned. They bought a house in Upper Arlington, near campus, with nanny's lodging above the garage. She sold her bungalow. Rarely leaving the house during her pregnancy, Esther took a sabbatical for fall quarter, ostensibly to work on her dissertation. She gave birth in December and resumed teaching at the start of winter quarter, January 1923. She earned her Ph.D. in the spring when her baby, Audrey, was six months old.

Esther pulled the Packard to the curb in front of the Plaza Hotel without turning off the motor. Audrey and Aimée stepped onto the curb.

"Audrey, I registered us under my maiden name," said Esther as she leaned over the seat. "Go up to our room and get settled while I take Aimée to the boat dock."

Aimée and Audrey hugged until Esther tooted the horn.

"I will write," said Aimée.

"Me too, see you at Christmas time…" Audrey's voice faded to a whisper.

"Have luck with the…, you know," whispered Aimée, squeezing Audrey's hand as she slid onto the bench seat and the doorman closed the car door.

Audrey stood on the sidewalk until the dusty, black Packard disappeared around the corner.

The doorman waited patiently, holding the grand brass-handled door.

In the hotel suite, she found the sofa pushed to one side to make room for the Steinway console piano her mother had rented. There were two bedrooms with a bath between, accessible from both.

Audrey was grateful for a pocket of solitude in this unfamiliar space that would be home for the next six months. She unpacked her two little suitcases, put her clothes in a drawer, positioned books on a shelf in her room and deposited her sheet music into the piano bench in the living room. After taking a bath and washing her hair, she stood by the window overlooking Central Park, wearing a hotel bathrobe while she combed the tangles from her long, wet hair.

Without thinking of her own situation, she watched women pushing elaborate wicker prams on the sidewalks that crisscrossed the bright green manicured lawn. An old lady in a wheelchair wearing a red hat and matching red sweater sat next to a hunched old man. The old woman's hands rested on a tartan plaid lap rug as the couple watched children play in the grass.

Watching the scene from the sixth floor, Audrey felt completely removed from the realities of life in New York City, or anywhere else on the planet. Her life was in limbo.

Audrey usually began her practice sessions with "Gymnopédies." She was halfway through when her mother returned.

Audrey noticed that her mother was exhausted from the long drive and the stress of the past few days.

"I'm calling room service. Let them in if I'm still in the bath. Be sure to tip the server."

Both wearing white terry bathrobes, Audrey and Esther ate their soup and bread in silence.

While Audrey rolled the dinner trolley into the hall, Esther opened the small mahogany secretary's hinged desktop, then from her satchel, gathered an empty notebook, a bottle of Waterman's blue/black ink and her favorite fountain pen. She sat down to write.

Audrey returned to the piano. Their temporary home filled with the scent of soup, ink and fresh paper and the reassuring harmonic vibration of piano strings.

"I found a couple in Manhattan who want to adopt a baby. I've been in touch with their attorney," said Esther's attorney when she visited his office.

"Don't tell me the attorney's name or the name of his client," Esther insisted. "And please be certain they don't discover our names or where we're staying. I demand complete and total anonymity."

Audrey glanced away from the piano keys when her mother returned to their suite. "The attorney found adoptive parents." She made an effort to make her voice sound upbeat and cheerful.

"That's good," said Audrey without stopping her practice, ignoring the confusion that gripped her.

As the days passed, Esther's aggravation and disappointment morphed into quiet acceptance. She found she enjoyed having time to focus on writing and she enjoyed the opportunity to talk with her teenage daughter.

Among hotel employees and restaurant waitstaff, they became known simply as Esther and Audrey. The only people in New York who knew Esther Dupré's true identity were the car dealer, where she sold her Packard, her attorney and the teller at the bank where Esther made weekly withdrawals to cover their accommodations and other expenses. Audrey went for monthly checkups, but she gave her doctor a false name and address.

They ate every meal together, either in the hotel café, at restaurants near the hotel, or ordered room service. Esther realized she was spending more time with Audrey during the pregnancy than she had during any other time in Audrey's life, even when she was an infant. She thought, *My career, my studies and my social activities always took time away from Audrey.*

Esther suggested getting tickets to *The Boys from Syracuse* on Broadway, "Weren't you working on a number from that musical?"

Audrey turned her face away. She and Ted were supposed to perform a duet at the spring concert. She couldn't bear seeing the stage production without him. "Let's book tickets to see *You Never Know* instead. Cole Porter and Robert Katscher wrote the music and lyrics. I'd like to see it."

After their early morning walks in Central Park, they avoided the slow, noisy elevator and climbed the stairs to their sixth-floor suite. *The New York Times* waited in the hallway by their door. They ordered breakfast from room service and Esther and Audrey read the paper from cover to cover while they ate. The walk, the climb and *The New York Times* became their daily ritual.

In the fall, as Audrey's condition became more conspicuous, Esther bought a long brown raincoat to camouflage Audrey's expanding body. They still took the stairs and both climbed with ease.

One morning in November, Audrey asked Esther, "Did you read the article a few days ago about the devastation in Germany? It's dreadful; rioters smashed Jewish businesses and synagogues; they call it *Kristallnacht*. It's not safe to be a Jew in Germany."

"President Roosevelt didn't say much about it," Esther replied, glancing at the paper in her lap. "But this morning, I see he's withdrawn the US Ambassador to Germany. At least he did *something*."

Esther sat at the mahogany secretary by the window, staring into the melancholy winter scene below, unable to focus on the novel she was writing. The snow-covered ground starkly contrasted with lacy, leafless trees as light snow fell. A dark path cut through the dim white blanket flanked by barren park benches. An old man in a brown coat and fedora slowly pushed an old woman in a wheelchair. The old lady wore a bright red coat and matching hat. Red mittens, a size too large, rested on a tartan plaid lap rug. The couple seemed to glow in the dim light. She wondered, *Will Eiffel and I grow that old together?*

Men in long dark overcoats and pinched fedoras hurried past the old couple, leaning into the cold air. Women, wearing cloche hats and calf-length raccoon-collared coats, hunched beside the men as they hurried beyond the park to the cold-looking stone buildings with warmly lit windows. All the while, Esther listened to Audrey practicing Franz Liszt's "Piano Sonata in B-Minor," which sounded rich and elegant, more like raindrops than snowflakes, but matched Esther's tranquil mood.

When Audrey finished the Liszt piece, Esther turned away from her desk and the view of Central Park. "*Ma chérie,* you seem too young to play with such intense emotion."

"I interpret the music Maman. I don't need to live it," Audrey mused. "Like an actor, I guess. Expressing emotion in my music has nothing to do with life experience any more than an actor has experienced a script." Then she added, "I'm still working on this piece. It's so difficult. I'm surprised you heard any emotion at all."

Audrey stood and walked to the bathroom, "I can't play more than one piece without using the facilities," she laughed. She drank a small glass of water, then slid back onto the piano bench and played "Clair de Lune."

Audrey had played it many times while they lived in Ohio, but hadn't practiced the piece since arriving in New York nearly five months ago. As she gently moved her fingers over the keyboard, Audrey felt the music in her soul and knew its tender texture reflected her mood of the day, today pensive but satisfied. She played the last note, then turned to look at her mother. "Maman, I have never seen you so moved by music."

Her mother's face was wet with silent tears, "Your papa and I were married to this piece." She quickly wiped her face with both hands. "A beautiful poem by Paul Verlaine inspired Claude Debussy to write the music." She recited the last stanza of the poem:

> *With the sad and beautiful moonlight,*
> *Which sets the birds in the trees dreaming,*
> *And makes the fountains sob with ecstasy,*
> *The slender water streams among the marble statues.*

"Given my love of poetry and your papa's occupation, we thought it appropriate, Clair de Lune… Light of the Moon…"

"You miss him terribly, don't you, Maman?"

She nodded. "I'm looking forward to living as a family in Paris," she admitted to Audrey for the first time.

David and Adina Sapozhnikov

New York, 1938

"I've been in touch with a lawyer whose client's daughter is expecting. They're hoping to arrange a private adoption without too many people knowing about the situation. The pregnant girl is only fifteen and has the best possible medical care. You might like to know the girl's mother is a college professor and her father is a scientist. The boy's parents are also educated. That's all I can divulge. Are you interested?"

"Yes! Of course. Of course!" David Sapozhnikov was in his office on Wall Street when his attorney called. His voice was uncharacteristically impassioned. "What a splendid gift, today is my wife's birthday. Thank you." Then, in his more customary, authoritative tones, he added, "What are the, ah, transaction fees? Should we come by tomorrow to sign the necessary paperwork?"

"There are no papers to sign at this time and no fees beyond my normal hourly rate. You're not purchasing a baby. The only signature will be on the birth certificate.

"The adoption details will remain strictly anonymous to both parties. I'll make the arrangements for the midwife, but the birth mother's parents are responsible for the midwife's services and for their own legal fees. Throughout the pregnancy, they will send updates to their attorney and I, in turn, will forward all communication to you and your wife. They plan for the girl to give birth at…" he cleared his throat, "at their temporary residence, not in a hospital unless absolutely necessary. I'll divulge the location when the girl goes into labor. When the transaction is complete, I'll invoice for my hours." The attorney paused for a moment. "Do those terms meet with your approval?"

"Yes, of course, that's fine," said David, then added, his voice shaking with emotion. "The child will never know."

David presented his wife with a long, narrow white box tied with yards of pink and blue satin ribbons trailing like streamers to the floor. Inside, two dozen long-stemmed white roses nestled in green tissue paper. On the birthday card, he had written, *Congratulations, we're having a baby!*

His wife, Adina, cried when he told her the story. Over their fifteen-year marriage, she had suffered several miscarriages; then just a few months before, in her ninth month, she endured a devastating stillbirth. Before she came home from the hospital, David had the baby paraphernalia removed from the apartment. The nursery had remained as empty as their hearts.

To distract her from her grief and disappointment, David had arranged a birthday dinner. Now the party quietly transformed into a private celebration, though the guests would remain unaware of the adoption plans.

David had invited eight couples to join them in a private room at Delmonico's Restaurant. He always enjoyed the ambiance and the food at Delmonico's; crystal chandeliers hung from the high ceiling and dark paneled walls contrasted with waiters dressed in all white, moving among the guests serving champagne, *foie gras* and toast points.

David had asked Adina's friend, Geneviève, to play her harp before and during dinner. Geneviève's gentle, healing music accompanied the tone of the evening from *hors d'oeuvres* to dessert.

When everyone took their seats, the waiters presented Delmonico's famous bread and garlic butter, along with black cod almondine, roasted fingerling potatoes crusted with rosemary and grilled asparagus. The wine, La Clarte de Haut-Brion Blanc, David imported from France just for the occasion, flowed generously.

During dinner, David casually mentioned to their friends they were planning an extended tour abroad.

"Are you sure it's wise to travel with the threat of war looming in Europe?" asked one of their friends.

"We plan to spend most of our time in Norway, we've always wanted to see the fjords," David assured his friend.

Actually, he had arranged for them to spend the next six months living in a cottage in Cold Spring, sixty miles north of New York City in the Hudson Valley while they waited for the teen-age girl to deliver. He hoped their absence in the social scene would reinforce the illusion Adina had given birth to the baby, due in December.

As busboys cleared the dinner dishes and white-gloved waiters poured Portuguese tawny port and coffee, a stocky young man, dressed in a tuxedo, entered the dining room pushing a cloth-draped trolley holding a huge, three-layer, chocolate cake. With a white towel draped over his arm, he lit the candles with a flourish, began singing "Happy Birthday," to Adina and directed the other guests to join in.

To entertain the guests, Bernard Berkowitz, a family friend and famous French tenor, sang "Giannin" from the popular musical "Firefly," then "O Sole Mio" in the original Neapolitan language. He concluded his performance with a fitting number: "Ah! Sweet Mystery of Life."

Adina stood and joined him. She never sang professionally, but her beautiful soprano singing voice often entertained guests during elaborate soirées and charity events held in their elegant penthouse on Park Avenue.

Adina and Bernard sounded very much like Jeanette MacDonald and Nelson Eddy in the movie, "Naughty Marietta," but no one in the restaurant, except her husband, knew Adina sang to their unborn baby.

Ah! Sweet mystery of life
At last I've found thee
Ah! I know at last the secret of it all;
All the longing, seeking, striving, waiting, yearning
The idle hopes, the joy and burning tears that fall!
For 'tis love and love alone, the world is seeking,
And 'tis love and love alone, I've waited for!
'Tis the answer, 'tis the end and all of living
For it is love alone that rules for evermore!

Before the Sapozhnikovs left for the upstate cottage, Adina put the butler and the housekeeper on paid leave to minimize the number of people who would know about the adoption. Riding in their French-made Delage sports car, on the way to Cold Spring, Adina put her hand on her flat belly and imagined the baby growing there. Tears spilled onto her cheeks as if her own hormones raged. They arrived at the rustic cottage early in the afternoon. It was quite small, especially compared to their Manhattan penthouse.

The sophisticated red Delage D8-120 Aerosport Coupe, with its smooth curved fenders and wide, white-walled tires parked in the bucolic setting, looked as out of place as a yellow-billed toucan in a maple tree.

Adina carried a basket of food into the cottage where highly polished pine floors and walls surrounded the well-worn wicker furniture. She put the groceries into the old, scratched and dented refrigerator and checked to be sure the gas stove worked. The cottage had a telephone line. The attorney could call with updates and contact them when the time came. She picked up the receiver and relaxed a little when she heard the dial tone.

Adina kept herself busy tinkering in the kitchen, preparing simple meals of vegetables she bought at the outdoor market and meat from the kosher butcher. They ate their evening meal on the screened-in porch while fuchsia sunsets reflected off the river. Instead of the constant traffic noise of New York City, they slept soundly listening to the river and to the strangely reassuring call of a barred owl, *whoo-wa whoo-wa, whoocooksforyouall.*

For the next five months, they enjoyed relaxing days without obligations or servants, just each other for companionship. David tried his hand at fishing and caught pre spawn bass Adina learned to prepare, following recipes from *Good Housekeeping* magazines she found on the cottage shelves. With healthy meals, no client meetings, parties, or charity events, they rarely drank wine or spirits and both felt healthier and more fit than they had in years. Still, David worried about her mental as well as physical recovery after the devastating still birth. He watched her closely as they walked paths through wooded hills and paddled a canoe on the river.

One blustery fall afternoon, they sat on a rock beneath a canopy of red and orange leaves, watching the river flow and listening to the birds while eating sandwiches they bought at the deli. Adina leaned on David's shoulder, "What if the girl decides to keep the baby, or something else goes wrong? I don't think I can bear losing another baby."

David hugged his wife. "Darling, we can't spend our time worrying about what could happen. Furthermore, the attorney assured me the fifteen-year-old girl and her mother want nothing more than to put this ordeal behind them so the girl can return to school. You must focus on your health and prepare to be the wonderful mother I know you will be." He leaned in to give her a reassuring kiss on the cheek.

Audrey's Baby

New York, 1938

Esther dressed for Thanksgiving dinner while Audrey practiced Mozart's "Rondo Alla Turca." The vehement tones and rhythm sounded like happy water dancing in a rocky stream.

"Maman, come watch—hurry!"

Esther rushed into the room, wearing her bra, slip and stockings, "What is it, *ma chérie?*"

"Watch! I can feel it dancing. Look," she said, laughing out loud as she continued to play. "It loves Mozart too."

Esther watched Audrey's belly move under her dark blue maternity smock.

"Maman, put your hand here. You must feel this. It's wonderful."

Esther tentatively reached toward Audrey's belly. When she felt the baby move with the music, she breathed, "Extraordinary."

Until now, they behaved as if it were a tumor waiting to be removed. In that moment, however, it was no longer an ordeal—**it** was a child, alive, listening, becoming part of the music. In perfect silence, mother and daughter both hoped it would inherit Audrey's gift.

"Where did this come from?" Esther asked, picking up the copy of *The Tale of Peter Rabbit* that Audrey had left on top of the piano.

Silence filled the room when Audrey stopped playing. "I brought it from Ohio. I hope you don't mind."

Esther's face pinched into a mask of concern. "*Ma chérie,* you realize you will not see it. You will never read to it."

"I know Maman," she paused with a deep breath. "But it will have *parents* who will love it and they will read."

Esther opened the book to the author's signature. "I was too young to remember Mrs. Potter, but I remember my governess reading this to me…" Her fingertips brushed Mrs. Potter's autograph. She closed the book.

"And I remember *my* nanny reading it," said Audrey.

Esther suddenly sat down on the bench next to Audrey, facing the window, hugging the book tightly to her chest. "Oh how I wish it were my voice you remembered reading *Peter Rabbit*…" Esther's breath consumed the sound, scarcely a whisper. "If I could turn back the clock."

Before Audrey could respond, Esther was on her feet, putting the book back on top of the piano, her emotions stowed as always. In a louder voice, she said, "We should give this book to the adoptive parents."

"I hoped we could… It will never know where the book came from, but the new parents will know we cared about it, even though I can't raise it."

"Maman, what's happening?" cried Audrey from the bathroom.

"*Ma chérie*, it's normal, your water broke. Labor is starting," said Esther. "Are you having contractions?"

"I am now!" moaned Audrey, as she bent forward, supported by her palms on the pedestal sink. Esther helped her to bed.

"Another already?"

Audrey nodded, her face turning red.

"You'll feel better if you don't hold your breath. Try to breathe during contractions. I know it's difficult. I'll call the midwife and let her know your labor has started."

Esther looked out the window as she dialed the number thinking, *I hope the blizzard doesn't prevent the midwife from coming.*

Next, she called the attorney who would notify the adoptive parents. "They must arrive before the birth," she reminded the attorney. "There should be no opportunity for my daughter to see the baby."

Before returning to Audrey's side, she stood by the window for a moment and allowed herself to feel the regret, *This could be my only opportunity to be grand-mère. I hope I've made the right decision.*

Audrey's contractions were coming about three minutes apart and a few were back-to-back. *What if the midwife doesn't arrive in time? If I hold that baby, I will never be able to give it up....* thought Esther. She wiped Audrey's face with a cool washcloth and called room service to order ice chips for Audrey to suck on. She wanted to pace the floor but didn't dare leave Audrey's side.

For the next two hours, Audrey's labor grew more intense. With increasing concern, Esther called the midwife again, but her husband said she had left the apartment soon after the first call. Esther returned to Audrey and helped her remember to breathe with each contraction. "I'm sure the midwife will be here soon," she reassured Audrey, even though she needed reassurance herself.

An hour later, she finally heard boots stomping in the hall. Esther opened the door to find the midwife brushing the sparkling snow from her shoulders. "Good evening," the midwife looked at Esther with a warm, reassuring smile, "The weather is dreadful out there. How's she doing?"

The midwife stepped into the warm hotel room as if she and Esther had been friends forever. She put down two disturbingly large duffel bags then she took off her coat.

"The contractions have been two minutes apart for over an hour and they're lasting almost a minute. I'm so glad you're here," Esther reported, trying in vain to sound calm.

After washing as well as warming her hands in hot water, the midwife stepped into Audrey's room. "It's nice to meet you but we will not exchange names. Just call me Mid for midwife." She smiled at Audrey with understanding, compassion and reassurance as she eased sweaty bangs from Audrey's forehead.

Mid slid her hands into gloves, put a crisp white sheet over Audrey's knees and checked her progress. "Sounds like you've worked pretty hard to dilate to four centimeters. Your goal is ten. Before another contraction starts, let's review the rules. After the baby is delivered, I'll move it to the living room. Neither of you will see it, hold it, or know its gender. Do you understand?" Her tone was stern, but kind.

"Yes, of course," said Esther.

Audrey nodded as another contraction took her breath.

"That's a good girl. Remember to breathe... breathe. Excellent! That's it. You're strong. Your doing great." Mid's voice was as steady as a metronome.

When the contraction ended, Mid washed her hands again

and went to work preparing for the delivery. She opened one of the duffel bags filled with supplies, pulling out a blood pressure cuff, stethoscope, fetoscope, a box of gloves, scales, suturing kits and other sterile instruments wrapped in white cloth.

Mid helped Audrey scoot closer to the edge of the bed and made her as comfortable as possible with lots of pillows. She put a waterproof sheet under Audrey, arranged supplies on the nightstand and positioned a baby scale on the desk in the living room.

Eyeing the piano bench, solid, level, just the right size, Mid transformed it into a dressing table with a thickly folded blanket and lots of thick white towels.

THE BLIZZARD

COLD SPRING, NEW YORK, 1938

"I've never seen such a blizzard!" David Sapozhnikov said, leaning toward the kitchen window as Adina made corned beef sandwiches for their lunch.

Later, as Adina finished washing the lunch dishes, they heard a knock. David opened the door and welcomed the landlord, Albert, accompanied by wind and snow. "You got a telegram; thought I should walk it right over. The phone lines are down because of the storm. Don't know how long it took that Western Union guy to get here. Hope it's not too important."

As Albert kept up his dialogue, David ripped open the envelope, read the message and handed it to Adina.

She read it and gasped.

GIRL IN LABOR STOP GO TO PLAZA HOTEL SUITE 600 ASAP STOP BE CAREFUL IN THE SNOW STOP

"Albert," said David, "We need to return to New York at once, can you help me dig out my car?"

"What's so important that you can't wait for this blizzard to slow down? Ya know there's lots of winding road between here and New York City…"

David put on his coat while Adina rushed into the bedroom to change into warmer clothes and pack their things.

"Believe me, Albert, we must leave, NOW!" David stepped into his boots, pushed the door open against the wind and Albert followed him out.

"In that case, I'll fetch a shovel from the shed," yelled Albert into the wind.

David began sweeping snow from the car with a broom he liberated from a drift on the porch. When the driveway was cleared as much as possible, he started the car. Albert helped Adina put their luggage in the trunk then she stepped through the deep snow and climbed into the car.

"Here, take the shovel," Albert said to David. "But I hope ya don't need it. Good luck!"

David put the shovel in the trunk, swung into the driver's seat, put the car in gear and mumbled an old Jewish prayer.

"I don't care how we look when we get there as long as we arrive before that baby is born," said Adina, her voice unnaturally shrill as she pulled David's stocking cap over her hair. "If the girl or her mother have a chance to hold the baby, they might decide to…"

"Just wipe those thoughts from your mind. We'll be there in time." He sounded more confident than he felt. David knew his wife was right. They had to be there before the moment of birth, or they risked the mother and grandmother changing their minds.

"David, can't you drive faster? We can't be late."

"I'm driving as fast as I can. This car wasn't made for snow and ice," he growled between clinched teeth.

Navigating through blowing snow on icy slopes in a Delage Aerosport Coupe with its long wheelbase and rear-wheel drive made the trip slow and dangerous. As he skated down a hill and around a curve, the right rear tire slid off the pavement. They were stuck.

"David, you shouldn't drive so fast on these icy roads!" Adina shrieked.

His wife had never been so critical of him, but he understood, their emotions were as raw as if she were giving birth herself; more so.

He took the shovel from the trunk and dug away the snow, exposing gravel. After several attempts, spewing dirty snow, the wheel found traction. The car lurched out of the ditch and fishtailed down the slippery, snow-covered road. Adina closed her eyes, gripped the dashboard and held her breath until David regained control.

"Oh David, I'm so frightened. What if we don't arrive in time? Please don't go into another ditch!"

Blowing snow reflected the headlight beams, reducing visibility to just a few feet. They inched their way toward Manhattan and what they hoped would be their new lives as parents.

As they entered the New York City limits, snowplows worked to clear the streets and the storm began to ease. Visibility improved but their anxiety doubled. They arrived at the Plaza Hotel at 7:02 a.m., quietly stepped past the dozing doorman and took the elevator to suite 600. Warm tears trickled down Adina's cold face, tears of joy, anticipation and fear.

David knocked. They waited. He knocked again. Still, no one came.

"My God are we too late?" whispered Adina. "Maybe they went to the hospital." Adina's hand trembled as she reached to knock on the door herself, as if the response would be different.

Finally, the midwife opened the door. "Sorry it took me so long. The baby is crowning," she said, catching her breath. "So glad you made it in time. Make yourselves comfortable." She waved toward the sofa and quickly disappeared into the makeshift delivery room.

Stabilizing each other in a firm hug, the Sapozhnikovs noticed the thickly folded blanket and towels on the piano bench and a baby scale waiting on the desk. On top of the piano, they also noticed the corner of a children's book peeking from beneath a folder of documents.

Only moments later, before the snow melted on David's hair, they heard the broken wail of a newborn.

They watched in awe as the midwife rushed from the girl's room carrying the naked baby. First, the midwife placed the howling infant on the scales and whispered, "it's a boy, seven pounds, five ounces, twenty inches long, 7:09 a.m." She moved to the thickly padded piano bench and placed the baby boy as if for inspection. She cleaned, diapered and expertly swaddled him in a receiving blanket and placed him in Adina's arms. His broken wails calmed and he opened his swollen eyes, meeting his adoptive mother for the first time.

The new mother held her cheek against the warm, tiny face, skin to skin. She deeply inhaled the new baby scent and longed to unwrap the blanket to look at his tiny toes and fingers, but time was of the essence.

Mid pushed the birth certificate across the top of the piano and indicated where they should sign. It was the only illegal aspect of the transaction.

The new father signed without hesitation and pushed the pen and paper toward his wife. Supporting the tiny head, the new mother relinquished the baby into the arms of her husband only long enough to sign the papers. Then Mid notarized the documents and handed the father a carbon copy of the birth certificate. "And the girl wants you to have this," she smiled, giving him the copy of *The Tale of Peter Rabbit*.

With the baby snug and warm in a pale green flannel bunting supplied by the midwife, David drove the two blocks to their Park Avenue penthouse. "The girl has been this close all this time," said David. "We could have walked from the hotel to our building. Instead, we're the only car on the street."

"Congratulations," murmured the sleepy parking lot attendant as David helped Adina out of the car. "This is wonderful. I didn't know you were… expecting," he said, smiling at the tiny bundle.

When they entered the lobby of their building, the doorman said, "Congratulations, I'm so happy for you." The new parents beamed as the doorman wiped a tear.

Once they were safely in their warm apartment, Adina removed the heavy blankets and freed the baby's arms and legs. Although both parents were born Jewish, the Sapozhnikovs hadn't been to synagogue in many years. Many *Hanukkahs* had come and gone without their notice. In that moment, however, the new parents looked into each other's eyes and without further comment, they let the baby's fingers clutch his mother's index finger with one hand and his father's index finger with the other hand. His eyes opened as if he knew he was home. They began reciting a prayer:

> *Blessed art Thou, oh Lord our God, King of the universe, who has given us life, sustained us and brought us to this day.*

In the dim light of their bedroom, Adina lowered their new baby onto their bed. They stood in a long hug while gazing at their sleeping son. "Today is Friday," said David, "The bris will be Saturday next."

"Yes, but we should keep the celebration low-key. Only the mohel should attend. I'm not ready to share him with our friends and colleagues. I've been thinking about what his name should be." Then, almost in a whisper, she said, "I think Sergei Sapozhnikov sounds nice."

"Yes, *Sergei Sapozhnikov*. It sounds like a famous artist or a movie star."

He called his attorney to let him know they were home with the baby.

The attorney had worked with David for many years and was aware of the heartache they had endured trying to have a family. "Congratulations, you will be wonderful parents. The child is lucky to have you. Later today, a delivery will arrive from Macy's. I placed an order for diapers, layette, formula and a bassinet to be delivered to your penthouse as soon as I knew you were home with the baby, my compliments."

Occupied by the wonder of finally becoming a mother, Adina spent the first few days alone with Sergei while her husband returned to his business responsibilities. She felt safe in the cocoon of her dimly lit bedroom. High ceilings with white crown molding framed the elegant room above their family heirloom furniture. Subtle cream on cream stripes covered the walls. Matching chintz draperies, fashioned by hand and imported from China, remained closed to the gloomy winter sky, a soft shield between the baby and the world beyond the window. An elegant wicker bassinet, a gift from their attorney, stood by her bed; however, she left her new baby there only long enough to take a quick bath, use the facilities, or prepare his bottle.

When he was fussy, she cradled Sergei in her arms and sang a Russian lullaby, *Bayu Baushki Bayu*. Although she sang quietly, Adina's powerful soprano voice filled the penthouse, a sound as tangible as water or the wall. Sergei's tiny mouth opened like a baby bird and his face bobbed toward the sleeve of her nightgown. She noticed her breasts tingled just as they had when she returned to the empty nursery a year before. As naturally as changing his diaper or rocking him to sleep, she pulled her nightgown aside, exposing her naked breast. He quickly found her dark nipple and suckled eagerly.

When David opened the front door after work that evening, the penthouse was completely dark. He circled the living room, turning on lights as concern clawed at his heart. Opening the bedroom door, he stood silhouetted by the yellow light from the living room while his eyes adjusted. His chest tightened with a feeling of dread. He shivered when he saw his wife in the rocking chair with her nightgown pulled aside, allowing the baby to nurse. After losing the last baby, his wife's mental state had been fragile.

Now he wondered if five months upstate had been enough time to heal.

He entered the room slowly, "Darling? Is everything all right?"

She looked up at him, her face radiant, "Never have I been so good! I am feeding him my own milk. Can you imagine? I didn't plan this; it just happened. He rooted at my breast and... my body knew..." Tears of joy flowed down her glowing cheeks, as milk trickled from Sergei's tiny lips.

David hadn't seen his wife this joyful since their wedding day. Slowly, his hand caressed her cheek and he bent to kiss her lips. Then he moved his hand to the nursing baby's crown. He knelt by the rocking chair and wept. "He truly is our son."

When their housekeeper, Jenny, came back to work at the beginning of 1939, Adina maintained the illusion of having given birth by wearing oversized clothing, spending a lot of time resting and nursing the baby.

No one else, however, beyond the doorman, parking attendant and mohel, knew about Sergei's arrival until spring. Her friends thought she had delivered without them being aware of her pregnancy. At her age and with her medical history, her friends and charity associates understood why she had been secretive about the pregnancy and delivery. They asked no questions. They simply cooed over the baby and accepted the miracle of birth.

On December 23, David came home from work to find the table centered with the silver *chanukiah* his ancestors had carried from Russia a century before. No one knew how long the family had cherished the beautiful heirloom before they left Russia. The ancient menorah with nine candles was dented and slightly bent but brightly polished.

Tears came to his eyes. He hugged his wife and son, "I agree, we should honor his first *Hanukkah*."

For eight nights, they said ritual Jewish prayers and lit the traditional candles.

Audrey and Esther, 1938

Audrey's long hair spread like spilled ink as Esther fluffed the pillows trying to make her daughter more comfortable. Audrey's bangs, wet with perspiration, clung to her forehead. Esther crawled onto the bed beside Audrey, "How do you feel?"

"Just a little crampy," Audrey murmured, her hand resting on her belly. "But I feel hollow. Empty." Her fingers moved to her heart, "I had no drive to become a mother, but now I wish…." Her voice cracked. Her tears came hot and quiet. Esther held her daughter as they both cried. The ordeal was over, but the torment lingered.

"Someday you'll meet the right fellow, fall in love and have a family."

"No Maman, I won't," Audrey said between muffled sobs. "I'll never…." Audrey glanced at the clock. It was 7:15 a.m., December 9, 1938. "Today is my sixteenth birthday…," she said. "Birthdays will never be the same."

Esther hugged and rocked her daughter until Mid returned to the room.

"They've gone," Mid whispered.

Through the fog of their grief, they heard only—*gone*.

Esther walked into the sitting room while Mid lifted the sheet to tend to the afterbirth.

Esther had stayed by Audrey's side throughout her labor, leaving only to use the facilities. Now, alone in the dim morning light, she sat at her desk. The room was warm, but she trembled. Outside, the sky was heavy and still. She held back her tears. If what Audrey said was true, Esther would never be a *grand-mère*. Before this ordeal, she had never paused to consider whether or not she wanted to be a *grand-mère*. Her studies always took priority, even over Audrey's childhood, but now she wished she could hold the baby and love it forever, but... the baby was gone.

Huge snowflakes floated past the widow as if released from an invisible portal. The streets below were silent, abandoned under a glassy sheen of ice. Esther watched a long, red sports car creep past the hotel, turn onto Park Avenue and disappear into a parking garage, unaware her grandson rode inside. *Why would anyone drive a fancy sports car in this weather? What could be so important?*

She dialed room service and ordered three servings of eggs Benedict, orange juice, toast and coffee.

Mid packed her supplies and equipment, put on her coat and waited.

Esther handed Mid an envelope. "Thank you..., Mid. Can you stay for breakfast?"

"Thank you, but I have another patient who may need me tonight. I need a little sleep."

Mid tucked the envelope into her bag, next to the sealed envelope with the birth certificate. Then she looked at Esther's sad face. "These things are never easy. I have yet to meet a mother or grandmother who doesn't have second thoughts... You must believe you made the right choice. The adoptive parents are lovely people. The child will have a happy home."

Mid reached for a hug and, uncharacteristically, Esther cried on her shoulder, then Esther stepped away, straightened her back and quickly wiped her face with both hands.

"We can't thank you enough for your help," said Esther.

"I'm sure your daughter will have no complications in her recovery. Her labor was long and hard, but her delivery was normal. Good luck to both of you."

ON THE *SS CHAMPLAIN*

December 1938

Esther and Audrey settled into their cabin as the *SS Champlain* set sail beginning the frigid winter voyage from New York to France. As they ordered dinner on the first night, the grand piano, bolted to the floor in the dining room, sat silent. Audrey asked the waiter, "Is there no one on board who will play the piano?"

"I'm sorry, Miss, our pianist became ill at the last minute and we left port without him."

"Would you like *me* to play?" asked Audrey.

"You are so young, Miss. Perhaps there is someone on board with more experience. I will inquire," he replied with thick French vowels that curled around each word.

Esther laughed out loud, "I assure you, there is no one on board whose performance you will enjoy more than my daughter's."

The waiter gave Esther a condescending look, rolled his eyes and waggled his hand at the piano. "Perhaps you could play until your dinner is served."

He turned toward the kitchen muttering to himself about the audacity of American passengers, but when Audrey began to play "*Gymnopédies*," he stopped abruptly. The music rose and fell like rain drops, reminding him of melancholy winter days in Toulon when he was a child. He looked around the dining room. All eyes had glazed as if Audrey's music lured every passenger into a space of deep reflection.

He returned to Esther and bent to whisper, "I must apologize, Madame. I have never heard the piano played more beautifully and it is clear," his arm swept toward the enchanted passengers, "Our guests are mesmerized."

Esther replied quietly in French, "It is Audrey who deserves an apology." She nodded toward Audrey with a proud smile.

"*Oui, Madame.*" He bowed and, unwilling to interrupt Audrey's performance, slipped through the service doors to the kitchen.

Later, a purser came to their cabin and offered to pay Audrey to perform for the passengers. She declined payment. "*Merci,* I will play as often as you like. I am happy to be able to practice during the voyage."

The next morning, the marquee signboard next to the dining room announced: *Featuring Miss Audrey Dupré on Piano.*

When rough seas made passengers too ill to eat, they still came to listen. Whether Chopin, Bach, or Mozart, the music soothed their discomfort.

Each day after breakfast and before dinner, while Esther worked on her novel, Audrey enjoyed cold, solitary walks on deck, using a long red pashmina to secure her wool cloche hat and keep her throat warm. The pashmina was a gift her father brought back from Nepal the year before. She tucked the ends into her winter coat, elegant but ill-suited for the cold sea wind. The buttons refused to close over her still-swollen abdomen. She held it closed and bent into the cleansing salty wind. Leaning against the railing, she watched the prow cut through the blue water and the dolphins leap in the wake, as if racing the boat toward France. Breathing as deeply as she could, she allowed her mind to be as empty as the churning waves that stretched beyond the horizon.

When not playing the piano or strolling the deck, Audrey took long naps while her mother filled a notebook. When they disembarked in Le Havre and boarded the train for the last leg of their journey to Paris, Audrey fastened all the buttons on her coat.

Her father met them at the train station a few days before Christmas. He hugged Audrey and kissed both of her cheeks, but his presence felt unfamiliar, distant. Usually, Audrey and her mother spent summers in their Paris apartment with him, but this year they had spent the summer in New York, isolated from the rest of the world, while he remained in Paris. She had spoken to him briefly on the phone, just to say hello, but it felt like years since they had been together.

In the taxi, her mother sat in the middle next to her father. While her parents talked, Audrey pressed her forehead against the cold glass and stared into the snowy streets, tuning them out. She was happy to be in Paris but her heart was broken.

After they stowed their luggage in the apartment, they walked to Esther's favorite brasserie, once frequented by Hemingway. They enjoyed duck *foie gras*, mushroom terrine, *rémoulade cervelas* and Merlot served in heavy tumblers. After dinner, they strolled the streets as heavy snow began to fall. Audrey remembered when she was younger, how much she loved Christmas in Paris with her father. She looked up toward the lights strung across the street. "Look, Papa, the snowflakes look like falling stars." He put one arm over Audrey's shoulders and caught Esther's gloved hand with the other and kissed it gently. "It's good to be a family again."

"I missed you," murmured Esther.

Dusted with cold powdery snow, Parisians bustled in and out of shops with their packages. A man peddled by with a small Christmas tree lashed to his bicycle. A toddler pulled a tiny red sleigh with his little brother clutching the sides in red mittens, followed by their parents, arm in arm, all warmly bundled against the cold, snowy air. No one seemed the least concerned with Hitler's growing shadow.

Breath suspended in the air like steam above hot cocoa, candles glowed in apartment windows. In the park, Christmas tree lights reflected on the fresh snow like millions of tiny diamonds. Audrey, still unsettled, tried to push memories of the last year's events back across the cold Atlantic.

Audrey and Aimée happily reunited later that evening when Aimée returned home. After a long hug, Aimée made a pot of chamomile tea. The young women sat on Audrey's bed and talked for hours.

"I went to *Théâtre* tonight with girlfriends. We saw Edith Piaf. Have you heard her sing?"

"I've been a little out of touch," Audrey said wryly, rolling her eyes.

"She sings French chanson. Even famous songwriters write songs just for her. She is amazing. We will go together sometime soon."

Aimée told Audrey about the mixers she had gone to and the

fellows she'd met, but that no one lived up to the butcher's son in Ohio. Audrey's maturity was deceptive; Aimée almost forgot that Audrey had just turned sixteen. Aimée was twenty.

They discussed books they'd read, including *The Tenant of Wildfell Hall,* which Aimée had read before they left Ohio and Audrey devoured during the car ride to New York. "It's disappointing to think that society still expects women to depend on their husbands for support. Women's lives haven't changed much in ninety years," Audrey grumbled.

"It's appalling we have no choices like men," said Aimée. "My parents, they had jobs, like your parents… but I want to fall in love, 'ave babies."

"Not me. I never want to get married or have children. I just want to play the piano, sing and teach music, especially children who wouldn't have an opportunity otherwise."

Still as close as sisters, they shared their fear of Hitler's advances and reports they had read about the dreadful persecution of Jews happening in Germany and Russia. They didn't mention their sudden departure from Ohio, Audrey's pregnancy nor the baby.

Sergei Sapozhnikov, 1939

Sergei's Childhood

While Sergei was an infant, Adina Sapozhnikov kept a sparse social calendar. She'd waited so long to have a baby she refused to miss a single first—the first time he rolled over or sat up, the first time he said mama or papa, his first steps, every magical moment. Eventually, she would hire a part-time nanny and resume her charity work, but not yet.

One afternoon, with two-year-old Sergei supported on her hip, she explored the shelf of children's books. Selecting *The Tale of Peter Rabbit,* she sat in the big wingback chair near the window in the living room and Sergei snuggled onto her lap. When she opened the book, she inhaled a sharp breath, noticing the author's inscription:

For Esther, Merry Christmas, December 1902.

She'd been so enthralled with her new baby; she'd never opened the book until now.

As she read, little Sergei put his pudgy dimpled hands on her face and said, "Mama sad."

"No darling, these are happy tears," she smiled, kissed his forehead and covered his tiny hand with hers as he wiped the tears from her face. "I am so happy to be reading this book to you, little one."

That night, after Sergei had gone to sleep, Adina handed David the book and asked, "Have you noticed this signature? It's the book the midwife gave us when Sergei was born."

The rims of his eyes suddenly turned red, as if tears might spill, "I'm ashamed to say I never looked inside." He inspected the little book. "This is a first edition, self-published by Beatrix Potter. Who do you suppose Esther is?"

"It's dated 1902, maybe Esther is his grandmother?"

"We'll never know, but it's clear someone wanted us to read to him... Not a day goes by that I don't marvel at how lucky we are to have him here with us." He kissed his wife. "This book reminds me that someone gave him up so we could be his parents."

She took her husband's face in her hands and wiped his tears away with her thumbs, then dabbed her own eyes. "We'll read it often, but we shouldn't let him play with it. It should stay with him, always."

Before the holidays, Adina planned a children's charity event. Cocktail parties were all the rage and many of her friends raved about a new book by James Beard, *Hor d'Oeurves and Canapes* and his catering company, Hors d'Oeuvre, Inc. She called his office.

"Hello, this is Adina Sapozhnikov. I'm planning a cocktail party on Tuesday, December second from 5:00 to 7:00, about fifty people in our home. Are you available for catering?"

"Yes, Mrs. Sapozhnikov, the second is open," said the secretary. "I'll put you through to Mr. Beard to discuss the menu."

After a brief discussion, James took control of the conversation. "Here's what I'll do..." He told her what he would be serving.

"That sounds wonderful, I'll leave the menu up to you, but we must end the evening with caviar if you can find it."

The day before the event, Adina asked David, "Do you think Sergei is old enough to join the party?"

"Absolutely! He's so comfortable with strangers, I think he'll love it. Besides, it's a children's charity event. He should be included."

Sergei wore a white shirt, little black satin bow tie, velvet jacket, matching short pants and highly polished high-top leather shoes.

As guests arrived, the caterer-waiters drifted among them with chilled champagne and platters of canapés including mushroom caps filled with blue cheese, salpicon of celery root, fingers of brioche covered with foie gras and a cheese platter with Stilton spread, cucumber spread and chicken marron served with toasted baguette slices.

Her long, dusty rose chiffon dress flowed behind Adina's smooth narrow stride as she mingled among her guests. She tried to keep the conversations light and merry, steering away from the war in Europe whenever she could.

While her guests enjoyed the elegant fare, Adina stood by the piano and sang Bellini's *Casta Diva* accompanied on the piano by her friend Irving. Her soprano voice filled the room with achingly pure luminescence. When she finished, the room fell completely still. Her performance moved some guests to tears. Then the room exploded with, "*Brava, Brava.*"

When the ovation subsided, Irving stood by the piano bench, "Rosa Ponselle couldn't have done better. Now, for a change of pace, Adina has agreed to sing my newest tune—"White Christmas."

Sergei stood next to Irving, his beautiful olive-green eyes hovering at keyboard level as he watched Irving's fingers dance over the keys.

While Adina performed, waiters set up a long linen-covered table laid with Beluga Caviar in clear glass bowls, snuggled in shaved ice. Around each bowl of caviar stood small separate bowls of hard cooked egg yolk and egg white, finely minced scallions, crème fraîche, lemon wedges and lightly toasted points of Russian black bread and Pumpernickel. Waiters wove through the crowd passing chilled coupes of French champagne and trays of test-tube-like glasses filled with frozen Russian vodka nestled in beds of shaved ice.

As Irving stepped away from the piano, no one noticed the chubby-cheeked, brown-haired, almost-three-year-old Sergei struggling to climb onto the piano bench. He pulled himself onto his tummy, then sat up, turned to face the keyboard and played *White Christmas.*

Adina, David and the guests turned to see who was playing. Sergei's parents couldn't believe their eyes—or their ears. "I assure you, we did not plan this," Adina told her guests. "Sergei has never touched the piano keys. Sometimes he sits on my lap while I play, but..." She smiled at her friend Irving, "Your song was his inspiration."

Sergei wiggled off the bench, his olive-brown eyes shining below long dark lashes as he took a bow. His forehead nearly touched his dimpled knees as everyone applauded.

"He looks so much like Adina," said one guest.

"And he's clearly inherited his mother's musical talent," said another.

"Yes, but he has David's chin," laughed yet another.

Adina and David beamed with pride. "We had no idea he had this talent," said David. "Can anyone recommend a teacher?"

Sergei began piano lessons on Saturday—the day before Japan attacked Pearl Harbor.

Audrey's Parents

As they spent more time together, Audrey saw her father in a totally different light. When she was little, he read to her, but after she started school, he had become a stranger, traveling a great deal, nominated for a Nobel Prize in science and respected by his students and the scientific community. He dressed the part, always looking dapper in his tweed suits and fedora.

But now, because of the unrest around the world, he stayed home. Spending so much time in his reading chair left his shirt and trousers rumpled. A small hole unraveled on one sleeve of his hunter green cardigan sweater, while one of the brown suede patches drooped from his elbow. Either he had never noticed, or he found the imperfections inconsequential. Audrey noticed that his unruly black hair and mustache had become steely gray and he needed a haircut. Without his professor persona, he seemed more real and approachable, more like the papa she remembered from her childhood.

Sometimes, Audrey took a break from her music and Eiffel put down his books. While Esther worked on her novel and Aimée attended culinary school, Eiffel and Audrey walked the streets of Paris. They wandered along Rue Cler just to smell the flowers, vegetables and fresh fruit. They paused near the entrance to the spice shop to inhale the scent of cloves, cumin and cardamom. A few doors down, they watched the chocolatier gently nestling an assortment of cherry cordials, pecan turtles and nutty fudge into a little white box.

She understood that Aimée's passion for preparing fine food, her mother's passion for literature and her father's passion for the cosmos matched her own passion for music.

Sometimes they would stop for a *café au lait* at a street café and discuss whatever was on Audrey's mind.

"Papa, the newspapers say this is a phony war. What do you think?"

"The war seems far away from Paris, but it is not phony. Hitler invaded Poland and he's sending Jews to horrible camps. No doubt he will soon invade France. I worry about French Jews, especially Bernard and others who live in our building."

June 1940

Eiffel decided to stay in the building while millions of Parisians, including most of their tenants, fled the city, abandoning their apartments and their lives, ahead of the Nazis invasion. "We are leaving our belongings except for a few items that will fit in our car," a tenant told Eiffel. His words came in breathless jerks, as if he had just run a marathon. "We hope we can find petrol to drive to Tours where my aunt owns a hotel," he said. "We will return when this war is over. Let us hope it is not long. *Au revoir.*"

"*Bon courage.*"

As German soldiers filled the streets and occupied every restaurant in Paris, there were rumors of violence and reports of arrests for no reason. Eiffel suggested, "We should leave the flat as little as possible. It's not safe."

"I will do most of cooking and with my fluent German, I should shop for food with our ration tickets," offered Aimée.

The abundance of food displayed in the markets diminished with each passing day. Aimée stood in line at the bakery before dawn, but when the store finally opened, she was lucky if she was allowed their full ration—one baguette per person per week.

Aimée took back streets and alleys to avoid the Germans. Sometimes, but rarely, her green mesh bag held three potatoes, an onion, two turnips, three eggs and one baguette, intended to feed all four of them for several days. On Audrey's eighteenth birthday, just before Christmas, Aimée managed to buy two extra eggs, but she could not buy flour or sugar to bake a cake.

Blackout curtains and curfew choked the city, leaving the streets dark and eerily silent. On a warm evening in April 1941, Eiffel, weary of reading by candlelight, rose from his chair and said to Audrey, "It is April in Paris and the City of Lights is in darkness. We have the opportunity to see the uninterrupted night sky like never before. Fetch a quilt and come to the roof with me, I have a surprise for you."

Eiffel held a single candle to light their way through the dark corridor and up the squeaky wooden steps to the roof. The thick wooden door creaked. Stepping gingerly, he moved to the edge of the roof and set up his tripod. Audrey spread the quilt as if for a picnic in the dark. When he snuffed the candle, the purple night sky settled around them. He rolled onto the quilt, one arm pillowing his head. Audrey put her head on his shoulder, remembering the only other time they stargazed together—before he became famous.

"I have never seen so many stars, Papa," Audrey whispered. "Look, a shooting star and another and another!"

"Yes, that is my surprise," he chuckled. "The Lyrids meteor shower is happening this week. We should see many meteors tonight and again tomorrow, but they are too fast to observe through my telescope." Then his voice became deep and harsh, "Hitler's army cannot stop them."

After a while, when their eyes had adjusted to the starlight, he stood and trained the telescope on Saturn, then stepped aside so Audrey could peer through the lens. She was as tall as her father; adjustments were unnecessary. "Galileo discovered the rings around Saturn in 1610. Can you imagine? He was the first human to observe those rings!" he said as Audrey saw them for the first time. Then he moved the scope's focus, "See this dot that looks like a star?" He stepped aside. "Actually, two stars swirling around each other create that dot of light. They are spectroscopic binary stars. My published research has been focused on spectroscopic binary stars. I travel to observatories around the world to study them."

As Audrey peered through the scope's eyepiece, she felt his passion for the dark sky, just like the feeling that overwhelmed her during the perfect execution of Liszt or Rachmaninoff. A sense of reverence and admiration squeezed her heart. Now she understood her father's dedication to his research and why he traveled the world. *Next to the vast universe, the Nazi threat seems strangely small and inconsequential,* she thought, *at least for tonight.*

"When the war is over and I continue my research, history will report that Eiffel Dupré discovered that the earth has another tiny moon. I will take you to an observatory where you can see it." His quiet voice sparkled with emotion. She had never heard him so thrilled about his work. "It is an asteroid captured by Earth's gravity. I first recorded sightings just after you were born."

"How big is your moon, Papa?"

"About twice the size of the *Arc de Triomphe*, a tiny primordial crumb compared to earth and her moon."

As the smog grew woolly and gray and the acrid scent of war mixed with the smell of turnip soup wafting up from the street, they gave up the telescope and reclined on the quilt again, happy to be outdoors—together. "My darling Audrey, did your mother ever tell you that my family immigrated to France from Italy?"

"No Papa, tell me the story."

"My grandparents, my uncle, Maman and Papa came to France, just weeks before my birth. Grandfather changed the family name to Dupré to sound more French and abandoned his Italian surname and language. I never learned what that name was. There are no written birth records, but I'm certain of my birthday, May 15, 1889. Maman told me I was born on the day *La Tour Eiffel* opened to the public. She and Papa were climbing the stairs when I decided it was time to join the world. I was born outdoors, under the stars, at the base of the tower. This is why my name is Eiffel Dupré. Just think, if they had been sightseeing elsewhere, my name could easily have been Versailles or Louvre."

A quiet chuckle escaped the thicket of his mustache, as he hugged Audrey.

"Eiffel Dupré sounds much better than Versailles Dupré or Louvre Dupré," she stifled a laugh. "They might have named you Champs-Elysées Dupré!"

He chuckled again and kissed her forehead.

Thinking of her papa as an infant reminded Audrey of the baby she gave away.

As if he knew her thoughts, he said, "Don't worry about the baby. I'm sure the adoptive parents will give the baby a happy home. You are only eighteen; you have plenty of time to fall in love and start a family."

"I was thinking about the baby too," she paused. "It's two and a half now. It seems odd, but giving up the baby confirmed I don't want to get married and have a family," said Audrey. "I've decided that music is my life's focus, just like the stars are your focus. Housework and children and having a husband to care for would interfere with who I want to be. I guess I'm not like other women."

Eiffel Dupré smiled to himself as he contemplated the veil of stars across the sky. When he met his wife, neither he nor Esther wanted marriage and a family. Tears of gratitude trickled toward his ears. "I love you and your mother very much, but our little family is not like other families," he whispered. Then, quickly changing the subject, he said, "My papa once told me that his great grandmother was a descendant of Galileo. And my mother's cousin was Raoul Pugno, an Italian composer and musician. It's no wonder you are a young virtuosa."

It was the first time Audrey heard her father say he loved her, the first time he acknowledged her musical genius and the first time he revealed his heritage. She savored every breath. "I love you too, Papa," she whispered, aware that, if not for the war, they would have had far less time to get to know one another.

"Come to the cellar with me. I have something important to show you," said Eiffel.

A Gestapo officer stubbed out his cigarette when he heard the door squeak on the neighboring roof. He watched a man setting up a telescope, but when the candle went out, the man vanished into darkness. Watching from behind a chimney, the officer assumed the man was alone. He reported his observation to his superiors, who quickly determined the man was Eiffel Dupré, the owner of the building, a famous scientist and possibly a spy.

Once inside, Eiffel pulled a match from his pocket, struck it on the sole of his shoe and lit the candle. They silently descended the wide marble stairs to the lobby, his hand shielding the candle's flame. Shadows flickered across the lobby like restless ghosts. The cellar door creaked open and the dusty old stairs groaned as they descended into the musty, dark underground chamber. He used the key from his pocket to open the wine cellar where his collection of fine wine rested on shelves.

"I have never trusted banks and have always kept cash on hand, just like my papa. During the depression, when my landlord could no longer maintain the property, I bought this building for a fraction of its value with francs I had locked in my safe." He knelt on the cool dusty floor and motioned for Audrey to join him. He moved the brick façade that camouflaged a heavy metal safe. "The four-digit combination is your birthday, 12-9-19-22. Try it. Start by turning the dial clockwise for at least four turns to clear the mechanism. Then stop at twelve. Turn counterclockwise to nine and so forth."

When the thick metal door squeaked open, Audrey gasped. "Papa, *tellement d'argent!*"

"There is enough here for us to live for years, if necessary," he said. "Although the newspapers insisted it was a phony war, I thought if the Nazis invade, we will need money when they are defeated. I closed my French bank account. There are US dollars in cash in my safe deposit box in Ohio as well. Do you have access to the account there?"

"Yes, Papa. Maman and I went to the bank before we left Columbus. They have my signature."

"These coins are gold, so if the French franc is worthless when this war is over, we will have gold to sell. Your maman knows about this hiding place, but tell no one else, not even Aimée."

He put a long chain with a key around her neck and pressed the key to the wine cellar into her palm. "Let's hope you never need this."

He groaned a bit as he straightened his legs to stand.

"I have another hiding place in my closet floor. I will show you tomorrow."

Aimée magically conjured meals with turnips, potatoes, onions and an occasional stale baguette. That morning, she had managed to bring home three eggs. Aimée served diminutive omelets filled with a few tiny bits of caramelized onion, then took her seat.

Before the war, Aimée would have prepared their omelets with two eggs each, filled them with sautéed spinach leaves and ham or bacon and garnished them with Mornay sauce. Now, Audrey didn't care.

Before taking a bite, she looked at her parents and felt overwhelmed with gratitude. The stress of her pregnancy and the war might have caused tension and angst and separated them further. Instead, she'd had the opportunity to recognize their gentle spirits. Time in New York, waiting for the birth, had drawn her closer to her mother. The German occupation kept her father at home allowing them to spend time together. He taught her about the cosmos he worshiped. Even with this meager meal, Audrey was happy they were all eating together.

From the breakfast table in their top-floor apartment, they didn't hear the four Gestapo officers pounding on the front entrance of the building.

The Arrest

Eiffel had hired the doorman, Shihab, partly due to his pleasant, helpful nature, but also because, speaking French, Arabic, Berber, German, English, Castellano, Russian and Dutch, he could communicate with the multinational tenants living in their building.

When the four Nazi officers pounded on the door, he unlocked it and said, *"Guten morgen offiziere, wie kann ich Ihnen helfen?"*

They pushed him aside. *"Wo ist Herr Dupré?"*

"On the top-floor," Shihab replied in German, pointing to the elevator.

Two of the officers guarded the elevator while the other two climbed the stairs. From the fourth step, one officer pulled his Luger from its holster, turned and shot Shihab in the heart, muttering, "Dirty mixed breed." With his dark skin and blue eyes, the Germans considered Shihab a mongrel.

When the Duprés heard the rock-crushing thud of jackboots echoing off the marble stairs, their heads turned in unison. At first, Audrey feared for their Jewish friends Bernard and Geneviève on the second floor, but the boots kept pounding up the stairs. Suddenly the officers kicked in the door, shattering the thick, white casing. Soldiers dressed in gray-green tunics grabbed Eiffel by each arm but ignored the women, as if Eiffel were alone in the room.

His round-rimmed glasses skittered across the floor. His slippers were left overturned beside his toppled chair.

Afterward, although they didn't remember leaving their chairs, Audrey and Aimée stood with their backs against the wall. Mrs. Dupré remained seated, dazed, in shock. It all happened so fast.

Audrey gazed at her father's omelet, with only one bite missing, his fork tossed on the floor. A quiet horror settled over her. She knew her father would rather die than cooperate with the Germans.

And, she realized, they would never again share a family meal.

The officers dragged Mr. Dupré down the stairs to the lobby and forced him to step over Shihab's dead body. His socks soaked up Shihab's blood leaving grizzly footprints.

From the top-floor balcony, Audrey watched the officers push her father into a truck and speed away.

"Mama, are you okay?" Audrey spoke English even though they usually spoke French now that they lived in Paris.

Esther's nod contradicted her shocked, uncomprehending stare.

Audrey tried to call the front desk. An eerie silence answered.

With their arms hooked together, Audrey and Aimée crept down the stairs, peeking toward the lobby to be sure all the Germans had left the building. They were horrified to see Shihab's body sprawled on the marble floor, a pool of blood smeared around him. Bloody footprints led across the lobby, down the stoop and all the way to the curb.

"What should we do?" Aimée's voice was unrecognizable.

"We can't leave him here on the lobby floor…" said Audrey, trying not to stare at the blood spilling from Shihab's chest. "I think we should wrap the body and take it outside; then I'll get Bernard. He'll know what to do."

In a daze, emotions checked by shock and fear, they rolled Shihab's body into a white sheet they found in his flat and carried him out the front door.

Audrey climbed the stairs two at a time to consult Bernard Berkowitz in 2C. He was a famous tenor with the Paris Opera. Before the occupation, Audrey often played the piano accompaniment when he sang at the synagogue or practiced his part in an opera.

Meanwhile, Aimée went to the cellar to gather a bucket, soap and rags to clean up the blood.

When Audrey knocked on Bernard's door, no one answered. She knocked again, "Bernard, it's me, Audrey. Please, we need your help."

The door slowly opened, revealing his pale face, "We heard the jackboots and hid under the bed. We thought they were coming for us. What has happened?"

"They arrested Papa and shot Shihab."

When Audrey and Bernard came downstairs, Shihab's body was no longer on the street. The blood-soaked sheet lay on the stoop like a garish, empty shroud.

"You did the right thing, carrying the body outdoors," said Bernard, withdrawing his glance as Aimée began to scrub the floor. "A horse-drawn wagon combs the streets every morning, gathering the dead." The famous tenor's voice sounded unusually hoarse and gravely.

"I had no idea," Audrey whispered. Her chest ached and she couldn't breathe. Feeling shattered and helpless, she trembled, though the room was warm. Rarely leaving the flat the past year, she knew little about the violence that the Nazis brought to her beloved Paris. The remaining tenants had whispered reports of brutality they had seen on the streets or heard of, but those things happened to other people, not the ones she loved. The realization that the savagery could impact her own life so tragically made her head spin and her stomach heave. She leaned over the waste bin to vomit.

Esther Goes Missing

"Are you feeling unwell again today, Maman?" Audrey put her hand on her mother's forehead. "You still have a fever. Let me walk with you to the doctor's office."

"You stay here with Aimée," said Esther as she put on her coat. "I can go alone. I'll be fine. They won't bother a woman walking to the doctor's office. It's not far."

Audrey and Aimée both insisted on coming along, but Esther stood firm. "I'll be fine! There's no point in all of us going out into the madness. I won't be gone long."

She kissed Audrey's cheek, straightened her hat and stepped into the stairwell without looking back.

Esther left the building at 10:00 a.m. For lunch, Aimée served a small bowl of soup, but Audrey couldn't eat. She paced back and forth in the living room, "She should be home by now. Something happened. I'd go look for her, but I don't know where the doctor's office is. I feel so helpless."

Each hour stretched like a day. Audrey kept peeking through the blackout curtains, watching the street below as if her mother might reappear by sheer force of will.

"Maybe they're just questioning her and they will release her today," Audrey whispered to Aimée, as if a lurking Nazi might hear.

Leaving Paris

June 1941

Even a soft knock on the door caused Audrey and Aimée to jump. When Audrey slowly opened the door, Bernard and Geneviève stepped inside.

"We are leaving tonight," whispered Bernard. "There is an underground network smuggling Jews to Switzerland. We are not safe here and neither are you. The Nazis have requisitioned many apartment buildings and are likely to come here any day. You and Aimée should be ready to escape."

Audrey reached to hug her friends, "I will miss you terribly. Come back when the war is over. *Bon courage.*"

That afternoon, Audrey whispered toward her soup, her spoon untouched. "Bernard is certain the Nazis will requisition this building." Tears splashed into her bowl. She looked up at Aimée. "He said we should be prepared to leave at a moment's notice, but what if Maman and Papa return and can't find us? How can we leave?" Her was voice barely audible.

"If Nazis want this building, they will take it. They will arrest us or worse! If Aunt and Uncle return, the Nazis will put them in the street or send them to camp. We have no choice, Audrey. If *boche* come, we must leave."

That night, Audrey crept to the cellar with a candle, carrying her winter coat over her arm. The combination lock on the safe clicked softly, as if it knew the urgency of stillness. She took a handful of francs and gold coins, then closed the safe and restored the camouflage. If the Germans forced them out, Audrey and Aimée would need money.

In the dark cellar, she lit a second candle, took the needle and thread from her pocket. With trembling fingers, she sewed the money into the lining of her coat.

They stowed two knapsacks packed with chunks of cheese wrapped in paper and jars of water so they would be ready to leave quickly if the Nazis seized the building.

As if her parents' books could keep them with her, Audrey gathered her father's book, *Les Étoiles,* written before she was born and *The Adventures of Tom Sawyer* he read as a boy. She held *Voices of the Night* and *Lyrics of Life,* her mother's most cherished books.

"I will always have you with me," she whispered as if her parents could hear her. She hugged the books to her chest before stowing them in her knapsack along with her winter coat with the money sewn inside.

As Bernard Berkowitz predicted, Nazis appropriated the building a few days later. When they heard the door crash open and jackboots in the lobby, Audrey took Aimée's hand and they fled down the back stairs and out the service entrance. They spent the night huddled together, listening to the distant bark of gun fire and rustle of rats. As daylight cast dark shadows, Aimée noticed a truck parked nearby.

"I have an idea," she whispered. "That truck, it is filled with empty wine bottles. Maybe it is going to Beaune, where I grew up."

When the driver returned to the truck, Aimée approached him. "*Bonjour Monsieur, comment allez-vous aujourd'hui,* can you give us a ride to Beaune?" she asked in French. "*S'il vous plaît?*"

He insisted on speaking German but agreed to take them— for a price.

Audrey's stomach twisted as the driver's smirk deepened.

"This is all we have," Aimée said in German, her voice flat as she handed him the francs.

His sinister snicker sent chills down Audrey's spine. Aimée climbed in first. The driver's rough paw lingered on her derrière when he shoved her into the bed of the truck.

The waxed green canvas tarpaulin snapped in the breeze as it closed over them. They huddled on top of empty wine bottles as the truck bounced along *Autoroute du Soleil,* a four-hour ride. With only their clothes for protection, bottle tops pushed into their flesh, leaving bruises as if a giant sea creature had assaulted them.

Gravel crunched. The brakes squealed. The motor stopped. A black silence wrapped them like a shroud. They groped in the dark to catch each other's hand. The truck driver's door squeaked open. Gravel bit his boots as he walked to the back of the truck. When the tarpaulin jerked aside, they jumped inside their skin.

As Aimée leapt to the gravel road, the driver seized her arm, grabbed her breast and sneered, "*Du schuldest mir.*"

Audrey didn't understand the German, but his intention was

clear. With a shudder, she eased out of the truck and stood in the dark, ready to run for help—she didn't know in what direction.

In the shadows, Audrey saw only silhouettes. She listened to the heated but quiet conversation between a lecherous monster and a hissing cat. Then—quiet.

Aimée stepped back. The driver returned to the cab. The engine started. The blue-tinted headlights cut through the dust. He slowly pulled away.

"How did you convince him?" Audrey whispered, her voice ragged.

"I told him if he didn't let go of me, I would scream and soldiers would arrest him," Aimée said in a flat voice. "Maybe he believed me?"

The Vineyard in Beaune

June 1941

Audrey followed Aimée through the quiet, starlit streets to an alley behind the hotel. Aimée tapped on an old wooden door. No one answered. She thumped a little louder but still, no one came.

"Let's hope the Nazis haven't arrested them," she whispered. Finally, she knocked as loud as she dared. The noise echoed off the surrounding buildings. Neighbors may have peaked, but no lights lit the windows.

Finally, an old man's unsteady voice came from behind the door, "*Qui est là*"

"Chef, *c'est moi*, Aimée."

Audrey heard the lock slide aside. The thick wooden door creaked slightly open. A gnarled old hand pushed a candle into the dark night. Its flame cast a flickering light across Aimée's face.

"*Ma Dieu,*" whispered the old man. His other hand emerged—wrinkled, spotted and knotted with age. His finger curled, inviting them inside. The door quietly closed. As the small flickering candle threw long shadows behind him, the lock clicked into place.

Aimée kissed the old Chef on both cheeks as the scent of bread and ash hung in the air. Soon, other members of Aimée's hotel family embraced her. The head housekeeper, Madame Laliberty, stepped into the candle's glow. Audrey saw no other faces, but Aimée recognized voices and scents of the aunties who had loved her all her life.

"I cannot believe it," whispered Chef.

When Aimée stepped aside to introduce Audrey, Chef moved the candle from Audrey's face to Aimée's face and then back to Audrey. In the dim candlelight, they looked like twins.

"Our fathers were brothers," Aimée said in French.

"Of course, the scientist," he said. "Delighted, *Mademoiselle* Dupré."

"The Nazis arrested Uncle and commandeered the building," Aimée whispered. "We have nowhere else to go."

Madame Laliberty, wrapped in a long, well-worn flannel housecoat, her white hair escaping the nightcap that framed her weathered face, whispered, "We must be very careful. Tomorrow, you will tell us your story. Tonight, I will show you to a guest room. Keep the blackout drapes closed tight. Use only a small candle. Never look out the window or pull the blackout curtains aside, day or night.

"There is chamber pot under bed. I will bring a pitcher of warm water. The wardrobe has clean clothes."

Madame Laliberty didn't mention that the young Jewish woman who originally owned that clothing had suddenly disappeared one afternoon, along with her Swiss husband, a wine merchant.

As Madame Laliberty lit a candle and turned to lead the way, Chef patted Audrey's back and hugged Aimée again. "I will bring soup and wine," he whispered. "You must be starving."

Madame Laliberty tied kerchiefs around their hair. "*Boche* want us to make wine for them, but they arrested our workers, sent men to fight and some to work camps. The vintner, he will be pleased to see you." She cupped Aimée face. "If *boche* come, don't look up. Keep working. If they see your pretty faces…" She shook her head, unable to finish. She took a deep, ragged breath as she led Aimée and Audrey into the vineyard and introduced them to the vintner.

Audrey quickly learned to cradle a cluster of grapes, clip the stem with sharp secateurs and gently place each bunch into a basket lashed bandolier-style over her shoulder.

The 1941 harvest was dismal—ruined by bad weather, missing workers and lack of supplies.

In her nineteen years, Audrey stayed fit by walking everywhere and climbing the stairs, but her hands had never worked beyond the piano keyboard. Her long, delicate fingers quickly chapped and blistered.

"My hands are so sore," said Audrey.

"Mine as well," said Aimée looking at her red, raw fingers. "I remember Maman's cure."

Aimée boiled a mash of water, grape skins, seeds, stems and leaves left from wine pressing.

"Ahhh," said Audrey as they submerged their hands and feet into the strange, warm mixture.

"Our skin, it will turn purple," Aimée warned, "But pain will go."

"The soup tonight has potato, a leek and a little milk but that is the last leek," announced Chef. "The Nazis, they took all but one old milk cow, all the horses and all but one chicken who hid in the tree." He glanced at the nearby Plane tree as if it had saved his life. "The Nazis, they missed our cellar. We hid potatoes, turnips, carrots, beets, cabbage, onions and garlic, but soon, the cellar will be empty."

The months of the occupation ground on and as Chef predicted, the larder supplies ran out. Audrey dug a few potatoes and turnips from the small garden, but not enough to feed Audrey, Aimée and the old people the Germans left behind. In the spring she tried planting between the grapevines, but the gravelly soil that provided good drainage for healthy grapevines offered dismal support for a vegetable crop. There were no animals to produce manure for fertilizer and no compost to amend the soil. In late summer, they harvested plums, but without sugar, the plum jam tasted bitter and spoiled quickly.

Audrey's hands suffered further abuse as she carried old bricks from a dilapidated shed near the barn to the hotel and down the stone stairs to a cavernous storage vault below. Like winemakers across the region, they were taking measures to keep the finest wines hidden from the Germans. Together, Aimée, Audrey and the old people installed a wall fronted with a faded and chipped statue of Our Lady of Grace. They camouflaged the new construction with dust and spiders to make the wall look old and authentic. The old vintner hoped their deception would leave thousands of bottles of their precious wine inventory intact and available to sell when the Germans were defeated, as he knew they would be.

To camouflage the newer, less valuable wine, Audrey helped brand bottles with the false labels. Then Aimée used a tea kettle to lightly steam the racks of falsely labeled bottles so that when they shook dirty rugs over them, the dust would stick to the bottles, making them look older and more valuable.

"Help catch spiders to do their work," said Aimée.

Audrey watched in revulsion as Aimée gently closed her palms over a spider in a dark corner, then released it onto the falsely labeled racks of wine.

"I'm happy to help however I can, but I cannot catch a spider!" cringed Audrey, backing away as Aimée released an especially large black arachnid onto the dusty bottles.

The next morning, Audrey returned to the cellar to shake more dirt over the webs the spiders had created overnight, praying Chef wouldn't ask her to catch more spiders.

Weeks later, when the Nazis came to buy wine, doddering Chef led them to the falsely labeled bottles. After the German's departed with the first load of low-grade wine with high-value labels, the household enjoyed a level of glee, knowing they were pouring second rate wine down the gullets of German officers—but their delight was diluted, knowing if the Nazis discovered the deception, everyone at the vineyard would certainly be executed.

Sergei's Music Lessons

New York, 1942

Isolated from the war that gripped Europe, four-year-old Sergei learned to read music by watching the notes on sheet music while his mother played the piano. His eyes tracked the notes across the page as if he had known all along how music worked. Within a few months, before he could tie his shoes, he was composing.

He learned to read books the same way—just weeks after he had learned to read music. His eyes tracked the letters as his mother read and soon he was reading on his own. At first, she thought he had memorized the stories, so she bought new books he had never seen but he read them without hesitation.

She felt she had little to do with his knowledge; he was born knowing so many things.

"He's not like other children and that's alright," said his father, David. "As his parents, I think all we need to do is keep him safe and give him every opportunity to experience the world."

"But he's only four years old!" Adina wrung her hands and scowled at her husband. "He still needs his mother." Even as she said it, she knew, he wouldn't need her for long.

Sergei and his parents attended operas, theater performances and movies. They started with Disney films, *Pinocchio*, *Bambi* and *Dumbo*. When they saw *The Sorcerer's Apprentice*, Sergei jumped from his seat into the aisle and directed the music.

The man sitting behind them leaned over David's shoulder. "He's remarkably good at that," he whispered. "I'm glad you didn't make him stay in his seat. It's a lot more entertaining this way."

"Amazing, isn't he?" whispered David with a big grin.

On Saturday afternoons, David tried to encourage Sergei to play catch in the park, but Sergei was physically awkward, with arms and legs that seemed too long for his body. His passion for music left no room for sports.

"I won't force him to play sports any more than I'll force him to practice piano. He seems to know what he needs."

Adina laughed, "Yes, except for eating his vegetables!"

They saw *Rhapsody in Blue* at Aeolian Hall and *Annie Get Your Gun, Kiss Me Kate* and *Oklahoma!*

At first, ushers would suggest they move to a section more appropriate for a toddler, but of course, David refused. Even at four years old, Sergei always had a first-row balcony seat where he could see the orchestra and jump into the aisle if he felt moved to conduct. More often, he sat spellbound, his gaze flicking between the stage and the orchestra pit. He absorbed it all. Adina and David were certain he understood the music far better than anyone else in the audience.

The butler chauffeured Sergei and his mother to his first day at the Braun Boys' School in Manhattan. He let her give him another hug, then pulled away from her grip as the teacher welcomed Sergei into the classroom. Sergei's classmates were the sons and grandsons of famous senators, actors and Rockefellers.

"Mama, can I stay home so I can learn something?" he said on the way home one afternoon.

"But Sergei, darling, that's why you go to school, to learn. You've only been there a few days."

He pulled his reading book from his satchel and handed it to his mother. *The ABCs.* "Today we studied the letter B." His tone was incredulous. "No one in my class knows how to read! Today I played the piano, but the teacher made me stop. It's just as well, that old piano has no dynamic contrast, it sounds like a cabbage."

In many ways, Sergei was a typical five-year-old boy, complaining about going to bed on time, unwilling to eat his vegetables and his room was always messy. His shelves were cluttered with board games: Chutes and Ladders, Sorry, Monopoly, Parcheesi and Backgammon. Meanwhile, he was composing music on manuscript paper. When his parents were asleep, he secreted books from his father's library, reading with a flashlight under the covers.

Adina and David hired tutors. When they announced they were withdrawing Sergei from school, the headmaster objected, "All boys have a right to an education."

"He's bored to tears. Don't you have some sort of evaluation instrument that can measure his abilities?" asked David.

Once Sergei demonstrated his reading skills and took placement tests in math, biology and chemistry, the authorities agreed he was better off with tutors and less of a distraction for the teachers and other students.

Sergei was so intense about his music and books that Adina bribed him to go for walks in Central Park with her. They hired a physical education teacher to help him balance his life, but he preferred to read and practice.

In the summer of 1949, Sergei enrolled in a music program at Juilliard where he studied piano as well as violin, cello, flute and oboe.

His full name, Sergei Sapozhnikov, confounded the faculty—unpronounceable, difficult to spell and impossible to remember. Within weeks, the staff and students at Juilliard simply called him Sergei. He became a legend among the students: the boy who played everything—well.

Adina was aghast when Sergei announced, "I'm taking the bus to Juilliard ALONE. I never have a moment's peace with all the people in and out of here. And you treat me like a baby!"

"But Sergei, you're only ten years old."

"Yes, I'm ten now and I can ride the bus by myself." He threw on his coat and slammed the door with the force of a boy who wants to be free.

She didn't stop him, but she called out, "Do you have bus fare?"

"Yes mother, I have what I need."

Audrey and Aimée

One warm sunny afternoon, as Audrey and Aimée came into the kitchen after finishing their work in the vineyard, Chef said, "Audrey, come. I show you how to enjoy fine Burgundy." Although Aimée had learned how to enjoy wine before she was ten years old, she followed them into the dining room.

"Today we taste red Burgundy, tomorrow we taste white," said Chef. "Yes?"

"But I thought Burgundy was red," said Audrey.

"Most Americans think so," chuckled Chef. "Burgundy wine is made in the Burgundy region of France."

"In Ohio, Maman always drank Chardonnay, where does that come from?" asked Audrey as she followed Chef to the dining room where he had gathered six glasses and opened two bottles of wine.

"Ah, that is a good question. If Chardonnay grapes grow in the Burgundy region, the wine becomes white Burgundy. But if grown elsewhere, it is simply Chardonnay."

Chef, looking bent and tired, poured a small amount of Pinot Noir into three of the bowl-shaped wine glasses. Before lifting his glass, he slowly shuffled to the dining room window and with a swift jerk of his boney arm, swept the blackout curtains to one side, exposing the late fall afternoon. All the way to the horizon, perfectly spaced rows of orange and yellow vines climbed the rolling hills. The three glasses of red wine sparkled as a bright yellow beam danced over the polished oak table, casting long glowing shadows beyond the glasses. Finally, his knobby arthritic fingers grasped the foot of his wineglass.

"The heat from your fingers will warm the wine. You must grip by the stem or the foot, just so." Then, holding his glass up to the bright window, Chef said, "First, gently swirl, watch its legs run down. Thicker and slower legs show more alcohol in the wine."

He put his nose over his tilted glass, "What do you smell?"

Awkwardly gripping the glass by the stem, Audrey swirled, trying not to splash onto the table.

"I smell… vanilla… and berries and… maybe oak?" said Audrey.

Aimée nodded in agreement.

"*Parfaite!*" said Chef. "Now taste."

Audrey brought her glass to her lips.

Chef raised one eyebrow as if to say *and…?*

"And I taste strawberry, raspberry and blackberry. This is lovely!" she said, taking another sip.

"*Tchin-tchin!*" chimed Aimée, lifting her glass.

They repeated the tasting lesson with fresh glasses and the other bottle of red wine.

"I don't smell the depth in this one. Its legs are thinner and the flavor isn't as robust. The texture isn't as smooth either. It's not bad but there's a significant difference."

"*Excellente*! This is the wine German officers took," he chuckled.

"So, this is why we camouflaged the labels. Won't they notice?"

"The *boche*, they cannot distinguish. All French vintners sell lower-quality wine and German officers have nothing to compare. They are happy to have wine, but maybe the *boche*, they would like more beer?"

The winemaking season ended when snow fell in the vineyard. The perfectly spaced rows of dark, leafless vines climbed the white rolling hills like black lace on white satin while the cobblestone streets became slippery mounds of white fondant candy.

Drinking weak coffee in the morning, made from chicory and grain and sipping watered-down wine in the afternoon, Audrey read every book she could find in the hotel. She pulled the blackout curtain aside just enough to illuminate the text until Madame Laliberty came by and closed the curtain with a huff.

In a dusty corner of an unoccupied guest room, she discovered Hemingway's *The Sun Also Rises* and *A Farewell to Arms*. In the room she shared with Aimée, she found a new copy of *To Have and Have Not* on the nightstand. The book had belonged to the wine merchant, arrested by the Nazis. He'd read as far as page thirty then marked his place with a postcard photo of the hotel, the same photo used on wine labels.

In the photo, rows of grape vines laddered the hillside beyond the hotel. Below the steeply pitched roof covered with multicolored glazed tiles in geometric patterns, typical of fifteenth century Burgundian architecture, the courtyard glowed in the sunshine.

The wine merchant had started a note, but never finished: *Dearest Mamma, Rachel and I are staying at this lovely vineyard.*

Tears gathered in Audrey's eyes as she put her hand on her heart. She wondered if this man, like her, would ever see his mother again.

She reread her father's well-worn first edition of *The Adventures of Tom Sawyer* and savored her mother's poetry books, *Poems and Other Writings* and *Lyrics of Life*. She even read *Les Étoiles*, the textbook her father had written in 1921. The text still made little sense to her, but as she turned the pages, she heard his voice and felt his enthusiasm, as if his breath warmed the words.

Three-year-old Audrey cuddled next to her father in his overstuffed chair, her knees tucked under her chin, her head resting on his tweed sleeve. He read aloud from Les Étoiles. She listened to his voice rise and fall as if he told the story of a mean Doppler Effect who chased Binary Stars around the big sun. "Spectroscopic binary star systems are usually," his voice rose as if Mr. McGregor entered the scene, "Detected by the mooovement of the emmmission and absorrrrption lines in the observed spectrum, caused by," he lowered his voice to a high pitched whisper, like mama rabbit, "The Doppler Effect as the stars move in their ooorrrrbit."

She understood not a word but, mesmerized by her father's rich baritone voice, she melted into the lingering woodsy, juniper berry aroma of his pipe tobacco and the scent of old paper.

As she grew up, he became less and less accessible, spending more and more time in his library on the second floor or away from home. By the time Aimée joined their family, when Audrey was thirteen, time with her father had become precious and rare. The scent of his pipe tobacco and old books became her anchor—a way to keep him near when he traveled half-way around the world, mapping the cosmos.

Wrapped in threadbare blankets against the coldest winter in history, Audrey crept to the parlor holding a flickering candle while Madame Laliberty's warning echoed, "We must avoid drawing the German's attention. You mustn't play the piano. We never know where they might be lurking and there seems to be no logic to what will interest or annoy them."

Audrey settled onto the bench and let her stiff fingers dance over the piano's fallboard as she played her favorites, in silence. Her imagination created beautiful compositions only she could hear.

As the spring sun melted the snow and warmed the vineyard, the old vintner taught Audrey and Aimée how to prune and tie fast-growing vines to tightly strung wires. Even wearing gloves, Audrey developed heavy calluses from the rugged work.

Looking at her fingers, blistered and raw, she wondered if they would ever play again. Two years had passed since she played.

One night in April, after everyone had gone to sleep, Audrey whispered to Aimée, "Come outdoors with me. I have a surprise for you."

"Now?" said Aimée. "In the dark?"

Audrey silently marched down the stairs with a small candle and two big quilts; Aimée followed like a curious kitten. Audrey spread one quilt on a patch of dewy new grass.

"Lay down and we'll cover up with the other quilt."

Audrey blew out the candle. They put their hands under their heads like pillows and their elbows touched.

"I have never seen so many stars," whispered Aimée, her eyes adjusting to the starlight cast across the dark sky. "Oh look! Shooting stars! They are everywhere!"

Audrey laughed a little too loudly, "Yes, this happens every April. Papa said some years are better than others. This is a particularly good year!"

"*Merci beaucoup*, Audrey," Aimée whispered. "So few things bring joy these days."

The next morning, Madame Laliberty found their bedroom door open and the room empty. "*Mon gracieux*, what has happened to the girls?" She trembled as she searched all of the guest rooms, then thumped downstairs as fast as her old legs would take her.

"Chef! Chef! Where are the girls? They aren't in their room!"

"Maybe they went for an early walk?"

"It's not yet daylight! Why would they go out in the dark?" her old voice trembled more than usual.

Out the kitchen window, in the pink predawn light, she saw the mound of quilts on the grass. Opening the kitchen door, she surveyed the yard, making sure no Germans lurked. "There you are, you crazy girls! What are you thinking?" Her voice sounded quiet but screechy.

Aimée peeked over the top of the quilt with sleepy eyes.

"I'm sorry if we frightened you, Auntie," she said. "We came out to see the stars. We didn't intend to fall asleep."

Audrey peeked from her side of the quilt. "Tomorrow night you must come to the yard with us. The shooting stars are magnificent," she said, rubbing her eyes with the back of her hands like a sleepy little girl.

"We have so much work to do," Madame Laliberty scolded. "Come inside for breakfast. The old hen left us a few eggs."

That afternoon, clear blue skies shimmered and the sun warmed Audrey's back. The soft breeze blowing through the wires sounded like her father's voice, as if she cuddled in his lap and his deep baritone voice read *Les Étoiles*. The breeze seemed to carry a whiff of pipe tobacco and the smell of old paper.

"Hello Papa," she whispered.

She smelled her mother's Chanel N°5 and heard her faint words, *Oh, how I wish it was my voice you remembered reading* Peter Rabbit. The sound of those words echoed through the growing vines.

Oh, how I wish.... thought Audrey, *Maman and Papa would have been wonderful grandparents.*

Aimée's voice brought Audrey back to the vineyard, "I finished my row, now I help finish yours."

"Thank you Aimée, but you go on in for lunch. I'll finish and join you in a bit."

"Are you feeling alright? You look flushed."

"I'm enjoying the sun on my back, the smell of the vineyard and the sound of the breeze," she said with a smile, but her eyes reflected no signs of joy.

The Germans are Leaving

August, 1944

During the night, rumbling noises near the vineyard awakened Audrey and Aimée. "What's happening? Do they come this way?" wondered Aimée as Audrey peeked around the curtain, despite Madame Laliberty's warning not to open the blackout curtains for any reason.

She saw an endless caravan of German tanks, jeeps and trucks with dim headlights, thundering down the dirt road, surrounded by clouds of moonlit dust. "Looks like the *boche* are on the move," whispered Audrey.

"Where do you think they are going?"

"Let's hope they're going back to Germany."

Audrey and Aimée tried to go to sleep, but their curiosity and the roar of the caravan kept them awake for hours.

The next day, Audrey and Aimée watched a muddy green jeep roar up the long driveway toward the hotel. One man stood shouting, holding the windshield with one hand and wildly waving the other.

"Should we run to barn?" said Aimée, dropping her hoe.

"I don't think so," said Audrey with her hand hovering above her dark bangs to block the sun's glare. "They look too happy to be dangerous."

As the jeep drew close enough for them to hear the shouts over the roar of the engine, Audrey heard one man say, "Paris is free, the Germans are leaving!"

Audrey, Aimée and the old people cheered and paraded through the hotel, ripping blackout curtains from the windows. In the sun-filled dining room, Chef opened two bottles of Burgundy.

"This wine is magnificent," breathed Audrey. "How did you manage to keep this from the Germans?"

Chef's foggy old eyes twinkled, "I stashed six bottles behind loose stones in the empty root cellar. We hid the rest of our inventory behind that brick wall and the statue of Our Lady of Grace.

Their meager dinner tasted better just because Paris was free. Madame Laliberty's hollow, wrinkled face became pink and radiant with the joy of liberation and the wine. "Audrey, it is time for you to play for us."

Audrey slid onto the piano bench. Her hardened hands hesitated over the keys, "My hands are so stiff." Slowly she played *Ah, vous dirai-je, Maman*, the Mozart piece she had learned when she was three years old. Audrey laughed when Aimée sang along, "Twinkle, twinkle little star."

Then Audrey played *La Marseillaise*, the French National Anthem. At first, filled with raw emotion, the weary vineyard and hotel staff stood around the piano and hung their heads as if in prayer.

"Encore," murmured Chef. Soon, their quivering elderly voices sounded young again, as their weathered faces glowed with relief and gratitude.

> *Allons enfants de la Patrie,*
> *Le jour de gloire est arrivé!*
> *Contre nous de la tyrannie*
> *L'étendard sanglant est levé, (bis)*
> *Entendez-vous dans les campagnes*
> *Mugir ces féroces soldats?*
> *Ils viennent jusque dans vos bras*
> *Égorger vos fils, vos compagnes!*

As the others savored their Musigny, Bouchard Père & Fils 1937, Audrey's fingers became intimate with the yellowed ivory keys. She cherished each note. Her heart swelled with the feel of the keys.

For the first time, she played the composition she had created in her mind during cold, dark winter nights in Beaune.

"I did not know you had such beautiful music inside you, Miss Dupré," said Madame Laliberty, her face wet with emotion. "I have longed for music even more than meat."

Return to Paris

When Audrey and Aimée decided it was safe to return to Paris, Chef offered to drive them to the train station in a jolting and sputtering 1935 Opel Blitz left behind by the retreating Germans. Madame Laliberty spread an old quilt over the ragged, filthy seat and left the windows down to mitigate the smell of diesel fuel and decay—rodents, smoke, mildew.

Audrey's fingers brushed the bullet hole perforations along the passenger side of the dusty green truck. "We are so fortunate," she whispered, locking arms with Aimée.

Chef and Madame Laliberty stood next to them in the sunshine and Audrey noticed their ages. Chef's stooped shoulders, wrinkled face and warbling voice reminded Audrey that he was an old man, about the same age as Madame Laliberty.

Reaching to give each of the girls a long, tender hug, Madame Laliberty said, "You must come for a visit in better times…" She stepped back, her gnarled fingers wiping tears from her wizened cheeks.

The young women climbed into the cab, looking very much like peasant sisters. Audrey's black hair hung like a brittle and dull horse's tail. Aimée's dark curls scattered around her face and down her back, looking more like scribbles than wispy willow branches. Aimée covered her well-worn colorless dress with a moth-eaten wool sweater she'd found in a closet at the hotel while Audrey stowed her old money-filled coat in her knapsack. They both wore the scarred and ill-fitting work-boots Madame Laliberty had found in the cellar when they first began working in the vineyard.

At the train station, Chef kissed them each on both cheeks. "With your help, we kept the 1937 vintage from the Nazis. Such a feat would have been impossible without your young strength." The package he gave them contained four bottles of his treasured Burgundy: Musigny, Bouchard Père & Fils 1937. "The grapes harvested here in '37 made the finest wine of my lifetime. It will age over time to even finer complexity. Be sure to store it properly."

He stepped back when they boarded and waved as the train pulled out. "*Au revoir mes petites.*"

During their train trip back to Paris, Aimée used the Sommelier's knife included in the package to open the first bottle. "*Santé*," Aimée toasted, offering Audrey the first sip of Musigny, Bouchard Père & Fils 1937.

"*Merci beaucoup*," said Audrey. She carefully lifted the bottle to her lips, but the swaying jolt of the train caused her to spill wine down her chin. They muffled their giggles like children playing hide and seek, momentarily forgetting the war and the loss.

As the train bumped over the rough tracks and passengers swayed to the rhythm, Aimée and Audrey savored one of the most coveted wines ever produced, straight from the bottle. Returning to Paris filled them with fear, joy and anxiety. They behaved like young students headed to their first adventure away from home. The clacking wheels and forlorn call of the whistle seemed more like music than noise.

When the bottle was half empty and their cheeks glowed from the alcohol, Audrey and Aimée noticed the train was eerily silent except for the wheels screeching and brakes hissing as the train made frequent stops. They began to notice the gaunt cheeks and blank stares of their fellow passengers and the stench of body odor and dirty diapers.

Audrey noticed three toddlers with red, runny noses and chapped little hands clutching the skirt of their frail-looking maman's colorless housedress, as if they might fall from the train. An old man, perhaps their grandfather, slumped beside them, his eyes carved deep into his skull. The little family huddled on the seat by the exit, their haunted eyes full of fear, ready to jump and run if necessary.

After taking another sip, Audrey contemplated the drawing on the wine label, the same drawing she had seen on the postcard she found in the wine merchant's book. On the label, the line drawing of the hotel, scratched and stained from years behind the loose stones, still retained its beauty. The sophisticated drawing and smoky fruit flavors of the smooth, elegant wine contrasted sharply as she gazed out the window at the bombed-out buildings, cratered fields, piles of blasted stone walls and scorched leafless trees, stretching as far as she could see.

Close to the tracks, emaciated women and children gazed at the ground as they walked, some barefoot, their sepia-colored clothing in tatters.

She couldn't contain her tears. Overwhelmed with gratitude, Audrey hugged Aimée. "I would not have survived without you and your hotel family." She took another gulp, "Santé," and passed the bottle to Aimée.

"I am thankful we survived together," said Aimée with her arm over Audrey's shoulders, "*Tchin-tchin!*"

Audrey tossed the empty bottle onto an overflowing trash bin when they disembarked in Paris. They carried their knapsacks with the remaining bottles carefully wrapped inside. Walking toward the apartment building, Aimée asked, "What if our building was bombed?"

"*Ne t'inquiètes pas* I sewed money into the lining of my coat. We'll get by."

"So that is why you wear that old coat," laughed Aimée.

"Let's not worry until we see the building." Audrey's voice sounded confident, but as they moved closer, her heart pounded and she rocked between joy and grief, happy to be returning to Paris but wondering if she would see her parents again.

The Art Déco balconies held withered flowers, their droopy long-dead blooms a ghostly reminder of the life that once filed the building. Despite broken windows, the exterior seemed to have survived in good condition.

Entering the lobby, Audrey steeled herself, trying not to think of her father's arrest, her mother's disappearance, or Shihab's blood-soaked body sprawled on the cold marble floor. She carried a fragile shard of hope, against all reason, that her parents would be waiting for her in the apartment.

Debris cluttered the lobby and the stairs. The apartment door hung from one hinge. Audrey gasped at the destruction inside the penthouse. The Nazis had ground cigarette butts into the fine Persian carpet her father had brought from Iran. Broken windows allowed rain to stain and warp the parquet floors. They'd smashed the furniture against the walls and ripped wood molding from around the windows and doors, using the wood for the fireplace. Broken dishes, glassware and garbage cluttered the living room and the vulgar smell of German cigarettes and jackboot polish permeated everything.

Surrounded by the debris and devastation, Audrey's Blüthner grand piano stood without so much as a cigarette burn—the only furniture left in the apartment. She put her hands on the black lacquered wood and felt the piano's heartbeat, as strong as her own. She lifted the lid to inspect its strings, then played a few tentative cords. The warm, resonant tones drifted through the wreckage, full-bodied and alive, a memory in every octave.

The piano's maker had used slow growing spruce harvested from high in the mountains. The dry wood would have burned hot in the fireplace on a frigid winter night while the Nazis occupied the apartment, but they didn't burn it.

Overcome, she lowered herself onto the bench, tears gathering. She bent at the waist, buried her face in her hands and shook with sobs of relief and gratitude. She knew at least one German officer loved music. Her piano stood perfectly tuned and unharmed.

Finally, as she gathered herself, she opened the bench and shivered when she found nothing but German folk music. While Aimée set the songbooks ablaze with a match she found on the floor next to the fireplace, Audrey summoned *Arabesque No. 1* from memory. The notes flowed like a clear mountain stream; her recovering fingers danced at the base of Debussy's musical waterfall.

Nothing to Buy

Although their mattresses remained, neither Aimée nor Audrey could bear to sleep on them. One by one, they dragged all the mattresses down the stairs and outside to the garbage piles on the sidewalk. They slept on top of their old coats on the floor under the piano.

At first, even though she had the money her father left in the safe, there was very little to buy. The war had left farmlands fallow and cratered by German bombs. Battles and bombing had destroyed factories, bridges and the railway infrastructure used to deliver goods. Shops stood abandoned. The empty market stalls seemed like gaping mouths—waiting for food.

The second day in the apartment, while Aimée went looking for food, Audrey sat alone on the living room floor, leaning against the wall beneath a broken window, beyond tears, stunned. The war was over. Her piano remained, but the Nazis had destroyed everything else in her life she held dear. Without Aimée, would she have survived? She didn't allow her thoughts to drift to the other obvious question: *what if they had all remained in America?* It was far too painful to contemplate.

The Germans had torn her father's clothes from hangers and left them in a pile of glass and debris on the floor. Wrapping his old green sweater around her hand to avoid shards of smashed telescope, she pushed the debris aside and tapped until she found a loose floorboard. Careful not to cut her fingers, she pried up a board. Hidden below, she found a roll of francs and bundles of small diaries dated from 1900 to June 1940. The broken telescope's glass had protected the hiding place. She clutched the notebooks to her chest.

"*Merci*, Papa," she whispered, grateful he had the forethought to hide his journals along with the cash.

In the living room, she perched on the piano bench and opened the oldest journal, dated April 1900. The handwriting, clearly nine-year-old Eiffel's, recorded cloudy nights, clear cold weather and shooting stars.

May 15, 1899 "Today is my tenth birthday. Papa and Maman gave me a telescope."

His observations became more detailed, with sketches of the moons spinning around Saturn and the relative size of Jupiter, Mars and Venus.

In the 1922 journal, before he knew he would soon become a father, he'd written a detailed description of what he believed to be an asteroid caught in Earth's orbit. He referred to it as *Eiffel's Moon.* In every subsequent journal, he made mathematical notations regarding its position and movement.

When Aimée returned from shopping, her shoulders sagging from exhaustion, they sat on the floor sharing a stale baguette and bruised, wrinkled apple.

"We should put the Burgundy in the wine cellar," suggested Audrey.

Aimée followed as they descended the stairs, carrying the three remaining bottles of Burgundy. The cool stone cellar would protect the wine from the apartment's fluctuating humidity and changing temperatures, but Audrey also wanted to see if her father's safe had remained hidden.

The Germans had broken the lock on the cellar door, consumed her father's wine collection and left a clutter of broken glass and debris.

As if in ceremony, moving beyond the war's torment, they carefully leaned the three wine bottles onto the only remaining shelf. They had no food except for the apple and baguette Aimée found at the market, but they had three bottles of the finest red wine ever produced.

When the wine was safely stowed, Aimée's knees buckled. Audrey helped her sit on the rickety wooden steps.

"What will we do, Audrey? There are no jobs in Paris and your tenants will not return to pay rent until this building is repaired. There cannot be enough money hidden in your coat to cover repairs. How will we survive?" Aimée put her face in her hands and surrendered to the deep, shuddering sobs she had held inside since the Germans dragged away her Uncle Eiffel.

Audrey sat next to her, put her arm over Aimée's shoulder, *"Ne t'inquietes pas, ma chèrie."*

She stood, walked to the other side of the cellar and used her boot to shove aside the heap of debris.

Aimée gasped when Audrey revealed the safe.

Audrey dialed the combination, her birthday and listened to the quiet clicking sounds.

Aimée squealed when the door swung open, revealing stacks of gold coins and bundles of francs. "*Mon Dieu!*"

"My father made me promise never to reveal this hiding place to anyone, even you, as if the *boche* might read our minds or see the quilt on our faces. But now, my dear cousin, you must know, we have more than we need to recover from the financial devastation."

She pressed gold coins and a bundle of francs into Aimée's hand.

"For you."

Apartment 3A

Early one morning, after Aimée left to find breakfast, Audrey brushed her hand over the exposed lath and plaster that wept like shattered bones and flesh from the sitting room wall. Staring at the white plaster dust clinging to her long fingers, she violently shook her hand, as if white blood stained her hardened skin.

Bits of fabric and puffs of stuffing from her father's favorite chair scattered like feathers plucked from a dead chicken, its bones burned for heat.

Audrey knelt on the dirty floor, next to the Persian rug her father had brought from Iran long before she was born. Her hand brushed over a hole burned in the rug where a boot must have snuffed a burning cigarette. In a fit of anger, Audrey rolled up the rug. Her knees left a parallel trail like train tracks through the dirt and dust.

Aimée came through the open door, "Look, I found flour, milk, coffee and a few eggs. Can you believe it? The Americans and the Brits brought in convoys of food!"

Staring at the ruined parquet floor under the window, Audrey whispered, "We cannot stay here," her voice as pale as her skin.

"You mean in Paris or in France? You want to return to America?"

"I mean this apartment. My father lived here before he married Maman and when I visited as a child, his spirit filed the space, even when he was traveling. Now it's as empty as the larder, his essence destroyed by the Nazis." Finally, she looked up at Aimée, her arm sweeping toward the bedrooms. "Anyway, we don't need all these rooms. Let's start fresh in 3A."

The door was missing, but the apartment had been vacant long before the Nazis invaded. The empty apartment held no implication or emotion since Audrey never knew the tenants. After living behind blackout curtains for a year in Paris and three years in Beaune, the light-filled windows and cheerful brightness invited them into the living room and two bedrooms, even on a rainy day.

"The rain has stopped, at least for a while. I need to take a walk. I'll be back in an hour or so," Audrey told Aimée.

Audrey opened the door to the street, expecting the smell of fresh rain and sweet flowers. Instead, the sour miasma of war took her breath. As she walked, the cloudy skies added to the war-weary shabbiness of both the architecture and the spirit of people she passed on the street.

Food stalls once overflowed with brightly colored flowers, fruits and vegetables, but now they held pitifully bruised and wrinkled produce. The spice shop window was boarded. The bakery had already sold out for the day.

She sat on a park bench, watching people rush by and for a moment she felt like Paris was returning to normal, but the unpleasant diesel fumes and the acrid smell of rubbish reminded her that nothing was the same.

A tall woman hurried by. Her wide-toed high-heeled shoes clicked on the sidewalk and her stylish dark hair coiled on top of her head into plump victory curls.

Audrey jumped from the bench and shouted, "Maman!"

The woman turned. Audrey stepped back, "Excusez-moi, désolée." Beyond the black hair and tall stature, the woman looked nothing like her mother.

Life will never be the same, she thought.

Audrey climbed the stairs to the third floor and found Aimée in the kitchen of 3A, washing her hands with harsh soap and hot water from the kettle. "Come, I'll show you what I've done."

The claw-foot tub, pedestal sink, tiled walls and floor, left filthy by the Nazis, sparkled like new, reflecting the light slanting through the high transom window. The scent of carbolic soap and cleanliness filled the small bathroom. They hugged each other; no words were necessary.

Audrey hired workmen to restore 3A, replacing the doors, molding and the fireplace mantel and painting the walls in neutral colors. When the work was complete, Audrey and Aimée, on their hands and knees, polished the wood floors to a high shine, washed the windows inside and out and sanitized every inch of the small kitchen. Audrey hired a burly team to move her piano into 3A and waited in the lobby, "I can't bear to watch," she admitted to Aimée.

Until Audrey could reclaim her parents' belongings stored in Ohio, she purchased little beyond new mattresses. They decided they could live with two once-white painted wooden chairs and a small battered and rickety table that Aimée found on the street corner. Aimée brought home two mugs and a coffee press, a few chipped dishes and dented cutlery, sheets, washcloths and bath towels. They ate most of their meals at a nearby café where Aimée found part-time work as a sous-chef.

Audrey began teaching piano and voice in the bright but sparsely furnished apartment. Her students had a wide range of talent and experience: youngsters who had never touched the keys and whose parents could never pay for lessons, talented adults and former orchestra members who had lost everything.

Audrey After the War

1945

Early one evening, a knock on the door startled Audrey and Aimée. They momentarily froze, then remembered the Nazis were gone. Audrey opened the door to find a bent and emaciated man. Skin stretched over his skeleton, with no flesh in between.

"*Comment puis-je vous aider?*" asked Audrey.

"I was wondering if I might return to apartment 2C?" the man said in French.

At first, Audrey felt a little frightened. The stranger's waxy skin looked greenish gray with deep brown under his eyes, but when he smiled, she recognized the gleam in his eyes. "Bernard! I am so relieved to see you. Of course you can return to your apartment!" she cried, wrapping her arms around his thin, fragile frame. Once stout and vigorous, Bernard looked like an old man. His shoulders stooped forward. What remained of his once-thick black hair resembled dirty straw scattered haphazardly on his scalp. She knew he had survived with little nourishment, probably in one of the camps she'd read about, but she said, "Did you find your way to Switzerland?" even though it was clear he had not.

His formerly stunning tenor resonance sounded deep, reedy and hoarse, nearly undecipherable. "I am fortunate to be alive. For now, let us only look forward. Maybe someday I will tell you our story, but today it is far too painful. Geneviève..." He took a deep breath. "Geneviève did not survive..." He gazed at the floor, then looked at Audrey. "I am relieved that you survived this terrible war. I must ask, did your maman and papa come home?"

Audrey shook her head. "Papa was killed, they thought he was a spy... Maman...? I have no idea...," she whispered.

In her heart, Audrey had known that her father did not survive the Gestapo, but to confirm, Audrey had gone to the records office. It didn't take long to verify that Eiffel Dupré faced a firing squad shortly after his arrest. She mourned the loss of her papa, but still held a tiny sliver of hope that her mother would return. For Bernard, she tried to remain strong. She knew he had survived horrific circumstances.

"I am so sorry… a dreadful war…" said Bernard, tears gathering in his dark, deep-set eyes.

Bernard hooked his arm with Audrey's and they descended the stairs toward 2C. He clutched the railing and moved one step at a time. When they entered 2C, where he had lived with Geneviève before the war, he said, "I've never been so glad to see a space so demolished."

Workmen had replaced the front door, put new glass in the windows and swept a pile of debris into the middle of the living room, however, lath and plaster glared from the damaged walls and the burned and water damaged parquet floor had yet to be repaired. "This apartment seemed so small when Geneviève moved in with me after our wedding. Now it seems quite spacious."

Audrey heard a soft gasp push from his fragile lungs and followed his gaze across the room. In a corner, behind the workman's tools and stacks of lumber, stood Geneviève's harp, protected by its black leather case. He shuffled toward it. Unzipped the dusty cover revealing the pristine wood and strings. Bernard crumbled to his knees.

"I'll bring you soup and bread," whispered Audrey, rubbing his hunched, quivering shoulders. "But for now, I'll leave you to your memories." The door closed without a sound.

One afternoon, two police officers came to Audrey's apartment. "*Mademoiselle* Dupré, do you know who this ring belongs to?" asked the detective as he doffed his *képi*.

Audrey held out her palm. When the gold band touched her skin, she gasped. Even before she looked at the engraving, her mother's energy shot through her body like a lightning bolt. The inside read: *Esther and Eiffel Dupré, June 26, 1920.*

"Yes," she whispered, as she rolled the wide band between her thumb and index finger, scarcely able to breathe. "It's my mother's wedding ring." She shivered, wondering about the matching gold band her father wore. "During the occupation, Maman went missing on the way to visit a doctor." Her voice became even softer, as if she spoke from a different time and place. The officer leaned closer to hear her. "I never knew the doctor's name or the location of the office. I assumed the Nazis arrested her. Thank you for returning it. Where did you find it?"

"At the home of Dr. Petiot," he paused. "I'm sorry to tell you *Mademoiselle*, the doctor used the confusion of wartime to lure victims while he stole their money and belongings. Sorry to tell you…, your mother must have been one of the victims he injected with cyanide instead of the expensive medication she undoubtedly paid for."

Audrey nearly fainted. Aimée lowered her to the floor, with her back to the wall. The detective had extinguished her last flicker of hope.

"*Je suis vraiment désolé pour votre perte*," said the officer, expressing his sympathy as he backed away.

"*Merci beaucoup.*" Aimée murmured as she closed the door.

They sat on the floor by the door for the rest of the day while Audrey remembered her mother. Tightly gripping the wedding ring in her fist, Audrey murmured, "I remember her telling the story of the first time I tried to play the piano. She was having a Christmas martini with her friend, *Mademoiselle* Claudette, who became my teacher. Oh, how she loved her martinis," Audrey smiled. "She wrote poetry books and novels but none of them were published. We will never know what she wrote."

"She loved you," said Aimée. "She was so proud of you."

Ted Grantham, Flying Ace

1945, Hawaii

In his nightmares, Ted spun around and around on a carnival Fly-O-Plane ride while he frantically tried to shoot down the cast iron ducks-in-a-row at the arcade. When he stepped off the carnival ride, General Eisenhower shook his hand and piled cheap stuffed animals into his arms. On the walls in his father's den, his mother hung his useless carnival trumpery among the dead animal trophies and military commendation medals awarded to his ancestors and his older brothers.

The night nurse opened a window, allowing fresh tropical air to waft through the ward crowded with wounded sailors. Ted heard gigantic waves crashing on a nearby shore and smelled fresh salty air mixed with the sweet, intoxicating fragrance of night-blooming dracaena. Even before he opened his eyes, he knew he was a long way from Ohio's maple trees and cornfields.

As the nurse leaned in to check Ted's IV, his eyelids fluttered open.

"Well, hello there Ace. Glad to see you're awake," she whispered. "Even if it is 2:00 a.m."

He could see the nurse's smile and her white uniform and hat in the dimly lit room, but her features were blurry. "Where am I?" he asked in an unsteady voice.

"Honolulu Naval Hospital."

"Did we take Okinawa?"

"Not only did we take Okinawa, the Japs surrendered," she smiled. "The war officially ended yesterday. From what I hear, you and your Hellcat took down more enemy planes than any other pilot, until you ended up in here. You're a hero!"

He tried to recall but his mind responded like a clump of steel wool. He smelled the olfactory assault of war. Like a maladroit orchestration, he heard the hum of approaching enemy planes, the edgy discord of air-to-air combat, the roar of machine guns and cannons and the ghastly whistling sound of his Hellcat spiraling to the earth.

"How long have I been here?"

"You've been in a coma since you were shot down in June, almost three months ago," she whispered. "You're lucky to be alive."

He had no memory of ejecting from the burning aircraft or being pulled from the China Sea into a small skiff by brave sailors who miraculously avoided burning oil and debris while the battle raged overhead. He suffered multiple lacerations, two badly broken legs and a severe head wound.

For the next three months, after waking from the coma, he endured intensive physical therapy as he learned to walk again. In October, Ted stood at attention as best he could, supported by crutches and tried to focus his still-blurry vision as General Douglas MacArthur pinned The Navy Cross on Ted's white uniform next to the Silver Stars and Distinguished Flying Cross.

"Congratulations, son. We couldn't have beat the Japs without brave flyers like you," said MacArthur, saluting, then grabbing Ted's shoulder and shaking his hand.

In early December, without notifying his parents in case there were delays, Ted caught military flights from Hawaii to San Francisco and eventually to Lockbourne Air Force Base in Columbus, Ohio. Then one of his buddies gave him a ride to Upper Arlington. As the transport truck stopped in front of the Grantham residence, the soldier commented, "Wow, man, nice digs…."

Then he saw the five flags hanging in the living room window, four with gold stars and one blue. "Sorry to see the gold stars, man, bet your parents'll be glad to see you!"

Ted found enough breath to say, "Thanks for the lift, have a safe trip home." He pulled his duffel from the back as if it weighed a thousand pounds, then waved to his buddy.

Hesitating at the front door, Ted squared his shoulders and held back tears, trying to breathe, his heart gripped by the four gold stars in the window. Until that moment, he was unaware of the fourth fatality. His four older brothers had all been killed: the first in North Africa in 1942, the second on an Italian beachhead 1943, the third at Normandy 1944 and the last, he later learned, in France, just hours before Ted's plane went down in the Pacific.

As Ted took another shuddering breath and reached for the door, it swung open and his mother collapsed into his arms. Unable to speak, her knees buckled and he helped her to the living room sofa. They huddled together in grief and reunion.

"Where's Dad?" he finally asked.

"He rarely comes out of his war room."

Ted and his brothers often heard their father bellow, "Be a man," but Ted knew he had heard it most often. Somewhere in the back of his mind, Ted hoped that the medals on his own uniform would definitively prove to his father, *I'm no sissy.*

Ted found the Admiral uncharacteristically slumped in his leather chair, staring at the dead wildlife decorating the wall in his den. The free-standing brass ashtray held an untouched cigarette, smoke curling from its long, undisturbed ash. His father looked pale and drawn. Days of gray whiskers made him look old and ruined. His hand rested on a group of medals won by Ted's dead brothers.

"Hello, sir," said Ted, automatically standing at attention in the doorway, his arm flying into a salute while the Blue Marlin's dusty sword pointed at the commendation medals on his chest.

The Admiral's gray head slowly turned toward Ted, as if he could not comprehend Ted's voice. He slowly stood and shuffled toward him. Ted reached out to shake his hand, but Theodore grabbed him in a bear hug and wouldn't let go. Ted felt his father tremble and heard muffled sobs.

"Welcome home son," sobbed the Admiral. "Welcome home."

Ted After the War

Ted stayed with his parents for the summer while his legs grew stronger and his vision improved. He and his mother, Alice, sang together, as they had when he was a little boy. Theodore no longer objected.

One afternoon, Ted said, "Mom, let's walk to the park. I need to tell you something and I don't want Dad to interrupt." The sun was bright, the air hot and humid. They smelled the zinnias, marigolds and Shasta daisies blooming along the path to the park. "Do you remember my girlfriend, Audrey?"

"Sure," she said, "a lovely, talented girl. All through school, you two were like an old married couple, making beautiful music together. I never knew why they left town so suddenly."

"They left because her mother didn't want anyone to know that Audrey was in trouble. I'm the father."

Alice sat down heavily on a bench. "Did she have the baby?"

"Knowing her mother, I assume she gave it up for adoption. She never contacted me."

"While other children played on the swings, slides and monkey bars, you two played music," said Alice. "Were you in love?"

"The first time I saw Audrey, I fell in love. She was in first grade. We would have been happy together. We shared a passion for music, but the war ended that passion for me."

A strange sounding "harrumph" pushed from her lips. "Your father ruined your passion for music… not the war." She took a deep breath. "I wish I could have convinced him…" Her voice was quietly angry, as if she spoke only to herself, then she quickly asked, "Does he know about the baby?"

"Yes, Dad said I had to marry her and I wanted to, but when we walked to her house, we discovered they had left town. Dad said I should keep it a secret, he said you'd be upset if I told you." They sat in silence for a few moments. "The child will be eight this December, wherever it is. I thought you deserved to know."

"I'm glad you told me. It's wonderful to know I'm a grandmother, even if I never meet the child." Alice leaned over next to the bench to pick a daisy. "Someday you'll have a family…" she said, patting his knee.

"I'm planning on it," said Ted, hugging her shoulders. "The sooner the better."

"One of them will play your great granddad's violin. Music is in our blood."

When Ted's older brothers had grown and gone and his father was away at sea, Alice taught Ted to read music, sing and play the piano. Every night during dinner, they listened to the radio and discussed their favorite composers. Then, while Alice washed the dishes and Ted dried, they harmonized to popular songs, like John Steel's "Love Nest,"

> Just a love nest
> Cozy with charm,
> Like a dove nest
> Down on a farm.
> A veranda with some sort of clinging vine,
> Then a kitchen where some rambler roses twine….

One night, Mendelssohn's "Violin Concerto," played by Fritz Kreisler, flowed from the radio, lyrical and joyful. Young Ted lay on his back on the wood floor, his hands pillowing his head. He felt as if the passionate, haunting melody gently lowered him onto the uncultivated grass growing on the rolling hills near his grandparents' country home. White clouds floated across the azure sky as a gentle breeze tossed his hair and tall grass tickled his bare feet. The electrifying coda caused tears to roll to his ears. He sat up and looked at his mother.

"What is it sweetie, are you crying?" said Alice, lowering her knitting into her lap.

"I want to play the violin," he said with passion in his youthful voice. "I must."

"I'm thrilled to hear you say so."

A few days later, she gave Ted a worn brown leather violin case tied with a blue ribbon. "My great grandfather played this violin and his father before him. A beautiful violin has no value unless someone who loves music plays it. I want you to have it."

Ted untied the ribbon, lifted the violin from its brown leather case, put it under his chin and drew the bow over the strings. Tears came to Alice's eyes as she realized he had an instinct and natural touch, creating sweet tones. "A violin is worthless unless it can make beautiful music."

Dayton, Ohio

Ted moved to Dayton, landed a part-time job at Wright Field and began studying for his BS degree in Aeronautical Engineering. He supported himself on his meager wages, a small military pension and refused help from his parents.

A team of burly movers hauled an old console piano, the only thing he bought, to his top-floor, semi-furnished, apartment in a run-down old house. The space had once been a bedroom with a walk-in closet. He shared a bath on the floor below and ate most of his meals at a diner a few blocks away.

After graduation, while he worked toward his Ph.D., Ted took a job selling aeronautical parts and equipment to airplane manufacturers. His first territory was just Ohio, but later included the entire US.

Listening to Mozart, Vivaldi and Chopin on the radio, Ted drove the flat and tedious country roads from Columbus to Dayton after spending Christmas break with his parents. When static became too much, he turned to a contemporary station in Dayton and tapped the steering wheel in time with Artie Shaw, Cab Calloway and Jimmy Dorsey.

As darkness fell, the temperature dropped and a dense fog filled the cold air. When Ted drove over the Miami River Bridge, just a few miles from his apartment, the Dodge spun out on black ice and slammed into a guardrail. His wounds were minor compared to his war injuries; he drove himself to Valley Hospital. He walked into the ER with blood dripping from a minor head wound and clutching his injured wrist.

A student nurse cleaned and bandaged his forehead while the attending physician, Dr. Wurtzburg, immobilized his left wrist in a cast.

Ted admired the student nurse's long eyelashes and the fresh scent of the brown hair she wore in a knot on the back of her head. Her fair skin, petite frame and outdoorsy quality made his heart beat a little faster.

Ted looked at the nurses' name tag. "Thanks for patching me up—Evelyn Reilly. Uhm, I'm wondering," he ventured, "can I call you? Maybe we could have a cup of coffee sometime?"

Evelyn wrote her number on the back of a prescription sheet, "I share a room with my best friend, Gertrude Anna. She's also a nursing student. If we're on the night shift, we sleep during the day. This is the landlord's phone number." She handed him the paper with a quick shy smile that melted his heart.

He called her the next day and over the following months, Evelyn had dinner with Ted whenever their schedules allowed. They spent their days off at museums in Dayton and Cincinnati.

A few months after they met, Ted took Evelyn to dinner at a new restaurant. As the waiter served champagne, Ted slipped from his chair and bent down on one knee, "Evelyn, I love you. I want to spend the rest of my life with you. Will you marry me?"

"Oh, Ted! I love you too. YES, I'll marry you!" she blurted.

They kissed as waiters and diners applauded.

As new leaves covered oak and maple trees with bright green and happy beams of light and shadow dappled the road, Ted and Evelyn enjoyed the leisurely three-hour drive to Columbus to announce their engagement.

"Mom, Dad, I'd like you to meet Evelyn. Evelyn, this is my mother Alice and my father Theodore."

"Nice to meet you, Mrs. Grantham, Mr. Grantham," said Evelyn, hoping she didn't look as nervous as she felt.

"Ted darling, why didn't you tell me you were bringing a friend?" said Alice Grantham.

"I wanted to surprise you," said Ted. He knew that his mother suspected Evelyn was "the one" but he planned to make the announcement during dinner.

After introductions, they all took a walk in the elaborate and fragrant English garden, filled with rosy, red foxglove, deep blue delphinium and multi-colored snap dragons. Ted's mother talked about the plantings. "These hydrangea blossoms will make a lovely centerpiece," she said as she cut a few stems.

With no interest in gardening and unable to hold his announcement any longer, Ted blurted, "We're engaged."

Alice gave them each a hug and wiped her eyes.

"Congratulations son," said Theodore, as he shook Ted's hand and gave Evelyn a brief hug. "Too bad I don't have champagne on hand!"

Later, Ted and his father went to the war room to discuss airplanes and politics, while Alice led Evelyn on a tour of the house. They passed closed bedrooms once occupied by Ted's four dead brothers. Evelyn had never been in a house with so many rooms and bathrooms.

"This is the guest room," said Alice. "Ted will bring your bag in here later. There's the bath. I hope you will make yourself at home."

Evelyn followed Alice to the kitchen where Alice pulled an ice cube tray from the freezer. As she poured scotch over the crackling ice in two highball glasses, Evelyn noticed how much Ted looked like his mother, the same blue eyes, mahogany brown hair, narrow face and long arms and legs.

"If you'll take these to Theodore and Ted, I'll start dinner."

Evelyn walked down the hall, following the sound of their voices and found the men in Theodore's study. She shuddered as she saw the thousand-pound Blue Marlin, the furry, dead animals and the war memorabilia hanging on the walls. Handing the men their drinks, she realized that Theodore's study told her more about Ted's father than words ever could explain.

Back in the kitchen, Evelyn watched Alice turn on the oven, heave a roasting pan from the rack above the stove and pull a rib roast out of the refrigerator. She watched her future mother-in-law bustle around the kitchen, wearing a pink and gray paisley apron that covered the front of her narrow black skirt and pale green sweater-set. Although she knew nothing about cooking a meal, Evelyn asked, "Is there anything I can do to help?"

"Sure sweetie, you can put the crudités together. He doesn't like me to serve *hors d'oeuvres* before dinner, says it spoils his appetite, so when we have company, I serve crudités as a side dish. Everything's ready in the fridge and there's a platter in that cupboard."

Evelyn easily found the platter, but she opened the refrigerator, having no idea what she was looking for. "I'm sorry Mrs. Grantham," Evelyn said. "I've never had crew da tay."

"Oh, that's no problem." Alice began pulling carrots, celery, asparagus and cauliflower from the refrigerator. "I put a clean tablecloth on the table in the dining room; you can set the table.

The dishes are in the china cupboard and the silver's in the center drawer."

Evelyn took four dinner plates from the glass fronted mahogany china cabinet and put them on the table. She pondered the purpose of the remaining sizes. Then she opened the silverware drawer, revealing an assortment of various sized and shaped spoons, forks, knives and serving pieces.

"You're awfully quiet in there," laughed Alice. She found Evelyn standing by the table holding four salad forks while tears dripped from her chin. "Oh, sweetie, it's alright," said Alice, throwing her arms around Evelyn. "Don't worry, I'll show you how."

"I'm sorry Mrs. Grantham, it doesn't look like I'll make Ted a very good wife." Putting the handful of forks on the table, she used the back of her hand to wipe away tears. "I spent my childhood and adolescence in the fields and barn with my dad and the animals on our dairy farm, not in the kitchen with my mother. Mom said I'd be sorry someday, but I never understood until now."

At the dairy farm, Evelyn and her father weeded the flower beds and groomed the lawn, preparing for Evelyn's garden wedding. She and her mother created an altar using an old table covered with a white linen tablecloth and an arrangement of flowers from the garden in shades of pink and deep blue.

As she dressed for her wedding, she thought about Ted, his dreamy, sparkling blue eyes, his charm, impeccable manners. He had an elegance about him she had never encountered. Although not traditionally handsome, his narrow face and blue eyes reminded her of Jimmy Stewart. Gentle and kind, he made her feel like a million bucks. Ted was the first boy she kissed.

"Now, hours before the wedding, she wondered how she would measure up to Ted's upbringing, to the family of overachievers who had died with medals on their chests. She had only calluses on her hands and half a nursing degree. She closed her eyes and breathed deeply to calm her jitters.

Evelyn's best friend and Maid of Honor, Gertrude Anna, floated toward the altar to the serene yet joyful "Canon in D Major" by Johann Pachelbel, played by the minister's wife on the army field organ Ted's father borrowed for the occasion. Tall, elegant and stunningly beautiful, Gertrude Anna wore a watery cerulean linen suit that highlighted her deep azure eyes and creamy, caramel complexion. She'd pulled her oiled, nappy hair into a shiny, smooth chignon below a cerulean half-hat that matched her suit and carried a bouquet of cobalt blue hydrangeas.

As the organist played Mendelssohn's "Wedding March," Evelyn took her father's arm. She carried a nosegay of pink peonies and blue hydrangeas. Evelyn's perfectly tailored, soft rose tweed calf-length pencil skirt and fitted jacket with a longish peplum accented her stylish, hourglass silhouette while a matching pale rose half-hat with a chin-length veil nestled in her brown waves and curls.

Even though the only guests were Gertrude Anna's parents the Turnbulls, Alice and Theodore Grantham and the organist, Evelyn shyly stared at the grass until she started saying her vows. Then she looked up into Ted's blue eyes. She felt the intensity of his love for her and hoped she could be what he expected in a wife.

An amber ribbon of light fell across the bed as Ted held Evelyn in his arms. Soft classical piano music, "Gymnopédie" by Erik Satie, played on the radio, reminding Ted of his high school sweetheart, Audrey Dupré. He considered telling Evelyn about the child they had conceived in 1938, but his heart swelled as he looked at Evelyn, smiling contentedly, nearly asleep in the crook of his arm. He tucked a strand of brown hair behind her ear and kissed her forehead. Telling her about the baby would only cause her pain. He decided she would never know.

Back in Dayton, Evelyn admired the beautiful Victorian mansions, shadowed by enormous oak trees and surrounded by well-tended flower gardens as she snuggled next to him in his old Dodge. *Why haven't we been here before?* she thought. When he parked in the driveway of a house in dire need of repair, she understood.

"It's not much, but it's home," he laughed as he opened her door.

Paint peeled from the siding and around the windows. Some of the faded green shutters hung from one hinge or were missing. No one had mowed the yard or weeded the beds since before the war.

They lugged Evelyn's belongings to the top-floor landing. Then he carried her across the threshold and kissed her before lowering her feet onto the threadbare carpet. Her eyes swept over the room's damaged furniture. A sideboard held a spoon, one small bowl, a can opener and a dented pan suitable for heating a can of Campbell's soup on the old hotplate. The refrigerator, with a big, round, noisy motor on top, was big enough to hold little more than a quart of milk, a half-dozen eggs and an ice cube tray.

"The bedroom's over there," he said as he brought her bags in from the hallway. "It was probably a walk-in closet originally." The former closet was just big enough for the double mattress on the floor. A rod and shelf extended over a tall narrow bureau. "I emptied the bottom two drawers for your things," said Ted. The space was so tight, she would need to sit on the bed and lift her legs out of the way to pull out the drawers.

"Where's the bathroom?" she asked, looking around the apartment.

"Downstairs, we share with the owner, but she keeps it really clean."

After meeting Theodore and Alice Grantham in their big, stunning home in Columbus, Evelyn, who had grown up in a spacious farmhouse with a room of her own, was shocked to see the apartment where they would live. Ted seemed so elegant and well-bred; his ramshackle apartment was shockingly out of character. She touched the frayed edge of a sofa cushion with the palm of her hand.

He noticed her concern. "It's not much, but I've been saving every penny I can. Someday soon, we'll buy a house."

Her apprehension melted away when he kissed her. The newlyweds found the bed.

Evelyn gave up nursing school when she married Ted and found she had little to do each day. Business kept Ted away from home at least four nights each week and often two weeks at a time. Alone most of the time, she curled on the threadbare sofa with novels from the library and listened to the clock tick-tick-tick.

One Saturday evening, when he was home for a few days, Evelyn persuaded Ted to walk to a nearby club. They danced to "Moonlight Serenade" and "Dancing in the Dark" but when the band played "Boogie Woogie Bugle Boy," Ted said, "I'm sorry darling, my leg hurts, let's sit this one out."

The bar teemed with postwar service men hungry for female attention. "Hey, you mind if I dance with your girl?" asked a young soldier in uniform.

"She's my wife," Ted grinned, squeezing Evelyn's hand. "But sure, if she wants to dance, it's alright with me."

Ted looked surprise when Evelyn didn't hesitate.

"Sure!"

Evelyn became the center of attention. As the men took turns spinning her around the dance floor, Ted rested his aching legs and nursed his scotch.

They were almost home when Evelyn asked, "Ted darling, you're awfully quiet. Does your leg still hurt?"

"How did you learn to dance like that?" Ted finally blurted. "You really cut a rug. You said you never dated."

"Oh, Ted! Are you jealous?" She giggled and stood on her toes to kiss him. "During nursing school, my best friend, Gertrude Anna and I danced in the boarding house when the landlords were out of town and they were often out of town. Tonight's the first time I did the jitterbug with a fella!" she laughed. "Thanks darling. After sitting in that apartment alone day after day, I had so much fun dancing. I hope you didn't get bored just watching." She hugged his arm as they walked.

"No darling, I enjoyed watching you have a good time." Reassured, he took her in his arms for a long kiss.

As she fell asleep with her head on his chest, she could hear his heartbeat speeding up before he drifted to sleep. Some nights he mumbled names she didn't recognize—brothers, maybe? Pilots? Former girlfriends? She didn't ask.

Ted's Violin

"Darling, I dust that old violin case every other day, but I've never heard you play. Will you play for me now?" asked Evelyn, giving Ted a soft smile and that look he could never resist.

He slowly opened the well-worn lid, closed his eyes and listened as if the old violin spoke to him. Even before he touched its rich golden finish, Ted heard silvery sweet tones and felt the mystery and passion, as if his great-great-grandfather stood in the room drawing the bow over the strings.

With the violin on his shoulder, Ted drew the bow over the A-string and adjusted the peg until it was perfect. Then he tuned the other strings, no need for a tuning fork or piano.

As he played Mendelssohn's "Violin Concerto," the old violin's lustrous, rich clarity made his heart ache and brought tears to his eyes. Playing the violin returned him to that mystical realm only music could conjure; a fleeting restoration of the passion he'd lost when Audrey Dupré was torn from his life. The music also reminded him of the secret he kept from his wife; the child would be ten years old.

When he finished, Evelyn said, "Ted darling, that was lovely. Can you play 'Ol' Joe Clark'? It's a fiddle tune Gertrude Anna's father played on Saturday nights when we were little."

Ted turned his back, disappointed that Evelyn knew nothing about music. Her appreciation was shallow. "No, I don't know that one." He gently lowered the violin into the case, aware that the velvet lining also cradled a part of his soul, a part of himself he could never share with Evelyn; a part of him she would never understand.

He paused as he closed the case for the last time. His heart said farewell to the violin and to the musical passion he had cherished. He carried the case to the bedroom, wrapped it in a blanket, put it on the shelf and closed his heart to a realm he would never open again.

"There's no point in dusting it every day; I don't remember much. Let's walk to the ice cream shop. I'm in the mood for a scoop of chocolate," he said.

As he helped her with her sweater, Evelyn said, "Ted darling, I'd like to finish my nursing degree. I have nothing to do all day and becoming a nurse has always been a passion of mine. What do you think?"

"Good idea! Everyone should have a passion and studying is an ideal way to spend your time while I'm away." He opened his worn leather attaché and found his checkbook. "This should cover tuition and books and maybe a little extra," he said, handing her a check. "The demand for nurses is always high. If anything ever happens to me, you'll have something to fall back on."

She gaped at the check, astonished at his generosity. She had spent lonely months in their dreadful apartment while he traveled the state selling airplane parts. It always felt like they had no money. Tears clung to her eyelashes as she leaned her forehead on his chest, folded her arms around his waist and whispered, "Thank you."

Nurse Evelyn

Evelyn's hand trembled with pride and disbelief as she endorsed her first paycheck and slid it to the teller, "Cash please," she said with authority. She and Gertrude Anna went out to lunch at the diner. "Order whatever you want, my treat."

"Congratulations!" smiled Gertrude Anna. "You're finally an RN."

They toasted with their coffee mugs. Then they went shopping for a new skirt and sweater. After that splurge, Evelyn deposited all her paychecks directly into Ted's savings account.

One evening, Ted and Evelyn went to the movies to see *The Philadelphia Story*. Evelyn noticed how much the ER's Dr. Wurtzburg looked like Cary Grant, except that the doctor had blond hair and hazel eyes. As a student nurse, before she met Ted, she'd had a schoolgirl crush on Dr. Richard Wurtzburg. As she watched the movie with Ted's arm over her shoulders, she felt a strange tingle when Cary Grant kissed Katharine Hepburn. She worried Ted would notice, but he didn't.

The same feeling happened every time Dr. Wurtzburg smiled down at her. He was a foot taller than Evelyn, with long dark eyelashes framing the mischievous deep hazel eyes that sparkled over the top of his surgical mask. She knew he was married with two little boys, but Wurtzburg flirted with the nurses and patients alike. He was so suave; men didn't seem to notice; everyone loved the charming Dr. Richard Wurtzburg. After she finished nursing school, Evelyn and Dr. Wurtzburg often worked together. She stood by his side for hours every day, helping him put on his surgical gown, handing him instruments and wiping sweat from his brow.

Then, day after day, she went home to the shabby third floor apartment and slept alone on the mattress on the floor. She loved Ted, but this was not what she had expected when she met the elegant war hero.

During a night shift emergency room rotation, a bus accident brought over twenty people to their five-bed ER. Evelyn cleaned and bandaged wounds and managed general triage while Dr. Wurtzburg tended to the more seriously injured. They worked well past the end of their shift. When they released the last patient, Evelyn and the doctor were both exhausted.

"You did an amazing job tonight, Evelyn. If you hadn't noticed the bruising under that woman's hair, she could have had major complications. They rolled her up to surgery just in time," he said. "Let me buy you breakfast."

She looked at her watch. "More like lunch. It's almost eleven. Won't your wife expect you at home?"

"She took the boys to her mother's house for a couple of weeks. What about your husband?"

"He's in Cleveland this week, the proverbial traveling salesman, something to do with airplane parts," she shrugged. "He hasn't been home much since we got married."

In the cafeteria, she ordered scrambled eggs with bacon and coffee with cream. "Same for me, please," he asked the server. Before sitting down, Wurtzburg took his plate, silverware and coffee mug off the tray and set his place at the table, sliding the tray onto the adjoining empty table. Evelyn normally left everything on the tray, but found his method far more civilized. She set her own place across from him, then gently slid her tray on top of his.

"This is my last week at Valley Hospital," he announced suddenly. "I gave my notice. I'm joining a private practice here in Dayton so I can get clinical experience. My plan is to move to Seattle in a year or two."

"Why Seattle? That's so far away," she said, failing to ignore the desire she saw in his charismatic hazel eyes. Conflicted feelings rising in her chest surprised her, part relieved he was leaving as well as an irrational sense of loss.

"It's a beautiful place, with mountains and water all around. I want a house with a view of the mountains and water. That can't happen in Ohio." Looking into her eyes, he asked, "Did you grow up around here?"

"Yes, I had an idyllic childhood on a dairy farm north of Dayton. I was up with the sun to help with milking, but rarely helped in the kitchen. When I was about eight, I even drove a team of Belgian horses while Mr. Turnbull shoveled cow manure from a flatbed wagon."

"Turnbull? Is that Gertrude Anna's father?"

"Exactly! During the Depression, my father invited the Turnbulls to live in the cabin on our property in exchange for help around the farm. Gertrude Anna and I were toddlers; I felt like I had a sister. Gertrude Anna and I have been best friends ever since."

As she told him about the dairy farm, he listened attentively, never interrupted and made eye contact she couldn't tear away from.

"Tell me about your childhood," she said.

He grinned, as if thrilled that she expressed an interest in his life. "My parents were tenement farmers, but even as poor as we were, Papa insisted his boys finish high school."

"How many siblings do you have?"

"Three brothers and three sisters."

"Being an only child, I can't imagine such a big family. Won't you miss them if you move to Seattle?"

"My parents are gone and my oldest brother, who I was the closest to, died in the war. The rest of my siblings have spread out across the country. There's no reason to stay in Dayton."

"Sorry about your brother."

He shrugged and looked at his cup of coffee.

"How did you end up in medical school?" she asked, curious how a poor farmer's son could afford an education.

"Ohio State gave me a full ride scholarship in the College of Agriculture. Then, after Pearl Harbor, my older brothers enlisted. I was lucky. The US Army was recruiting intelligent men to become medical doctors. My chemistry professor recommended me for a military scholarship. When I enlisted, the Army paid for medical school. I had no aspirations to study medicine, but I sure couldn't refuse a free education. By the time I earned my MD, the war was over."

As he talked, her heart rate slowed and her shoulders dropped as she became surprisingly comfortable with sexy Dr. Wurtzburg.

When she looked at her watch again, it was 2:00 p.m. "Good grief, look at the time! We need to get some sleep before our shift starts again."

"Thanks, I enjoyed this," he said, covering her hands with both of his.

"Me too," she admitted, unable to look away from those lusting hazel eyes.

Alone in the apartment that night, she couldn't stop the flickery, fleeting butterflies she felt when she thought about Dr. Wurtzburg.

The ER was unusually quiet the next night. "Others can cover for us. Let's take a break and get a bite to eat," he suggested to Evelyn.

On the way to the cafeteria, he stepped into the doctor's lounge, pulled her in behind him and locked the door. To her own surprise, Evelyn did not resist his advances. As if living in someone else's body or not in a body at all, she dissolved into his captivating charm.

In the doctor's lounge, Dr. Richard Wurtzburg and Evelyn Reilly Grantham lay on their backs facing the ceiling, her nurses' hat and white bobby pins scattered on the floor, her white uniform and his trousers and lab coat draped over a chair. "I've longed to do that since the first day I met you," sighed Richard.

"Me too," murmured Evelyn, although feelings of guilt, confusion and regret tugged at her conscience.

"But I love my wife. I don't know what came over me."

"My husband is the only man I ever even kissed," she said. "And I love him deeply. This isn't who I am. How did I get here?"

"I'm sorry I lured you into this Evelyn. We can't let it happen again." His lips met hers, one more time.

"It's good you're leaving soon," but her body lingered even as she tried to distance herself. She stole one last, passionate kiss.

Evelyn's Guilt

"Oh, Gertrude Anna, what have I done?" cried Evelyn as she admitted the shameful liaison. "I love Ted and Doctor Wurtzburg said he loves his wife. What's wrong with me?"

"You've had a crush on that doctor since we were in nursing school."

Evelyn remembered the day she and Gertrude Anna met Dr. Wurtzburg.

It was the first day of Doctor Richard Wurtzburg's residency at Valley Hospital. As Evelyn and Gertrude Anna walked down the hall, he came out of a patient's room and nearly bumped into them. "Good morning, ladies, lovely day isn't it?" he'd said, flashing his big smile and alluring hazel eyes. When he was out of sight, they swooned together. Evelyn whispered, "Who was that gorgeous creature?"

Now, sitting in the cafeteria, Gertrude Anna said, "Ted left you alone in that god-awful bachelor pad of his, it's no wonder you needed attention. Let's just hope your cycle starts on time."

"Gosh, that would be a disaster. What will I do if…? I'll never forgive myself and neither will Ted."

"Ted's so in love with you, I think he'd forgive even this. He'd blame himself."

The next day, when Evelyn finished her shift at 9:00 a.m., Ted was waiting in their apartment with a bouquet of daisies. He swept her off her feet and carried her to the bed. Their comfortable intimacy reminded her how much she loved him. She tried to focus on Ted instead of her guilt.

After lovemaking and a good sleep, they walked to the neighborhood bodega for an ice cream cone.

"This feels like a celebration, darling," she said.

"Well, it might be. I was going to wait until I knew for sure, but I can't wait to tell you. I'm being considered for a promotion, with less travel, a salary instead of straight commission and I'll be on the management track. If I get the job, we can buy a house and start our family."

"Our family?" she giggled. "We've never talked about having children."

"I want a big family, don't you, darling?"

"Uh" she hesitated. "Yes, I guess," she whispered. "When will you know about the promotion?"

"I'm meeting with the CEO at corporate headquarters here in Dayton in a few days. I'll be home until the meeting. Can you get time off?"

"Actually, yes. I have two days before I start the day shift and I can ask for one more day."

"Marvelous!"

While Evelyn tried to suppress her guilt, the two of them behaved like newlyweds, making love, talking about the future, or just being silent together. She wasn't herself, more attentive, more careful, less spontaneous. But Ted was so happy to have a few days with her, he didn't notice.

Back at the hospital, Evelyn and Gertrude Anna managed to take a break together. Looking around to assure no one could overhear, Evelyn whispered, "If Ted gets promoted, he wants to buy a house! How will I tell him about–you know...?"

"Are you late?" Gertrude Anna whispered.

"Only a day, but if I don't start by Saturday, I'll lose my mind! I'm usually so predictable."

"You will never tell Ted," Gertrude Anna gripped Evelyn's shoulder, "even if..."

"A secret like that would ruin our marriage."

"Just try to stay calm and act normal until you know."

The next day, Evelyn met Gertrude Anna in the cafeteria for lunch. She leaned over her lunch tray and mouthed, "I just started."

"Great! Forget it ever happened," whispered Gertrude Anna, patting Evelyn's hand on the table.

"I am so relieved. Nothing like that will ever happen again!"

When Ted's promotion came through, he quit using condoms. It didn't take long to learn a baby was on the way. He was thrilled.

"Oh, Ted, this is the perfect house," said Evelyn when they found the Craftsman bungalow in the suburbs of Dayton. Maple trees arched over the street and the house had a backyard where children and a puppy could play. A porch spanned the front of the house with thick tapered columns supporting the low-pitched roof. Evelyn especially liked the living room with the beautifully finished natural wood cabinets flanking the fireplace. She didn't mind the small kitchen; her cooking requirements were minimal.

Morning sickness lasted only a few days and she had more energy than most expectant mothers she knew, giving her plenty of time to organize their new home before the baby came. She ordered furniture for the baby's room from the Sears catalog, lined the drawers with lavender scented shelf paper, then folded tiny onesies and cloth diapers into the dresser drawers.

Two weeks before her due date, she thought Braxton Hicks pre-labor contractions kept her awake, until a trickle of fluid told her real labor was starting. "Ted darling, I'm sorry to wake you, but it's time for the baby."

She giggled when Ted leaped out of the bed, stubbed his toe on the dresser and danced around putting on his pants. "I think we have plenty of time darling, don't hurt yourself."

"Where is the little bag you packed? I'll put it in the car, then help you down the stairs."

As Evelyn slipped into a cotton maternity dress, she said, "Ted darling, I can walk down the stairs and you can carry my bag. I'll be fine."

Not much happened for the first few hours they spent in the labor room. They walked up and down the hall, waiting, waiting, waiting.

Gertrude Anna found them staring at the babies in the maternity ward. "I only have a moment," she said, giving Evelyn a hug. "Our maternity ward is always so busy during a full moon. Your labor is early, others are late… Dr. Wurtzburg's wife is in labor and having a tough time, she might end up with a C-section. Dr. Wurtzburg is on a flight back from Seattle, so I promised her I'd stay on until she delivers. I best get back in there." She hurried down the hall, then turned to wave, "Good luck!"

Finally, when contractions began in earnest, Ted helped Evelyn remember to breathe and massaged her legs when they cramped. Finally, as a nurse wheeled her to the delivery room, leaving Ted behind to wait, he kissed her forehead.

They named their baby girl Gertrude Reilly Grantham after Evelyn's best friend, Gertrude Anna and Evelyn's maiden name, Reilly.

Gertie Reilly Grantham

Dayton, Ohio

Ted and Evelyn's first child, Gertrude Reilly Grantham, was a petite five pounds, eight ounces, with a cap of soft, dark hair. Ted proudly pushed his newborn, nestled in a yellow wicker pram, under the arch of red-orange maple leaves in their Dayton, Ohio neighborhood, while Evelyn enjoyed rest and quiet. When the maples leafed out again and the air smelled of lilacs and mowed grass, he put Gertie in her new stroller so she could see and smell every red tulip and yellow daffodil.

Their first son, Teddy, was born in 1951 and Robert followed in 1952. Ted was proud to have sons, of course, but couldn't help favoring his little girl, maybe because he never had sisters.

Ted never missed a parent-teacher conference or class pageant and while Evelyn worked as a nurse at the hospital, he took Gertie door-to-door to sell chocolate mint, shortbread and sandwich cookies for her scout troupe's fundraiser.

Month after month, Ted sat at the piano with Gertie on his lap, trying to develop Gertie's musical talent, but he realized she had not inherited his interest in music. It never occurred to him that one of his sons could become a musical genius.

For Gertie's third birthday, Ted designed a playhouse. From the outside, the two-story facade looked like a miniature version of their craftsman home, with white tapered columns and green shutters on tiny double-hung windows, complete with a porch light. On the inside, however, if he crawled through the front door, he could stand comfortably.

He ordered lumber and supplies but realized, given the time he had to devote to the project and the pace he was going, she would be in high school before he finished, so he hired a carpenter to complete the work. The carpenter also created miniature wooden appliances and a sink with a metal tub that could hold water.

"Oh Daddy, I love my new playhouse," said Gertie as she threw her arms around his neck. He sat at a miniature chrome dinette set in a tiny chair upholstered with red Naugahyde while Gertie set the table with her pink Hazel-Atlas tea set and tin flatware. Ted had stocked her playhouse with miniature copper-bottomed Revere Ware, exactly like the big ones her mother used, including a saucepan, skillet, teakettle and percolator. "Would you like coffee wiff cueem?" she asked, as she stood beside her little wooden stove, wearing her apron, rehearsing for her life's work.

One afternoon, Ted got a call at the office from Evelyn, "Is everything all right darling," he said.

"Oh yes, darling, it's just that a nurse has called in sick and they've asked me to stay until the substitute arrives. Can you fix dinner for the children? The babysitter needs to leave by five. I was going to make creamed tuna tonight. There are cans of tuna and cream soup in the pantry and bread in the breadbox, recipe card is in the file on the counter. I'll be home before bedtime."

Ted left the office early, chuckling to himself; Evelyn needed a recipe card even to make cream tuna on toast. He stopped at the grocery store and the butcher shop to gather ingredients for spaghetti and meatballs.

"I'll be fixing dinner tonight," he announced after the babysitter left. "Spaghetti and meatballs."

"I love ska-betty," said Gertie. "Can I help?"

"You sure can! I'll show you how to make—MEATBALLS," he laughed pushing the package of meat toward her.

While the boys returned to their blocks in the playroom, Gertie dashed to her playhouse to fetch the ruffled apron her Grandma Alice had given her for her birthday.

Ted helped her wash and dry her hands. "Now, can you unwrap the meat?"

As if opening a birthday present, her tongue poking out the side of her mouth, Gertie removed the white butcher paper wrapped around two pounds of ground chuck.

Ted pinched off a lump of meat and rolled it between his

palms, "Like this, try to make all the meatballs about the same size."

Standing on a folding metal stool, her little hands made meatballs much smaller than her daddy's example, but he said, "Your meatballs are perfect!" He helped her lower the meatballs into the hot marinara sauce with a big spoon and they stirred the sauce more than necessary just for Gertie's enjoyment. "Now help me put the spaghetti into the boiling water." He lifted her so she could lower the pasta into the pot. "Careful not to splash."

Ted let Gertie set the table, then called down the basement stairs, "Come on up boys, dinner's ready."

After that night, Gertie and her brothers looked forward to their mother working late and their dad fixing dinner.

Return to Ohio

1950

Audrey and Aimée decided it was time to visit Columbus, Ohio, to sort through family belongings they had left behind in June 1938 when Audrey announced her pregnancy.

Audrey boarded the plane at Paris Nord airport wearing blunt-toe, high heels and a dark blue smartly tailored jacket with a stylish peplum. Aimée wore flat shoes with a more comfortable skirt and sweater.

The glamorous air hostess in a sharp navy-blue suit and high heels welcomed them aboard. After settling into their spacious seats, the hostess, who had switched to flat shoes and removed her hat, pushed a cart down the aisle offering drinks. Audrey and Aimée enjoyed Pinot Noir, along with a small bowl of mixed nuts. About an hour into the flight, the stewardess served dinner. They drank another glass of Pinot Noir with the soup, salad, braised duck breast, roasted vegetables and *crème brûlée* for dessert, all served on fine china.

Aimée socialized in the cocktail lounge after dinner while Audrey kicked off her shoes and reclined her seat all the way back. The hum of the engines lulled her, but the pervasive foul smell of cigarette, cigar and pipe smoke kept her from falling asleep.

After hobbling through customs on swollen feet that wouldn't fit back into her shoes, Audrey claimed their baggage from the skycap and gave him a generous tip. Another skycap rolled the bags to the curb on a trolley and hailed a taxi. She tipped him as well. She was certain these young skycaps had served in the American military. She couldn't help noticing their eyes—still wide with war, still carrying something unhealed, not to mention other more obvious wounds, a scarred face, a missing finger and a serious limp. A generous tip seemed the least she could do for the men who helped liberate Paris from the Nazis' grip.

Audrey and Aimée checked into adjoining rooms at Hotel Hartman. "I'm going to take a long hot bath and send these smelly clothes to the hotel laundry," said Audrey.

"The hotel does laundry? We did not offer laundry in Beaune," said Aimée.

"You'll find a bag in your closet, like this," she pulled the canvas laundry bag out of her own closet. Put your clothes in there, including underwear, if you want and they'll come back fresh and clean in the morning, before you wake up.

They enjoyed a quick cup of coffee and a Danish in the hotel café then took a taxi to the storage facility. Standing in front of the unit with their arms locked together, they braced for the ghosts to erupt from inside.

A cavalcade of fragrance marched into the sunshine. First, the fresh, juniper berry and woodsy notes of her father's pipe tobacco, then her mother's Chanel N°5 perfume with hints of roses and tropical ylang-ylang, followed by the sweet and savory scent of onions browned in butter. With barely enough breath to utter the words, Audrey whispered to Aimée, "It smells like home."

As if suspended between the past and the present, Audrey's chest ached with extreme sadness, but as they worked, there were also moments when her heart filled with joy; photos of a day on the beach with her papa when she was little, a well-worn book of French poetry her mother loved, or the box of sheet music from her first piano lessons.

As they slit the tape on cardboard cartons and sorted through her parents' belongings, she sensed their presence so strongly, she felt as if they might walk out of the shadows behind the furniture and boxes.

Aimée and Audrey worked for four days, sorting through every box, setting aside rugs, glassware, dishes, pieces of furniture and art for the movers to repack and ship to Paris. They set aside items to donate to charity.

Audrey opened the box marked "gold tea set and assorted items." Below a thin layer of excelsior packing, she found a framed sepia image of her smiling parents taken on their wedding day. She hugged the frame to her chest and turned away from the busy workmen, catching her breath. "I'll be taking this home in my luggage," she quietly told the foreman.

"Yes ma'am." The enormous, muscular, brutish-looking foreman wore dirty denim overalls and his shirt had sweat-stained underarms, but his voice sounded incongruously compassionate. He said, "I'll wrap it in paper and set it aside for you." His kind eyes clearly expressed: *I understand the pain of your loss.*

Audrey pointed to the box where she found the picture. "This tea set once belonged to my father's great-great-grandmother. Please pack it carefully for the journey to Paris. It's especially precious to me."

She peeked into a black-and-white striped hatbox and quickly closed it. "Also be careful with this hatbox," she said. "Be sure it doesn't get crushed." She didn't have the strength to sort through the secrets her mother stored inside. It was too raw, too soon.

"Yes ma'am."

"Thank you," she muttered as she walked away, knowing if she looked that kind man in the eye, she would lose her composure. When the movers brought Aimée's trunk into the sunlight, Audrey's breath caught in her throat. "Oh Aimée, I'm so sorry. Maman should have shipped your trunk along with the piano."

Aimée hugged Audrey's shoulder, "Your maman was not herself after your... surprise. But this is good. If she had shipped the trunk, the Germans would have destroyed all of my treasures. I am grateful."

After living with nothing but mattresses on the floor, a rickety old table and chairs and boxes instead of bureaus for their clothes, Audrey imagined the French provincial furniture from her childhood bedroom arranged in Aimée's room in apartment 3A.

She shipped an Art Déco mahogany dresser, nightstands, two Tiffany lamps from her parents' bedroom and the iron bed that had once belonged to her father's parents. From the library, she kept two wingback chairs upholstered in sage green brocade and from the dining room, she shipped six of the twelve mahogany chairs upholstered in black leather with flared backs and balancing wide seats. The wingback chairs upholstered in sage green brocade provided comfort and she could arrange them in groups in the living room/dining room area. She made arrangements to sell the remaining chairs and the huge dining table and shipped a smaller mahogany drop-leaf table instead. She selected only a few treasured pieces from the living room, since her grand piano would occupy much of the space in apartment 3A.

On the third day, a muscular moving man carried the velocipede rocking horse into the sunlight. "What should we do with this thing, whatever it is. Looks like a tricycle and a rocking horse all in one."

Audrey nearly stopped breathing. She touched the horse's head and ran her palm down its scratchy hemp mane. "This was my father's toy when he was a child," she managed to say in a thin voice. "Please pack it carefully."

Audrey imagined her father as a boy, riding the velocipede on the great driveway in front of her grandparents' home in rural France. Thankfully, the velocipede rocking horse remained safely stowed in the Ohio storage unit while the Nazis occupied their apartment building. No doubt it would have become firewood.

That night, while Aimée had dinner with the butcher's son, Audrey ordered bread, soup and a bottle of Pinot Noir from room service. Content to have time alone, she sat in the upholstered chair, with her feet propped on the ottoman, blindly staring out the window at Columbus traffic and listening to classical music on the radio while she sipped a glass of wine, letting her mind clear. She drank another glass as she ate her tepid vegetable soup, then she closed the drapes to the waning daylight, took a long hot bath and put on her cotton nightgown. As she poured the third glass of Pinot Noir, the day's nostalgic reminders defeated her protective veneer.

Methodically, as if sleepwalking, she folded the bedspread, put it on a chair, then tucked her weary frame between the crisp white sheets. Although she had lived what seemed like a lifetime, she was only twenty-seven years old. Her mother would be fifty-one and her father sixty, had they survived WWII.

For the first time since the Nazis smashed their way into the apartment to arrest her father, she allowed the sensations of responsibility, accompanied by unbearable pain. Her parents might still be alive if she and Ted Grantham had practiced their duet instead of surrendering to adolescent curiosity and hormones. As the war escalated, if she and her mother had remained in Ohio, certainly her papa would have left Paris and stayed with them in Ohio until the war ended.

The fourth glass of wine delivered the torpor she sought; however, sleep offered no rest or release. In her nightmares, a lurid, laughing Nazi with dull blond hair, wearing a green tunic and tall shinny jackboots, used his Luger to shoot the velocipede rocking horse, then hacked it with an ax as if chopping wood. Flames licked the horse's wooden body. Its rope mane flashed into ashes as her father's precious books, scientific papers and her mother's manuscripts turned blood-red in the dark. Liquefied wheels morphed into bullets used by the firing squad to slaughter her father, whose blood flowed garish and bright into the dark red flames, the flames morphing into the serial killer's furnace where her mother slept.

Audrey awoke from the nightmare as if screaming, her mouth wide open, soundless, unable to breathe.

With her swollen eyes rimmed in red, hidden behind sunglasses, she visited Merchants National Bank where her parents had left the majority of their wealth. Audrey gained access to the accounts and the safe deposit box with her proof of identity and signature. The teller remembered Audrey and her family, but when Audrey removed her sunglasses, the teller saw the palpable sorrow and made no further inquiry. The teller's cheerful professionalism faltered. Her voice softened as she opened the vault.

Sitting alone in a small, windowless room, Audrey began sorting through her parents' safe deposit box. Her father had left a great deal of cash, which didn't surprise her. The surprise came when she learned that her mother had inherited the Mancini's vast estate. Twenty-seven-year-old Audrey was a wealthy woman. But she thought, *I'd give up a lifetime of financial security if Maman and Papa....*

She awoke the next morning to find an envelope the hotel concierge had slipped under her door. Holding the crisp hotel stationary between both palms, she dropped onto the bed. Even before she read the note, she knew Aimée would not return to France. Warm, quiet tears dripped from her chin as she opened the envelope. The note from Aimée read:

"I have checked out of the hotel. We will meet you at the storage facility at 10:00 a.m."

We... Aimée is part of a couple, thought Audrey. She remembered introducing Aimée to Roger, the butcher's son, when Aimée first arrived in Columbus.

Aimée and Roger were waiting for her when she arrived at the storage unit. With his arm hugging Aimée's shoulders, their faces beaming with joy, Roger announced, "Our love was interrupted but not destroyed. We will be married tomorrow."

"Congratulations," Audrey said. She gave the prospective groom a hug, steeling herself against another breakdown. Then, Aimée grabbed her and sobbed, "I wanted to tell you last night, but I just couldn't. I will miss you terribly."

Audrey stepped back and took Aimée's face in her hands, wiping away Aimée's tears with her thumbs. "It's time for you to have joy in your life. I am so happy for you!" She wiped warm tears from her own face with the back of her hands. "Of course I might starve without your cooking," she shrugged. The joke cracked the sorrow like a shell, offering brief relief before they collapsed into each other's arms while Roger rubbed Aimée's back.

After a brief ceremony at the Franklin County Courthouse, Audrey treated the bride and groom and his brother to brunch at the Hartman and surprised them with champagne and a three-tiered wedding cake, which they shared with the hotel guests and staff.

Roger's brother stood to offer a toast, "Congratulations! I wish Father were here. He would be so pleased to see you happy together. Brother, take the day off. I can manage the shop alone for one day."

Audrey stood. "You deserve to be happy and I am happy for you." Lifting her champagne flute, she added, "But I am feeling sad as well. I'll miss you more than words can say. Now go," she hugged Aimée, "before we both melt into a puddle of tears again, your carriage awaits." She forced a laugh, hugged them both one more time and waved as Aimée and Roger climbed into the horse-drawn coach Audrey had engaged for the occasion.

Audrey hired a truck to deliver Aimée's trunk to her new home along with a set of fine English bone china she knew Aimée loved. Fighting to stay composed in front of the workmen, she watched as the gate on the moving truck rolled closed, then she returned to the hotel to pack her luggage and check out.

She could not imagine her life in Paris without Aimée. They had quickly bonded like sisters when Aimée first came to Ohio in 1935 and they supported each other during the war. Aimée had been her anchor.

After losing her parents and enduring the war, Aimée deserves joy in her life, she reminded herself, but she laid on the bed and sobbed.

On her way to the airport, Audrey asked the taxi driver to drive past her childhood home in Upper Arlington. "This is the house where I grew up," she said, as he slowly drove past.

The house on Hillside Drive never felt like home. She remembered enjoying summers in Paris with her parents at her father's apartment. She loved to walk the Paris city streets, especially at dusk when warm lights glowed in apartment windows, cafés teemed with Parisians enjoying local cuisine and the sound of laughter, conversation and popping champagne corks filled the air. Paris—with the rich scent of food—was home. She longed to return.

"Should I pull over, ma'am?"

"Thank you, but that's not necessary. Turn right at the next street, please."

As the driver turned the corner, she asked him to pull over for a moment under the bright orange, scarlet and chartreuse canopy that arched above the street near the Grantham's big brick colonial. She wondered if Ted's parents still lived there. Just then, the front door opened. Ted walked across the porch. He looked filled out, more mature and less awkward, despite a slight limp, but his body had never caught up to the length of his arms and legs. He looked distinguished in a wide-lapel suit and fedora. Next to him, a woman carried a new baby swaddled in a pink blanket. His hand gently held her elbow. A foot shorter than Ted, the woman's brown hair fell into deep waves under her half-hat, while a pearl necklace hugged her throat. Her rose tweed pencil skirt fell to mid-calf and the peplum of her fitted jacket emphasized her slim waist. They reminded Audrey of an advertisement she'd seen for *It's a Wonderful Life* with Jimmy Stewart and Donna Reed. There was a peaceful, synchronized air around them. *It's obvious they are happily married*, Audrey thought.

"Take me to the airport, please," she said to the driver, her voice sharp and sudden, causing him to jolt to attention.

The Shipment

When the shipment from Ohio arrived, movers spent two days unpacking. They positioned the furniture according to Audrey's direction. When the men left with the empty boxes and packing materials, she asked them to take away the rickety table and chairs she and Aimée had used since the war ended.

As the sunset cast golden light, she wandered through the apartment, adjusting a vase of flowers, moving a group of books, rearranging a collection of framed images on a side table. Her steps slowed as the rooms took shape. She tried to make it her own, but there was a whisper of a shrine to her parents.

This is the perfect moment to enjoy the second bottle of Burgundy. She descended the marble stairs to the wine cellar and returned with a bottle of Musigny, Bouchard Père & Fils 1937. Carefully, she opened the bottle, filled a beautiful antique wine glass, the only one left of a once-cherished set and took a sip. "*Magnifique,*" she said aloud. "*Merci, Monsieur* Chef."

She meandered through the apartment, turning on lamps, lighting candles and sipping the Burgundy. She stood in the door of what would have been Aimée's room. The elegance and sophistication of the canopy bed and French Provincial furniture looked more at home here than in Ohio, but Aimée was not coming back to Paris to enjoy it.

Audrey wandered into the living room, sat sideways on the piano bench and tapped "Twinkle, Twinkle Little Star" with one hand, while sipping the wine. She moved to the window and turned to scrutinize the space. Her parents had never lived in these sunny rooms, but their furniture and other belongings now accompanied her grand piano.

Audrey's hand rested on the velocipede rocking horse, as if touching her father's shoulder. Then she sat at her mother's writing desk. The smell of ink from Esther's favorite fountain pen seemed to waft around her and she heard the scratch of its nib. She sensed their presence so tangibly, she nearly fetched two more glasses to pour wine for them. "Oh, how I wish I could share this lovely wine with you," she whispered.

Audrey received a birthday card from Aimée, including a note, the first one Aimée had written totally in English.

Dearest Audrey,

As you can see, my English has improved! I have been taking night classes and Roger helps me too.

As I wrote before, I helped in the butcher shop every day and I started making soup to sell to our customers, but during the last few weeks the smell of the meat made me so nauseated I had to run to the bathroom. Turns out—We're having a baby!

I'm thrilled but morning sickness is keeping me home, eating saltine crackers and sipping ginger tea. Can you imagine me hating the smell of food!?

Have a wonderful birthday! Miss you so much!!
Roger sends his love.
Love, Aimée

Audrey sent a Christmas card with a note,

Dearest Aimée,

Congratulations—I'm so happy for you!
Sounds like your dreams are coming true!

My news is far less exciting. The building is completely occupied and I hired a new doorman who does small repairs. He is not as friendly as I'd like but he speaks many languages which I need since my tenants are multi-national.

I'm still teaching voice and piano and occasionally playing for the opera when their regular pianist is unavailable. I love it!

It took two months for the household goods to make the trip from Columbus to Paris. Maman and Papa's furniture fits perfectly. The bedroom set in the guest room (I still call it Aimée's room) is also perfect. I'm so glad we moved to 3A.

I look forward to lots of photos!
Love, Audrey

As the months went by, Audrey received photos of Aimée as she grew bigger and bigger, but the correspondence came less and less frequently until Audrey received a birth announcement, including a photo of Aimée beaming, holding two bundles.

> *Audrey,*
> *Peux-tu le croire? Identical twin girls!*
> *I'll send photos as often as I can but, you can imagine, we are quite busy with feeding and diapers (oh so many diapers!) The babies were born three weeks early and weighed slightly less than five pounds each but they are quite healthy and clearly, their lungs are fully developed!*
> *We named them after you and your mother and hope they grow up to be as brilliant, kind and generous.*
> *Visit as soon as you can!*
> *Miss you so much!!*
> *Love,*
> *Aimée and Roger*

On the back of the image Roger had written:
August 8, 1953
Aimée holding Esther and Audrey

Standing by the tall living room window, Audrey watched the sunset turning red, as if the clouds were soaked with spilled Bordeaux. The rooftops, buildings and *La Tour Eiffel* glowed with saffron dust. She clutched the black-and-white photo of Aimée and the babies to her chest. For several minutes, her mind remained nearly blank, as if conflicting memories caused deep meditation.

So much had happened in the fourteen years since Aimée, Audrey and her mother left Ohio. Audrey still missed Aimée's company, but Aimée had achieved her dream; she had a beautiful family.

At the age of almost thirty, Audrey had also achieved her dream of becoming a respected classical musician. She loved the voice and piano students who came to her flat every day and she enjoyed playing piano for the opera when they needed a substitute... *But...* she thought, *What if Maman had been more accepting when I announced the pregnancy? What if there had been no WWII? What if Ted and I had married and raised the baby? What if we could play music together every day and go to that enchanted realm no one but Ted understood?*

The pain suddenly escaped the closely guarded portion of her heart. She longed to listen to Ted tell her about his day and she yearned to discuss her most private thoughts like they had when they were children. As if Ted stood next to her playing his violin, the haunting, passionate melody of Mendelssohn's "Violin Concerto" filled the darkening room. She dropped onto the wingback chair and allowed regret and sorrow to consume her.

Audrey's Opera Career

"Miss Dupré, the opera is in need of a pianist," said the managing director when she answered the phone. "We plan to hold auditions next week, however, if you are willing to become our pianist, auditions will be unnecessary. You are the best there is."

"Thank you, Maestro, I would be honored."

"The salary is—"

"Maestro," she gently interrupted. "I don't want a salary. Donate anything you would pay me back to the opera. I insist."

They discussed the winter schedule and she agreed to play for the first rehearsal.

Alone in her apartment, Audrey made herself a cup of tea, sat in the wingback chair and allowed herself a moment of reflection. She looked around the room at the beautiful furniture that once belonged to her parents, but she'd tried to make it her own.

Although it had been fifteen years since she gave birth, it seemed as if she had just boarded the ship for the long voyage to Paris. The war was years behind her, but sometimes she felt as if she and Aimée had fled to Beaune only yesterday.

She looked at her fingers clutching the warm mug of tea. *My hands have recovered, but my heart will take forever to heal.*

She heard a gentle knock at the door.

"Hello, Bernard, come in. You're looking well." They kissed each other on both cheeks. "Would you like a cup of tea? The pot is still hot."

"That would be lovely." He followed her into the kitchen and watched her pull a mug from the low shelf.

As she poured, she said, "I agreed to play for the Paris opera this season," she told Bernard. "Have you considered singing again?"

"Even if I could re-train my voice, I no longer have the energy or desire. The opera is lucky to have you. Will you continue teaching here in your flat?

"Yes, of course. I could never give up my students."

"Glad to hear it. Friends I met when I sang for the New York opera, Adina and David Sapozhnikov, would like their son, Sergei, to study music while visiting me this summer. They're looking for a teacher. He is quite talented and his mother is an angelic soprano. If you don't mind, I'll give Adina your name and address."

A few weeks later, Audrey opened the letter from Adina Sapozhnikov. She walked across the living room as she unfolded the sweet-smelling linen stationery. She sat on the piano bench to read the letter, ignoring the strange fluttering in her heart.

> *Dear Mademoiselle Dupré,*
>
> *Our son, Sergei, will visit our friend Bernard Berkowitz, who is a tenant in your building. Bernard has recommended you as a music teacher. We are wondering if you have the time to instruct him daily, perhaps for an hour or more if possible.*
>
> *Please let me know if you are available during June, July and August and what the fees will be.*
> *Very Truly Yours,*
> *Mrs. David Sapozhnikov*

Audrey responded:

> *Dear Mrs. Sapozhnikov,*
>
> *My friend Bernard speaks highly of Sergei and his talent. I would be delighted to include him among my students. When he arrives, we will work out the best schedule for both of us.*
>
> *Regarding fees, I do not accept payment from my music students. It is a labor of love. Instead, please send a donation to the Paris Opera Company.*
> *Sincerely,*
> *Audrey Dupré*

"Good afternoon," said Sergei, shaking Audrey's warm hand. "I have heard wonderful things about you from our friend Bernard Berkowitz. I'm honored to be one of your students this summer."

During their handshake, Audrey felt a visceral jolt of affection, like lightning through her body, but on the outside, she remained composed, as always.

It was evident from the boy's impeccable manners that he had grown up in the company of money and dignified social aesthetics. He carried an ease she often saw in her students who had been spoken to as equals since birth. He was thin and tall, with thick wavy brown hair that grew over his collar, unusual in the 1950s. Long, dark lashes shadowed his sparkling olive-brown eyes and his face was smooth, with no trace of whiskers or blemishes.

When Sergei sat down at her piano, she closed her eyes as he played a flawless rendition of Chopin's extremely difficult "Etude in G# minor." Its trilling thirds vibrated into her heart. She clutched her arms across her chest, her breath shallow, unsure whether it was the notes or something older than the music that stirred her so deeply. Sergei's intrinsic understanding and heartfelt execution moved everyone who listened to him play. However, Audrey's feelings went beyond his talent. *Why does this enormously gifted Jewish boy make my heart ache so intensely?* she wondered. The feeling was something between grief and longing.

That summer, she challenged him with Liszt, Chopin and Islamey and coached his singing voice so he would feel the music from inside himself. He was a remarkably strong tenor, especially for one so young.

To make singing more fun and add variety, on Wednesdays, after his lesson, they sang popular American tunes together, harmonizing and laughing:

> *It had to be you*
> *It had to be you*
> *I wandered around*
> *And finally found*
> *The somebody who*
> *Could make me be true,*
> *Could make me feel blue,*
> *And even be glad just to be sad*
> *Thinkin' of you.*

On Friday afternoons, they played the duet of his choosing. "Mozart 'Sonata for two pianos K.448,' what else?" laughed Sergei.

They played the piece often, but since she had just one piano, they shared the keyboard. Elbows touching, minds entwined, lost in musical abandon, it didn't matter which hands were hers.

Adina Sapozhnikov's Revelation

New York, 1955

Adina Sapozhnikov was delighted when Sergei's former teacher, *Mademoiselle* Dupré, agreed to come to Sergei's graduation celebration. "Sergei has raved about you since his summer in Paris. We would love for you to stay in our guest room," offered Adina on the phone.

"Thank you, that's kind of you, but I have reserved a room in a hotel. I'll be taking an early train to visit my cousin in Ohio."

When Audrey arrived in New York, Sergei convinced her to play Mozart's "Sonata for two pianos K.448" at his graduation performance.

He walked onto the stage and stepped to the microphone. "When I was fifteen, I had the honor and privilege to study music in Paris with a special teacher. On Friday afternoons, we played a duet of my choice, which was almost always Mozart's "Sonata for two pianos K.448." I'm pleased to announce that my teacher has come all the way from Paris to perform with me tonight. May I present *Mademoiselle* Dupré."

Audrey floated onto the stage, tall, thin and elegant in a long black dress with white satin collar and cuffs, very much like a tuxedo. Her warm smile, gentle voice and welcoming olive-brown eyes contradicted the severity of her Edith Head hairstyle with heavy bangs across her forehead and a wide bun, secured at the nape of her neck. The audience leaned forward, captivated.

Audrey and Sergei hugged, then moved to their respective benches facing each other over two shining ebony pianos huddled together like yin and yang.

Sergei sat, then stood up and wiggled his head as if confused, causing his hair to fall across his forehead.

Audrey looked up, her fingers poised above the keys, then

her arms extended out with her palms facing up, as if to say, "What's wrong?"

He ran his fingers through his hair and shook his head again.

Audrey threw her head back in a staged laugh, scooted to one side and patted the bench next to her.

As he passed the microphone, he told the audience, "When we practiced in Paris, we had just one piano."

He settled next to her and they began the musical part of their performance.

At the first note, tears filled Adina's eyes. Soon she was nearly sobbing, struggling to hold her breath and be still.

David put his arm over her trembling shoulders, "Darling, it's graduation, not the end of the world," he whispered, hugging her closer to him.

"That's not it, David," she whispered in a low, hoarse voice, "I'll tell you later."

Audrey and Sergei enjoyed an uproarious standing ovation, held hands and took their bows.

Adina's crying was evident to everyone at the reception, among the other tearful mothers. "Your performance was lovely," Adina told Audrey. "He really does love Mozart." They enjoyed a brief conversation, then Audrey said good night and took a taxi to her hotel.

Later that evening, when they were finally alone in their bed, David asked, "So tell me," he whispered gently, "why were you so overcome?"

"Ms. Dupré is his mother."

David sat up, "That's ridiculous darling... I admit their eyes are very similar, but... did she say something to you?"

"Oh, I'm certain she has no idea but..."

"Well then..." he said.

"No darling. It hit me like a thunderbolt the moment Sergei sat on the bench next to her. Then, during the reception, I asked her about her family. Her parents died in the war, her father was a scientist and her mother's name was Esther, like the inscription in *The Tale of Peter Rabbit*."

David exhaled deeply as Adina rubbed his back.

"It's alright darling. In a way, I'm happy we met her," she said. "Now we know where Sergei inherited his exceptional talent and she is a lovely, warm, kind, generous woman. She was a child when she gave birth."

David lay back down on the bed and hugged his wife. "Maybe *Mademoiselle* Dupré is his biological mother, but… we will always be his mama and papa."

Audrey Visits Aimée

Columbus, Ohio, 1955

Aimée and her family lived in the apartment above the butcher shop where her husband's father once lived. Audrey climbed the stairs and stood in the hallway listening to Aimée's two-year-old twins laughing and playing in the apartment. She smiled and realized that she couldn't imagine what it would have been like to grow up with a sibling.

Aimée and Audrey hadn't lived like sisters until Audrey was thirteen, when Aimée came to live with them in Ohio after her parents were killed in the car accident.

She knocked and heard a tiny voice from inside, "*Maman, la porte.*"

Audrey laughed out loud, happy that the little girls were learning French.

Aimée opened the door and tears suddenly formed in her eyes, "*Mon Dieu!* Audrey, what a wonderful surprise!"

They caught each other in a long, firm hug while the little girls stood behind their mother, clutching her skirt.

Aimée turned to them, "This is your Aunt Audrey."

Audrey bent to meet the girls eye to eye. "It is wonderful to meet you," she said in French, as she sat on the floor.

One little girl stepped forward, "*Je m'appelle aussi* Audrey," her black hair curly like her mama's.

Gathering the tiny, dimpled hands into her own, adult Audrey said, "Nice to meet you, Audrey. You are my namesake."

"*Oui*," replied the twin in a tiny, shy voice.

"Then you must be Esther. You are my mother's namesake."

Little Esther nodded, too shy to speak.

Audrey knew from letters that Aimée had told them stories about Auntie Audrey and her mother, Esther.

"You and your sister look very much alike," said Audrey.

"*Oui*, we are twins," said little Audrey.

Lost for words, Aimée stood watching her daughters and Audrey. "I am so glad to see you!" she said, moving her hands to her heart.

"One of my students invited me to attend his Juilliard graduation in New York so I decided I'd take the opportunity for a surprise visit."

"I can't believe you're here! Are you hungry? Do you want lunch or coffee?"

Audrey gathered Aimée into another hug. "Oh, Aimée, I have missed you. Please just sit down and talk to me." She lowered herself to the sofa and patted the space next to her. "How is your life?"

Little Audrey and Esther climbed onto their mother's lap. Identical dark eyes stared inquisitively at Audrey.

Aimée hugged the girls, "These two have made my life complete." She kissed the girls on top of their soft, dark curls.

"Your maman and I lived together before she knew your daddy, before you were born," Audrey said in English.

"In Paris," little Audrey announced. The girls easily switched to English.

"*Mais oui.*" Audrey's voice caught slightly. "We shared an apartment in Paris."

While the girls took a nap, Aimée began fixing dinner and they finally settled into a more relaxed conversation. Aimée talked about her husband and her daughters, Audrey talked about her students and the opera. "Your timing is perfect! This afternoon we're going to visit the house we made an offer on. You can see where we'll be living for the rest of our lives... if the deal goes through."

Roger left the shop in his brother's hands and they piled into the car to visit the house they hoped to buy.

"It's my dream house," gushed Aimée. "It's a white, two-story, with five-bedrooms! Maybe we'll have more children to fill it?" she giggled as she patted Roger's shoulder, so excited, her French accent became stronger. "It has a huge, wraparound porch and the two acres of woods will be ours too. It's in Gahanna and only a twenty-minute drive to the butcher shop, but Roger hopes to open another butcher shop in Gahanna and maybe a deli. When the girls are older I can cook if I still want to." She finally took a breath.

"When do you plan to close?" asked Audrey.

"Next week if the financing comes through. We're using Merchants National Bank, where your parents had their account. People there are always friendly and accommodating."

Aimée served *pot-au-feu* for dinner. "How do you manage to prepare such a scrumptious meal while caring for twins?" asked Audrey.

"If I don't prepare dinner while they nap, we don't eat," she laughed. "And it helps to be a butcher's wife." Aimée patted Roger's broad hand.

They did the dishes together while Roger gave the girls a bath.

After Audrey read to the twins and they fell asleep, she said, "Well, it's getting late and it was a long train trip. I should call a taxi."

"I wish we had the room for you…"

"In the new house you'll have plenty of room," laughed Audrey. "Maybe next time I visit we'll start piano lessons." Audrey stood and reached for the telephone.

"I'll drive you to the hotel, I insist," said Roger.

"That's kind of you," said Audrey.

Audrey was at Merchants National Bank when it opened the next morning.

"Miss Dupré, so nice to see you," said Mr. Hollenbacker, the bank manager she had known her entire life. "Have you moved back to Ohio or are you just visiting?"

"Hello Mr. Hollenbacker. I'm visiting my cousin, but there is something I'd like to discuss with you."

"Of course, come into my office. Would you like a cup of coffee or tea?"

Later, Audrey was in the apartment with Aimée and the girls when Roger came upstairs to have lunch and play with his girls, leaving his brother in the shop. "I'm excited about moving to our new house, but I'll miss visiting with my girls at lunchtime," said Roger, hugging Aimée.

"How soon do you plan to open the new shop?" asked Audrey.

"That depends on our finances, as soon as we can afford it," said Roger. "Maybe in a year or two."

As they ate their roast beef sandwiches and the little girls pushed meat and green beans around in their bowls, Audrey said, "I want to tell you a story."

Roger and Aimée looked up from their sandwiches.

"Losing my parents during the war was devastating. Aimée helped me get on with my life. She helped me prepare the building for the tenants' return and organize our apartment for my students. I don't think I would have survived without Aimée."

"Audrey, I couldn't have survived without you, either."

"We helped each other, but please, let me finish my story. When we came back to Ohio for our belongings and you two were married, I wanted to help you get started, but I didn't want to interfere with your lives. Now I have the perfect opportunity." She pulled an envelope from her pocket. "This is a belated wedding gift." She handed an envelope to Aimée, who passed it to Roger to open.

He pulled out a blue paper folded around a document. "What is it?" asked Aimée.

"It's the deed to our new house," whispered Roger. Then he quickly added, "Audrey you can't do this."

"Well, I can and I did. You own the property free and clear, but you'll need to sign some documents, of course. I also left an account for your new butcher shop, as well as the beginnings of a college fund for the girls."

"But… Audrey…"

"Aimée, you saw that stack of gold coins in my father's safe. That was only a small part of my parents' estate. I have no other heirs. Your family should have it now; seems silly for me to will it to the girls when I leave the planet and I don't plan to leave until I'm at least 100."

Gertie Grantham In High School

Dayton, Ohio, 1966

Ted Grantham's daughter, Gertie, never missed a football or basketball game, but not because she loved high school sports. George Taylor was on both teams.

She had a small record player in her room and, over and over, driving her brothers mad, she played her favorite song, "Wishin' and Hopin'" by Dusty Springfield:

> *Show him that you care just for him*
> *Do the things he likes to do*
> *Wear your hair just for him, 'cause*
> *You won't get him*
> *Thinkin' and a-prayin', wishin' and a-hopin'*

George was on the vocational track and she was in liberal arts, so they had no classes together. She made sure she smiled at George as he passed her in the halls, stood behind him in line at the water fountain and often ate lunch alone, hoping he would notice her. In the fall of sophomore year, he finally did.

He carried his lunch tray past her, then turned around and slid his tray across from her. "Okay if I join you?" He said in his deep masculine voice.

She squeezed out, "Of course, George." At first, other words stuck in her throat. The bell rang just as he sat down. She ignored it, knowing she would miss Home Economics class. That day, he finally asked her to the after-game dance.

A few weeks later, he gave her his class ring. They were *going steady.* At the five and dime she bought yards of angora yarn to match every outfit, wrapped his ring to fit her finger and wore it proudly.

One Saturday morning Ted joined Gertie as she ate a bowl of Cheerios. "What's going on, Muffin? You look disappointed."

"George asked me to the Senior Prom."

"Shouldn't you be happy?"

"Sure I am, but Mom and I were going to go shopping for a dress today. That was her on the phone. She has to stay to help a patient in crisis."

"I'll take you shopping! I don't know much about dresses, but I can offer my opinion, if you want me to."

Store after store, gown after gown, Ted nearly fell asleep while Gertie tried on everything in her petite size. Finally, she stepped out of the dressing room wearing a full-length, cream satin dress embroidered with blue flowers. "You look lovely," said Ted, sitting up straight and grinning at his daughter.

"Oh, Daddy, isn't it beautiful? It's like the Givenchy Jacqueline Kennedy wore. I hope it's not too expensive."

"If that's the dress you want, that's the dress you'll have."

On prom night, George put a gardenia corsage on her wrist and she pinned a matching boutonniere to his wide lapelled, baby-blue tuxedo that had black trim on the collar, slanted pockets and side seams.

Ted took pictures of Gertie coming down the stairs in her prom gown. He took pictures of her in front of the fireplace. He took pictures of Gertie and George together, then he asked Evelyn to take his picture with Gertie and one of the boys took a picture of Ted, Evelyn and Gertie.

George held the door of his dad's '57 Chevy open for Gertie, something he never did, then slowly drove to the dance.

As a disco ball scattered starlight around the gymnasium, their classmates crowned them Prom King and Queen. The high school ensemble played Paul Mauriat's "Love is Blue" and George and Gertie danced alone in a spotlight that shone through George's already thinning blondish hair.

After graduation in 1968, George's flat feet kept him out of Vietnam. Although he was a high school quarterback, he lacked the grades and physique to play college football. He started looking for a job.

On Gertie's eighteenth birthday, George picked her up in his dad's brown and beige '57 Chevy. She wore her hair long and down her back because that's what George liked and her outfit was blue, his favorite color. After they shared a hamburger (no pickles, no lettuce, no tomato), fries (no ketchup) and a vanilla milkshake at the Big Boy drive-in, George drove to an overlook on the outskirts of Dayton. Almost before the engine stopped, he turned on the bench seat and blurted, "Let's get married." He pulled a ring with a diamond chip from his pocket and put it on her finger.

"Oh, George, yes, let's get married!"

When Gertie announced her engagement, Ted gave her a hug. "I hope you'll wait until you're at least twenty and George has a job."

During the next two years, Gertie worked as a hostess in a fancy restaurant and saved every penny of her wages and tips, while Rike's department store at the new Salem Mall hired George as a clerk, selling men's clothing.

Gertie made a doctor's appointment to get a prescription for birth control pills, but her regular doctor wouldn't prescribe them.

"You're not married yet," he said.

"Yes, but everyone says I'll need time to adjust to them."

"I'm sorry Gertie, come back after the wedding and I'll see what I can do."

Gertie found the number for an OB/GYN in the Cincinnati phone book and George drove her to the appointment she made under the name Mrs. George Taylor. After the appointment, Gertie met George in the waiting room. She held up the prescription slip and smiled, "No problem."

At first, the pills made her nauseous, like morning sickness, but she eventually adjusted to the elevated hormone levels.

Gertie wanted a small wedding, with George's sister as the only bridesmaid and a cake with white frosting roses on top instead of the dreadful bride and groom mannequins. For the ceremony, George wore an ill-fitting rented black tuxedo, while Gertie's frilly white dress resembled a coconut marshmallow cupcake.

After a weekend honeymoon at a local motel, they moved into his parents' basement. She vacuumed and dusted every day, ironed George's shirts with just the right amount of spray starch and laid out his clothes each morning while he showered. When the store promoted George to department manager and with help from Ted and Evelyn, they bought a house in the suburbs of Dayton, Ohio, a few blocks from her parents' home. Gertie quit her part-time job, stopped taking the pill and threw herself into full-time housewifery and gardening.

She planted lettuce, carrots, peas, russet potatoes and lots of zinnias, marigolds, cosmos and mums. George loved plum jam, so she bought a small plum tree. Near the back fence she dug a big hole for the tiny root ball, fertilized and watered the diminutive tree, little more than a stick. She knew it would take several years for the tree to produce fruit. *We will live in this house while we grow old together. There will be plenty of time for the tree to bear fruit,* she thought.

While Gertie and George were planning their lives together, Gertie's youngest brother, Robert, enlisted in the Army and served as an infantryman in Vietnam. During his second tour of duty, he met Chau. A year later, he returned to the US with his Vietnamese bride.

To welcome her brother home from the war and to express her support for his marriage, Gertie called Robert. "George and I would like you and Chau to come to dinner on Saturday night."

Gertie wanted everything to be perfect. Welcoming her brother with a home-cooked American meal, she set the table in the dining room with her best china and picked flowers for a centerpiece. She served what had been his favorite meal: roast beef, baked potatoes and green beans, along with her pride and joy, homemade yeast rolls.

Chau pushed the food around her plate and didn't touch the rolls. She wasn't accustomed to using silverware or eating meat and over-cooked vegetables. Her English was perfect, but they had nothing in common. Gertie mentioned that she and George had just seen the movie *Klute*, with Jane Fonda. "I loved her hair cut," said Gertie.

Robert froze. His fork in mid-air. "That's the haircut she

wore when they photographed her sitting on an anti-aircraft gun." His fork clinked on the edge of his plate. "That gun was used to target American planes!"

"Oh my," Gertie breathed.

Chau's pretty face turned to stone.

George tried to change the subject. "We saw Walter Matthau in *A New Leaf.* It was really funny."

Chau and Robert hadn't seen it. They all listened to the clink of silverware on china, searching for some common point of conversation. Finally, Gertie stood, "Well then, are we ready for dessert?" She served apple pie à la mode. Chau poked it with her fork and took only one bite.

Everyone was glad when the dinner ended.

On his way out the door, Robert hugged his sister and whispered, "I appreciate the effort, Sis."

In 1972, Gertie and George's first child, Suzie, was born and three boys followed over the next few years. Gertie strained vegetables from her garden, fruit from the local farmer's market and leftover pork or beef to feed the babies, not trusting products that came in a jar. When her children were older, she made bread for their lunch box sandwiches. Each morning, after they left for school, she made the beds, vacuumed, dusted, ironed and baked Toll House cookies or brownies with fudge frosting for their after-school snacks.

Gertie remembered Evelyn quickly preparing meals after work, serving Gorton's frozen fish sticks baked with Ore Ida tater tots, or sometimes sliced Spam with canned beans. Gertie planned her meals around the preferences of her husband rather than convenience. The children preferred creamy peanut butter and George liked Miracle Whip, so that's what she stocked in the pantry. Their meals were bland and spice-less, potatoes, vegetables and roasted meat as George expected.

The woman's movement gained momentum, but Gertie felt proud to be a housewife. She absorbed *The Total Woman* by Marabel Morgan. Morgan wrote, *It's only when a woman surrenders her life to her husband, reveres and worships him and is willing to serve him, that she becomes really beautiful to him.* Gertie didn't question it. Caring for George and her family made her life worthwhile.

By the time Gertie's husband, George, was thirty, his blondish hair had disappeared from the top of his head, leaving a frame of dirty-blond curls above his ears. With his lack of exercise and Gertie's cooking, George's waistline had expanded. On his days off, he loved to go fishing. Wearing his favorite outgrown red flannel shirt, he floated down the river looking like a pudgy fire hydrant with glasses.

Gertie packed his favorite lunch: Wonder bread with bologna and lots of Miracle Whip, a bag of Lay's potato chips and a package of Twinkies. Sadly, George preferred Wonder bread over Gertie's homemade bread and Twinkies were his favorite snack, no matter what she baked.

When George had a successful day on the river, Gertie cooked the fish for their dinner. If he caught catfish or crappie, she coated the fillets with egg, dredged them in cornmeal and fried them in Crisco. If he brought home bass, she baked the fillets in a Corning Ware casserole with slices of lemon and Oleo margarine.

On Friday nights, even when the boys were little, George took his three sons to a local high school football game. They had their favorite teams, but they didn't care which team won, they just liked to watch the game. On the boys' birthdays, George took the family to The Steakhouse for dinner, "Order whatever you want, it's a birthday celebration," said George.

When one of the boys ordered Coca-Cola, Gertie interrupted, "Order anything you want to eat, but milk instead of Coke." For dessert, the waitress brought a cupcake with a candle to the birthday boy and all the waitresses sang Happy Birthday.

Their daughter, Suzie and George had their own traditions. They spent Sunday afternoons together, just the two of them. When she was tiny, before her brothers were born, he took her to the park in the wicker pram that had been Gertie's. For Suzie's third birthday, Gertie's father, Ted, surprised them by having Gertie's playhouse, built in 1953, moved to their backyard near the plum tree.

Suzie had Gertie's wavy dark hair, but she was tall for her age and she'd rather read to their dog Bosco than fantasize about cooking, ironing, or tending baby dolls. George knew Suzie would soon outgrow the playhouse.

To encourage what he considered *appropriate feminine behavior*, George bought an EasyBake oven and a little apron for Suzie's fourth birthday.

Suzie opened the present from her daddy. "What's this for?" she asked, taking the device out of the box.

"It's an EasyBake oven. You can make cakes all by yourself in the playhouse."

"Cakes without flour? Or eggs?

"Everything you need is in this packet, just add a little water."

She examined the device, "How do I set the temperature?"

"Sweetie, you just turn it on and it bakes the little cake." He held up the packet and the little cake pan.

"Thank you, Daddy." Giving him a kiss on the cheek, she slid the toy oven back into its box and never touched it again.

Every year, on her birthday, Suzie and George enjoyed lunch at McDonald's. George let Suzie order what she wanted and gave her the money to pay for their to-go order. "You can put the change in your piggy bank when we get home," said George.

They walked to a nearby park and sat on a bench. Suzie threw little pieces of bread to a crow who decided he wanted more and swooped in for her bag of fries.

"Look Daddy," Suzie laughed, "that crow stole my fries! Can we get some more?"

"Sure, sweetheart, we'll get more fries on the way home. Do you want to play for a while before we go? I'll push you on the swing."

"I'm ten now Daddy. This is a baby park."

Their last father/daughter date was on her sixteenth birthday. He took her to Rike's in-store restaurant for her birthday lunch. As a Department Head, he enjoyed an employee discount. Compared to McDonald's, or even The Steakhouse, the dining room was elegant, with white tablecloths and waitresses dressed in black skirts and white shirts.

"I'll have French onion soup," said Suzie, looking up from the menu.

"I'll have the special with meatloaf, green beans instead of cauliflower and a baked potato with butter, no sour cream."

Suzie enjoyed chocolate cake with a candle on top. George ordered a banana split without a banana and vanilla ice cream instead of chocolate.

Sergei's 40th Birthday

New York, 1978

Sergei arranged for his Concert Tour to end in New York so he could spend December with his parents and celebrate Hanukkah and his fortieth birthday.

David Sapozhnikov was having trouble walking due to the arthritis in his hips. The morning of the concert, Sergei brought a wheelchair into his parents' penthouse.

"I don't need a wheelchair!" David growled. "I just can't walk as *fast* as I once did."

"But Papa, it'll be easier for Mama and more comfortable for you. I reserved front row balcony seats. You can sit together where the chair won't block the aisle and we can take the elevator." Sergei didn't mention that the elevator was reserved for disabled patrons.

In the long black limo on the way to the performance, Adina asked, "I hope Debussy's 'Clair de Lune' on the program tonight."

"It is now," Sergei smiled at his mother.

Sergei began the concert with Mozart's "Ave Verum Corpus" and "Exsultate, Jubilate," followed by parts of Bach's "Christmas Oratorio." After playing a bit of Mendelssohn and Reinecke, he stood at the microphone. "There is an addition to the program tonight. My mother requested Debussy's 'Clair de Lune.'" He waved toward the balcony, "For you Mom!" Applause echoed throughout the hall as the faces of Sergei's loyal fans tipped toward his mother. He motioned for her to stand. She nodded demurely to the crowd as the deafening ovation continued.

As he finished "Clair de Lune," the stage lights dimmed.

"Oh dear, we're having a brown out!" he laughed, as unflappable on stage as always. "That's fine. I love playing by candlelight."

Just then, the first violinist stepped onto the stage, pushing a trolley with a three-tiered cake glowing with forty candles.

"This is not the candlelight I was thinking of!" Sergei announced with a startled grin.

Three singers dressed in lovely gowns joined the violinist who turned to the audience, "Please join us in wishing Sergei a happy fortieth birthday."

The entire audience burst into song, as Sergei stood by his piano, *verklempt,* his hand on his heart.

The following evening, at a soiree Adina had arranged so their friends could visit with Sergei, one of their long-time friends mentioned, "I was here the first time Sergei played the piano and he still looks like you, Adina. Will you sing "White Christmas" while Sergei plays?"

"We'd be delighted," Adina replied.

She took her place by the piano. At seventy-eight, she was as lovely as the first time Sergei played, thirty-seven years before.

Sergei sat on the piano bench, raised his hands, then comically hunched over the keys and played as if he were a three-year-old.

Everyone laughed. Adina arched her brow, feigning disapproval. He straightened up, played the prelude and she sang, "I'm dreaming of a white Christmas… just like the ones I used to know."

Gertie and George on the River

Dayton, Ohio, 1988

Since their wedding day, George and Gertie had made Saturday night date night. In the early days, when they had no money, they walked in the park and shared a scoop of vanilla ice cream. Later, the kids slept at her parents' house on Saturday so George and Gertie could have dinner at The Steakhouse, see a movie and spend uninterrupted time together.

One Saturday afternoon, while the children were with Ted and Evelyn, Gertie and George had a picnic on his rowboat. She fastened her life jacket and he held her hand while she stepped in and settled in the bow. Her shoulder-length brown hair, streaked with early gray, reflected the golden afternoon sunlight.

He handed her the picnic basket and pushed off the dock as he jumped in. With the basket balanced on her Bermuda shorts, she held tight to the gunnels. When he leaned over to kiss her, she squealed, "Oh George, please sit down. You'll tip the boat over."

"I stand up in this boat all the time." He stood and rocked it slightly. She closed her eyes and shrieked. "Oh George, please don't. It's so tippy! It feels like we'll both fall in. You should wear a life jacket too, George."

"It's perfectly safe. I don't need a life jacket. I can swim."

Gertie opened the basket, handed him a bologna sandwich, a bag of potato chips and a Coke—then held a death grip on the boat as if her life depended on it. She didn't eat her sandwich until they were safely back in the station wagon.

On the days when George went fishing and Gertie planned her dinner around his catch-of-the-day, he normally came home by 2:00 or 3:00 p.m., giving Gertie plenty of time to prepare the fish and giving him time to mow the lawn or play catch with the boys in the backyard. One afternoon in the summer of 1988, George still wasn't home at 5:00 p.m.

Suzie prepared grilled cheese sandwiches and Campbell's tomato soup for her brothers while Gertie paced the floor, worrying about George. At 6:00, Gertie called the police.

Gertie, sixteen-year-old Suzie and the boys, aged fourteen, twelve and ten, waited together in the living room. One of the boys turned on the TV, but they had no interest in watching *The Wonder Years, Growing Pains*, or any other program. Their vigil lasted until 10:00 p.m. when two policemen rang the doorbell.

"May we come in?" one of the officers said in a calming voice. "I'm sorry to tell you ma'am, but we found your Ford station wagon at the marina. The empty rowboat was downstream, with his glasses and an open tackle box. One line was still in the water".

Gertie nearly collapsed. They helped her to the sofa and offered to call someone for her.

"No thank you," said Gertie, "there's really no one to call." Her whole life revolved around George and her four children.

After the police left, Suzie asked, "Should I call Granny Evelyn and Granddad?"

"No, that's not necessary. The police will find him and everything will be okay." Alerting Ted and Evelyn would mean the worst had happened and she couldn't face the possibility.

After a sleepless night, she tried to do her housework and cook for the children, sure that the police would find George with a bumped head and amnesia like she'd seen on *Days of Our Lives*. She considered no other explanation; she allowed no other thought to enter her mind.

Around 4:00 p.m., the police came by to report that an angler had found George's body caught in debris near shore. George was only thirty-eight years old.

While Gertie sat with the boys on the sofa, all of them crying, Suzie called her Granddad Grantham.

He heard the distress in her voice. "Hi, sweetie. What's the matter?"

"It's Daddy," she said between sobs. "He's dead."

"Is your mother there with you?"

"Yes. The boys are here too."

"I'll be there in ten minutes."

Ted called Evelyn at work and waited on the line several minutes until she came to the phone. "Hello darling, what's going on? They said it's an emergency."

Ted told her about Suzie's phone call. "I don't know yet what happened. I'll pick you up on my way there." They parked in Gertie's driveway and hurried to the door, Evelyn in her nurse's uniform, Ted in a business suit.

Suzie explained, "The police found his boat yesterday, but Mom told us they'd find him and he'd be okay, but today, they found his... body."

The next few days were a blur for Gertie and her family. Her parents helped with meals and Suzie proved to be strong and pragmatic. "I'd go to the grocery, but the car is still at the marina," Suzie told her granddad.

"Ted darling, you take Suzie to get the car and I'll stay here with Gertie and the boys," said Evelyn.

"Good idea. Are you sure you're up to it Suzie?"

"Thanks Granddad, I'm fine."

They found the old Ford Country Squire station wagon with its dull yellow paint and faded faux wood panels at the marina where George had parked.

"Let's leave my car here until we fill up the Ford," Ted suggested. He also had the tires checked and the oil changed. Suzie drove him back to his car, then she drove to the grocery store and home again.

Suzie found things for her brothers to do and they were happy to help. "Will you bring in the rest of the groceries, please?"

"Help me peel the potatoes?"

"How about pulling some carrots in the garden?"

In September, when Gertie's children had gone back to school, Ted took a day off. Wearing a button-down shirt and khakis, he parked in front of her house, put a big pot of yellow mums on the stoop and rang the bell. When she answered the door in her pink terrycloth bathrobe and fuzzy slippers, he stepped over the threshold. "I thought maybe you could use a little company today."

She fell into his arms and he held her as she broke down. They sat on the sofa together and he hugged her while she sobbed, "I miss George so much! What will I do?"

"I know... It will take time...." He hugged her close while she cried. Then he asked, "Have you had breakfast? Let me fix us something to eat."

As always, he turned to food to comfort her. "French toast used to be your favorite. It'll make you feel better." She sat at the kitchen table, dunking a Lipton tea bag into the hot water he poured for her.

Ted understood that, beyond losing the love of her life, Gertie had no means to support her family and no work experience beyond housewifery and motherhood.

When they finished breakfast, he washed all the dishes, left them drying in the rack and they went back to sit on the sofa. "Don't worry about the financial side of things. I'll help out."

Ted Grantham's Diagnosis

Dayton, Ohio, 1988

In the weeks following George's death, while Gertie struggled with her grief, Ted frequently took a few hours away from the office to have breakfast or lunch or just a cup of coffee with her. As a result, he was behind in his work. He was finally getting caught up when his secretary came into his office.

"Dr. Wilkinson's office has called several times. They said it's important that you make a follow up appointment today."

"Thanks Madge, call to see if he can see me late this afternoon."

His intercom buzzed a few minutes later. "Yes Madge?"

"The doctor can see you at 4:45."

"Thanks Madge, now can you come in here please? We need to catch up on dictation before my appointment."

Dr. Wilkinson welcomed Ted into the office. "I'm glad you finally came in. So sorry to hear about your son-in-law. How's Gertie doing?"

"As well as expected, I guess, she's devastated. Now, what was so important that I needed to come in today? I have a lot of work to catch up on."

"I won't beat around the bush. I'm sorry to tell you this Ted, you have testicular cancer. It's unusual. We usually see this in much younger men."

"Do I need surgery?" asked Ted.

"I'm sorry, it's too late for surgery. This could go pretty fast; it's already metastasized to your lungs and liver." He patted Ted on the shoulder. "I sure wish I had better news."

Suddenly, the work that seemed crucial a few moments before now felt insignificant. Ted drove home in a fog.

"What's happened?" asked Evelyn, as he came through the door. She knew by the look on his face, something terrible had happened.

Ted held Evelyn close as she broke down. She knew very well what the future held.

In October, Ted called the family together, insisting that Robert and Teddy come home for a family reunion. They ordered pizza and sat by a blazing fire in the living room.

Finally, Teddy remarked, "What's the big deal? Why did Robert and I have to fly home for *pizza*?"

"I have some news and wanted us all to be together," said Ted. "I have cancer that has metastasized to my lungs and liver."

"Ugh, that can't be good," remarked Teddy.

The rest of the family gazed at the fire. No one knew what to say. Gertie and her daughter Suzie cried.

Before her brother Robert returned to California, he and Gertie had coffee together.

"I'm sorry I can't stay and help," said Robert, "but our baby's due in three weeks. I need to get back."

Teddy caught a flight back to Florida without saying goodbye.

Ted tried various treatments. The drugs his doctors prescribed made him violently ill. Evelyn quit her nursing job to take care of him. It soon became apparent that he might not survive the year, but he was determined to live past Christmas. "Gertie and her family have had enough grief this year, I'm not going to spoil Christmas."

Ted died in January; he was sixty-three.

Gertie left messages for her bothers. "Please call me, it's important."

When Robert returned her call, she told him the sad news.

"Sorry it took so long to call you back, the baby's had a cold and we don't get much sleep," said Robert. "I'm sorry Dad never got to meet our son William. Give Mom a hug for me. I'll call her later." Gertie could hear the baby crying in the background.

Teddy never called, so Gertie finally left a message. "Teddy, I'm sorry to tell you this in a message, but Dad died yesterday. Call me and I'll give you details about the memorial."

Teddy didn't return her call and didn't show up at the service.

By the end of his life, Ted was the CEO of the aeronautical parts manufacturing company he started to work for while he was in grad school. He made a good salary, had a sizable life insurance policy and company stock. His family didn't know, however, that for thirty-five years he'd saved his meager military pension and amassed a fortune investing in mutual funds and IBM stock. Per his will, his estate was divided among Evelyn, Gertie, Robert, and Teddy.

Evelyn's Grief

Evelyn was just sixty-one and in excellent health when Ted died, but her grief was debilitating. Without Ted, she often forgot to fix herself lunch or dinner and became quite thin and frail.

With Gertie's encouragement, Evelyn sold her house and moved into Gertie's guest room. They hoped the rhythm of family life and the children's perpetual energy might help her recover.

Evelyn gave Teddy power-of-attorney because he was her oldest son and a CPA. He paid her medical bills and sent Gertie a weekly allowance during the nearly ten years that Evelyn lived with Gertie and her family.

Evelyn loved Gertie's cooking, especially since she had never been interested in cookery herself. As always, Gertie served meals her children preferred and kept the house spotless.

One night, after Gertie and the children had gone to bed, Evelyn finally had the strength to go through a box of papers Ted had left in his den. She filled a waste basket with things that meant nothing to her, but then she came upon a letter addressed to her. Too bereaved to open it, she tucked it in her dresser drawer as if his spirit were sealed inside. Every night, Evelyn took the envelope from her bureau drawer, held it to her cheek and listened to Ted's fountain pen scratching his thoughts onto the heavy stationery; she watched his tongue lick the envelope.

Only months after Evelyn lost Ted, his parents, the Admiral and Alice Grantham, died within hours of each other. They were nearly one hundred years old, still lived in their eight-bedroom home in Columbus, cared for by full-time in-home staff who lived in the rooms once occupied by the five sons they had outlived.

Evelyn remembered the cookbook Alice gave her the first time they met. She smiled and thought, *it didn't help my skills very much.*

The family gathered in the attorney's office for the reading of the Granthams' will. The will directed the attorney to divide most of the estate among Evelyn, Gertie, Teddy, Robert, William and Gertie's four children.

"Who the hell is William?" growled Teddy.

"That's our son," said Robert, looking at the blue bundle in Chau's arms.

Teddy continued to protest, complaining that Gertie's inheritance was way more than his because she had four children and he had none.

"I'll sue!" he shouted as he threw back his chair and stormed out. He slammed the door so hard Evelyn winced, certain the glass would shatter.

The attorney assured Evelyn and the rest of her family that the Grantham's will was sound, "There is nothing Teddy can do."

Each day, while Gertie did her housework, grocery shopping, or attended her club meetings, Evelyn walked. She usually passed by the high school at lunchtime and sometimes chatted with the students. Other days, she stopped at the park and watched the children on the swings and slide. The little ones would wave and shout, "Hi Granny, watch me, watch me!"

"Jimmy, you're so good on those monkey bars!" said Evelyn.

"Jenny, look how fast you can run." Sometimes she'd catch children at the bottom of the slide or push them on the swing. Then she'd sit on the bench with the young mothers.

One day, when Jimmy fell from the monkey bars, Evelyn told his mother, "You stay here and chat. I'll help Jimmy." Then the children climbed onto the merry-go-round and she pushed until they were all dizzy.

"You make the park more fun for all of us," laughed Jimmy's mother. Evelyn became known to everyone in the neighborhood as Granny Evelyn.

One blustery fall afternoon, Evelyn admired the canopy of red maples, orange oaks and the sweet-earthy scent of fall. She turned south at the corner of Rose Street and Maple, but after walking for twenty minutes, she found herself back at the corner of Rose and Maple.

She walked for two more hours and began to panic, *Where am I? What's happening? I can't remember the way to Gertie's house!*

Just then, Gertie drove by on her way home from a Woman's Club meeting. She pulled to the curb and rolled down the window, "Hi Mom, that was a long walk!"

Evelyn opened the passenger door and crawled in, "I'm exhausted. It's so strange. I walked and walked, but I couldn't find the right street."

Memory Care

As the months passed, Granny Evelyn became more and more difficult to care for. She'd leave the burner on under a dry teakettle, or forget to turn off the water after taking a shower. Once, while Gertie was out, the tub overflowed. The water would have ruined the ceiling if she hadn't come home in time to clean up the mess.

The ultimate defeat came one bitter, winter night when the doorbell rang near midnight. "Hi Mrs. Taylor," said a neighbor, Jimmy. "I found Granny Evelyn wandering in the Kroger parking lot." Jimmy had known Granny Evelyn all his life. Embarrassed by the old woman's nudity, she wore only a lacy nylon slip and high heels, he helped her into the house and fled before Gertie could thank him.

Gertie took Evelyn to the doctor and, as she feared, the diagnosis was Alzheimer's.

Following the doctor's recommendation, Gertie began the emotional process of moving Evelyn to a memory care facility. She phoned her brother Teddy in Florida. "Mom's been diagnosed with Alzheimer's and the doctor recommended that I move her into memory care at Village Garden Senior Living. Sometimes she doesn't remember who I am or how to brush her teeth. We need you to make the financial arrangements at Village Garden. I checked and they have…"

He interrupted. "I don't understand why my future inheritance should be wasted on a retirement home," growled Teddy. "There's no reason why Mom can't stay where she is."

Gertie told him about Evelyn's nearly naked midnight stroll in sub-freezing temperatures, thinking the story would raise some sympathy for their mother's deteriorating condition. It didn't.

"You're just being lazy. I forbid it," he said and hung up the phone.

Gertie paced the kitchen, trembling with rage. She realized she'd spent her whole life avoiding anger—especially with Teddy. *I never get angry*, she thought, *I don't even know how to get angry*. Now, however, she was so mad at Teddy she couldn't even cry.

She breathed deeply and tried to calm herself as she placed a call to Evelyn's doctor's office. "My brother, who has power of attorney, is not convinced that our mother should move to Village Garden," she informed the receptionist. "Could the doctor call him and explain the severity of the situation?"

"He'll be happy to," said the receptionist. "This happens a lot more than you might think."

"Evelyn isn't safe," the doctor told Teddy. "Gertie isn't safe either. Evelyn could start a fire in the kitchen or her bedroom. As the disease progresses, she'll need help managing basic bodily functions. She needs twenty-four-hour professional care and Gertie isn't qualified. The Village Garden staff is equipped to provide the care Evelyn requires. It's the best solution."

A few days later, Gertie got a notice from Village Garden— Teddy had signed the papers without so much as a phone call.

In February, under a steel-gray sky, Gertie moved Evelyn to Village Garden. The streets were icy, so Suzie's boyfriend drove Gertie, Evelyn and Suzie in his four-wheel-drive SUV and carried boxes into the room. Suzie unpacked and hung Evelyn's clothes in the closet and helped Gertie hang a framed picture of the Olympic Mountains that Evelyn had always liked.

Gertie tried to make the space as homey as possible with colorful bedding, pillows and an afghan.

After the nurse took Evelyn's blood pressure and checked her heart, Evelyn shuffled to the big window, wrapped her arms around her waist and seemed mesmerized by the blast of colors in the snow, the jungle gym in primary colors and the children wearing brightly colored snow suits. She seemed to have no idea where she was and didn't care.

A few days after the move, Teddy called, "What are you doing with all the Grantham stuff?"

"There isn't much to worry about, Teddy. Mom sold her furniture and gave away most of Dad's things when she moved in with us years ago and you know how frugal Dad was."

"Send that Civil War musket to me. I have a contact here in Florida who wants to buy it." He didn't ask, he demanded.

For once, Gertie didn't hesitate. In a crisp voice that didn't sound like her normal tender tones, she told him, "I can't do that

Teddy. If you would have stayed to hear the reading of Granddad's entire will, you would know that Granddad Grantham left money to the Military Museum. They devoted a room to Grantham family memorabilia. I gave the musket, the sword and all the medals, letters and other papers to the museum, except for Dad's commendation medals. I sent those to Robert."

"Without consulting me?"

"Why would I consult you, Teddy? Robert enlisted and served in Vietnam while you dodged the draft, it seemed only fair." Her tone was harsh, but she felt authentic and strangely satisfied.

"What about those blue and white dishes that belonged to Great Grandmother Grantham?" he asked.

"Mom gave the dishes to me when she moved in with us. She said I should have them since I'm her firstborn and only daughter," said Gertie. "I still have Granddad's hunting trophies stored in the basement, the moose head, deer heads and stuffed marlin. I'm happy to send them to you."

"Don't bother," Teddy snarled and hung up the phone.

Suzie and Tom

Cincinnati, Ohio, 1993

Suzie was at the library studying, when a student accidentally dropped a massive chemistry book on the floor beside her chair.

She jumped and whispered, "Shush."

"So sorry," he whispered. "I meant to sit at the other end of the table where I wouldn't disturb you. I'm so sorry."

When she looked up, her irritation dissolved. Tom was 6'4" with fair skin, blond hair and big bright eyes, more violet than blue. His easy smile and calm energy melted the tension.

"Sorry I growled at you," she said quietly. "My final literature paper is due this week. I'm a little jittery."

"I understand. My chemistry exam is tomorrow morning. Is it okay if I sit at the other end of the table? Promise, I'll be very quiet."

"Of course," she smiled and returned to her studies.

An hour later, she whispered, "I'm going to get something to eat. Are you ready for a break?"

From that day on, they were together.

After graduation, Tom got a job as a high school chemistry teacher and she became a licensed Speech-Language Pathologist.

A year later, they drove from Cincinnati to Dayton for Sunday dinner with Gertie and to visit Granny Evelyn. Suzie noticed how much Granny Evelyn had deteriorated since their last visit and the toll it had taken on her mother.

After helping with the dishes, Suzie said, "Wish we could stay longer, Mom, but Tom has papers to grade and I have some work to catch up on. Thanks for a lovely dinner."

During their drive back to Cincinnati, Suzie said, "I'm sorry Tom. Mom seemed so stressed I couldn't tell her we're engaged. I've never seen her so exhausted."

"I have an idea," he grinned. "Let's play hooky on Friday and elope."

"Great idea," she grinned back, with tears welling, "I love you so much!"

After the ceremony at the Hamilton County courthouse, they drove to Dayton and surprised Gertie. "Tom and I got married this morning!"

"Oh, I'm so happy for the two of you," said Gertie, wiping tears as she hugged Suzie, then stood on her tiptoes as Tom bent his 6'4" frame for a hug. "We'll plan a reception when Granny Evelyn settles down a bit."

Suzie saw the flicker of disappointment behind her mother's smile, but she knew—deep down—they'd made the right decision.

Suzie, Tom and Suzie's brothers all had dinner at Village Garden to celebrate Evelyn's seventieth birthday. During dinner, Suzie announced, "We're having a baby!"

While Gertie began to laugh and cry at the same time, Evelyn took another bite of roast beef and asked, "When are you two going to start a family?"

Suzie looked at Tom, "In about seven months, Granny," said Suzie, as her brothers snickered.

"Oh, that's nice. Now when are you going to start a family?" Evelyn repeated.

When the staff served the birthday cake Gertie had baked, with seven tall thin candles, Evelyn asked, "What's that for?"

"It's your birthday, Mom."

"How old am I?"

"You're seventy. Happy birthday, Mom." Gertie took a picture while Suzie and her brothers helped Granny blow out the candles.

Forensic DNA

The silver streaks in Audrey Dupré's black hair caught the morning sun light as she sat at the table with her coffee, croissant and *Le Parisien*. At seventy-six, she still wore heavy bangs across her eyebrows and a bun coiled on the back of her head. The strong light from the tall windows revealed lines around her eyes and mouth, but her skin remained remarkably smooth and vibrant, her olive-brown eyes as bright as ever.

As she sipped her coffee, she began reading an article in the Paris Newspaper:

May 10, 1999
NEW DNA TESTING METHODS
REVOLUTIONIZE FORENSICS
DNA profiling is now being used by Paris detectives to help solve cold cases. Evidence collected at a crime scene is compared to the suspect's DNA. Although DNA evidence alone is not enough to secure a conviction, DNA can be used to include or exclude a suspect. Police predict that someday soon, DNA profiling will be the gold standard for identifying and convicting perpetrators.

Here's the science: Chromosomes contain markers where short DNA sequences are repeated multiple times. The number of repeats at each marker varies from person to person and each person has two copies, called alleles, of each marker, one inherited from their mother and one from their father. "With the latest advances, we can now use saliva, sperm or hair follicles where before we needed blood samples," said Police Chief Boutroux. "We are hoping we can use the updated methods to identify the victims in the 1945 Petiot case."

After the war, a foul stench and smoke led police and firefighters to the home of Dr. Petiot where they found a roaring furnace burning human remains and additional remains scattered around the basement and buried in shallow graves in the neglected terrace behind the house. Victims' suitcases, clothing and jewelry cluttered the property. Dr. Petiot was apprehended, tried, convicted and executed in 1946.

We hope to use DNA testing to help confirm the identity of Petiot's victims. Forensic evidence was stored in hopes of someday using this sort of technology. "The problem is, of course," said Chief Boutroux. "we don't have samples to compare to. We're asking families of his suspected victims to provide us with samples that might still have the victim's DNA, for example, hair from a hairbrush. If that isn't possible, a cheek swab from an immediate family member, son, daughter, brother, or sister, can provide a fairly conclusive match."

Audrey put the newspaper on the table and pushed her croissant aside. The notion that the police might still have samples of her mother's remains fifty-five years later, made her queasy.

She'd spent fifty years teaching music and playing piano for the Paris Opera. But reading the article awakened her longing for the truth along with her grief.

Moving to the writing desk that had been her mother's, she took an envelope from a small drawer and wrote:

Regarding 1945 Petiot case,

Hair samples from Mrs. Eiffel Dupré

She added her address. Carrying a folding stool into her bedroom, she climbed to reach her mother's black-and-white striped hatbox. The round hatbox had been on the top shelf of her closet since she shipped the family belongings to Paris in 1953, but it had remained unopened since before she announced her pregnancy in 1938.

Sitting on the bed, she gathered the strength to look inside. She rested one hand on top of the box while her other hand traced the sophisticated red lettering on the side, *Mercerie de Paris*. When she opened the lid, her mother's spirit materialized, as if rising out of the box. Audrey heard her mother's laugh and smelled her Chanel N°5.

Audrey lifted the wide-brimmed summer hat that nestled inside, pushed her bangs out of the way and put the hat on her head. She glanced at the mirror above the dressing-table—her mother's dressing-table.

Everything blurred as if time spun backward. The face that stared back at Audrey was her mother's face as it might have been had she lived to be seventy-six. Audrey quickly removed the hat, gently placed it on the bed next to her and fluffed her bangs back into place.

As she suspected, she found the sterling silver dresser set in the hatbox. Each tarnished piece was lavishly decorated with a floral design and held an ancestor's monogram. She remembered her mother sitting at this dressing-table holding the hairbrush in one hand and the hand mirror in the other while she brushed the back of her hair.

As if the silver brush were made of fragile spun glass, Audrey used tweezers to carefully remove long strands of her mother's black hair and placed them in the envelope. Tears welled as she sealed the hair inside.

She descended the marble stairs and stood on the sidewalk in the sunshine as the doorman hailed a taxi for her. She would deliver the sample in person.

"The police station, please," she said to the driver.

Months later, when the postman delivered an envelope from the police department, she left it on the side table until her last student left. Then she poured herself a glass of Pinot Noir, sat at the writing desk and opened the envelope. The report confirmed a

DNA match, verifying that her mother died at the hands of a serial killer and not the Nazis.

Audrey settled into the wingback chair by the window where she could glimpse *La Tour Eiffel.* Her mind wandered to the months she spent with her mother in New York, waiting for the baby. They'd walked together in Central Park. Over breakfast and *The New York Times*, they'd discussed literature, war, politics and immigration. She tried to remember conversations they'd had during the entire fifteen years before that and realized she couldn't think of any. She and her mother had never enjoyed each other's company as they did during those months in New York.

SIMONE

As Audrey Dupré gathered her sheet music and turned off all the lights except for the ghost light traditionally left on stage, a nun emerged from the shadows, followed by a young girl.

Startled at first, Audrey asked, "Can I help you?" Her rich voice reverberated through the cavernous auditorium.

The nun moved toward the stage as if floating, her silent, soft-soled shoes hidden below the long black habit. Only the gleam of her white wimple and under-veil gave her shape in the dark.

A girl followed with her chin tucked toward her collar, her fingers clasped in reverence. A well-worn, knee-length cotton dress tugged across the girl's shoulders. Her white-blond hair hung in a heavy plaited rope down her back. "Yes, mademoiselle. Excuse me," the nun replied in soft, hesitant French as she neared the stage. "I was wondering if you could teach our little girl to sing?"

The location was unusual, but not the request. Audrey was willing to spend a few minutes with the girl before walking home for dinner. "Come up here child," Audrey said, with outstretched arms, her voice warm and inviting.

Skin like alabaster, eyes like aquamarine crystals and long white eyelashes gave the child an angel-like quality as she moved out of the dim light behind the nun and ascended the stairs toward Audrey.

The child glanced back at the nun.

The nun brought her hands together in prayer and smiled reassuringly.

"What is your name?" Audrey asked in French.

"*Je m'appelle* Simone."

"What would you like to sing for me, Simone?"

"*Ave Maria, s'il vous plaît.*"

"Would you like accompaniment?"

"*Non, merci, Madame.*"

Audrey nodded.

The girl closed her eyes, focused on her task and began to sing a cappella.

Ave Maria,
Gratia plena
Maria, gratia plena

Ave, ave dominus
Dominus tecum
Benedicta tu in mulieribus
Et benedictus

Et benedictus fructus ventris
Ventris tuae, Jesus
Ave Maria

As if released simultaneously from the heavens, the earth and this diminutive ragamuffin, the powerful yet delicate voice, infused with passion and intensity, filled the atmosphere.

On the first note, Audrey closed her eyes. Her chest ached and her eyes burned; a visceral consequence of music so perfectly performed. In fifty years of teaching, Audrey had never heard such bell-like clarity—certainly not from a child.

For several moments afterward, the prayer hung in the air, palpable and pure. Finally, Audrey broke the spell. She held the girl's hands in both of hers and whispered, "Simone, I would be honored to be your teacher."

"Merci, Madame."

Audrey felt the girl's otherworldly grace, unlike anything she had ever known. She hugged the little girl, then descended the stairs to arrange for her lessons and to learn more about the child.

"Late one night in 1987, there was a knock at the door, when I answered, I found a baby in a basket, swaddled in a pink blanket, her umbilical stump still soft and yellowish," the nun told Audrey. "A note pinned to the blanket read, *'C'est* Simone, please take care of her for I cannot.'"

"You are eleven?" Audrey asked Simone who nodded shyly while the nun put her arm over the girl's shoulder.

"Simone has always been small for her age but quite precocious," she smiled down at Simone. "She learned to read quite young and," she laughed, "she understands maths better than most of the nuns at the convent. Every day, Simone's bell-like voice fills the nave. We decided her voice is a God given miracle. She must sing for all of God's children, not just the nuns of our small priory."

Until the trip to meet Audrey, Simone had spent her life under the watchful eyes of well-meaning nuns. She had complete freedom to roam the cloister, refectory and gardens, but like the nuns, she never left the convent. She slept on a narrow cot in a long, dark dormitory with no windows and no heat. In summer, she helped in the garden, pulling weeds and harvesting carrots and potatoes. In the winter, they taught her the basics, reading, writing and arithmetic. It was a quiet world of soft-soled shoes on stone floors, muffled voices and music.

The outside world was a marvel to Simone. On the way to her first lesson, chaperoned by a postulant, Simone pressed her forehead to the cold bus window and watched the chaos of people, cars and delivery trucks. She listened to the cacophony of horns, high heels clicking on concrete and laughter. A multitude of voices blended to sound like the wind. The aroma of exhaust, flowers and food was enough to make her dizzy, so different from the convent's scent of candle wax, incense and stone.

Simone gaped at the apartment building where Audrey lived and taught, with its balconies filled with red geraniums and its ornate balusters. Simone had seen such buildings only in books.

For an hour every afternoon, Simone studied voice and piano. Madame Dupré gave the postulant a donation to replace Simone's outgrown clothing with new dresses, shoes, boots and a winter coat.

One evening, Simone accompanied Audrey to the opera. While Audrey played the piano in the orchestra, Simone sat in the front row, with strict instructions to stay seated until Audrey came to fetch her after the performance.

Simone wore the deep blue velvet dress with a white satin collar and patent leather shoes Audrey had bought especially for

Simone's first opera. Simone's thick platinum blond hair fell over her shoulders and down her back like luminescent moonlight.

When the music began, Simone's heart swelled and beat wildly. She saw the composition, as if colorful rainbows danced on the stage and felt the music vibrating through her body, as tangible as the chair she sat in. Simone knew at that moment; opera was her calling.

Afterward, Audrey came to sit next to Simone while patrons streamed out of the opera house and into the night. She noticed that Simone's face was flushed and blotchy. Her watery eyes shimmered. As they stood to leave, Simone flung her arms around Audrey's waist, "Auntie…," she whispered, but no other words would come.

"I know, Simone," said Audrey, gently massaging Simone's trembling shoulders. "The thrill of discovering opera… how well I know."

With her arm still resting over Simone's shoulders, Audrey hailed a taxi. The driver waited while Audrey walked Simone to the convent door, then took her home. She climbed the stairs to 3A, holding the rail with one hand and her long black performance skirt out of the way with the other.

In her bedroom, she changed into a nightgown. Sitting in front of the dressing-table mirror, she removed the small batons that held her bun in place and her long black and silver hair spilled down her back. As she brushed her hair, a profound sense of contentment seized her heart as if her life's work had led her to this day, the day Simone fell in love with opera.

Adopting Simone

During her next lesson, Audrey said, "I think it might be easier for the nuns if you stay in my guest room after the opera so that we don't wake the sisters after the performance. Would you like that? Come, I'll show you the guest room."

She watched Simone run her hand over the chenille bedspread covering the four-poster bed that had furnished Audrey's childhood bedroom in Ohio.

Simone's aquamarine eyes grew even larger than usual, "*Oui, I would like this very much*," whispered Simone. "*Merci beaucoup.*"

After Simone's thirteenth birthday, Audrey met with the nuns. "I have become quite fond of Simone and I would like to offer her a home and an education beyond music, but only if this is what she wants as well. She would have her own room, attend school and we would continue her voice and piano lessons."

After several discussions with both Audrey and Simone, the nuns agreed. Audrey officially adopted Simone and her name became Simone Dupré.

Audrey was seventy-eight, but she felt more like a mother than a grandmother. Simone's youthful energy revived Audrey's spirit. They took walks together, usually ending along Rue Cler, enjoying the collection of scents: spices, chocolate, fruits and vegetables. They lunched together at their favorite brasserie, outdoors with the sun on their faces.

After coming to live with Audrey, Simone went to school during the day, then stood by Audrey's piano, working with her breath, practicing scales and developing endurance.

Simone was like Audrey, she preferred music to any other activity. She found her classmates' interests trivial, dull and childish. After practicing, Simone read books from Audrey's shelves, books she never would have found in the convent, Anne Brontë, Hemingway, Longfellow, Tolstoy and Coates.

Simone helped Audrey with minor tasks around the apartment and accompanied her to opera rehearsals and performances.

Usually they walked, weather permitting and always took the stairs, never the elevator.

Occasionally, they went shopping. One day, Audrey selected a dress and stepped into a dressing room to try it on. When she came out, Simone said, "I'm sorry to say, Auntie, that dress makes you look quite old. I'll find a better one for you."

Audrey removed the dress, waited in her slip, laughing, remembering. In her youth, while other girls giggled about fellas in their school or dressed in the latest fashions, Audrey studied piano and voice. She never joined the other girls when they went shopping, never cared too much about fashion.

Spending time with thirteen-year-old Simone reminded Audrey of Aimée's arrival in Ohio when Audrey was thirteen.

Memories of her childhood before Aimée felt brittle and dim, like flowers pressed in a book. The time she spent with Simone felt like returning to a place she had never been.

Loaded with shopping bags, Audrey and Simone stopped at the tea shop on Rue Cler for a cup of sweet flowery tea and *Calisson d'aix-en-Provence*, treats made with ground almonds, candied melons, candied orange peels, honey and orange blossoms. Noticing the look on her face, Audrey knew Simone had never tasted such decadence.

On another shopping trip, Audrey purchased two laptops. They learned to use them together as Simone shared what she'd learned at school.

Audrey's usually nimble fingers awkwardly pecked at the keyboard until she learned to type. It wasn't long until she scheduled her student's lessons via email and managed her schedule online. She canceled her newspaper subscription; all she needed to know she could find online.

In the spring, when Simone passed her *baccalauréat* exam with high marks, Audrey asked, "What do you want to do now, Simone? You can study anything and anywhere you want, I'll cover tuition and expenses."

"I'm drawn to Russian history and music," said Simone. "And I'd like to study at the Sorbonne."

"Of course, that's wonderful. Maybe you can live in the student dorm, or we can find an apartment for you close to campus."

"If you don't mind Auntie, I'd rather stay in my room here."

Audrey reached for a hug, "You know how much I love having you here with me, but don't feel that you must."

By her junior year, Simone spent less and less time in their apartment. Audrey was happy that Simone had developed a group of friends with similar interests but felt that living with her, now eighty-five, might be cramping Simone's social life.

"I've been thinking…" Audrey said as she nibbled her morning croissant, "you know I am delighted to have you live with me, but today is your twentieth birthday and, well, you're old enough to have your own apartment. The tenant in 3C has moved out. It's yours if you want it. You are more than welcome to spend as much time as you like with me and come and go as you do now, but you could also retreat to your own space, study at all hours and invite your friends over without worrying about disturbing me."

"I do worry. My friends are a musical and vocal bunch," said Simone.

They walked across the hall to 3C. "The cleaners have finished putting it to rights; it's ready for you to move in, if you want."

Simone walked across the room to open the folding door that hid a small refrigerator and stove and then pulled down the Murphy bed. "Oh Auntie, thank you, this is perfect," she beamed, giving Audrey a hug, "and I'm still close if you need me."

SERGEI SAPOZHNIKOV RETIRES

New York, 2003

Weary of traveling the world, Sergei Sapozhnikov quit touring and became a music teacher at his alma mater, Braun Boys' School in Manhattan. He felt as if he had never experienced adolescence—his youth had been consumed by practice, travel and performance. Not because his parents drove him to practice and perform. Far from it. From an early age, he was obsessed with music, with no interest in sports. Now, teaching at his former school offered the opportunity to enjoy the energy of the students and celebrate the youthful experiences he missed, as if returning to a place he had never been.

He attended every varsity soccer match and quickly became a favorite teacher. He often tried to participate; his lack of experience brought good-natured laughter to the field.

One spring, Sergei tried to play baseball with the students. Dressed in his usual suit and tie, Mr. Sapozhnikov—known to the boys as Mr. S.—took the bat and stepped up to the plate. A thirteen-year-old student pitched the ball.

Sergei swung and missed. Then swung and missed again.

The young umpire shouted, "Strike two!"

Sergei connected with the next pitch. The sharp crack of the bat echoed then they heard glass shattering as the ball flew through a window on the other side of the field.

The umpire shouted, "Automatic home run!" Both teams came off the bench to escort Mr. S. around the bases.

After the game, the boys practiced for the traditional talent show to be performed the week before graduation.

Watching the boys' dress rehearsal, his mind floated back to the day he graduated from Juilliard. He remembered how his own mother had wept and how emotional she seemed at the reception. She was far weepier than the other mothers whose sons were graduating. Something about watching him perform with his former teacher stirred her deeply. Sergei had no idea why. Soon after, he began touring and left the moment behind.

Gertie Grantham's Thanksgiving

Dayton, Ohio, 2017

The week before Thanksgiving, Gertie gently hand-washed linens that once belonged to her Grandma Alice Grantham, her father's mother. Off-white embroidery and cutwork decorated one corner of each napkin and all four corners of the tablecloth. *The linens must have been elegant in their day,* she thought. As she lovingly ironed each piece, a wave of nostalgia gripped her heart.

As if the fragrant steam wafting from the ironing board carried the scent of Thanksgiving, Gertie imagined generations of Grantham family members sitting around an enormous oak table covered with crisp, white linen. She envisioned the Grantham's blue and white wedding china heaped with turkey, mashed potatoes, gravy and vegetables from the garden.

Gertie had always worried her four children would break the blue and white dishes or lose pieces of the silver Evelyn had given her, so the dishes and silver remained safely stored in the basement. But now that her children were grown, it felt silly not to use them.

After unpacking the dishes, Gertie carefully lowered a stack of blue and white dinner plates into hot soapy water. As if bathing a newborn, she wiped each dish with a soft washcloth. She dipped each piece into the hot rinse water in the second sink, then placed it in the drying rack.

To make room in the china cupboard, she carefully packed pieces of carnival glass George's mother had given her. She had never liked its iridescent glaze and garish colors. *They're probably worth more than the china,* she thought as she wrapped each colorful pitcher, bowl and candy dish in bubble wrap and lowered them into a plastic storage bin.

The day before Thanksgiving, Gertie's kitchen filled with the aroma of spicy berries and sweet, cheerful citrus as she ground cranberries and navel oranges using her Grandma Alice's old metal grinder attached to the kitchen table. Grandma Alice started making the famous cranberry salad in 1957 when she found the recipe in *Ladies Home Journal.* Gertie could make it in her sleep. While the fruit mixture chilled in the refrigerator, she dissolved Jell-O in hot water. She smiled, recalling the ads for J-E-L-L-O on the *Jack Benny Show* when she was a little girl. Her hand involuntarily touched her face as she remembered her father's scratchy wool jacket rubbing her cheek. Cuddling next to him, breathing the medicinal carbolic hint of Lifebuoy soap, his deep infectious laugh vibrated when Jack Benny said, "Now Rochester!"

Her father and George had both been gone for nearly thirty years, but the grief felt as solid as the table she stood next to. She pushed thoughts of George and her father out of her mind while she gathered ingredients for pumpkin pies and yeast rolls.

Finishing the do-ahead meal preparation, Gertie set the table, lit the white tapers held by silver candlesticks and stood back. In the candle's glow, she admired the blue and white dishes and silver cutlery. Grandma Alice's embroidered tablecloth fit the table perfectly and the silver sparkled in the candlelight. Before going to bed, she blew out the candles and drifted into her garden with a flashlight to cut the last yellow mums for a centerpiece.

Slowly, she climbed the stairs. She took a quick shower and crawled into bed. Her back ached from standing in the kitchen all day. But as tired as she was, she couldn't fall asleep. As she often did, she pondered, *What would my life be like if George were still here?* Tears rolled from her eyes as she waited for sleep.

Gertie's three sons and their wives watched football in the family room while Gertie basted the turkey and completed the final dinner preparations. She preferred having the kitchen to herself and her daughters-in-law had learned to stay out of her way.

She moved around the kitchen, machine-like, with the football announcer blaring in the background, as always on Thanksgiving Day.

For a moment, she paused by the kitchen window. The plum

tree she planted for George, when they first bought the house, had grown huge. She made plum jam every summer. Her heart ached as she gazed at the leafless tree, thinking of George.

She remembered trying to stuff the turkey during her third pregnancy, while she held Suzie on her hip and George junior threw Cheerios all over the floor from his highchair. The tree was just a stick.

George Sr. had spent quality time with each child. He'd been a devoted father, but he wasn't much help around the house. She didn't expect it. However, that Thanksgiving Day—with two babies and another on the way—he didn't offer to take care of the children while she prepared Thanksgiving dinner. She wondered now, *Why didn't I ask him to help?*

For the Thanksgiving holiday, Gertie wore a large floral print dress stretched over her generous bum, clip-on earrings, nylons and black pumps. She protected the outfit with Grandma Alice's old pink and gray paisley apron that covered the entire front of her dress. Her tightly curled, blue-tinted hair resembled an English barrister's wig.

Suzie and Tom arrived at 1:00 with their three children. The teenagers, who also towered over Gertie's elfin frame, gave their grandmother a quick hug. They knew they weren't welcome in the kitchen while Grandma Gertie was cooking and made a beeline to the basement family room to watch the Bears and Lions game with their uncles. Suzie's little dog, Baxter, a blond Cairn Terrier, sat in the dining room as if he knew where the food would go next.

"The table's beautiful, Mom," said Suzie with her arm over her mother's shoulder. Suzie was taller than her mom by six inches. There was a family resemblance, but Suzie's hair floated in long dark waves and she was trim and muscular.

"I don't remember these dishes," said Suzie's husband, Tom. "Are they new?"

Gertie gazed at the dishes; her eyes filled with pride. "They've been in my family for 125 years. I decided we should use them. Your Grandma Grantham would like that."

Tom helped Gertie pull the twenty-pound turkey out of the oven. She covered it with foil to let it rest while Suzie put the green bean casserole in the oven. Gertie mashed the potatoes with lots of butter and heavy cream, using the old wire masher her Grandma Alice once used. As she worked, she remembered the mashed potatoes her mother made from a box and served with canned gravy. Gertie felt a surge of pride as she whisked the roux into the hot pan drippings, creating perfectly delicious brown gravy.

When everything was ready, Tom carried the turkey to the table while Suzie called downstairs, "Dinner's ready!"

"Just a minute, the game's almost over," came a male voice from the basement as the others trickled up the stairs, the younger boys, more interested in food than football.

Finally coming up the stairs into the dining room, her oldest son took a deep breath and said, "Smells great in here, Mom!"

Gertie's sons, now in their forties, towered over her, all tall and handsome, with blond hair, hazel eyes and captivating wide smiles. The oldest reminded Gertie of Cary Grant.

Suzie's kids were young teens and as gentle as a herd of startled buffalo. Her three brothers, even in their forties, could be equally awkward. "Okay you guys, these dishes are over 125 years old. Be careful! Don't break anything!" Suzie cautioned.

Tom carved the perfectly golden turkey while the dining room filled with the sound of laughter and the smell of succulent turkey, tart cranberries and citrusy orange peel. Half-empty serving dishes covered the sideboard, but the stuffing was nearly untouched. Suzie's boys filled their plates the second time and even a third, with helpings of turkey, mashed potatoes and gravy, but they never touched the stuffing.

Life is as it should be, thought Gertie, watching her grandchildren enjoy the meal she had prepared, *except George never met them.* Unwilling to deal with her pain, she stood and said, a little too loudly, "Anyone ready for pumpkin pie?"

Suzie and Gertie washed dishes while everyone else returned to the family room. Suzie dried each piece with a well-worn dishtowel and put the dry dishes into the china cabinet where Gertie had made room for them.

Gertie brought the bowl of stuffing into the kitchen, then gathered the tablecloth and napkins and put them down the laundry chute. She pushed the chairs into place around the table while Suzie put the leftovers in the refrigerator. "Suzie," said Gertie, "do you want to take that stuffing home with you?"

"No one eats it, Mom."

"Well then…," tears spilled from Gertie's eyes. She felt as if she was throwing George himself into the waste bin.

"I'm sorry Mom, I didn't mean to upset you." Suzie hugged her mom, surprised by the tears.

"Oh sweetie, it's not your fault. I made this recipe because your dad liked it…" Gertie scraped the rest of the stuffing into the garbage. "It's time to find new recipes."

Gertie hung her apron on its peg in the pantry then went to the basement family room, "Time to visit Granny Evelyn," she announced.

"Last time she thought I was Granddad Grantham and she thought Suzie was a neighbor from forty years ago. Do you really need us to come with you?" said George Jr.

Gertie, always one to keep harmony, reluctantly let them stay home. Tom insisted on driving Suzie and Gertie to visit Granny Evelyn.

When they walked into the dining room at Village Garden, the unpleasant tang of aging humans, medication, disinfectant and roasted turkey filled the air. They watched a nurse lead Evelyn into the dining room to eat her Thanksgiving meal. Evelyn looked at them blankly and nodded with a half-smile, as if they were strangers standing in line at the grocery store.

The server placed a turkey dinner in front of Evelyn. With wild eyes, she stared at the food, like a baby given her first plate. She scooped mashed potatoes and Jell-O into her mouth with her hands and tried to take off her clothes, smearing gravy and red Jell-O all over the front of her hunter green sweater.

"Oh, Mom," said Gertie, jumping up with tears in her eyes. She used her napkin to pull Evelyn's gooey hands away from her sweater but ended up with mashed potatoes smeared over her own clothes. Suzie pushed the plate out of reach and tried to wipe Granny Evelyn's hands with her napkin as Granny whined and reached for the plate. Tom went to find help.

Gertie looked around the room. Old people and their families filled the cafeteria, each dealing with their own personal issues. No one seemed to notice—that she was aware of.

"Evelyn is more agitated than usual," the nurse told Gertie. "Looks like you'll need to keep your visit short today." The nurse helped Evelyn out of the chair, "Come with me Evelyn, let's go to your room and clean up." They disappeared down the corridor toward the memory care wing, the nurse cradling Evelyn's elbow.

Watching from behind, Gertie thought, *No one would guess what just happened.* Eighty-nine-year-old Evelyn looked healthy, her back erect, her stride sturdy and in step with the nurse, less than half her age.

DNA Revelation

Years before Ancestry.Com, Grantham family members had traced their history back to England in the 1700s. They knew that Ted's eighth-great grandfather had been a Revolutionary war hero. Proud of her father's prestigious heritage, Gertie had joined the local chapter of the Daughters of the American Revolution (DAR).

With Evelyn in a memory care facility, there was no one to answer Gertie's questions about her mother's lineage. The Reilly family was a mystery. The focus had always been on the Granthams—the paternal side of her ancestry. Gertie heard on *The Today Show* that DNA testing was becoming mainstream, but she didn't know how to begin.

The next time Suzie visited, Gertie asked her to order a DNA test, since Gertie didn't use a computer. "I'm glad you're doing this, Mom. I've always been curious about our ancestry. The boys and I are all tall and they're blond and fair, even though both you and Dad were—let's face it—short," she squeezed her mother's shoulders.

"Will Ancestor send us a written report?" asked Gertie.

"No. You'll log in to your Ancestry.com account to see the results."

"You'll need to help me with that too," said Gertie.

When the package from Ancestry.com arrived, Gertie opened it and read the directions. She would need to spit into the vial. It sounded disgusting.

Following the instructions, she waited until morning, then she gathered her courage and filled the little DNA vial. When her spit reached the blue line, she snapped the lid closed and shook the vial as directed, until her spit turned blue. Then she sealed it in the package, ready to send out in the noon mail.

A few weeks later, Suzie called, "Hi Mom, is it okay if I come for a weekend visit? Tom and the boys are going on a camping trip and Emily is spending the weekend at the lake with her friends."

"Of course! I'll put a roast in the oven."

"No Mom! Let me take you out for dinner on Friday."

"What time will you be here? I don't like to eat too late."

"I'll be there by four, Mom. We can go to The Steakhouse."

"That would be nice."

When she hung up, Gertie remembered that George always took Suzie to the Rikes dining room rather than the Steakhouse. *Maybe she would enjoy something different*, she thought. *I'm not sure I like the food at the Steakhouse all that much. It was the restaurant George always liked.*

Instead of a roast, Gertie made cinnamon rolls. Her well-stocked pantry held all the ingredients she needed. It still didn't occur to her that Suzie might prefer an egg-white omelet or granola for breakfast.

On Saturday morning, Suzie and Gertie sat at the kitchen table drinking coffee. Suzie ran her finger over the cream cheese frosting and licked her fingertip.

"You know," said Gertie, "I've been thinking, it's too bad Teddy didn't have any children, there's no one to carry on the Grantham name."

"Uncle Robert's son, William, is a Grantham."

"Yes, but William's mother is…."

"Mom! William is just as much Grantham as I am."

It was difficult for Gertie to comprehend. Future generations of the Grantham family would be part Vietnamese.

"Hey, let's see if your DNA test results are back yet," Suzie suggested as she pulled her iPad from her bag hanging on the back of a chair.

Suzie logged in to the account and discovered the results were available, but she hesitated. "No, Mom, the results aren't here yet," she fibbed.

To understand the report, she needed to study the data. The names of relatives were unfamiliar to her and they were not from England. If what she suspected was true, her mother would be devastated. Suzie needed time to consider how to break the news.

Back in her home office, Suzie spent hours going over all the data. Their ancestors were mostly German, Italian and Irish. Her mother's paternal grandparents immigrated to America in the 1880s. Gertie had always believed that her Grantham ancestors were from England and that she was a descendant of famous Revolutionary War heroes. Nothing in the DNA report supported the family legend.

A few weeks later, Suzie finally drove to her mom's house to go over the DNA results. She'd put it off as long as she could.

During the one-hour drive from Cincinnati, she considered her conundrum. *How do I tell my mother that the man she thought was her father—wasn't?*

After they ate a bowl of homemade vegetable soup and yeast rolls, Suzie tried to be as gentle as she could, "Mom, I've thought a lot about this, but there's just no easy way."

Suzie logged in to the account and they reviewed the data together.

"Are they saying that Ted Grantham is not my father. Admiral Grantham is not my grandfather?" The pitch of Gertie's voice rose with each word and became a high-pitched squeal. "They made a mistake!"

She sat for a moment, scarcely breathing, then asked, "Who do they say my real father is?"

"I think Granddad Grantham would say he was your *real* father. He loved you: you know that. It looks like your biological father was Dr. Richard Wurtzburg," said Suzie, pointing at the screen.

"German!?" Gertie shrieked.

"He and his wife had five children. One of them is a girl exactly your age. It's remarkable, you and your half-sister have the same birthday and you're both named Gertrude," said Suzie as she scrolled through the data.

"Well, none of this can be right…. Excuse me, please," said Gertie, as if leaving a group of strangers at a bridge table.

When her mom didn't come back downstairs, Suzie found her curled on the flowered bedspread. Dim light filtered through the wispy, sheer, under-curtains. "Can I get you anything, Mom?" asked Suzie as she slipped off her mother's black pumps and covered her with the mauve and turquoise afghan Gertie crocheted years before.

With her steamy, wet face hidden in the bend of her arm, Gertie said, "Thank you, dear. I think I need to be alone for a while," her voice muffled further by the ruffled throw pillows.

"After walking Baxter, I'll fix dinner."

"I'm. Not. Hungry," said Gertie.

Hearing his name, Baxter came into the room. He stood with his paws on the edge of the bed and tilted his head one way and the other. He understood Gertie was upset.

"Come on Baxter, let's go for a walk," Suzie said to her constant companion. He followed her downstairs where she attached the leash to his collar. They passed the blue dishes in the china cabinet and Suzie remembered how badly Uncle Teddy treated her mother when Granny Evelyn moved to Village Garden. Considering the DNA results, thinking of Uncle Teddy sent a menacing shiver down Suzie's back.

An hour later, when Suzie and Baxter returned, Gertie was sitting at the kitchen table with a cup of Lipton tea. "Let me take you out for dinner," said Suzie.

"No, thank you," said Gertie. "I'm not at all hungry and, if you don't mind, I'd like to be alone today."

"Okay Mom, I understand. I'll head back to Cincinnati, but promise you'll call me if you need anything."

"Yes dear," said Gertie, gazing at her teacup.

Trying to Cope

After Suzie left, Gertie filled the tub with hot water and hung her dress and underwear on a hook. Before soaking, she stood looking at her naked self in the full-length mirror on the back of the bathroom door. Over the years, her waistline had thickened.

She was only thirty-eight when George died, but her hair had quickly turned completely gray. She'd asked the hairdresser to cut it short and give her a perm. The hairdresser had recommended a rinse to give a bluish tint to Gertie's perm-curly, helmet-like coiffure, thinking the blue tint would make it less brassy. By the time Gertie's youngest graduated from high school in 1993, Gertie's prematurely gray, old-lady hair do, thick waistline and frumpy wardrobe made her look nearly as old as Evelyn.

As Gertie pulled a shower cap over her fluffy blue-ish hair and stepped into the hot bubble bath, she thought, *My body isn't what it once was. And I'm not who I thought I was.* Her mind raced back to her childhood. She watched TV cuddled next to the man she loved, who she thought was her father. She played in the little playhouse he had lovingly built for her. *None of this DNA business can be true*, she thought.

As the weeks passed, Gertie convinced herself that the DNA report was false. She threw herself into her woman's clubs and made cupcakes for a bake sale to raise funds for disadvantaged children. As if being more involved would save her, she joined a DAR committee.

She crocheted baby blankets for charity while she watched her afternoon TV programs, *Days of Our Lives* and *All My Children*. At 4:00, she set the table, placing a serving bowl filled with leftover potato salad and a platter of leftover pork roast.

Even when she ate lunch or dinner alone, Gertie never stood by the sink or ate from Tupperware. She set the table, lit a candle and sat down.

Gertie started to feel somewhat normal, as if the Ancestry report had been a bad dream. Denial had always been her best defense.

Then Teddy called. "What's this I discovered about your paternal gene pool?" he said in a scornful voice. "Looks like you inherited an estate that you had no right to."

"Hello, Teddy," she could hardly breathe. Her confidence against his insults had vaporized the moment she heard *inherited an estate.*

"When Mom dies, I'll make sure you aren't included in her will. I can do that, you know. I have power of attorney. She should've died years ago. And I'll talk to my attorney about recovering what you pocketed from the Grantham estate."

"Yes, Teddy, I know you have power of attorney and you're right, Mom's had Alzheimer's for over eighteen years. You forget that I've been taking care of her ever since Dad died, while you went fishing in Florida." She ignored his questions about the validity of her inheritance.

"I'm sure you were happy to have her there since George was dead too; two old ladies, sitting around knitting and eating homemade bread," he said, his voice even more vindictive than usual. Gertie didn't have the energy to listen or the power to hang up. "Mom even gave you Great Grandmother Grantham's dishes because you were supposedly their first-born, ha!"

"What would you do with the dishes Teddy? Your wife divorced you and you have no children; you don't even know how to cook—who would you leave them to?"

"I'd sell 'em. They're 125 years old, probably worth something."

"They're worth a lot to me and my family," she breathed, not really speaking to Teddy.

"Yes, but now we know that you and yours aren't really Granthams."

"Goodbye Teddy. I'm hanging up now."

She sat on the flower-patterned sofa in the living room, staring at the beige wall. As a child, he had bullied her. Then, when their mother moved into Village Garden, she had gained strength against his insults. But now that he questioned her identity, her validity, the strength she had gained melted away. She felt more vulnerable than ever.

The phone rang again and she mechanically answered, "Hello."

"Is this Gertrude Grantham?"

"That was my maiden name," said Gertie with a tone of disdain, thinking it was a solicitation call.

"Well, my name is Trudy Wurtzburg Hart. You don't know me, but I think I'm your half-sister."

Gertie slammed the receiver so hard, the old harvest gold Princess phone nearly pulled off the kitchen wall.

She called Suzie, "How did that woman know my phone number? Why can't we keep all of this private? Did you tell Uncle Teddy about the DNA?"

"Hello, Mom. I haven't told anyone about the DNA test, not even Tom, but the phone call from that woman is all my fault. When I set up your Ancestry account, I entered your phone number since you don't use email. I never considered anything like this. I'm so sorry."

Gertie hung up, again.

A few hours later, Suzie and Baxter came to Gertie's door. "I'm so sorry Mom. I've already changed your contact info on the account. I'll call that woman and tell her not to call you again. Do you have her number?"

"No, I don't have her number. Why would I?"

The old wall phone in the kitchen didn't have a caller ID screen, so Suzie dialed *69 to retrieve the phone number of Trudy Wurtzburg Hart.

Trudy Wurtzburg

On a warm afternoon, Trudy Wurtzburg's mother kept her children out of the house while her two-year-old took a nap. She knelt in the flower bed weeding around the daffodils and emerging tulips while the boys, six and eight, played catch and four-year-old Trudy ran around the outside of the house, her little arms pumping, her blond ponytail half undone. On her fourth lap, her mother asked, "Trudy, what are you doing?"

"I'm essercising."

Wondering where her four-year-old daughter had learned the word *exercising*, she turned the activity into a counting lesson. "Let's see how many times you can run around the house. You're up to four so far."

She sprinted around the house as if she could outrun her older brothers. Even at age four, Trudy yearned to surpass her identity beyond her family and her gender.

When her baby sister woke from her nap, Trudy showed no signs of slowing. "Wonderful!" said her mother, catching Trudy with a big hug. "That's twenty, let's see how many laps you can run tomorrow. Now come inside and let me fix your ponytail."

In junior high, Trudy signed up for the girls' basketball team, but in those days, girls played half-court "to avoid overexertion." Wearing uncomfortable navy-blue jumpsuits, the girls in her gym class performed calisthenics without breaking a sweat. Trudy did her own workout at home after school, jumping jacks, lunges, push-ups and basketball with her brothers and their friends, her thick, blond ponytail swaying as she dribbled down the court.

In 1966, the municipal pool finally allowed her to join the swim team. She won ribbons in butterfly, backstroke, breaststroke and freestyle—even against the boys her age.

After high school graduation, Trudy enrolled in premed at

the University of Washington. She didn't want to become a doctor, like her father, Richard Wurtzburg, but she liked the sciences and wanted the scholastic challenge.

In May of 1970, her Junior year at UW, she was walking through the student union reading a newspaper article when she bumped into a young man also reading the paper. He was only a few inches taller than Trudy, but his presence seemed large and powerful. His brown eyes were intense. Glasses perched on his narrow face.

"Are you reading this article about the protest in Ohio?" she pointed to her newspaper. "It's terrible! The national guard—"

"Shot peaceful protesters," he finished her sentence. "Why would—"

"—they do that?" she finished his sentence.

"It's horrific—," they both said at the same time. They stood silently, side by side, leaning against the wall, horrified at what they were reading. The National Guard had shot and killed four students in Ohio while the students peacefully protested the US government's expansion of the Vietnam War into Cambodia.

"There's a rally tomorrow. Are you going?" he asked.

"Yes, I haven't missed one yet and this is all the more reason to make our voices heard," she said, waving the newspaper in the air.

Finally, he extended his hand, "Hi, I'm Elliot Hart."

"Trudy Wurtzburg."

Their handshake lingered and their eye contact held.

"Wanna meet me here and we'll walk to the rally together?"

"Sure," said Trudy. "Sounds great."

After that day, whether protesting the Vietnam war or studying for finals, Trudy and Elliot were together whenever possible.

Two years later, after graduation, Trudy and Elliot had a casual summer wedding with fifty guests in her parents' backyard. Trudy came across the lawn barefoot on her father's arm, wearing a strapless leather mini-shift overlaid with a white guipure lace tunic with dolman sleeves. She carried white roses, mingled with stephanotis, tied with streaming satin ribbons in deep rainbow colors. Her long, straight hair hung to her waist like buttery Chinese silk. Elliot wore a Madras plaid shirt tucked into khaki shorts and well-worn Birkenstock sandals.

A photographer took lots of photos as they ate cake and toasted with champagne. Then the newlyweds escaped to Elliot's apartment on Capitol Hill in his MG Midget. Trudy turned in her seat and tossed the bouquet toward her sisters as the little red convertible roared out of the driveway.

That fall, Elliot started dental school and Trudy began her career as a licensed dental assistant. After Elliot achieved his DDS, he joined the same practice.

On weekends, Elliot and Trudy frequently spent Friday nights at a B&B in Port Townsend on the Olympic Peninsula, then drove to the Washington coast and set up their tent at Kalaloch where they relaxed, drank their favorite Chardonnay out of coffee mugs and watched gulls and eagles float by as wispy fuchsia sunsets melted into the Pacific Ocean's sapphire surf.

Thanksgiving Day, November 22, 1973, Trudy was lifting the turkey out of the oven when her first contraction hit hard. Drippings sizzled in the hot oven and turned the floor into a greasy mess, but she kept the bird in the roasting pan.

As Elliot helped Trudy into his red MG, he said, "Don't worry honey, I'll clean up the mess before you and the baby come home."

"I spilled turkey juice all over my top, it smells terrible," she grumbled between contractions. "That's the last turkey I'll ever cook!"

With her new baby boy snuggled warm and dry in his spacious buggy, Trudy walked the streets in the Northwest rainy winter weather while cedar and fir trees reached for the heavy clouds overhead. In the spring, when he was old enough to sit up, she bought a stroller and continued their long outings on the streets of the eastside, including bay-side parks where they watched rafts of colorful ducks and Great Blue Heron feed near shore.

Trudy enrolled in a Swimming for Tots class so Elliot Jr. could learn to swim. He loved being in the water as much as she did. "Elliot swam across the pool by himself today," she told Elliot Sr.

"When you finally have your sailboat, we can all swim together."

Trudy and Elliot Sr. pitched their tent at a campground in Port Townsend to attend the Wooden Boat Festival. Elliot Sr. carried three-year-old Elliot Jr. in a backpack as they walked up and down the pier, toured a huge, tall ship and admired the meticulously crafted smaller wooden boats bobbing by the docks at Point Hudson. "The wood is so beautiful, it seems a shame to get it wet," said Trudy.

Later, as Elliot Jr. slept in the tent, they enjoyed a glass of Chardonnay while Elliot Sr. grilled vegetables and steaks on the Coleman stove. Sitting at a picnic table, they watched the green and white Washington State Ferry float across Puget Sound. "I wonder if there's any need for a dentist here," Elliot contemplated. "We could open a dental practice in this little town. Just a thought."

"A dream," whispered Trudy.

The dentist they both worked for announced his retirement and asked Elliot and Trudy if they were interested in taking over his practice. They spent a long weekend discussing the pros and cons of starting a dental practice from scratch in Port Townsend versus taking over the practice where they had established a reputation. Ultimately, it seemed prudent to stay.

Trudy and Elliot bought a house on the eastside and their dream of living in the seaside village vanished like a seashell at high tide.

Brain Tumor

On Elliot Jr.'s seventh birthday, Elliot Sr. left the party at Chuck E Cheese clutching his head in pain from a sudden, excruciating headache. He waited in the car until the party ended.

Trudy found Elliot laying on the backseat clutching his head. She was terrified. "What's wrong?"

"It's a little better just getting away from all the echoing noise in there."

"I'm taking you to the ER!"

Trudy arranged for Elliot Jr. to go home with friends and drove Elliot Sr. to the ER. The medical staff immediately admitted him, offering pain relief and conducting an MRI, blood and other tests to find the cause of his sudden, severe pain.

"Your tests reveal an inoperable malignant brain tumor. I'm sorry. Nothing can be done," said the doctor, his voice flat and clinical, as if announcing the weather. "You should get your affairs in order."

Stunned, Trudy and Elliot Sr. sat motionless. Tears streamed from their eyes as they both stared out the window, avoiding the pain of looking at each other.

Trudy crawled onto the bed and swung her arm and leg over him, getting as close as she could. His arm came around her shoulder and they stared into space.

Finally, Elliot murmured, "Let's sell the practice and spend as much time as we have…,"

Over the next few days, they sought second and third opinions and although other doctors delivered the news more gently, the diagnosis didn't change. They followed the third doctor's opinion and agreed to surgery to ease the pain and hopefully give him a sliver of time with his family.

While Elliot Sr. was well enough, they returned to the Washington Coast and set up camp in their favorite spot on Kalaloch bluff. Elliot Jr. played on the tide-packed sand, throwing sticks into the foamy waves for his yellow Labrador to fetch, while Trudy and Elliot Sr. snuggled on a quilt, next to an old-growth driftwood log, sipping Chardonnay from red coffee mugs. At sunset, they watched dark, menacing clouds—like a bruised shroud—drift over the claret sinking sun.

On the way back to the eastside, they stopped in Port Townsend at an old pub with red Naugahyde booths, a jukebox that played nothing but '50s oldies and the best hamburgers and fries in the state of Washington. Then they walked to an ice cream shop; mint-chocolate-chip for Trudy, butter-pecan for Elliot Sr. and a banana split for Elliot Jr.

Eventually, even morphine couldn't dull the pain. After a long, painful fight, Elliot Sr. died at home in the spring of 1984 with Trudy and Elliot Jr. by his side.

For months afterward, Trudy didn't go to the gym, the pool, or go for walks. She cooked simple meals for Elliot Jr. and when he went back to school that fall, she felt more lost than ever. Hollowed out, she felt like a stranger in her own skin.

"I've always been an athlete," she told her therapist. "I'm only thirty-three, but I can hardly walk through the grocery store without a rest."

"Have you considered yoga?" suggested the therapist during one session. "It might help you center and work through your grief."

Skeptical but willing to try anything that would help, Trudy enrolled in the therapeutic yoga class the therapist recommended, in a small private studio near Elliot's school.

She found yoga relaxing and slowly, she gained strength and balance. She also found she liked the teachers and other students. They were calm and open, uninterested in impressing each other, which was a rare phenomenon in their community, where grocery stores teemed with women in stylish haircuts and perfect makeup and men in professionally laundered dress shirts, all wearing $400 designer jeans.

She had lived on the eastside since her parents left Dayton, Ohio, when she was a few months old, but Trudy never felt like she belonged.

As her grief became less debilitating, Trudy took a job as a dental assistant and continued her daily yoga practice while Elliot Jr. started high school.

He was a brilliant student, like his father and his Grandpa Wurtzburg. Before his sixteenth birthday, Stanford offered Elliot Jr. a full-ride scholarship.

That fall, Trudy took two weeks off from work, allowing plenty of time to shop for what he needed, pack the car, drive to California and settle Elliot into his dorm.

While Elliot drove, they listened to his choice of music. He played Metallica's "Master of Puppets" over and over, then switched to Guns N' Roses' "Appetite for Destruction." It all sounded the same to Trudy, loud and annoying, so deafening they couldn't have a conversation if they tried. When they stopped near Portland for gas and a hamburger, Trudy welcomed the silence.

"If you don't mind, I'll eat my lunch in the grass over there," said Elliot.

Trudy knew Elliot Jr. was anxious about starting college and, as much as she wanted to help him, she tried to give him the space he needed.

With Trudy behind the wheel, they turned south onto I-5. "Thank goodness it's my turn to pick the music," she laughed. She turned to a channel that played her favorites.

Elliot rolled his eyes. "Geez Mom, do we have to listen to John Denver and Neil Diamond?"

"Not if you'll talk to me." She turned off the radio with a snap.

"What do you want to talk about?" He sounded grumpy.

"How do you feel about living so far from home?"

"It's okay."

"You can call me anytime, day or night. And if you decide this isn't what you want, I'll come back for you, no questions asked. There's no pressure. You know that, right?"

"Yeah, sure, I know."

They rode several miles in silence, the horizon occasionally blurring as Trudy fought back tears. She wanted to give him space but they might not see each again for months. Finally, she muttered, "That was a short conversation."

"Look Mom, I just want to get there and meet people and get started. I don't feel like talking about it."

"Sorry Elliot. I didn't mean to push. I'm anxious too."

"Can we just listen to music?" he grumbled.

"Sure, check out the CDs in the console. Maybe Bruce Springsteen? Or Steve Winwood? Or maybe Bon Jovi?" she suggested. "Please, just pick something that doesn't have loud electric guitars, no more Metallica." Trudy kept reminding herself that he wouldn't be sixteen for two more months and he was too stressed to be his usual, convivial self.

"Is John Coltrane acceptable?" he said. "He's an oldie."

"Sure."

While Trudy checked in at the Holiday Inn in Ashland, Oregon, Elliot stayed in the car listening to Metallica.

Trudy carried their small duffel bags to the room, changed into her swimsuit, then took the extra room key to Elliot. She tapped on the vibrating window twice. He finally turned off the music and gave her the car keys.

"We're in room 210; here's your key. I'm going for a swim before dinner. Join me if you want to. It'll feel good after being in the car all day."

Trudy swam for a while, although not as many laps as usual. When she returned to their room, she found Elliot stretched out on a bed, wearing his swimming trunks, sound asleep.

After a shower Trudy put on shorts and a T-shirt and wrote him a note, *Join me in the restaurant,* but when she returned to their room, he was still asleep.

At 5:30 a.m. she heard him shuffling around in the room, but she stayed still while he took a shower and left the room.

From the window, Trudy watched the water splash over Elliot's long, thin frame, so obviously fifteen, as he swam back and forth in the sparkling early morning light. After only a few laps, he pulled himself out of the pool, sat on the edge of a chaise lounge, elbows on his knees and stared at the water while the concrete under him darkened. Trudy put on her jeans and T-shirt and left him a note, *Join me! I'm having breakfast in the restaurant.*

She was half-way through her omelet when he sat down across from her. "I'm starving," he said and picked up the menu without looking at her.

"Order whatever you want. I'll just read my book until you're ready." He finally looked up with a grumpy expression, but something in his eyes said, *Thanks for understanding.*

She finished her omelet and quietly read while he devoured sausage links, a stack of pancakes, scrambled eggs and orange juice.

Elliot became more tense and irritable as they neared campus and the radio volume increased.

"I'll help you unpack."

"That's okay, Mom. I'd rather do it myself."

"Do you know how to use the washer and dryer? Be sure to separate whites and darks..."

"Yes mother," he interrupted.

"Since your roommate won't be here till tomorrow, can I take you out to lunch before I go?" She tried to sound cheerful.

Elliot put his hands on his mother's shoulders. "Mom, I'm fine. I'll have lunch in the cafeteria." He didn't ask her to leave, but it was time to go.

"I'll miss you, Elliot." She took his face in her hands. "Your father would be so proud of you!" Then she kissed his cheek and hugged him one more time. "Call me if you forgot anything," she said as she left his room, trying to look happy and strong but failing miserably.

She didn't hear him follow her down the hall. When she stepped into the stairwell, she heard him call, "Mom!"

She turned around, straightening her back and wiping her face, "Yes."

"I love you," said Elliot Jr. as the door closed behind them. "Thanks for... everything."

"I love you too, Elliot, more than you can ever know."

After one long, last hug, she took the stairs to the parking lot, then sat in the car for half an hour and let the tears fall.

Trudy started the Subaru and decided to drive to Redding that afternoon. North of San Francisco, an accident blocked the road. As she sat in traffic, she turned on the radio. The first tune to play was Natalie Cole singing *Miss You Like Crazy.* The lyrics struck a nerve so raw, her whole body trembled. She exited the freeway at the first opportunity and, through the blur of tears, headed for the Pacific coast. *I don't need to hurry home*, she thought. There was no reason to rush back to a life that felt unrecognizable. She spent that night at a boutique hotel in Bodega Bay and after a leisurely breakfast, she drove north until she came to Eureka, a charming seaside town, where big Victorian homes reminded her of Port Townsend, WA.

She found an ocean-side B&B.

"The only available space is a lovely big room with a view of the ocean," said the innkeeper. "It's our most expensive room and the most private."

Trudy handed over her credit card and checked in for three nights.

The innkeeper recommended restaurants where she could have dinner.

"Tonight, all I need is a bowl of soup and a glass of chardonnay," said Trudy.

"Then our little café off the lobby should be perfect. Our soup today is clam chowder. And the cook made bread this afternoon."

"I thought I smelled fresh bread, thank you," said Trudy, accepting the room key.

She enjoyed an early dinner in the hotel café, then walked through the tiny town and found a bookstore that sold new and used books. She bought *Love in the Time of Cholera* and *The Thorn Birds*, then stopped at the wine shop for a cold bottle of chardonnay.

With a book and a hotel coffee mug filled with chardonnay, she settled into an Adirondack chair, secluded from other guests, watching foamy waves flow onto the beach and retreat into the vast nothingness. As gulls shrieked and the ocean waves sighed, she opened *Love in the Time of Cholera*, but loneliness smoothed her concentration like the incoming tide. She sipped the wine and gazed at the ever-changing ocean view. Pearl-like clouds hovered on the horizon, reminding her of camping at Kalaloch on the Washington Coast with her husband and Elliot Jr.. Sorrow poured from her eyes, unchecked.

Fumbling in her pocket for a tissue, she tried to make sense of her life. Totally free and unencumbered, she could sell her house and live anywhere she wanted. There was no place she wanted to be except close enough to see Elliot Jr. as often as possible without smothering him. But she knew, once Elliot graduated from college, he might find employment anywhere in the world. This was no time for impulsive choices.

On the third night in Eureka, after two cups of Chardonnay, she fell asleep while watching an idyllic saffron sunset.

In her dream, dark turbid clouds tipped in gold, roiled across the horizon like India ink through honey. In the opposite direction, a snow-covered mountain burst through a golden fog that hugged the ocean. She saw herself wearing black leggings and a lavender tank top, sitting in a cross-legged pose, *sukhasana*, her thumbs and index fingers touching, the back of her hands resting on her knees. The atmosphere calmed, allowing her mind, body and spirit to reach total harmony. A small group of men and women materialized out of the golden fog. Slowly, she moved into a new pose with her legs straight in front of her, *dandasana*, then she lifted onto her hands and knees, *marjariasana*. Bathed in the breath of a calm sea, the men and women assumed each pose while breathing the soft, salty air and listening to the gentle waves murmur over a rocky shoreline.

When she awoke, she could hear the surf magnified by the fog bank that had rolled in after dark. The damp air felt clean and unobstructed and encouraged her mind to follow. She felt a presence, unseen but undeniable and whispered toward the sea, "Thank you. I hear my calling. I know what I must do."

On a terrestrial level, Trudy's epiphany included cutting to part-time hours at the clinic and enrolling at Bastyr University in Seattle to earn a Master of Science degree in Yogic Studies. She hoped that someday, when Elliot Jr. started his career, she could open her own yoga studio not too far from where he settled.

In some of the yoga classes at Bastyr, students found the postures by imitating the teacher. Trudy's favorite class, however, was Iyengar yoga, where the teacher corrected misalignment and students held poses longer. Props, including bolsters, blocks, straps and chairs, provided extra support, allowing beginning, injured, or elderly students the opportunity to participate and enjoy the benefits of yoga.

Regardless of the Yogic lineage, she believed in the necessity to unite the body, mind and spirit, all aspects of human existence, whether the student was Catholic, protestant, Buddhist, or atheist.

Upon graduation, she began teaching yoga at the Athletic Club after work. Her yoga classes filled with professional men and women who wore colorful active-wear purchased just down the street at Nordstrom department store in the up-scale Eastside

Shopping Mall. The students joined her classes to vary their workout routine and improve their physical shape. They had little interest in her emphasis on the therapeutic benefits of mind and body connection. She tailored her classes to meet their needs and gave up on anything spiritual. She thought, *is this why I spent time and money earning a master's degree?*

Attracted by the shape of her body in a swimsuit, men at the club asked Trudy out to dinner. At Canlis' in Seattle, she enjoyed the best steak she'd ever eaten while watching small sailboats race in the breeze on Lake Union. Salty's in West Seattle served a tasty whiskey crab soup with a view of the Seattle skyline reflected in Puget Sound and Ray's Boathouse at Shilshole marina, where mesmerizing sailboat masts swayed with the rhythm of the bay, she dined on perfectly prepared Copper River Salmon. The meals were impressive. Her dates were not. No one measured up to becoming Elliot Sr.'s successor or Elliot Jr.'s stepfather, much less her own life-partner. The men she dated had no interest in her efforts to live an authentic and balanced life.

Port Townsend

One Friday in July, after working at the dental office, then teaching a yoga class, Trudy drove to Port Townsend to attend a two-day yoga workshop at Madrona MindBody Institute. She pitched her tent in the Fort Worden campgrounds, then walked along the beach and sat on a huge driftwood log. Breathing fresh ocean air, she watched the sun slowly set. Twilight still lingered when she zipped herself into her sleeping bag at 10:00 p.m. Lulled by the gentle waves at high tide, she heard a whisper—something essential hovered. She knew she was getting closer. She slept soundly until 5:00 a.m. when the morning sun reflected off the tent.

After class on Saturday, Trudy perched on the rocks north of Point Wilson Lighthouse, where the Strait of Juan de Fuca churned into Puget Sound. A deep crimson sunset reflected on the sea like glistening sequins, stretching to the horizon.

As the colors reached their peak to the west, she turned east and watched the moon cast a yellow path, like spilled buttermilk, across Puget Sound and the wet sandy beach. Trudy felt as if she had finally come home for the first time in her life.

Trudy's son, Elliot Jr. graduated from Stanford with a Ph.D. in Electrical Engineering, then completed another Ph.D. program in Computer Science at Harvard. Upon graduation, a multinational technology company in Redmond recruited him to work in their Think Tank. In less than eighteen months, he became their VP of Technology and bought a house on Lake Sammamish.

Now that Elliot was settling into his adult life, Trudy considered her alternatives. She spent a weekend exploring Port Townsend, contemplating her future. She enjoyed heart-stopping views in every direction, the Strait of Juan de Fuca and Mt. Baker to the north, Cascade Mountains and Puget Sound to the east, Mt. Rainer to the south and the snow-capped Olympic Mountains to the west.

On Sunday, she hopped onto a little red trolley for a tour through the storybook town. The driver/guide slowly passed huge Victorian mansions built by investors and sea captains in the 1800s.

"Citizen-leaders and investors predicted that this hook of land marking the confluence of Strait of Juan de Fuca and Puget Sound would become the busiest port on the west coast—but the railroad spoiled everything," said the guide. "Seattle became the hub and this little seaside village became an artist colony. Over time, a tourist industry developed. Investors converted the mansions into hotels and B&Bs, but the flavor of Port Townsend's artist community remains."

Trudy made a decision.

Trudy gave her notice at the clinic.

That afternoon, she drove home feeling as free as an albatross sailplaning over the vast ocean. She parked in the middle of the two-car garage, walked past the utility room into the big open expanse of the living room/dining/kitchen area. The ranch-style home had three-bedrooms, two-and-a-half-baths and a large family room and if you stood on the deck, you could see Lake Washington. Within two weeks, the house sold for well over a million dollars.

In Port Townsend, a real estate agent showed Trudy several houses that held no interest, but then they entered a twenty-five-year-old two-bedroom rambler, perched on a not-too-high bluff in the North Beach area. Set on two-acres of waterfront property, the little house needed work but included a high fence to keep the intrusive black-tailed deer away from the well-established orchard, raised-bed gardens and mature blueberry and raspberry bushes. The little house also had a 400 square foot workshop that could be a yoga studio. Both buildings faced the sea, with windows looking toward the heart-stopping views of the Strait of Juan de Fuca and snow-covered Mt. Baker.

During her second visit to the property, the owner's daughter was in the house, sorting through her father's belongings.

"We moved Dad to a retirement center close to my home in California. Dad loved this place. He wanted me to keep it, but my life's in California and my husband thinks that traveling to Port Townsend is like going to Mars."

"Who's this little guy," said Trudy, kneeling to pet a small fluffy white dog who lifted his paw as if to introduce himself.

"This is Bentley the Bichon. He was Dad's companion. Now Dad's too senile to take care of him. I need to find him a good home. He's only four."

"Well, I've thought about having a dog ever since our old Lab died…,"

"Think it over. I'll be here for at least a week organizing Dad's things."

Just then, the Realtor rushed in from the deck, "Come look at this!"

The entire Orca J-Pod fed just offshore. Huge black and white whales breached and splashed back into the sea while the young stayed close to their mothers. The Realtor couldn't have scripted a better performance.

Trudy made an offer, including Bentley.

Trudy and Bentley rode the ferry across Puget Sound and drove to Port Townsend every week to monitor the renovation. The contractor put in new windows, replaced the dark paneling with insulation and drywall and installed radiant heat under new bamboo floors throughout. Trudy selected stainless steel appliances, granite for the kitchen and bathroom counter-tops and bamboo cabinetry.

The night before the movers delivered her furniture, Trudy unrolled her yoga mat on the warm living room floor with both the outdoor and indoor fireplaces blazing. Bentley cuddled by her side with his chin on her knee, as if he had been her companion all his life. Her hand rested on his soft white fur. Freed from the affluent eastside atmosphere, she breathed deeply, let it out slowly. Then again. *Finally*, she thought, *I'm home.*

BENTLEY

Every day, as they walked the beach, Bentley led Trudy to his favorite driftwood logs and tide pools. Occasionally, at low tide, they found orange sea stars. Once they found a dead octopus, but Bentley knew that these sea creatures were not to eat.

She loved the ever-changing view. Some days the water mirrored the sky's brilliant blue, while snow-covered Mount Baker glowed like a beacon on the horizon. She remembered the mountain in her dream.

Massive cargo ships ferried to and from far off ports. Luxury cruise liners headed to Alaska's Inside Passage from Seattle's port. Submarines from Keyport drifted past, escorted by buzzing gunboats with armed soldiers waving fisherman out of the path of the imposing vessel.

One morning, Bentley bounded onto the bed at 4:00 a.m. with a quiet woof and nudged Trudy's arm.

"Bentley, what is it? Do you need to go out so early?"

He nudged her again, his woof sharper, more insistent.

When she sat up, she saw the faint colors of dawn. "Did you wake me up to see the sunrise over the Strait of Juan de Fuca?"

He barked and turned in circles, then sat on the pillow and looked at her as if to say, *Obviously, now get dressed and let's go.*

She quickly made a cup of coffee, pulled on jeans and a jacket over her nightshirt and walked to the beach with Bentley on his leash. *This must have been the old man's routine,* thought Trudy. *What a lovely way to start a summer day.*

As they neared the shore, just feet away, an eagle took flight, clutching the salmon she'd been eating. Trudy gripped her mug and swallowed the lump in her throat. She had never seen the world so tranquil and bright, certainly not at 4:00 in the morning. "Thanks Bentley," she murmured.

With the Point Hudson lighthouse in the distance, she hopped onto on a massive driftwood log, worn gray and smooth by years of pounding surf. Bentley jumped up and rested his chin on her knee. The tangibly soft air caressed her skin and the aroma of seaweed, wet sand and salt air offered a sense of freshness that awakened her soul. The soft breeze felt chilly, but the sun warmed her face.

A sense of contentment settled over her, a sense she thought she'd lost along with her husband. *Elliot would love this as much as I do,* she thought, wiping a tear.

She rubbed Bentley's silky white coat. "I'm glad you didn't let me miss this. Let's watch the sun rise again tomorrow."

In the short days of winter, before darkness fell at 4:00 p.m., she sat on a bench near the bluff with a mug of Chardonnay and Bentley in her lap, watching moody moonrises reflected in the tranquil, cold, high tide. Low clouds like silver gauze often hid the mountain and blurred the horizon, blending the sky and sea into a pewter haze.

In the middle of the night, that first November on the bluff, foghorn blasts brought Trudy out of a deep sleep as huge cargo ships communicated their presence to each other in the gloom. Bentley didn't stir. Another morning, she awoke surprised to find seaweed stuck to her big ocean-facing windows high on the bluff. The newspaper reported that overnight, a king tide had coincided with high north winds allowing the ocean to demonstrate her power further inland than ever before.

Trudy loved preparing Thanksgiving dinner for Elliot Jr., especially since it was also his birthday dinner. Avoiding the traditional and boring turkey and trimmings, she spent hours poring over her *Barefoot Contessa* and *Bon Appétit* cookbooks and searching Epicurious.com for inspiration. She came upon Duck à l'orange, created with orange cream sauce and flaming brandy. A salad recipe with arugula, endive, crispy pancetta and roasted hazelnuts with apple cider vinaigrette served with toasted ribbons of butternut squash, made the perfect side-dish.

Early on the Tuesday before Thanksgiving, she drove an hour to Central Market in Poulsbo. The electric doors opened to an exhilarating harmony of fragrance. Aisles of colorful fresh produce reminded her of an outdoor market she once visited in Paris, with almost any fresh, organic fruit imaginable. Besides the usual apples, oranges and lemons, the produce section displayed red mangoes, green melons, yellow star fruit, exotic looking dragon fruit, dimpled kumquats, fuzzy peaches and several types of berries.

The vegetable aisles were equally impressive, with many varieties of onions and shallots, garlic large and small, fennel, snow peas and fresh asparagus.

She found the greens and squash she needed for her salad and the butcher at the meat counter wrapped a fat, organic duck and thin slices of pancetta. The cheesemonger recommended paper-thin crackers with Wensleydale cheese for *hors d'oeuvres*.

She stood, stunned, admiring the eggplant display. Long, graceful, bright lavender Chinese eggplant mounded between squatty, streaked Sicilian eggplant and long, finger-sized eggplant from Japan. The only variety she was familiar with was the plump, shiny, purple aubergine from Italy. She added one of each to her cart, thinking she and Elliot could experiment.

In the deli department, she watched a young woman put balls of dough into a Willy-Wonka-like machine; fresh tortillas came out the other side. She bought a package of warm whole-grain tortillas to make wraps for Elliot's lunch on Friday.

Her grocery cart filled with fresh whipping cream, two dozen farm fresh eggs, delivered to Central Market by the farmer that morning and chunks of dark chocolate for the Bûche de Noël, Elliot's birthday cake.

While standing in the checkout line, her phone beeped with a text from Elliot Jr.: *what can I bring?*

She responded: *I have it covered just bring your beautiful self.*

Elliot Jr.: *red or white?*

Trudy: *both!*

She put fresh sheets on the bed in the guest room and looked forward to having Elliot all to herself for a few days, even if he brought his laptop and spent hours working at the dining room table, they would be together.

Wednesday morning, he texted: *taking 7:30 to avoid ferry lines be there by 9:00 am*

She texted back a smiley face.

Her iPhone rang a little after nine. "Are you lost?" she asked Elliot.

"No, I'm on the Hood Canal draw bridge about twenty yards from the biggest submarine in the US fleet. This is amazing. I've never seen a sub so close."

Trudy could hear the wind on his cell phone. "I watched that sub sail by on the strait in front of my house. Intimidating, isn't it?"

"I have no idea how long the bridge will be closed to traffic, but I'm the second car, so when it opens, I'll be ahead of the gridlock."

"See you in a couple of hours then. I'll have hot coffee ready."

"Will it be too early for a glass of wine?"

She laughed, "Of course not, it's your birthday-eve!"

Thanksgiving morning, Elliot's twenty-eighth birthday, they relaxed on the deck bundled in down jackets, drinking coffee next to the outdoor fireplace. Bentley slept on Elliot's lap with his muzzle resting between his paws as they watched the featureless morning sky transmute to the color of dark, wet slate. Icy rain made a kissing sound on the metal roof as high tide thundered on the rocks below. "The raindrops sound like they're starting to freeze. I'm glad we don't need to go anywhere," she breathed.

"Um-hum." Elliot sounded relaxed and content as he sipped coffee from a steaming red mug, gazed into the frigid haze and slowly stroked Bentley's back.

Trudy smiled; her heart warmed by her son's contentment.

Trudy's new friend and neighbor, Wendy, stopped by for tea one afternoon.

"I'm so glad you could adopt Bentley," she said as she picked him up like a baby over her shoulder. "He's part of the neighborhood. Everyone loves him."

"Yes, he's introducing me to the beach and the neighbors. Do you think anyone will object if I open a yoga studio in the little outbuilding?"

Trudy had started the permitting process, which would include approval from her North Beach neighbors.

"The neighbors won't mind at all, especially back here where's there's plenty of parking." Wendy laughed. "But you can't turn around in this town without bumping into a yoga teacher."

"Let's walk over there. I'll show you the space." Wendy, Trudy and Bentley crunched along the short, gravel path from the house to the little building.

While Bentley sniffed around the room, Trudy and Wendy looked out at the steel blue sea, cyan sky and white clouds hovering near the mountain peak. They quietly sipped Rooibos tea from big red mugs. A cargo ship passed slowly and a fleet of sailboats, like tiny white party hats, hugged the shore near Whidbey Island. A bald eagle floated past at eye level. "Where can you practice yoga with this kind of view?" Trudy gazed out to sea as she took another sip of tea, hugging the warm mug with both hands. "I want to teach yoga in this beautiful space."

"I think you should," Wendy said, as the second eagle glided effortlessly past the window. "If you build it, they will come."

They both laughed and toasted their red mugs.

WALLY

Once the City of Port Townsend approved her plan, Trudy hired a carpenter, Wally, to transform the old workshop into a yoga studio. He was tall and thin, with a thick graying-blond ponytail sliding down his back, with lots of escaping curls. His face was round and pale with wide-set eyes and square chin. His relaxed smile and calm, positive energy made him easy to spend time with.

Wally created a small stoop and awning where students could remove their shoes before stepping inside. He installed a floating bamboo floor, cubbies for stowing shoes and Trudy's iPod sound system and built shelves for the yoga props. The only mirror in the studio was behind the bathroom door; there was a window over the sink. The panoramic view beyond the bluff was visible whether you sat on the toilet, stood at the sink, even in the glass brick shower.

Trudy and Wally sat on the new wooden stoop sipping iced tea in companionable quiet. He finally admitted, "I teach yoga at the gym downtown. I'd love to teach in this environment," he said as he looked out to sea.

"I guess I'm not surprised that you're a yoga teacher. You understood my vision exactly." She hesitated, "Do you think I can fill the classes?"

"There are so many yoga studios in this town, you'll have competition."

"I've heard and I've taken classes in several studios since I moved here, hope there's room for one more."

He took a folded piece of paper from his shirt pocket. "Here's the invoice. I can take a check, Visa, or you can use PayPal."

The header read Emerson Ralf Creations.

"Who is Emerson Ralf," asked Trudy.

"My first name is Emerson, my mother's maiden name. She insists we're descendants of Ralph Waldo Emerson."

"How did you get the name Wally?"

"Sadly, my middle name is Waldo. Dad's called me Wally for as long as I can remember."

"Emerson Waldo Ralf." Trudy turned her face away and suppressed a giggle. "Your mother had a sense of humor."

"I guess," he shrugged. "I don't think she really married Dad just because his name was Ralf, but it's always been a family joke."

Wendy dropped in to see the newly finished studio. "This is beautiful but where's the heater?"

"Under the floor. Radiant heat throughout."

"Brilliant! A student unrolls their mat on a warm floor with an intimate group of ten… Brilliant. If you want, I can photograph the space and create marketing materials."

"You can do that?"

"Sure, I make a living as a freelance graphic designer." Wendy looked around the room and across the sea toward Mt. Baker, shining white in the distance. "It's going to be a perfect evening for a photo shoot. Why don't you change into yoga clothes real quick and I'll run home for my camera gear?"

"Great! Meet back here in ten minutes."

While Trudy quickly changed into her yoga clothes, she thought about Wendy's career and realized that when she met people in Port Townsend, she discovered who they were, not what they did for a living. A refreshing thought after living on the eastside for so many years.

As the sun set, the sky glowed fuchsia and gold with deep blue streaks, all reflected in the sea and the snow-covered mountain. Trudy couldn't have asked for a more picturesque evening to capture the look and feel of the studio and its stunning view.

Wendy designed a logo using a silhouette of Trudy in a simple seated pose, with Mount Baker and the sea glowing in the background. She made flyers to post at the bakery and the food co-op and set up a website with lots of images and a link to Trudy's Facebook page.

"You need to give me an invoice for all the work you've done."

"Can I trade for yoga classes? How about three classes per week for a few months?

"Years of unlimited classes sounds more like it! You even created a website!"

"How about three classes a week for six months? After that, I'll pay like everyone else," suggested Wendy.

"If you're comfortable, so am I," Trudy hugged Wendy. "Thanks so much, you did a beautiful job!"

The spring weather couldn't have been more perfect for Trudy's open house. The garden was full of new plants, the apple trees were blooming and Mount Baker rose bright white in the distance.

Her new students were all ages, various professions and socioeconomic refinements. Some practiced with her weekly, others three times a week, a few practiced every day. Her students reported less back pain, less knee pain and improved balance and strength. By fall, she had a waiting list.

One Saturday morning, Trudy and Bentley walked to the studio to meditate and do her own yoga practice. It took her a while to notice, but Bentley mimicked her every move. "You are an amazing little beast," she laughed. He sat completely still, looking out the window during her meditation, then moved into his own version of her yoga practice. His downward facing dog pose looked more like a dog's play bow. When he put his back legs flat on the floor behind him and stiffened his front legs, his pose looked very much like her cobra, *bhujangasana*.

Back in the house, Bentley curled on his cushion next to her bed while she took a shower and enjoyed the view through the glass brick wall. She paused naked in front of the full-length mirror. Her willowy frame, sinewy arms, muscular legs and flat tummy had survived aging, but... The skin on her arms and legs looked like crepe paper, as if her skin no longer fit her body. No amount of lotion corrected the situation. She cupped her big breasts and lifted them to their former height. *My body sure has changed. Before, I could hold a pencil under each breast. Now I could hold a whole damn notebook,* she thought. She rested her hands on her hips. *I haven't had sex for sooo long...* She felt a whimper in her loins, "Face it. You. Are. Horny," she said aloud to her reflection.

Since moving to Port Townsend, Trudy found her meditation practice more satisfying, probably because she was finally living as a whole person—body, mind and spirit. As she came back into the house one evening, feeling alone, she thought of Wally, the handyman.

She called him, "Hi Wally, this is Tru. I was wondering if you would create a wooden sign for Tru Hart Studio?"

"Sure, I'd be happy to."

"I'd like to put it on the outside of the studio and make it big enough to see from 58th Street. Some of my students have had trouble finding me."

"I can drop by on Saturday around 4:00 with some sketches, if that works for you."

While Wally opened his sketchpad on the dining room table, Trudy opened a bottle of Chardonnay and poured them each a glass. When she handed him his wine, their fingers touched and she felt a spark between them. She looked into his beautiful blue eyes, but he quickly looked away.

"I like the way you used the logo Wendy created and the dimensions look good, but you spelled my name wrong." She took the pencil from his hand, crossed out True Heart Studio and wrote Tru Hart Studio.

"Tru? Your name is Tru Hart…? How appropriate," he grinned at her, then quickly looked away.

"Sounds better than Gertrude Wurtzburg Hart, don't you think? My friends and family call me Tru. You should too."

He handed her his estimate without looking her in the eye. "My services include installing the sign wherever you want it."

Wally was exceedingly sexy. Hormones crackled with unspoken tension, as if they were in a middle school classroom. His thick blond hair, pale blue eyes and sexy lips reminded her of Brad Pitt in *Legends of the Fall*. She nearly spilled her wine.

Finally, he stood up, "Trudy, ah, Tru. I'm trying to maintain a professional relationship here, but you're making it extremely difficult."

"How so?" She couldn't suppress her mischievous grin.

"Ah, well, I'm… well, I, I need your business—you know—financially and besides… I'm…"

"I wondered if you felt it too," interrupted Trudy. "Don't worry, Wally, I'll pay you to create and install the sign and I've already recommended your work to everyone I know in Port Townsend. Now then, would you like to have dinner with me tonight? I'm an excellent cook." She looked him straight in the eye.

"Yes, but well, I'm…"

"Wally, we're both over sixty. I haven't had sex for over twenty years… but it doesn't go away, ya know…?"

He grabbed her, more roughly than he intended, hugged her to his chest and kissed her long and hard.

"Now that's what I'm talkin' 'bout," she laughed.

She made a chicken stir-fry with snow peas and red peppers. After they cleaned up the kitchen—he insisted on helping—she opened another bottle of wine. They sat on the living room sofa in front of the two-sided fireplace and talked until 2:00 a.m. With remarkable ease, they made their way to the bedroom, as if they had been together for years.

Even Bentley knew something had shifted. In the middle of the night, he abandoned his usual sleeping pillow on the floor next to Trudy and curled on the bed between them.

Wally and Trudy began doing yoga together every evening, even after they both taught classes. They meditated together every morning. The sign he created was exactly what she needed and so was his companionship.

One night, as Trudy fixed dinner, Wally paced around the living room. "What's up Wally? You're as nervous as a lion in a cage."

"There's something I've avoided telling you…."

Trudy walked around the kitchen counter into the living room and handed him a glass of wine. "Don't tell me," she said sarcastically, taking a sip of chardonnay, "you're married."

"Well, yes, technically."

She opened her mouth, but no sound came out. She placed her trembling glass on the coffee table and dropped onto the sofa. Finally, she said, "You don't wear a ring. I just assumed… I wouldn't have…" her voice trailed off, her eyes rising to meet his. Without saying another word, her face said, *Tell me more.*

"I don't wear my ring because of the carpentry work I do… My wife, Diane, has Alzheimer's. We've been married for over thirty years. We never had kids, we're both teachers." Information poured out of him as if a dam had broken. "She started having trouble remembering words and sometimes used the wrong word in a sentence.

"There was a dead tree in our yard that she wanted to cut down. She called it a stag instead of a snag and once she ordered

Caesar salad without neutrons. We laughed about the cool words she came up with. She had just turned fifty and, I'm embarrassed to admit, I teased her about growing old."

"The two of you had a special relationship."

"Yes, we did."

They sat in silence for a while, then more about Diane poured out of him. "She'd retired from teaching when her back started bothering her, but now I know, there was more to it.

"One day we were riding our bikes on the Larry Scott Trail, out by the paper mill. I was behind her and watched her stop pedaling and fall over as if she forgot how to ride a bike. I left our bikes in the weeds and took her to the emergency room with a broken wrist.

"The doctor ran all kinds of tests and determined it wasn't a stroke. It was hard for us to hear she had early-onset Alzheimer's. We read everything we could find about Alzheimer's, but had to admit there was nothing the doctors could do. She said she felt as if she lived inside a foggy bowl. Sometimes she could see things clearly and then the glass steamed up as if she wore her reading glasses in the shower. It was a scary and difficult time for her. She could function most of the time, but I can only guess at her feelings as she watched the slow decline from within. Once the disease completely took control, her fear settled and she went back to her naturally happy self—almost."

Trudy sat quietly, hugging her knees while listening.

"One night, a few days after the diagnosis, when she was intensely coherent, we discussed our future together. 'I wish I could just end my life when the time comes. It seems ridiculous to pay for... anyway, don't hesitate to put me in a home and get on with it. I want you to have love, if I'm... not... here.' I couldn't imagine living without her.

"Our neighbors understood the situation and kept an eye out for her when I was teaching shop at the high school and night classes at the community college. One day she started to make scrambled eggs for her lunch, then went for a walk and left butter melting on the stove. A neighbor, who was working in her garden, saw Diane leave and smelled the browning butter. She stepped inside the kitchen door and turned off the burner—the advantage of small-town living.

"That's when I resigned my position at the high school and hired someone to stay with her in the evenings while I taught the woodworking class, but over the next year, taking care of her became a twenty-four-hour a day job, like sleeping with one eye open. I exhausted our retirement savings. I exhausted myself as well. Yoga was the only thing that kept me sane, but I didn't even have time for that.

"My doctor warned me that caring for her had sapped me physically, as well as financially. If I kept going like I was, I'd be too sick and worn out to take care of her."

The pain in Wally's eyes filled the room like thick smoke. Trudy put her arm around him.

"So, there it is," he said. "You're cavorting with a married man." He snickered a sad sound. "If you want me to leave and never come back, I understand."

She held his hand as they sat quietly for several minutes.

"Can I meet her?" she asked, reaching for the box of tissues.

"Sure," said Wally, wiping his eyes, surprised and reassured.

The next day, Trudy and Wally had lunch at the Bay View restaurant. As they watched a Great Blue Heron stalk the glittering shore of Port Townsend Bay, they ate in silence, both adrift in thought. Afterward, he drove to the nearby memory care center.

The lobby smelled of disinfectant and another scent Trudy couldn't identify. Diane was in the dining room, eating a bowl of vegetable beef soup. Cut-off jeans and a faded blue T-shirt along with her blond pixie haircut, made her appear far younger than sixty-three.

When he touched her shoulder, she stood up. "Hello Steve, how're Marilyn and the kids?" Diane asked, giving him a quick hug. Trudy thought, I would never guess anything was wrong.

"They're fine, how are you, Diane?" Wally leaned close whispering to Trudy, "Her brother Steve died in Vietnam. Marilyn is her other brother's wife."

"Never better. The chicken soup is great today—want some?"

"No thanks, we had lunch. I'd like you to meet my friend Trudy."

Trudy extended her hand, "Nice to meet you, Diane." Her hand was cold but her nails were beautifully manicured.

"Nice to meet you too, what did you say your name was?"

"Trudy."

"Would you like soup?"

"No thanks."

"What's your name?" She asked several times.

Trudy and Wally sat at the table with her. As Diane finished her meal, she chatted about the frosty winter weather and the beautiful snow, even though it was late June. She asked several times if they wanted soup. Diane called Wally "Steve", but then "Nick", her other brother's name. She never called him Wally.

Back in the car, Trudy broke down. Inside-out sobs shook her whole body. She couldn't breathe. Wally rubbed her shoulders while she processed her grief, tears glistening her face.

"How difficult this must be... for you... When they diagnosed my husband with terminal brain cancer, we knew what would happen, he would die and I would go on raising Elliot Jr. alone. It was horrible... but finite...." She dropped the side of her right hand like a hatchet into her left palm. "I watched his decline and I held him as he died."

She struggled to breathe. "This is worse than death, her heart beats, she looks healthy, but she isn't... here... Thanks for introducing me to Diane. How do you find the strength to cope...?"

It was a rhetorical question, but he answered. "Knowing you has helped more than you can imagine."

She scooted across the bench seat to put her head on his shoulder. She held his hand in both of hers.

"I feel like I can breathe again, but then... I still love—who she was. I want to ease her suffering but there's nothing I can do. And I feel guilty because I'm learning to be happy without her.... Does that make me a bad person?"

Trudy's DNA Report

During a weekend visit with Elliot Jr. at his home in Redmond, Trudy and her son enjoyed scones she'd made with her first blueberry harvest. They sat on the deck watching the Bufflehead, Wood Ducks and Canada Geese float on Lake Sammamish, with the Cascade Mountains in the background.

"I watched an interesting documentary on DNA research last weekend," said Elliot. Trudy's little white dog, Bentley, rested in his lap. "Have you ever considered doing a DNA test?"

Trudy didn't notice the mischievous glint in his eyes. "I saw the same documentary, but with my weird family—you excluded, of course—I'm afraid of the results. We might be part of Ted Bundy's family tree."

"You do have some strange siblings, especially Uncle Walter, but I doubt that anyone's a serial killer."

"I'm joking, of course," said Trudy, "but it is unsettling. What if we find out I'm likely to have Alzheimer's or that your Uncle Walter is a demented pedophile?"

"We already know he has issues," laughed Elliot. "He sure likes dating much younger people."

"What if he left DNA at a crime scene and the police follow my DNA to him—creepy."

"That sounds like an episode of *Law & Order SVU*... You don't really think your brother..."

"No, not really, but when you test your DNA, the possibilities for bad news are endless and your information is... out there..." She waved her hand over her head before taking a bite of her scone.

"But couldn't there be good news too? Like your ancestors came from Egypt or you have a famous great uncle you never knew about. Don't you want to know if we're related to Albert Einstein?"

"If you're related to Albert Einstein, it's definitely on your father's side," she laughed. "Alright, Elliot, I'll do it if you'll do it."

Elliot laughed, "I knew that's what you'd say." His eyes twinkling, he reached into his pocket and pulled out two DNA test kits. "I ordered these last week after I watched that documentary."

"What if I'd said I didn't want to?"

"Oh, I knew your curiosity would win in the end." When he grinned, her heart ached. The older he became, the more he looked like his father, with glasses perched on his narrow nose and a beautiful smile that lit his entire face.

"You know me too well!"

Elliot Jr. made sure his mother was up to date on everything high-tech. He'd given her the new Portal Plus so they could chat face to face via Wi-Fi. The tall, narrow flat screen stood like a big picture frame on a small desk by the kitchen. The Saturday their DNA data became available, Elliot called Trudy. She was in the kitchen, fixing her lunch when the device beeped, "Hi Elliot," she said from across the room, causing her son's face to appear on the screen.

"Hi, Mom!"

"Just a minute while I put cream in my coffee," she said. The device's camera followed her from the coffeepot to the fridge and back before she seated herself in front of the screen. "Have you logged in to check the results of our DNA tests?"

"The email notification came this morning, but I haven't taken the time."

"Me either. Let's do it now if you have time." They logged in so they could both see the results on their respective monitors. Elliot was at his home in Redmond. She was in Port Townsend.

"This device is fantastic," she said. "I love being able to see you while we talk." Then she gasped. "Would you look at that! Does that mean what I think it means?"

"Looks like I have an aunt I never knew about."

"Neither did I... I didn't consider this scenario. Good grief! Another sibling! Your Grandpa Wurtzburg was a busy boy in 1950. His other daughter is exactly my age." Her heart raced as she considered the data on the monitor. She tried to take a sip of coffee, but her hands trembled. She dribbled coffee down the front of her sweater.

"Are you going to contact your mysterious half-sister?"

"I don't know," she mumbled, her mind racing with the significance of this revelation, her pulse pounding in her ears. She considered her father's infidelity. *Did Mom know? What was the newly discovered sibling feeling? Are there others?* she thought.

"Hello, are you still there? I can see you, ya know?"

"I'm just thinking—Dad had an affair! Did Mom know about it? Did the girl know her father—my father? Are there other siblings that aren't in the database—yet? Oh, so many questions!"

Discovered Siblings

Trudy decided to contact her newly discovered half-sister in Ohio—there was no email address in the profile, so she called the number. "Is this Gertrude Grantham?" she asked.

"That was my maiden name," the woman replied, her tone clipped. The question, "Why are you calling" clearly implied.

"Well, my name is Trudy Wurtzburg Hart. You don't know me, but I think I'm your half-sister."

The line went dead. She stood listening to the dial tone, feeling a little rejected but also understood the stun of this discovery. Gertie must be as shocked as she was.

A few hours later, the woman's daughter, Suzie, called. "Mom's pretty upset. Hearing that Granddad Grantham wasn't her biological father was a huge shock. I don't think she believes it. Maybe someday you and I can talk about it?"

"I'd like that very much. Let me know when you're ready."

After she hung up, Trudy sat for a moment, absorbing the strangeness of it all. She picked up the phone feeling the need to share the information with the siblings she grew up with.

She called Mark. Four years older, he was an actual rocket scientist, retired from a lifetime as a Boeing engineer.

"Hi Tru."

"Hi. How have you been?"

"I'm doing as well as any a retired seventy-two-year-old can expect. What's up?"

"You'll never guess what I discovered. My DNA test revealed that we have a half-sister in Ohio, Gertrude Grantham Taylor. She and I were born on the exact same day."

"Did it ever occur to you that I might not want to know that I have a half-sister in Ohio?"

Trudy gripped the phone, turned her head away to look at Bentley asleep on his pillow. "Ah," she stammered, "actually, no Mark, it never occurred to me." She started to say I'm sorry but stopped herself. She wasn't sorry, not at all.

"I don't need another sister at this point in my life. What do you expect? Should I send her a Hallmark card? Or book a ticket and show up on her doorstep?" he growled. "Have you talked to her?"

"No, I tried, but she hung up. Her daughter, Suzie, called me back and apologized. She asked that I not contact her mother, but she gave me her own email address. She's curious to know more about her biological family."

"Why?" he grumbled.

"I thought you'd find this as fascinating as I did."

"What did you say her name was?" he asked sharply, like a detective demanding evidence at a murder scene.

"Grantham."

"When I graduated with my Ph.D. Dad gave me a business card, a guy named Ted Grantham, from Ohio. He helped me get my first interview at Boeing. I wonder if it's the same guy."

Ted Grantham had flown from Dayton, Ohio, to Seattle to meet with clients. He climbed out of a taxi at the Westin Hotel just as a black BMW pulled up to the valet station. A confident-looking blond man, dressed in jeans and a crisp, Oxford, button-down shirt, handed his keys to the valet. The porter took his avocado green American Tourister luggage and the man carried his black leather attaché to the check-in counter. Ted hoisted his duffel out of the taxi's trunk and followed.

"I have a reservation for Dr. Richard Wurtzburg," Ted heard the man say to the hotel clerk.

As the clerk slid the registration card across the counter, Ted said, "Excuse me, are you the same Dr. Wurtzburg who worked at Valley Hospital in Dayton, Ohio twenty-some years ago?"

"I am," said Richard, reaching to shake Ted's hand. "You here for the infertility conference?"

"No, I'm Ted Grantham, we met at the hospital the day our girls were born. The only reason I remember is, we both named our daughters after my wife's best friend, Gertrude... something."

"Ah, yes, Gertrude Anna, wonderful nurse. Nice to see you again, Ted. How is your Gertrude?"

"Wonderful but we call her Gertie," said Ted, pulling his wallet from his back pocket. "She's expecting my second grandchild." He showed Richard a wallet-size photo of their family taken at Gertie and George's wedding.

As Richard reached for his wallet, the hotel clerk said, "Excuse me, gentleman, would you mind finishing with check-in and stepping aside. Others are waiting."

"Oh, sorry." They both quickly finished, accepted their room keys and moved toward the elevator.

"How about a drink in the bar?" suggested Richard. "It's on the top-floor, stunning view of the mountains."

"Sure, why not? I don't have client meetings till breakfast, just let me put my things in my room. Meet you in the bar in five minutes."

Richard took the elevator to the bar. The valet had taken his luggage to his room. Taking a seat by the window, he ordered Guinness on tap and drummed a spoon to "Mama Told Me Not to Come."

When Ted joined him, Richard said, "I never tire of this view. I grew up in rural Ohio and even after twenty years, this still seems like paradise."

"It's spectacular, especially compared to Ohio. I grew up in Columbus, still live in Dayton." Ted ordered a scotch on the rocks and a glass of water. The conversation stalled as they listened to Creedence Clearwater Revival's "Bad Moon Rising."

When "Come on Baby, Light My Fire" blasted from the sound system, Ted waved to the waiter. "Would you mind turning that down? Thanks." He turned back to Richard. "I used to love all kinds of music, but this new stuff is just noise.... Where are you living now?"

Richard chuckled. "Less than twenty-five miles from here, across the Evergreen Point Floating Bridge." He pointed east across Lake Washington. "I'm attending an infertility conference. Staying in the hotel keeps me completely away from my practice and I avoid driving home after a few drinks." He lifted his frosty mug and took a swig.

Ted pulled snapshots from his wallet. "My son Robert's in Vietnam and Teddy's going to Ohio State. Gertie just wants to have babies."

Richard offered a family photo with Olin Mills stamped in gold lettering on the lower-left corner. The Wurtzburgs' five children surrounded Richard and his wife. The kids wore bell-bottom jeans with sweatshirts from their respective schools. "We have four in college and one in elementary school," laughed Richard. "Trudy will graduate from UDub in June and Mark went back to school after he watched Apollo 11 land Neil Armstrong on the moon and more importantly, bring him home. He's almost finished with a Ph.D. in Aeronautical Engineering."

"I have a Ph.D. in Aeronautical Engineering. I was a Navy pilot in WWII. After the war, I left the Navy and started selling airplane parts. I'm still with the same company." He took a sip of his scotch. "What does your son want to do?"

"He wants to work for Boeing here in Seattle."

"I do a lot of business with Boeing. When he's ready, tell him to call me. I might be able to help arrange an interview with the right man." Ted pushed his business card across the table.

"Thanks, that's generous of you. I'll tell my son."

"I hope to see you sometime this summer," said Trudy, dropping the DNA discussion with her not-so-pleasant brother. "You should come for a visit and see my house and yoga studio here in Port Townsend. You're welcome to the guest room." She was trying to be sisterly, but Mark didn't get it.

"What possessed you to buy a house on the edge of civilization? You're in the middle of nowhere and you're not getting any younger. Do they even have Internet service out there?"

"Yes, we have Internet in Port Townsend and all the usual modern conveniences—electricity, running water. And I have a magnificent 180-degree view of the Strait of Juan de Fuca and Mount Baker. I'd have to be Bill Gates to own a view property like this in Seattle.

"If it doesn't erode into the ocean," he grumbled.

"Oh, sorry, there's someone at the door, call me when you have time to chat. Gotta go, bye."

There was no one at the door. Trudy wanted to end the conversation with her not-so-pleasant brother. When they were young and living at home, she tolerated his negativity, but now, she could just end the conversation. *The advantage of growing older,* she thought.

Her sister, Rebecca, had the opposite reaction. "How wonderful to have another sister. Let's fly out to meet her! Oh, this could be fun! A girls' trip to Ohio—what do you say? Just imagine the stories."

Rebecca was only two years younger than Trudy, but the sisters were nothing alike. While Trudy was tall, willowy and blond and never worried about gaining weight, Rebecca had short legs, a small waist and constantly fought the size of her hips. Her hair was auburn and curly and she had their mother's blue eyes.

Every time the family gathered, Rebecca would subtly critique Trudy under the guise of sisterly advice. Trudy usually left early to avoid saying something she'd regret.

"Women our age just shouldn't wear long hair," Rebecca had said, fluffing her short, curly do. "It's not flattering and makes women look like they're trying to be younger than they are."

Trudy's hair was long, worn up, off her neck.

"It's ridiculous," Rebecca had said later that day. "Everyone on the eastside believes their kid is gifted." Rebecca knew that Trudy's son, Elliot, had been in the advanced placement program since kindergarten.

Rebecca didn't seem to notice that they couldn't be in the same room together and made ludicrous suggestions for time together—like a trip to Ohio.

"Our half-sister wants nothing to do with us," said Trudy. "Can you imagine the shock if you found out that Dad wasn't really your biological father?"

"I suppose that would be a shock. It seems odd that Dad had two daughters with the same name and it's such an odd, old-fashioned name too, Gerrrtrooodud," said Rebecca, drawing out the name as if tasting something revolting.

Trudy closed her eyes, took a deep breath, then another. Finally, she said, "I wonder how we got the same name."

"Are you surprised that Dad cheated on Mom?" asked Rebecca.

"Sure! I thought he loved Mom. Remember how they snuggled in front of the TV when they thought we were in bed? I knew he was a hopeless flirt, but I always assumed he was harmless."

"When I was in high school, I remember women flirting with him, even when Mom was with him, but he was so charming, no one seemed to mind. Now I wonder what Mom might have been thinking…. Have you told our brothers about the DNA results?" asked Rebecca.

"I called Mark, but he wasn't happy with the news."

"Mark's never happy about anything," she laughed. "Should I tell Walter? He listens to me," implying that he doesn't listen to Trudy. Her voice carried her signature faux sweetness.

Trudy sighed, "Sure, better you than me."

She was relieved that Rebecca would pass the news on to their other brother. She hadn't talked to Walter since Trump was elected. The last Thanksgiving they were all together, just after the 2016 election, Walter, a sixty-eight-year-old Economics professor, brought a twenty-year-old coed to the family dinner. The year before, he'd brought a young male student.

Walter was a vocal, aggressive conservative Republican and before the turkey came out of the oven, he shouted at Trudy, calling her a crazy, woo-woo liberal.

Trudy had nothing against his being bisexual or dating much younger people, but she couldn't tolerate his political values. Even worse, he was manipulative and predatory and didn't hesitate to borrow money he had no intention of repaying. She couldn't help wondering what their newfound Ohio sibling, Gertie and her family, would think of their brother, Walter. She was having second thoughts about sharing the information with him, knowing he might exploit the newly discovered relatives.

The youngest in the family was Meredith. After earning a law degree from Harvard, Meredith became a high-powered, high-paid, divorce attorney in Manhattan. Tall, beautiful and intense, she looked like their father. She inherited his brilliant mind but lacked his natural charm.

Trudy picked up her iPhone to call Meredith, then put it back on the table. *Maybe another day*, she thought. After talking with Mark and Rebecca, she had no energy left for Meredith. She decided to text: *Mert, had DNA tested and found half-sister living in Ohio. Call me if you want more info.*

A few minutes later, Meredith texted back. *saw the match, not relevant. Hope Thanksgiving was uneventful*

Typical Meredith—efficient, unsentimental.

Happy to avoid talking to Meredith, Trudy flipped on the outdoor fireplace and took a steaming red mug of hibiscus tea to the deck. Deeply breathing the tranquil sea air, she began to relax. She'd informed all her siblings. Mark didn't want to know about their father's dalliance, but Rebecca wanted to meet the newly discovered sibling. Meredith found the information inconsequential and Trudy feared Walter would seize the opportunity.

Leaning on the railing, the warm tea helped her ground herself after her family's emotional chill.

Aging Audrey

As Audrey aged, her knuckles swelled slightly, but her long, slender hands remained graceful and strong. Her ability to play the piano endured. After her eightieth birthday, however, she retired from the opera. She accepted no new piano and voice students, but continued to support her long-time protégés.

Audrey and her adopted daughter, Simone, sang together every day before Simone rehearsed for the opera. "What shall we sing today?" asked Simone.

Audrey's voice had become breathy, her range had diminished and her vocal endurance had weakened. Still, she smiled, "I think I can manage *Marriage of Figaro.*"

Meanwhile, with Audrey's insistence on breathing techniques and hours of scales, Simone's artistry and vocal allure deepened, her voice ripened.

Audrey and Simone often walked to the Opera house, but after Audrey's eightieth birthday, to save time, they hailed a taxi. They still walked to their favorite brasserie on Rue Cler for lunch as often as they could. Audrey always ordered *salade niçoise*, sometimes with tuna, sometimes sardines, sometimes smoked salmon. They rarely ate sweets, but occasionally, when the draw of chocolate grew stronger, they walked another block to the bakery for a chocolate chunk cookie. Afterward, they strolled back to the building and climbed the stairs.

Returning from lunch on her ninetieth birthday, Audrey paused. "Perhaps, it is time for the elevator." Audrey sounded like her usual bright self, but Simone saw the flicker of defeat behind Audrey's smile.

Simone slid the squeaky accordion gate aside. They stepped into the little iron cage and Audrey's long, boney finger ceremoniously reached to press number three. Like a wrought-iron birdcage, it lifted them to the third floor.

Audrey had never used the elevator. Even as a child, she loved climbing the winding marble stairs. Her maintenance man had replaced the original elevator mechanism but the small, Art Déco cage remained vintage, its geometric scrollwork matched the winding stairwell's hand railing and the small balcony balustrades on the building's exterior.

"Auntie, some of my friends have had their DNA tested and learned about all sorts of interesting relatives they didn't know about."

Audrey hesitated. A shadow crossed her face. Her throat tightened, remembering the DNA test that proved her mother had been killed by a serial killer during the war. She pushed the memory back into the dark corner of her heart.

Finally, she agreed. *Maybe Simone will find her mother or father*, she thought, not sure how she felt about that. In the back of her mind, she wondered if, by some miracle, she might find the baby she gave up for adoption.

Simone set up accounts for both of them and posted their samples.

The results revealed nothing about Simone's mother or father, but her heritage was distinctly German and Swedish.

Audrey's test revealed she was mostly Italian—no surprises—yet.

Evelyn's Memory Care

Evelyn Reilly Grantham shuffled back and forth by the window in her room at the Village Garden Memory Care Facility. She wrapped her boney, translucent arms around her waist as if holding herself together. Gertie sat with her mother for an hour or more every morning, reading aloud or knitting. They didn't interact, but Gertie believed her mother knew she was in the room with her, in the heavy, familiar silence.

One morning, Gertie arrived later than usual to find that her mother had a visitor. The woman's dark skin was smoother than Gertie's and her short black hair had only a few gray threads. Gertie didn't notice, at first, that she struggled to lift her thin frame out of the straight-backed chair. She was taller than Gertie—but then, everyone was.

"You must be Evelyn's daughter. You look like her," she said with a wide warm smile and high cheekbones. Her voice deep and confident, "I'm Gertrude Anna. Your mother and I are BFFs...."

Gertie blinked.

"You know, *best friends forever*?" the woman added.

"I... I... must be named after you?" Gertie stammered, her eyes wide. Not only was her mother's best friend an African American woman—she looked younger than Gertie. *She must be mistaken,* thought Gertie. *She must be another memory patient.*

"Yes, you are my namesake. Your mother is special to me. It's so difficult to see her like this. My body's brittle, but I still have my mind. Evelyn's in great shape physically with no mind at all...," her voice softened to a whisper.

Filling the silence, Gertrude Anna continued. "We met when my stepdad went to work on her father's dairy farm during the Depression. Then, after high school graduation, we were roommates during nursing school and then worked at Valley Hospital in the '40s, after the war."

Gertie was speechless, again, struck by how little she knew about her female relatives. The family stories had always revolved around the Grantham men.

Gertrude Anna smiled. "I was delighted to find her in the dining room when I moved into Village Garden a few months back. She quit nursing when Ted was diagnosed and we no longer saw each other everyday like we did when we worked together. The nurses allow me into the memory care wing so I can visit her every afternoon. I'm early today."

Gertie finally noticed the walker Gertrude Anna leaned on. "Please," she waved toward the chair, "sit down." She helped Gertrude Anna lower herself onto the straight-backed chair.

Still stunned by the beautiful Black woman who claimed to be as old as Evelyn, Gertie perched on the bed.

"Are you okay?" Gertrude Anna finally asked. "You look pale."

Gertie blinked, shook her head and blurted out, "Yes. Sorry. I'm just... surprised. You're... you're so beautiful."

"If I could, I'd trade places with her," said Gertrude Anna in a soft voice.

"I... I... I'm... sorry. I know so little about my mother... Well, I'm stunned."

"I saw you and your family with her on Thanksgiving," said Gertrude Anna. "But it was a difficult day for Evelyn, for all of you I imagine. I didn't want to intrude. Were you with your children?"

"Oh, Thanksgiving? That was my daughter, Suzie and her husband, Tom. My three sons and grandkids stayed home. I'm glad. That was the worst we've had." She glanced toward the window at the snow blanketed schoolyard. "I don't even know where my mother went to elementary school..."

"The Reilly's had a farm north of Dayton. Tipp City. We went to school there."

Gertie's breath caught. She'd almost forgotten that Reilly—her own middle name—was her mother's maiden name. Gertrude Reilly Grantham. She dropped it when she became Mrs. George Taylor in 1970, nearly fifty years ago. With a shock, she realized she had dropped her own name completely. Her mail still came to Mrs. George Taylor.

"We did our nurse's training at Valley Hospital. She told me your father paid tuition and expenses so she could finish her last semester of nursing school. He was so kind and loving. I remember how excited Ted was to have a baby girl."

Gertie gave her a blank stare, her mouth slightly open, as if ready to ask a question.

"You look pale—are you okay?"

A chilling thought struck Gertie like a thunderbolt. *This woman might know my biological father.* A crushing weight pressed on Gertie's chest. She gasped for breath.

Gertrude Anna pressed the call button. Within seconds, two nurses rushed in, surprised to find Evelyn by the window, hugging her waist as usual, while Gertie lay curled on the bed in a fetal position, clutching her chest and gasping for air. Her panic attack looked very much like a heart attack. A nurse checked her vitals. Her pulse was racing. Her blood pressure spiked. The nurse notified the doctor who admitted her to the hospital floor at Village Garden as a precaution.

By early afternoon, Gertie's daughter, Suzie, arrived from Cincinnati, surprised to hear the medical team focused on her mother, not Granny Evelyn.

With Gertie stabilized and sleeping peacefully, Gertrude Anna and Suzie found a quiet corner in the dining room.

"It's amazing how good the food is here. Have you eaten?" asked Gertrude Anna.

"I'll just have coffee," said Suzie, her voice thin. "Can you tell me what happened?"

"She seemed... stunned to find me in your grandmother's room. She told me she knew very little about her mother's life. When I mentioned how excited Ted Grantham was to have a baby girl, she either had an anxiety attack or heart attack—either way, it was dramatic."

Suzie slowly poured cream into her coffee, gently stirred with a spoon, put the spoon on a napkin. She gazed at the steam curling from the mug, as if the steam could explain everything.

"Hello? Hello?" Gertrude Anna leaned closer. "Are you going to collapse with an attack too?"

"Can I share something with you?" Suzie said, nervously folding a paper napkin into tiny squares. "I'm sure Mom wouldn't approve, but I think you might be able to shine some light on our history."

Gertrude Anna nodded, "Sure."

Suzie cleared her throat, still gazing at her coffee. "A few months ago, Mom had her DNA tested… part of her research for her DAR membership."

Suzie looked up when Gertrude Anna inhaled a ragged breath.

"Now it's your turn for a doctor," Suzie joked. "What is it?"

"Don't tell me… Gertie discovered that Ted Grantham is not her biological father?"

"You know!" Suzie said, her eyes wide. Her grip tightened on her coffee mug.

"Oh, child… there are so many secrets." Gertrude Anna slowly replaced her mug on the table, took a deep breath and told the story, her voice heavy.

"I saw Evelyn and Dr. Richard Wurtzburg slip into the doctor's lounge. I heard the lock click. Evelyn told me about it later." Her dark eyes shimmered. "He was handsome. Charismatic. Probably more dangerous than we knew.

"Fortunately, just after it happened, he left the hospital for a job in a clinic. Evelyn was beside herself. She'd never even kissed anyone but Ted. They lived in a tiny room on the top floor of a run-down house and he was rarely there that first year. After the tryst, Evelyn was a nervous wreck. But when she had a cycle, she tried to put it all behind her."

"She had a period… after…?" Suzie said, her voice small.

"Well yes and no. It's not unusual for an expectant mother to have some spotting when her cycle would have started. She assumed it was a normal cycle and tried to put the whole thing out of her mind. The baby weighed five pounds and was two weeks early; or so we thought. But now we know the baby was two weeks late.

Suzie listened, still folding and unfolding the napkin.

"Dr. Wurtzburg's wife gave birth to a daughter the same day. He was out of town for a job interview, so I helped Mrs. Wurtzburg through her labor and C-section. She named her baby after me." She glanced at Suzie. "That's how they were both named Gertrude."

"But they called her Trudy," whispered Suzie.

"How did you learn about Trudy?" asked Gertrude Anna, her eyes narrowing with curiosity.

"I put Mom's phone number on her Ancestry.com account. She's not exactly technical. She doesn't have email. Trudy Wurtzburg Hart called Mom when she got her own DNA test results."

Gertrude Anna blinked. "She called your mom?"

Suzie nodded, looking down at the coffee mug. "Mom freaked out. Hung up. I don't think she'll ever forgive me," her voice trembled. "She thought the data was wrong and she could keep it a secret, but when Trudy called… it was hard to deny the truth."

Gertrude Anna gave a knowing nod.

"Whatever happened to Dr. Wurtzburg?" asked Suzie.

"Trudy was a few months old when he and his wife moved to Seattle, Washington. They raised five children. Trudy was number three." Her eyes welled with tears. "For years, she sent me Christmas cards with photos of their family—those kids lined up in matching ski sweaters." She paused. "This must be unbearable for your mother. I can see what kind of woman she is—and, oh my goodness, Daughters of the American Revolution?"

Suzie gave a half-laugh, half-sob. "Yeah. That's been the hardest part. Granddad Grantham's family history dates back to before the Revolutionary War. That impressed Mom."

Suzie took a deep breath. "Speaking of Granddad, I came across another interesting tidbit." She took a deep breath. "Granddad Grantham's high school sweetheart gave up a baby for adoption in 1938."

"Ted Grantham? Wow, you just never know—what is it they say? Still waters run deep?"

Suzie nodded. "I haven't told Mom about him. His name is Sergei. I emailed him and he called me, from Paris."

Gertrude Anna sat up taller, "Paris?"

"He lives there. And get this—he lives next door to his biological mother. Granddad's high school sweetheart! We talked for a long time. What a delightful man. Last year, he had his DNA tested and found out he was adopted at birth. His parents even signed his birth certificate and he has a photo of them holding him when he was just a few hours old. They must have been there when he was born." Suzie wiped her eyes. "Sergei said he adored them. Without that teen pregnancy, they wouldn't have had a family. The best part is that DNA research led Sergei to his birth mother."

"She's still alive?" asked Gertrude Anna.

"She's ninety-six and he's eighty. He was born on her sixteenth birthday."

"If she was only fifteen when she got pregnant, it's no wonder she gave up the baby," said Gertrude Anna. "In the 1930s? I doubt her parents gave her any choice."

"Even when I was in high school, it was a big deal if one of our classmates got pregnant. I can't image what it was like for her in the thirties."

Gertrude Anna nodded. "What's Sergei's last name?"

"Sapozhnikov."

Gertrude Anna's eyes went wide, "The great piano virtuoso?"

Suzie laughed, "That's him. He mentioned he was researching the origin of his musical talent; I didn't realize I was chatting with THE Sergei. Isn't it wild? He could have been Sergei *Grantham*!

Suzie looked at Gertrude Anna. "If you don't mind, I have something else I'd like to discuss with you." Suzie reached into her bag and pulled out a wrinkled envelope, yellowed and soft with age and placed it on the table between them. "When I helped Mom move Granny Evelyn to Village Garden, I found this in Granny's dresser drawer. I asked Mom, but she refused to open it. She said it was addressed to her mother, so it wasn't her place."

Suzie stared at the envelope waiting on the table between them.

"I kept it all these years. For some reason," she shrugged and shook her head, "I grabbed it on the way out today. Maybe it'll help us understand the family mystery." She looked up. "Will you read it... please?"

Gertrude Anna nodded, reached for a table knife and gently slit it open. She unfolded the letter, her hands quivered slightly. She slipped on her reading glasses, hanging from a chain around her neck and glanced around to make sure they were alone. In her deep, lyrical voice, she read aloud with an actor's inflection and emotion.

May 10, 1987

My Dearest Evelyn,

There are things I need to say and I don't trust time to wait for the right moment.

I need to tell you a secret I've carried for a long time. I fathered a child with my high school sweetheart, Audrey Dupré. She was fifteen. I was seventeen.

Her mother moved away suddenly when Audrey told her she was expecting and I never heard from her again. I was never sure where they went, however, the mover let it slip that he was shipping the books to Paris. Her father had an apartment there. That was in June 1938, just as Hitler was stirring up chaos across Europe.

I've always hoped they survived the war. I assume the baby was adopted and of course, I never knew if it was a boy or a girl.

However, now, thanks to the cancer, I'm certain it was a boy. When I was first diagnosed with testicular cancer, the doctors discovered that I have a rare condition that makes it nearly impossible for me to father a daughter. No wonder our family has been all men for generations.

I thought they were wrong of course. We have Gertie.

After a great deal of thought, I realized it doesn't matter. I traveled so much after our wedding and I left you alone in that awful apartment for days, even weeks. I'm certain you were lonely.

None of that matters now. I love Gertie. I raised her as my own and I'm thankful I had the opportunity to be her father. I would have legally adopted her had I known.

I suspect you didn't calculate the timing and failed to realize she could be another man's child, but still, I believe with all my heart that you loved me.

Thank God for the car accident that brought me to the ER that night. I have loved you since that day.

It looks like I won't live a long life, but I'm thrilled that I spent the last forty years with you, my darling.

I love you.

Ted

Suzie and Gertrude Anna sat in silence for a few moments, both quietly wiping their eyes while the weight of the letter settled around them.

"You were right," Suzie whispered. "He loved her no matter what." She stared out the window at the cold pewter sky. "When Mom's feeling better, will you help me a share this with her?"

"Of course, sweetheart. She deserves to hear his words."

Suzie found a pen in her bag, unfolded and smoothed the napkin and tried to diagram their family tree.

"Okay, so here's the family tree—as I understand it. Ted Grantham, my Granddad (but he's not really my Granddad) had a high school sweetheart, Audrey Dupré, who gave the baby up for adoption—Sergei—the man I talked to in Paris. The musical genius, but he's not related to me after all."

She drew a line through his name.

"Ted Grantham married Evelyn Reilly and had Uncle Teddy and Uncle Robert, but they're my half-uncles because," she paused almost afraid to say it out loud, "because Granny Evelyn had an affair with Dr. Wurtzburg and gave birth to Gertrude Reilly Grantham Taylor, my mom. So, Dr. Wurtzburg is my biological granddad, not Ted Grantham."

She drew a circle around Dr. Wurtzburg and a line through Ted Grantham.

"Dr. Richard Wurtzburg had five children with his wife, including Trudy, the woman who phoned Mom. They're my half aunts and uncles. This is so confusing! Overall, I have three half aunts and four half uncles—right? Oh, I shouldn't forget my dad's sister. She's *really* my aunt, unless there's hanky-panky on Dad's side we don't know about, yet," she laughed.

"Looks like you have it mapped out," smiled Gertrude Anna.

Suzie's tone shifted. "When Uncle Teddy found out about the DNA results, he threatened to take our inheritance away because Mom's not really a Grantham. Can he do that?"

"I seriously doubt the court would decide in his favor," offered Gertrude Anna, gently placing both hands over the drawing, as if protecting Gertie and her family.

"Your family is filled with love, Suzie, anyone can see that. Your Uncle Teddy's bitterness can't erase that love—not now, not ever."

When Suzie and her mother visited Granny Evelyn a few days later, Gertrude Anna was already waiting for them in Evelyn's room.

"Do you remember the letter I found when Granny Evelyn moved to Village Garden?" asked Suzie.

"No, not really," said Gertie, already wary.

"At the time, you refused to open it because it wasn't addressed to you, but after everything we've learned, Gertrude Anna and I decided we needed to know what was in the envelope."

Gertie gave Suzie a fearful look, her brows tightening with concern.

"Let me read it to you, Gertie," Gertrude Anna said in her deep voice. She shifted her chair, put on her reading glasses and steadied herself, then looked across the room. "Evelyn, I want you to listen too."

As Gertrude Anna read the letter aloud, her voice rich with

compassion, while Evelyn paced back and forth in front of the window, hugging herself as always. Then Evelyn's arms slowly dropped to her sides.

"He's right," she said in a slow, wispy voice that sounded like it came from a deep well, the first words she had spoken in over a year.

Gertie, Suzie and Gertrude Anna sat completely still, as if any shift in the air would cause Evelyn to leave them again. Their three faces slowly turned.

Tears ran down Evelyn's wrinkled face as she shuffled toward them and sat on the bed next to Gertie.

"I never considered that our first baby wasn't Ted's..." Looking into Gertie's eyes, her gnarled fingers gently cupped Gertie's cheek. "He loved you so much," she whispered.

"Oh Mom...," Gertie whispered, brushing the tears from Evelyn's drawn, hollow face.

Too soon, the blank stare returned to Evelyn's eyes. She slowly returned to pacing by the window, hugging her waist and watching the children on the playground as if watching a movie.

Through blurry tears, Gertie stared at the dent on the bed next to her and touched her cheek where her mother's hand had been. "I wish you could have stayed longer," she whispered into the empty space her mother had briefly visited.

After Gertie and Suzie left, Gertrude Anna sat quietly, watching Evelyn pace by the window. Then, just as suddenly as before, Evelyn shuffled to her bed and laid down. Gertrude Anna pulled an afghan over her friend, slowly lowered herself to sit next to her on the bed and held Evelyn's pale, cold hand between her own warm palms. "I'm so glad you've been my best friend all these years," she told Evelyn. "I love you."

Evelyn smiled. "I love you too," she said in a deep, rasping whisper, warbled by old age. "Thanks for reading Ted's letter, Gertie needed to know how much he loved her." Then she closed her eyes, "I'll be going home now."

Gertrude Anna reached for the alert button but stopped. She held Evelyn's limp, cold hand. Her dark fingers stroked Evelyn's pale arm and smoothed a gray wave from her forehead. She whispered, "God speed dear friend."

Evelyn's Memorial

Suzie helped Gertie arrange a memorial service at the Village Garden's chapel. Family members stood at the podium and told stories of Evelyn's kindness to others and her dedication to nursing. Tom made a joke about Evelyn's cooking and everyone laughed. *She would have liked that*, thought Gertie.

Evelyn's two sons, Robert and Teddy, were absent.

Suzie asked Tom, "Will you take Mom and the kids home and come back for me in about an hour? I'd like to sit alone in the chapel for a while. Oh and don't forget to walk Baxter. His leash is on the back of a chair in Mom's kitchen. Thanks, sweetie."

"Sure." Tom gave Suzie a quick kiss and herded the three children toward the parking lot. Gertie was sitting on a bench by the door. "Come on Gertie, I'll take you home. Suzie wants to be alone for a while."

Suzie sat in the chapel thinking of her Granny Evelyn, her mother and everything that had happened. She knew how she felt knowing she wasn't really Granddad's granddaughter. She could only guess at her mother's feelings. She worried that Uncle Teddy would bring a lawsuit and checked her purse to be sure Ted's letter was safely stowed.

When she stood to leave, she saw Gertrude Anna leaning on her walker, halfway up the aisle.

"I was just trying to decide whether or not to disturb you. Are you ready for a cup of tea?" asked Gertrude Anna.

"Sounds perfect."

"Would you mind bringing it to my room? A waiter will put it on a tray for you. I'm quite tired."

While Gertrude Anna lumbered back to her room, Suzie went to the café for mugs of tea. The waiter included two peanut butter cookies on the tray.

Gertrude Anna's room looked like Evelyn's, but more lived-in with lots of books, magazines, a laptop computer and sketches Gertrude Anna had done.

Gertrude Anna sat on a straight chair while Suzie sat on the bed holding the mug with both hands and her knees curled under her. "Your sketches are quite good," said Suzie, looking around the room. "I didn't know you were an artist?"

"Thanks, but I'm not really. All my life I wanted to learn to draw but never had the time. I've been going to the classes they offer here."

Suzie sipped her tea and nibbled on the cookie while gazing out the window. "Outliving your friends must be very difficult."

"Yes… it is… Evelyn and I were friends for over eighty years."

"But now you have Mom and me," Suzie smiled. "We'll visit often, I promise."

They sat in silence for a while, each remembering Evelyn in her own way. "Granny Evelyn came to live with us after Dad died in a fishing accident. I was sixteen, my littlest brother was only ten. Granny was always there for us but never in the way."

"She was so devastated when Ted died," said Gertrude Anna, "as if he was the rock that made her life possible. She needed the activity of her grandchildren to keep her occupied. I was still working at the hospital."

"I remember my Granddad Grantham very well." Suzie took another sip of tea with her eyes full of tears. "He adored Mom and she adored him. That's what counts. There are tons of family albums filled with pictures of the two of them. He loved her and all his grandkids. How can I help Mom understand that her value in the real world has nothing to do with her DNA test results?"

"Gertie is stronger than she thinks she is. She'll figure it out."

"I never asked, do you have a family."

Gertrude Anna sat in silence, looking out the window. Finally, she quietly admitted, "I have a daughter. I haven't seen her for fifty years. She sends birthday and Christmas cards. I know she's in Chicago, but she never puts a return address on the envelope. I don't know how she found out I moved in here.

"Just like Gertie, I was shocked when I saw my DNA results," said Gertrude Anna, sharing her own secrets. "My mother's ancestors were slaves in Georgia, but she was light-skinned. I didn't know for sure until the DNA test, but I always suspected her father was the wealthy, white homesteader. My biological father was a white businessman. I never met him and my mother never discussed it.

"We lived in a Black community on the eastside of Columbus, Ohio, where we were outcasts because they thought we were half white. During the Depression, we moved to Tipp City to work on Evelyn's parents' farm. Your Granny Evelyn and I were the same age and drawn together like sisters. My long life would have been totally different without Evelyn as my best friend."

"Why did your DNA results shock you?"

"The test revealed I'm 35% Italian, 20% Russian, 15% Dutch, 11% Native American, 10% Turkish and 9% Kenyan."

"Wow," whispered Suzie. "I don't know what to say... you've lived your life as an African American, but that's the least of your heritage."

"My daughter has white skin, deep blue-green eyes and smooth, silky brown hair. She graduated from Columbia with a law degree and landed a job in Chicago. She didn't invite me to her wedding, but she sent photos. I'm sure she didn't want her white husband's family to know she had a dark-skinned, woolly-haired mama. She never had children."

"I'm so sorry..." Suzie whispered. Trying to change the subject, she said, "I can imagine you and Granny Evelyn as three-year-olds, playing with the baby chicks and running through the orchard in bare feet with your pigtails bouncing."

Gertrude Anna faded into herself, remembering her daughter as a toddler. They sat quietly for a moment with the hum of the computer and the muffled traffic noise beyond the snow-covered lawn.

A knock on the door made them jump.

Suzie opened the door. "They said I'd find you here." Tom stepped back, compelled by the swirling energy. He knew he had interrupted an important moment. "Uh, I'm happy to wait in the car until you're ready," he said, taking another step back.

"It's okay, sweetie," said Suzie. "Come on in." She gave her husband a quick kiss.

Gertrude Anna smiled up at Tom from her straight-back chair. "We've been having a lovely chat." She looked tired and frail in the dim afternoon light. She reached up and Tom gave her hand a squeeze.

"I'm sure you're ready for some rest and alone time after this stressful day," said Suzie, bending to hug her new friend. "We'll come to see you tomorrow before we head back to Cincinnati."

Evelyn's memorial was over and Suzie and her family had gone home. Weary to the bone, Gertie felt a deep sense of grief but at the same time, released from the constant overwhelming stress of her mother's Alzheimer's. She gripped the banister to help hoist herself up the stairs to take a shower and go to bed, even though it was barely 5:00 p.m. She waited for the water to get as hot as she could stand as she pulled a shower cap over her frothy coiffure.

Before putting on her nightgown, she noticed her body in the long mirror. Her breasts, never large except when she was nursing her babies, were still perky for her age. She pulled off the shower cap and studied her old-lady hairdo. *I'm not old enough to wear my hair permed like this*, she thought. *I haven't been living in the real world since George died.* To her reflection, she said aloud, "It's time for a change."

The next day, she joined a fitness center designed for women like Gertie. Now that she wasn't visiting her mother at Village Garden, Gertie went to her gym every morning and took advantage of the nutrition classes they offered. In the afternoons, instead of watching her soaps, she took long walks. For the first time in her life, she read nutrition books and planned meals only for herself, ignoring George's ghost.

One day, after her workout, she came through the house and noticed it was as outdated as she was. She called an interior designer she knew from her Woman's Club, "I'm sick to death of my blue-flowered wallpaper and matching bedspread. Can you help me redecorate my bedroom?" They scheduled a meeting to look at samples. "And bring some ideas for the kitchen, it's time to replace the harvest gold appliances and that dreadful linoleum with the green and yellow tattersall pattern."

Her hairdresser, Joanne, had done Gertie's hair since before George died. "I love seeing you every week Joanne, but... can you straighten this perm? I want to grow it out, add some brown streaks and learn to do my own hair. It gets all sweaty every day when I work out."

Joanne raised her eyebrows, "Work out? What's got into you girl?"

Gertie gave her a bashful grin, "It's time for a change."

"Sure, I can straighten it, but we shouldn't add color until the perm grows out, your hair will look fried by the chemicals. If you're going to do your own hair, you'll need shampoo, conditioner and styling mousse," Joanne pointed to her retail supplies. "I don't sell round brushes or blow dryers, you'll find those at the drug store."

Gertie stopped at Rite Aid on the way home. She put a large and a smaller size round hairbrush in her basket along with a blow dryer and added a new lipstick in a tawny shade George never liked. Near the checkout counter, she stopped at a display of hats and tried on several, looking at herself in the little mirror. *This is perfect,* she thought. Above the bill, it said, *Life is Good.* She added the baseball cap to her basket.

Every day after her workout, Gertie went home to shower, wash her hair and practice with the round brush and blow dryer. On the days when her new do didn't turn out the way she wanted it to, Gertie wore her baseball cap for the rest of the day.

In the spring, Gertie added asparagus, thyme, oregano, dill and basil to her garden and replaced russets with sweet potatoes.

When Suzie and her family visited, they picked green beans from the garden and used the steamer Suzie gave Gertie for Christmas. She experimented with spices she had never tasted like cumin and coriander. "Now I realize, I've missed so much," Gertie laughed as she sniffed the saffron. "I don't bake much anymore, but I still need to have a little chocolate now and then," she told Suzie.

"Me too! I gave up sugar and gluten, but I could never give up chocolate," said Suzie. "One of my Keto cookbooks has the perfect recipe for gluten-free brownies." They gathered maple syrup, almond flour, chopped walnuts and 85% cacao at the health-food store and made a batch together.

"I'm going to visit Gertrude Anna this morning, wanna come along?" Suzie said one Saturday morning after helping her mom style her hair.

"Not yet, sweetie. I can't face Village Garden just yet. Maybe in a month or two."

When Gertie finally visited Gertrude Anna, her hair had grown into a bouncy, layered bob with streaks of brown and she was thirty pounds lighter. She'd traded her dowdy flowered dresses and sensible black pumps for narrow legged jeans, brightly colored sweaters and comfortable ballet flats.

Gertie's transformation did not surprise Gertrude Anna. "You look wonderful. How do you feel?" she asked, happy to see Suzie and Gertie.

"I didn't do this to look good, I did it to feel good and I do," said Gertie. "When my husband died and then my dad, I felt as old as Mom and I started to look even older, as if being old would ease the pain of losing George and keep the rest of my family safe."

"We all deal with grief in our own way," said Gertrude Anna. "Maybe your DNA results caused the shock you needed to live a happy life again. The letter confirmed Ted was your father no matter what DNA says."

"Yes, at first, I reacted to grief, but now I know, it was more than that. A few months ago, Suzie taught me to pay attention to labels at the grocery store. I never did that before. I always bought the brands George liked, even after—especially after—he died. A few days ago, I was standing in the grocery store, reading the labels on both mayonnaise and Miracle Whip. I started laughing. So much that people started looking at me. I doubled over, nearly hysterical. The store manager came out of his office and asked if I was okay. I told him I was more okay than I'd been in thirty years.

"I pulled myself together, bought the mayonnaise and sat in the car hugging the jar. I don't even like Miracle Whip. The laughter turned to tears. Once I married George, I never questioned the choices I made. I never questioned my life's intention. I never knew what I liked, never even considered what I *might* like if I had the opportunity to choose for *myself*.

"He never said a negative word about Mom's cooking or the hours she spent at her nursing job. We respected Mom for her dedication, but deep down, I thought he expected more from me and I was drawn to the challenge. His devotion to me inadvertently blocked any self-knowledge I might have developed. Don't get me wrong, I love being a mom and grandma." She flung her arm over Suzie's shoulder. "And I loved my dad. He wanted to be a good father—it was the '50s!

"I know now, he never considered an alternative for himself either. Dad joined the Navy because Granddad Grantham expected him to have a military career, but I think Dad loved music more than we ever knew."

A warm smile brightened Gertie's face. "When I was small, I sat outside the bathroom door listening to him sing in the shower.

His voice was amazing. I don't know why he stopped. When he died, Mom gave me his violin wrapped in an old blanket. She only heard him play it once, but his talent was incredible. Until then, I didn't know he'd ever played the violin."

"Do you still have it?" asked Suzie. "Emily's been wanting to take violin lessons."

"Sure, Suzie, you can have it. Take it home with you. You might want to buy a new case, it's pretty worn. Emily should learn on her Granddad's violin, even if she couldn't have inherited his talent.

"Dad was a perfectionist. I didn't try new things for fear of disappointing him, but yesterday I signed up for two classes at the YWCA. Introduction to Computers is designed for people like me who have avoided them until now. And I'm taking a beginning watercolor painting class twice a week. I don't care if my stuff is any good. I'm not talented like you are," she looked around the room at Gertrude Anna's drawings, "I just like to paint. The teacher said it's okay if it's just color therapy," Gertie laughed.

"Who are you and what have you done with my mom?" said Suzie with tears in her eyes.

Suzie had avoided telling her husband, Tom, about Gertie's DNA results. Now that her mother was doing so well, she decided it was time to discuss it. "Mom made me promise to keep her DNA results a secret, but it's just too weird. Granddad Grantham was not her real dad," she blurted as if she'd been holding it in too long.

"Wow! That must have shocked Gertie. Do you know who her biological father is?"

"Yes, he's a doctor named Richard Wurtzburg in Washington State. There's more. I had a long conversation with Gertrude Anna after Granny Evelyn's memorial. Gertrude Anna knew Richard Wurtzburg and was aware that he and Evelyn had a one-night fling when they worked at the same hospital in Dayton."

"That doesn't sound like Evelyn."

"But that's not all. I discovered at least ten random records, all in the early '70s, indicating Dr. Richard Wurtzburg as the father. He couldn't have gotten around that much when he was fifty years old!"

Tom's face twisted into a weird mask.

"What? You look like you swallowed a dead goldfish."

"Well. Um. This guy could have been a donor..."

"A sperm donor?"

"Why not?" Tom inhaled deeply.

"Mom couldn't be the product of sperm donation, Granny Evelyn admitted her tryst to Gertrude Anna and anyway, doctors weren't even doing artificial insemination in 1949."

"No, sperm donation wasn't available until much later, but the other records... from the '70s...," said Tom, stalling for time.

"You're scaring me, Tom. You still have that dead-fish-look on your face."

"Look, I've got to tell you right now. When I was a sophomore in college, before I met you, I needed money, so I made a little cash donating sperm.... They never asked for my name. I thought no one would ever know. I'd forgotten about it."

"So, our kids could have half-siblings running around somewhere?"

"'Fraid so."

"Geez Tom! We have to tell them before they're blindsided."

The Violin

"Let's start by learning the parts of the violin," began Mrs. Zorn, Emily's violin teacher. When she lifted the violin, she took a sharp breath and peered into the F-holes, adjusting her bifocals. "Where did you find this violin," she asked, her voice almost breathless.

Emily, Gertie's thirteen-year-old granddaughter, bubbled with information. "It belonged to my mom's Granddad Grantham, but she never heard him play it. My Great Granny Evelyn said he was really good. She gave the violin to my Grandma Gertie and she gave it to my mom."

"I'd like to talk with your mother after your lesson," said Mrs. Zorn. "Let's leave the violin in the case while we discuss the parts of the instrument." She handed Emily a drawing of a violin, with arrows pointing to the parts from the scroll to the chin rest and gave her another sheet with the arrows, but no names. Emily's assignment was to learn the parts and fill in the blanks without looking at the first sheet.

"You should probably sit down to hear this," said Mrs. Zorn when Suzie arrived.

Suzie looked at Emily, wondering what had happened.

Emily looked up at her mom and shrugged, also curious about Mrs. Zorn's weird behavior.

"I suspect this is a...," Mrs. Zorn paused with her palm lightly resting on the leather case. "It could be a real Stradivarius. There are a lot of knockoffs out there but if it *is* a Strad... Well, a Strad sold at auction a few years ago for," she paused again, "for over a million dollars. This could be worth even more, especially if it's been in the family for generations as Emily suggested. You might want to have it appraised and perhaps find something more appropriate for Emily to bring to her lessons."

Suzie and Emily gaped at Mrs. Zorn. Finally, Suzie uttered, "Thank you, Mrs. Zorn. We had no idea…."

A local appraiser confirmed that it could be a real Strad, but he wanted to send the violin to a New York appraiser for confirmation. "It could be worth a lot of money even if it's a fake," said the appraiser. "It's an extraordinary instrument."

Suzie didn't want to let it out of her sight, let alone send it to New York. She and Tom discussed what to do with the violin. "It doesn't seem right that I should keep it," said Suzie. "Regardless if it's real or not. It should belong to one of Granddad Grantham's true ancestors."

"So, if your Granddad Grantham's beneficiaries include your uncles, Robert and Teddy and the famous pianist Sergei, who do you think should have it?" asked Tom with a grin.

"When you put it that way, it's a no-brainer!" laughed Suzie. Then she became more serious, looking Tom in the eye. "Don't think I'm weird, but when I touch the violin, I can feel its… energy… as if it has a spirit of its own. I can hear its music."

"You're not weird," whispered Tom. "I feel it too."

Suzie drove to her mother's house with the (possibly) three-hundred-year-old violin buckled in the front seat and her thirteen-year-old daughter, Emily, buckled in the back seat with Baxter. She felt nervous with the instrument in the car, but she didn't want to tell her mom about the violin over the phone and she wouldn't let the instrument out of her sight.

Gertie hugged Suzie and Emily when they came through the door. "You brought the violin! Are you ready to show me what you've learned?" Gertie asked her granddaughter, Emily.

"Well, sort of," Emily grinned. Emily put the case on the table.

Suzie opened the clasp. "We want to show you something." She held the violin in the light from the window. "See those markings?"

"What are you showing me?" asked Gertie, peering into the f-holes, adjusting her reading glasses.

Suzie slowly lowered the violin back onto the faded velvet lining. "You know that Granddad Grantham's mother's ancestors were from Italy, right? Well, I did some genealogical research and found evidence suggesting that Grandma Alice was a descendant of the great violin maker. Mom, this violin is probably a Stradivarius. It could be worth over a million dollars. Even if it's a fake it could be valuable."

Gertie plopped down onto a kitchen chair and put her hand on her chest, "Oh, my," she breathed. "Now that you mention it…, I found Granddad and Grandma's marriage license when they died, working on my DAR genealogy, I wanted to know when they were married."

"I remember you telling me they were married really young, in 1907. Do you remember Grandma Alice's maiden name?"

"Alice Anita Stradivari, but I never dreamed…." She took a deep breath. "What should we do with the violin?"

"I've been doing some research. There are people in New York we could contact if you want to sell it, but I think I have a better idea. It's a long story, I need a cup of coffee, you want some?"

"That would be nice. Emily, would you like some orange juice?" said Gertie.

"Thanks Grandma Gertie."

They settled around the kitchen table and Suzie began her story. "Turns out, our family is even more convoluted than we imagined," she paused. "Ted Grantham and his high school sweetheart…, Audrey Dupré…, had a baby they gave up for adoption."

For the second time in less than an hour, Gertie put her hand on her chest and breathed, "Oh my."

"Have you ever heard of the famous pianist, Sergei?"

"On the radio?"

Suzie nodded. "Well, Sergei is Granddad Grantham's biological son, born on December 9, 1938, but David and Adina Sapozhnikov, his adoptive parents, signed the birth certificate. He never knew he was adopted until he did his DNA test."

"How do you know so much about Sergei," Gertie asked.

"I found his email address on Ancestry.com and sent him a message. He called me from Paris. We had a long, lovely chat. It was just before Granny Evelyn died and I didn't think there was any reason to upset you even more."

"Thank you for that," Gertie said, tucking her salt and pepper hair behind her ears with both hands. "My nerves couldn't have taken any more DNA results! So, I have a stepbrother that isn't actually my stepbrother because Ted Grantham isn't my biological father, very confusing." Then she looked over at Emily, "Oh dear, should we be discussing all this…"

"I've heard the story before, Grandma. I think it's so exciting. My history teacher gave me an A+ on the essay I wrote about our family history," chirped Emily.

"I need more coffee," Gertie jumped up and turned her back to them as she headed for the coffeepot. "Are you hungry? Should I make scrambled eggs?" She almost fell back into her old habit of cooking during stressful situations.

"Mom, are you okay?"

"Oh, I'm fine." Gertie turned back toward them. "Just another shock in the DNA saga, but… well… I realize there's no hope of keeping it all secret. Emily, you want more juice?"

"No thanks Grandma."

"What do you think we should do with the violin?" asked Gertie, as she sat down with a fresh cup of coffee.

"The rightful heirs are Uncle Teddy, Uncle Robert and Sergei," said Suzie.

"Well then, that makes it clear!" laughed Gertie. "If we can be sure Sergei is who he says he is, you should offer it to him, but what will Teddy do?"

"Granny Evelyn gave the violin to you and you gave it to me. Even if he finds out, he can't do anything. If I give it to one of Granddad's rightful heirs…, there's still nothing he can do. Anyway, nobody knows we have it except for Emily, Tom, you and me and the violin teacher who brought it to our attention. We haven't even told the boys. I asked Mrs. Zorn not to tell a soul. She understood that it's pretty scary having a million-dollar violin just lying around."

Suzie paused as a sickened expression spread across her face and she looked at her daughter. "Emily, did you mention the violin in your family history essay?"

"Well, I might have… but I got an A+."

Suzie put her face in her hands and shook her head, "I'll make reservations for a trip to Paris. The sooner I give this violin to Sergei, the better."

Sergei's DNA

More interested in his musical background than his Jewish heritage or Russian origins, Sergei Sapozhnikov sent in his DNA sample. When his results came back, he discovered, without a doubt, that he was the son of Audrey Dupré. It suggested that his father was Ted Grantham.

As a boy, learning that his parents had deceived him would have made him angry and disillusioned. Now, nearly eighty, he was shocked and surprised, but in no way disappointed. He loved his parents and he knew they loved him. Now he questioned whether his musical talent had come from his biological parents genetically or environmentally from the parents he knew and loved.

Sergei found an obituary for Ted Grantham who had died at sixty-three in Columbus, Ohio. The family had traced their heritage back to England before the Revolutionary War. The report listed military majors, captains and privates but couldn't tell him if the Granthams had any musical interest or ability. He also noticed that, for over 100 years, there were no female family members except for the women the Grantham men married.

Sergei was thrilled to discover that Ted Grantham's mother, Alice, was a direct descendant of the famous Italian luthier and craftsman, Antonio Stradivari.

He turned to his biological mother's lineage, mostly Italian. The name Audrey Dupré rang a bell in his memory… at first, he couldn't place it. Then he remembered his summer in Paris in 1953. Sergei had studied piano with his friend Bernard Berkowitz's landlord, Madame Dupré. He didn't know her first name, but he remembered the closeness that developed between them during the summer he studied with her.

While in Paris for a performance at the Palais Garnier in the summer of 2018, Sergei felt powerfully drawn to his former teacher's address. Sixty-five years had passed since he studied with Madame Dupré. If still alive, she would be nearly one hundred years old. It was extremely unlikely that she still lived in the same building, but he couldn't ignore the magnetic attraction.

The building where she had lived and taught in 1953 stood as elegant in 2018 as it was when Napoleon hired the architect Haussmann to renovate Paris. The stone building had tall windows anchored by Art Déco ironwork balconies, each holding vivid red geraniums, glowing yellow petunias and bright purple verbenas.

"Do you know anything about Madame Dupré?" he asked the doorman.

The doorman replied in heavily accented English, "Who should I say is calling?"

"Oh, the family won't know me. Madame Dupré was my teacher in 1953 and I was wondering if…"

"Your name please, sir?" interrupted the doorman, peeved with the English-speaking visitor.

"Sergei Sapozhnikov."

"Wait here, please," he said, wagging his hand toward the modern and uncomfortable-looking rose, turquoise and chrome lobby furniture.

A few minutes later, a beautiful woman floated down the marble stairs and into the lobby. She wore a dress with a fitted white bodice and black and white polka dot circle skirt, remarkably similar to fashions in 1953. Her pale blond hair twisted at the nape of her long neck into a thick chignon. Her thick white eyelashes and aquamarine eyes gave her an otherworldly aura. She carried herself like a runway model in the most elite Paris fashion house, or, he thought, like an operatic diva. He didn't notice she was only five feet tall until she stood next to him.

"*Êtes-vous Monsieur* Sapozhnikov?" She pronounced Sapozhnikov like a Russian speaker, which he rarely heard.

"*Oui.*"

"*Suivez-moi, s'il vous plaît.*"

Following her to the third-floor apartment caused a deeply spiritual feeling of déjà vu. His heart beat a little faster and he felt as if he floated outside of his body, as if time swept him back sixty-five years.

He remembered, as a fifteen-year-old boy, climbing the marble stairs, holding on to the circling curve of Art Déco railing all the way to the top then looking down into what seemed like the spiraling path of a nautilus shell.

The graceful young woman opened the door to apartment 3A and gestured toward an old woman. Silver bangs hid her eyebrows and a silver bun coiled on the back of her head. Madame Dupré sat before a polished grand piano in an ebony swivel chair, custom-made to support her back while she played. An old red pashmina draped over her slightly stooped shoulders.

The high ceilings with wide crown molding created a feeling of spaciousness in the room. The walls were papered in creamy sage. Hunter green draperies, swagged with tasseled, gold velvet ropes, flanked three tall windows while the sun cast sunny shadows. Pots of red germaniums bloomed profusely on the tiny balconies. Between two white painted doors, a pair of wingback chairs gathered around a mahogany cocktail table. Near one window, looking out of place, stood an elegant velocipede rocking horse.

"*Madame, je suis heureuse de présenter Monsieur Sapozhnikov*," said the young woman, introducing Sergei.

The old woman swiveled toward them, then stood slowly, however, more quickly than her ninety-six years might have predicted. She greeted him with a shaky voice and thin, boney, cold but firm handshake. "Your level of achievement has inspired many of my students," she said. "It's good to see you again, after all these years."

"*Merci beaucoup*, Madame," he said as he bent into his signature bow, nearly touching his forehead to his knees. The deep salutation became his trademark when he was only three. As he stood up, he pushed a thick clump of longish gray hair back into place, also part of his signature. "I was only fifteen then. It's wonderful to see you again." He kissed her parchment-covered hand. "Thank you for all you did for me that summer."

"Yes, I remember, you were young and so was I," she laughed. Audrey grasped his forearm and, as if he had helped her thousands of times, he gently lowered her back to the swivel chair by the piano.

"Please, sit here," she said, motioning to a mahogany chair upholstered in black leather that matched the dining chairs on the other side of the room. Her olive-brown eyes were as bright as ever, her smile still enchanting. "I have followed your career. What brings you here? I can see something is troubling you."

"Well, you see... earlier this year..., I learned, through DNA testing, that I was adopted... and..."

"Where, what month?" she interrupted, her voice stronger and deeper than before.

"My birthday is December 9, 1938."

As he went on, her frail shoulders trembled beneath her red pashmina.

"I grew up in Manhattan thinking that David and Adina Sapozhnikov were my biological parents. I saw photos they took on the day I was born. My birth certificate has their signatures, but..."

He watched Audrey's expression change as she intensely studied his face and her spirit morphed from one emotion to the next in quick succession, disbelief, sorrow, joy, liberation.

"Do you still have *The Tale of Peter Rabbit* signed by Beatrix Potter?" she asked, her voice quivery and thin.

He thought for a moment. "Why yes, my mother read it to me often, but she kept it in perfect condition. I knew it was special to her. When I was older, I realized that it's a first edition, quite valuable. It's displayed on the bookshelf of my study in New York... Why do you ask?"

"The book was a Christmas gift to my mother, Esther, your grandmother, when she was a toddler. We wanted you to have it."

The room fell silent. Even the traffic noise beyond the balcony seemed muffled. Sergei sat, wide-eyed, fighting the sting in his eyes and the flutter of his heart.

"You were born at the Plaza Hotel, suite 600, on my sixteenth birthday," she continued. "Three days later, my mother and I sailed to Paris and I enrolled in a school for girls to study music.... I never knew if I gave birth to a son or daughter. The midwife wouldn't let me...," her voice evaporated.

"I never dreamed I would find you," he said. "And you were my teacher—this is the same room where I studied so long ago." He gazed out the window at the glowing red geraniums, fighting tears.

"I'm fortunate to own the building. My father bought it for a song during the Depression. While German officers occupied it during the war, my cousin Aimée and I escaped to Beaune. When we returned after liberation, the building was empty except for piles of trash and two musical instruments, Geneviève's harp that stood in Bernard's apartment and my piano, unharmed."

Her pale, blue-veined hand lightly stroked the music rack as if the piano were a cherished toddler.

Sergei looked at her, his ninety-six-year-old birth mother. He didn't know where to begin.

"Shall we start with a cup of tea?" she asked.

"Yes, please."

Simone appeared carrying a silver tray with a small plate of petits fours and an exquisite French porcelain tea service that she placed on the little table between Sergei and Audrey. Twenty-four-karat gold created a wide band on each piece. Hand-painted flower and fruit still lifes circled the teacups and the center of each plate. Simone poured Sergei and Audrey each a cup of tea, then left the room.

"The porcelain is exquisite," he said, holding his cup with both hands.

"The tea service has been in my family since the early 18th century."

"And the Germans didn't destroy it for the gold?"

"No, we left it in Ohio during the war. I was born there. My mother was American. Maman was teaching French at Ohio State when I told her I was expecting. To avoid disgrace, as she perceived it, we left for New York forty-eight hours later. Fortunately, we stored the tea set with our belongings. I remember it so well, displayed on the étagère next to the piano. It should be used rather than displayed. My father would like that."

"Tell me about *my* father," he said. "Did he like music?"

Audrey's face gathered a distant gaze as she remembered her school days. "When Ted Grantham played his violin, he brought grown-ups to tears. He walked me home from school almost every day and we practiced our music together, even in elementary school. He told me once he preferred the violin over the piano because he could stand and walk around while he practiced. His flexible fingers were perfect for playing the violin. He could spread his pinkie perpendicular to his ring finger."

"Like this?" Sergei lifted his hands and stretched his fingers until his little finger was at a 90° angle. "And this?" He put his hand on the table next to him and lifted his pinky to touch his thumb over the back of his hand. "I thought it was some sort of weird deformity, I've never shown anybody."

Audrey laughed, "Yes, I understand. Only his mother and I knew of his, as you say, deformity. He got bullied enough without the other boys knowing about his flexible fingers."

"Where did he study music?"

"His mother taught him to play the piano and the violin. With her support but against his father's wishes, he joined the high school orchestra instead of playing sports. He could have been a professional classical musician, maybe even a soloist. He was that good. Most graduates enlisted during those years, but Ted had no choice even without the war. His father didn't recognize his musical talents or if he did, he didn't want music to be central in Ted's life.

"Ted joined the Navy about the same time I left Ohio. He wanted to be a pilot to prove to his father he wasn't a sissy just because he loved music. I know he survived the war because I saw him in Columbus coming out of his parents' house, with his wife and child, I assume. He was limping a little. He didn't see me. I sat in a taxi on my way back to Paris after sorting through the storage unit where this tea set was stored. I wish he could have shared his talent with the world."

"Were the two of you in love?" asked Sergei.

"We loved each other even as children. I remember the first time I heard him play Mendelssohn's *Violin Concerto*." Audrey's eyes closed as if she listened to the sweet, introspective music, then a chuckle came from deep inside her. "He was nine. I was six. I couldn't believe that anyone could create such a beautiful sound. We were neighbors, best friends and shared a love of music all through school.

"When I announced my pregnancy, my mortified mother believed that a baby would ruin our lives and that adoption was best for the baby as well. Ted and I were so young...." her trembling voice faded, "Do you have a family of your own?"

"Music has been my only muse... I never married. My parents were Jewish, but I never saw the inside of a synagogue until I played a solo concert at Temple Emanu-El in New York when I was ten. Other than preparation for my bar mitzvah, I had no training. I grew up mostly oblivious to my religion. Mother was a socialite with an amazing singing voice and Father, I guess you'd call him a business tycoon. He was brilliant when it came to buying and selling companies and making money. I grew up in a New York penthouse on Park Avenue. When I showed a talent for music, they gave me every opportunity to flourish."

"Did they force you to practice?"

"No more than they forced me to breathe," he laughed. She gave a knowing nod.

"They didn't force me to play sports either. I was ten or so when they enrolled me in a weekend program at Julliard, but only because I wanted to. I loved performing; I still do. They've been gone for over thirty years now... Did you marry and have a family?"

Her silver head wobbled. "No, I was almost twenty-two when I returned to Paris after the war. I could have returned to America. I had an American passport, but Paris felt like home to me. I had no interest in becoming a wife. I focused my life on teaching piano and voice to children who wouldn't have had the opportunity otherwise.

"Simone is one of my students. As a newborn, someone abandoned Simone on the steps of a convent. The nuns recognized her musical talent and brought her to me. I officially adopted her when she was thirteen years old and she came to live with me. I had the opportunity to be a grandmother without being a mother," she smiled. "She sings for the Paris Opera Company. If you like, I'll ask her to perform for us—later."

"I would like that," he said, then returned to the subject at the top of his mind. "My DNA report said I'm over seventy-five percent Italian but if you're French and Grantham was English how can that be possible?"

"My mother's parents emigrated from Italy before Maman was born. I remember them, Luigi and Gianna Mancini. They died when I was about ten.

"My Grandfather Dupré immigrated to France from Italy in 1889. He predicted Italian banks would fail because of the tariff wars with France. He fled the country with his family and their assets and changed their name to the more French-sounding, Dupré."

"So, your heritage is Italian, not French. Do you know your father's original Italian name?"

"No, Papa's father never told him." She thought for a moment, "I wish I knew the origin of Ted Grantham's musical talent."

"My DNA report showed that his mother was Italian and a descendant of Stradivari."

"Well then, that explains where Ted inherited his talent," she laughed. "It's so sad Ted's father didn't support his genius."

They sat quietly, listening to traffic noise and considering the magnitude of their ancestral discoveries.

A smile spread across Audrey's wrinkled face. "When the war ended, my cousin Aimée and I left Beaune with four bottles of fine Burgundy. We drank from the bottle of the first one while we were on the train on our way back to Paris." She laughed, remembering the rocking train and the precious red wine dribbling down her chin. "We behaved like kids…. I opened the second bottle when my parents' belongings returned from Ohio." Audrey waved her thin, crepey arm. "The remaining two bottles must be worth thousands of Euros by now. I'm saving the last bottle for my one-hundredth birthday. Today is a fine day to open the third bottle."

"I would be honored… I'm surprised it wasn't confiscated."

"The vintners all over France cleverly protected their fine wine inventory. Aimée and I helped build a brick wall and she caught spiders to cover the old bricks with cobwebs and dust. I was too squeamish to catch spiders, but I helped in other ways. The Nazis confiscated the dairy cows and chickens and all the food they could find, but never found the cellar of fine wine. I'd be dead had they discovered the secret stockpile hidden below the hotel."

Simone entered with a tray holding the dusty bottle of Musigny, Bouchard Père & Fils 1937, two Waterford, balloon wine glasses, a sommelier's knife and a clean cloth.

"Will you do the honors?" Audrey asked Sergei. "And Simone, you must join us."

While Simone fetched another wine glass, Sergei removed the foil, very carefully removed the cork and gently wiped the top of the bottle with the soft cloth before and slowly pouring a generous taste into Audrey's glass. She held it by the foot and swirled with her nose close to the rim. She noticed the beautiful dark reddish purple reflected in the crystal facets. She tasted and exclaimed, "Exquisite, even better than I remember. It has the texture of fine velvet and the nose is rich and harmonious."

When Simone returned, Sergei tenderly tipped wine into the three crystal glasses.

"To my son."

"To my mother."

The three crystal glasses gently chimed. They savored in silence. Audrey and Sergei stared into each other's eyes as if they could mitigate the years of separation. Deep lines in Audrey's aged face reflected a long life of kindness and generosity, but her face also revealed shadows of sorrow and grief.

Finally, Audrey's face revealed her deep joy. Tears brimmed and trickled down her wrinkled cheeks, blushed by the wine. Her deep, elderly voice trembled with emotion and age. "When you studied with me in the summer of '53, I felt strangely close to you, but I had put memories of your birth and the war's delirium out of my mind and focused on teaching and playing piano for the opera.

I never suspected a Jewish boy from New York City could be my biological child. Now I realize how much you look like Ted....” She reached for him with thin bluish arms. Her old red pashmina fell onto the spindle-back swivel-chair. Sergei bent to embrace her fragile frame. They held each other for a long time.

“Mozart?” Audrey whispered on his shoulder.

“Perfect.” He arranged the piano bench next to her.

Simone watched their blue veined, age-spotted hands dance over the ivory keys. She closed her eyes and thought, *No one hearing their music would guess Audrey is ninety-six, or that her son is eighty.*

An orphan herself, Simone felt their powerful energy. Her eyes filled with tears and her heart ached. As they played, she cast her eyes to the floor, saying a silent prayer for the nuns who brought her to Madame Dupré. Then she stood, walked across the room and opened the tall windows, allowing the music to float to the fringes of Paris.

“Sergei,” said Simone when they finished, “why don’t you move in with us? The apartment between Auntie’s and mine is vacant.”

“What a splendid idea,” said Audrey. “Even if you’re not here full time... It’s yours if you want it.”

“I love that idea! Show me my new home,” he laughed, swallowing the last drops of red wine in his glass.

They walked next door and Simone unlocked the door to 3B.

He walked around the space, admiring the same tall windows and stepped onto the Art Déco balcony where the previous tenant had left pots of bright red germaniums. “I don’t need to return to New York right away. I’ll buy the furniture I need and have my apartment manager ship some of my things.” He gently hugged Audrey and Simone. “Now we are a family.”

Suzie Meets Sergei

By the time Suzie and her family left Cincinnati for Paris, Suzie had used Skype to video conference with Sergei several times, discussing the violin and the trip she planned.

At the airport check-in counter in Dayton, the agent remarked, "I'm sorry ma'am, you have too many carry-on bags, you'll need to check one."

"We're only staying a few days. We don't want to wait at the baggage carousel and we don't want to take the chance of losing luggage like the last trip we took." Her voice was kind but firm.

Holding the violin case, wrapped in a blanket like a baby, she leaned in and whispered, "This violin belonged to my… well, it's valuable. Can it have its own seat?"

"Last minute tickets are…" The agent studied his monitor.

Suzie listened to the clacking of the computer keys. He adjusted his glasses. "Oh honey, the only available seats on this flight are in first class. How 'bout you buy a first-class ticket and I'll give you an upgrade on your coach seat so you and the violin can be together?"

"That would be great!" She fumbled in her crossbody bag for her wallet and pushed her credit card toward the agent.

Tom whispered to Suzie while the keys clacked. "Aren't you being a little extreme? We can check my bag. No big deal if it gets lost."

"Then we'll need to wait at baggage claim and waste the time we have with Sergei. I told him we weren't checking any bags; he'll be waiting for us."

"Okay sweetie, it's your violin."

While affectionately squeezing Tom's arm, Suzie looked at the agent, "I'm sorry to cause so much trouble."

"No trouble at all," the agent said as he pushed their boarding passes over the counter. "You and your family have a pleasant flight." Then, with a twinkle in his eyes, he lowered his voice, "Snd have a free glass of first-class champagne for me! *Au revoir.*" He wiggled his hand toward the gate.

"How much did that cost us?" asked Tom.

"Never mind, it's worth it," she kissed his cheek.

When the TSA agent at airport security asked Suzie to put the violin through the x-ray tunnel, she nearly fainted. She whispered to her husband, "Tom, you go first so you'll be there when it comes out the other side. Don't let it out of your sight."

They disembarked at Charles de Gaulle Airport in Paris. Tom and the kids carried their bags while Suzie gripped the violin like a baby with both arms.

They found Sergei waiting in the terminal, holding a neatly printed sign that read SUZIE.

"It is wonderful to meet you in person, Skype just isn't the same. I hope you had a pleasant flight," he said as he shook her hand.

"*I* sure did," she laughed. "The violin and I both had first class seats." She introduced Sergei to her family.

Emily said, "Nice to meet you, Mr. Sapnovz, Mr. Sapnz…"

"Please, call me Sergei."

"Nice to meet you Mr. Sergei."

They traveled through the streets of Paris admiring the beautiful architecture. When the town car pulled up to the curb, but before the doorman was even close, they all jumped out and stared up at the building in awe.

Sergei led them up the winding marble stairs to the AirB&B suite on the second floor. The doorman managed their luggage, but Suzie never eased her grip on the violin.

Once inside the suite, Suzie pushed the blanket-wrapped violin case toward Sergei. "Before we do anything else, we want to give you the violin."

"This is amazingly generous. I don't know what to say. *Merci* is so inadequate. It seems strange that your grandfather is my biological father, even if it turned out that he wasn't really your biological grandfather. It's confusing," he looked at the violin case. "And remarkably, his mother was, that I am, a descendant of Antonio Stradivari."

"As I told you on the phone, we feel like the violin really doesn't belong to us. It should be in the hands of someone with music flowing through their veins. You can do as you wish with it, sell it, give it to a museum, or play it. The violin is yours now."

He clutched the violin to his chest and bowed his deep signature bow. "Well…," he said, standing up straight, wiping a tear, clearing his throat. "Please, I'd like for you to be my guests for dinner tonight at my favorite restaurant. A town car will arrive in an hour, if that is agreeable?"

"That will work for us, I just want to be sure we get to meet Madame Dupré sometime while we're in Paris."

"Audrey retires quite early these days. She is ninety-seven and usually at her best in the morning. Would tomorrow morning at 8:00 be too early? You could join us for croissants and coffee and meet Simone, her adopted daughter, as well."

"That will be lovely," said Suzie. "Thank you."

"Perfect." He looked at his watch. "I'll meet you in the lobby in and hour. *Au revoir jusque-là.*"

Crisp white linens covered round tables surrounded by comfortable-looking French provincial chairs while French doors opened to the courtyard, allowing the rosy, early evening light to fill the room. "It smells heavenly!" said Suzie.

As they took their seats, Sergei said, "The chef and owner, he has put together a special menu for us, I know you will enjoy the cuisine." He glanced at the teenagers with a hopeful look in his eyes.

Suzie's oldest son, nearly eighteen, said, "Don't worry, Mr. Sergei, we didn't grow up on hamburgers and fries like some kids back home. I never had fries until I started first grade. A friend's mom took me to lunch at McDonald's. Anyway, since she booked the tickets, Mom's been trying French recipes," he laughed. "I'm looking forward to the real thing!"

The server poured champagne for everyone. Emily and the boys looked at their parents with questioning eyes.

"Okay but after this, it's water," said Tom, lifting his glass for a toast. Emily took a sip, made a face and passed the glass to her father. The boys wanted more.

In the center of the elegantly set table, leaning against the diminutive, yellow flower arrangement, they found the menu printed on a small card.

Sergei asked, "Do you want me to explain each course?"

"I'd rather not know." Fifteen-year-old Emily spoke up first. "Then after we've finished you can tell us. It'll be more fun if we guess."

Each dish was perfectly paired with a different wine selected by the chef. "If we're going to have a different wine with each course, better pour ours short. I'd like to remember the end of the dinner," laughed Tom. "We don't drink very often."

Emily contemplated the first beautiful entrée placed in front of her. A golden-brown crust shaped like a fancy muffin or biscuit, but when she pressed her fork into the flaky outside, steam escaped, revealing finely ground meat and vegetables. She scooped a small taste, "This is amazing!" Emily breathed and everyone nodded with their mouths full. "I don't know what this is. I've never tasted anything like it, that's for sure, but I love it."

"What do you suppose it is?" asked Sergei with a patient smile.

"If it's something weird, please, don't tell me. I know it's meat, vegetables and there is vinegar in there."

"Close enough," laughed Sergei, lifting his wineglass, keeping the ingredients to himself: deer, wild boar, pork, poultry liver and wild mushrooms along with vinegar, herbs, shallots, garlic and cognac.

When the waiter brought the next course, it looked like hard-boiled brown eggs in silver egg cups, but on closer inspection, they found each fragile eggshell with a zigzagged edge, held flakes of king crab meat in lemon/ginger mayonnaise, garnished with a tiny green leaf. Suzie took a bite using the little fork. She leaned back in her chair and closed her eyes to savor the flavors. "I've never seen food so elegantly presented or tasted anything this delicious. It's crab with lemon and ginger, but how did they do this?"

"I'm sure it is the chef's secret! This is quite a famous dish."

Nearly four hours later, as they finished layers of flaky puff pastry filled with Bourbon and vanilla custard, topped with buttery caramel, the chef came to the table, dressed in his remarkably white chef's coat. Suzie and her family overflowed with praise.

"I am so pleased you enjoyed your dinner," he said with his heavy, French accent and a small bow. "It is our pleasure to serve you." He stood behind Sergei, resting his palms on his shoulders, "Sergei has been a special guest here for many years. We are happy he is living in Paris now."

As they left, the chef handed Suzie the menu card. "A souvenir of your dinner with us, I hope you will return," he said as he bowed.

Pâté en croûte de gibier à plumes
et légumes au vinaigre

Œuf « King Crab »,
mayo au gingembre-citron

Soupe d'artichaut, escalope de foie gras poêlée,
émulsion à la truffe noire

Noix de coquilles Saint-Jacques,
salsifis rôtis et bigorneaux en persillade

Filet de volaille jaune des Landes,
croustillant de cuisse au foie gras
et tagliatelles de céleri

Notre millefeuille à la vanille Bourbon,
caramel au beurre demi-sel

In the car on the way back to the suite, Suzie studied the menu card. "I want to remember each dish."

"So, tell me, which was your favorite?" asked Sergei.

"That crusty pie-like thing with the meat and vegetables inside," said Emily.

"The artichoke soup," said Tom. "I've never tasted anything like that."

The boys agreed with their sister. "Or maybe dessert was my favorite," laughed the oldest.

"And you, Madame? What did you like best?"

"The crab wins for flavor and for presentation—that was beyond amazing!" Suzie said, pointing at the menu card.

She asked Sergei, "How about you Sergei, what was your favorite."

"I loved it all very much but especially the perfectly paired wines!" he laughed a little louder than normal with slightly flushed cheeks. Clearly, he had enjoyed the wine.

Suzie and her family joined Sergei, Simone and Audrey for breakfast in Audrey's apartment. The housekeeper prepared omelets filled with mushrooms and drizzled with Mornay sauce, along with warm, buttery croissants, cold juice and *café au lait.*

"This is very generous of you, Miss Dupré," said Suzie as they took their seats around the table.

"It is wonderful to meet Ted's family after all these years. I'm delighted you could come."

Sergei said, "I'm hoping you can tell us a little about your Granddad's life?"

"We loved him dearly. He was a kind and loving man, generous but frugal. He drove the same car for as long as I can remember and I don't think he and Granny Evelyn ever bought new furniture or went on any trips, but I know he helped Mom financially when Dad died. Granddad loved to babysit for my brothers and me when we were little and made us spaghetti and meatballs, but he always called it *ska-betty,* Mom's word when she was little. We played all kinds of board games like Monopoly or Clue and he let us win. Sometimes he let us stay up late to watch old movies and he made popcorn. We knew he loved us."

"Did he sing or play his violin?" asked Sergei.

"The only time I remember hearing him sing was at Christmas time. He played the piano and we all sang carols, but I never saw his violin until Emily was thinking about taking lessons. Mom pulled it out of the closet and gave it to me."

"Did he stay in the military?" asked Sergei.

"No, Granddad Grantham was a Navy Flying Ace, but his plane was shot down during the Battle for Okinawa. Both of his legs were broken and a head injury affected his vision. He couldn't fly any more. He earned a Ph.D. in Aeronautical Engineering—that's about all I know about his career, except that I think he became CEO of the company he worked for."

"Emily," said Audrey, changing the subject away from war and back to music, "are you learning to play the violin?"

"I wanted to learn but I wish I had Great Granddad's talent. I think I like the piano better."

"Well either way, keep practicing, you need to have music in your life." Audrey turned toward Suzie. "Did he teach you to play the piano?"

"No, Mom said he tried to teach her to play but she was afraid she wouldn't be good enough and never learned. I was more interested in books."

"So sad," whispered Audrey, shaking her head. "So, so sad."

"What was he like as a little boy?" Suzie asked Audrey.

Audrey smiled and sipped her coffee. "Sweet. Kind. Teachers loved him. In elementary school the other boys were mean to him, but he didn't let that bother him. I saw him angry only once. An older boy, much bigger than Ted, tried to grab his violin. That boy had a bloody nose before he knew what happened. The boys never bothered Ted after that."

"Did you know my Great Grandparents?" asked Suzie.

"Ah, yes, Alice and Theodore Grantham III," Audrey answered. "I met Theodore only a few times. He considered music a waste of time. We practiced at their house only when the Admiral was out to sea. I remember listening to Mrs. Grantham's bell-like voice and when she played the violin, tears came to my eyes even when I was nine years old. She taught Ted everything he knew about music. I think she gave up her job teaching music when she married Theodore before WWI. They had five boys, the oldest was almost twenty years older than Ted if I remember right. What did you think of your uncles?"

"I never met my great uncles," said Suzie. "Granddad was the only brother who survived WWII. Mom said Great Granddad

Grantham was never the same after he lost his other sons. When I knew him, he worked in the garden, watched football games and never said much. They both died on the same day when I was seventeen. They were married for eighty years."

"Delicious breakfast," said Tom, pulling the conversation away from death and the war. "Thank you. After dinner last night, I didn't think I'd ever be hungry again, but I was wrong!"

The boys and Emily nodded in agreement.

Suzie looked at Sergei. "I wonder, do you play the violin?"

"When I studied at Julliard, I learned to play a lot of instruments, oboe was my worst. I loved the violin and my parents bought me one, but I was born to play piano."

"Before we leave, would you mind playing something on Granddad's violin? I've never heard anyone play it."

"Sure, seems the least I can do considering your generosity. I'll be right back."

He went to his apartment next door and returned with the violin, a music stand and sheet music. "I practiced a little after you gave it to me yesterday. I couldn't resist, as if it called to me. Then when I put it on my shoulder, the violin seemed to play of its own volition, breathtaking."

When Sergei drew the bow over the strings, Mendelssohn's *Violin Concerto* bathed the room with ineffable warmth and passion.

Audrey closed her eyes as Sergei played, her face tranquil with intense satisfaction as she followed the music to the mystical realm only music could conjure.

When Sergei finished, silence fell like stardust.

Finally, Suzie whispered, her voice nearly inaudible, "That was lovely."

Tom and the children silently nodded their appreciation, as if the sound of their voices would disturb the musical mist still floating around them.

Audrey broke the spell, "Sergei, why did you select Mendelssohn?" Her voice sounded horse and wavered more than before, as if she floated far away.

"It's the only sheet music I have for violin," he shrugged.

"The piece is lovely and you play far better than you led us to believe. Thank you, Sergei." Her voice evaporated like fog at sunrise.

As Sergei lowered the ancient violin into its case, Audrey struggled to lift herself from her spindle-back chair. Tom rushed to give her a hand, but ninety-seven-year-old Audrey refused his help. "Thank you but I am quite capable of standing on my own."

Tom stepped back and looked at Simone, who smiled and shrugged.

Sergei talked to Emily about playing the piano, while her brothers huddled around beautiful, blond and petite Simone and Tom and Suzie gazed out the window at the Eiffel Tower.

While everyone was occupied, Audrey quietly shuffled toward the violin, the red pashmina draped over her hunched shoulders. She opened the leather case and rested her hand on the warm wood. The commotion in the room faded from her awareness. Seventeen-year-old Ted stood by her piano playing "Falling in Love with Love" as she sat on the bench singing the lyrics. *I weave with brightly colored strings, To keep my mind off other things.....* That was the day Sergei was conceived.

It seems like yesterday, she thought, *how could eighty years have passed?* She closed and latched the lid and shuffled back to her spindle-back chair.

Suzie sat down on the bench next to her and cradled Audrey's cold, boney hands in both of hers. "I'm so grateful we could spend this time with you. We loved Granddad Grantham very much. It's heartwarming to know that you loved him too."

A year later, Suzie drove to the post office to sign for a registered letter.

The letter waited on the kitchen table while she took Baxter for a walk, gave him a scoop of kibble, emptied the dishwasher, wiped the counter and made herself a cup of tea. She stood by the table sorting the mail, putting the junk mail in the recycle bin. She took the bills to her home office.

Finally, she sat down, sipped her mint tea and opened the letter from Paris.

Dear Suzie and family,

I am sitting here fondly remembering the lovely meal we shared a year ago. I have returned to the restaurant many times, but no visit can surpass our evening together.

When I had the violin appraised, markings proved where it originated. We are certain that it never left the possession of a Stradivari family member. And even more remarkable, Stradivari also made the leather case. It is difficult to fathom how it survived all these years in such good condition!

I arranged for the Strad to go to an Italian museum. It will be cherished, kept in ideal environmental conditions and occasionally played by top violinists.

Please accept the enclosed cashier's check for half of the total value of the violin and its case. This is the only way I can feel comfortable with your generosity.

I hope we have the opportunity to meet again someday soon. Give my regards to Tom and the children. You have a family to be proud of.

Sincerely,

Sergei Sapozhnikov

Suzie did not know how long she sat at the table, trembling, staring at the check made out to her.

When Tom came home, Suzie said, "Let's go for a walk before dinner." When they turned onto the trail through the woods, as they often did, she pulled the envelope from her zippered jacket pocket. "Look what came in the mail today," she said as if it were junk mail from an unsolicited insurance company.

"Now who's sending us junk mail?" he laughed. Then he stopped walking. "What's this?"

"Oh, that's a check for twenty-two million dollars. Sergei paid us for the violin. The case was also quite valuable."

They stood on the trail, staring alternately at the check and each other. "How can you be so casual?" he asked.

"If you could see my blood pressure and heart rate, you'd know I'm not all that casual." She put the check and letter back into the envelope and zipped her pocket up tight. "I'm numb, in shock, disoriented," she said. "I guess I'll get excited when we figure out how to share the money with the rest of the family. We should probably start with tax advice," she said. Then she laughed, patting her pocket, "Guess this covers the violin's first-class airline ticket to Paris."

"Holy crap!"

Eiffel's Moon

Paris, 2020

Audrey read an article in *The New York Times* online about the Lyrids Meteor shower, reminding her of the night she spent on the roof with her papa before the Nazis arrested him. And she remembered the night she introduced Aimée to the shooting stars while lying on a quilt in the vineyard.

The article included reports of a previously unrecorded asteroid orbiting the earth. Audrey googled the Swiss scientist who was quoted in the article and emailed his address, asking him to contact her regarding the mini-moon he had discovered.

When he called her a few days later, Audrey explained, in her wavering, aged voice, the purpose of contacting him, "My father was Eiffel Dupré." She thought she heard him gasp, but she went on. "The night before the Nazis dragged him away, he told me about an asteroid caught in earth's orbit. After the war, I found journals he hid before the Nazis came. Would you be interested in seeing his notes?"

She heard silence on the other end. "Are you still there?"

"Oh, yes, sorry," he said.

"Papa would be so happy to know that something became of his research."

"Please forgive me, your information caught me off guard. Your call is well-timed. As you read in the article, no one in the scientific community believes that the asteroid has been in earth's orbit for more than a few years. Professor Dupré's notes would be most valuable to us."

"If you like, you're welcome to come to Paris to see the journals, but I am not ready to let them leave the building. The problem, of course, is the Covid-19 pandemic. We have been isolated since early March. At my age, I need to be careful."

"Since mid-March, my father, who is ninety-five and I have been isolated at our country home outside of Geneva. We've been careful since the beginning of the pandemic, for the same reason."

"When would you like to visit? I think we'll be fine if we all wear masks."

"Is tomorrow too soon? It's usually a six-hour drive from Geneva to Paris, but I'm sure the isolated streets will make the trip much faster," said the scientist. "We will start early."

"That would be fine, I look forward to meeting you both."

"I'll call you with our ETA as we get close to Paris."

Simone answered the door at 1:00 the next afternoon. A chubby man with long gray hair, a hospital mask over his red beard and pale skin stood next to a stooped gentleman, leaning on a cane, his mask pulled up over his mouth and nose like a turtleneck.

"Madame Dupré is expecting you," Simone said through a mask that matched her outfit.

They settled into the chairs Simone had placed six feet apart around Audrey's spindle-back swivel-chair by the piano. The housekeeper served tea, wearing gloves and a mask.

The old man started talking to Audrey, but his mask muffled his raspy voice.

"Sorry to say," Audrey interrupted, "I'm having trouble hearing you. If you stay six feet away, I think we will be safe if you remove your mask while you speak, otherwise I doubt I will understand anything you say,"

The old man pulled the mask from his face, gathering it around his wrinkled throat.

"I was saying, I met your father when I was twelve years old. My father was a music professor at the University of Geneva. When Professor Dupré attended a gathering of local professors welcoming the revered scientist, my father brought me along, much to my mother's chagrin. She thought it quite inappropriate for a child to attend."

The old man smiled, showing his crooked yellow teeth. "After the soiree, Professor Dupré stopped to shake my hand. I remember it so well, he said, 'Hello young man, thanks for coming. Are you interested in the secrets of the universe?' I only nodded, too star-struck to speak. He said, 'Come along, I'll set up the telescope so you can see the planets close up.' That night set the course of my life's work."

With veins like purple cords, the old scientist reached forward to take Audrey's hand, then, remembering the pandemic, leaned back in his chair. "I am so thrilled to meet you. Your father was a great man in so many ways."

"*Merci beaucoup, Monsieur.*" Audrey's arm swept toward the side table. "Please, I'm sure you will find his notes quite interesting, even the entries he wrote when he was a child." Her voice wobbled with age but rang strong and clear, even through the mask.

The younger scientist, himself over seventy, helped the older man stand up and they ambled across the room to the table stacked with variously shaped notebooks. They paused and stared at the journals, as if requesting approval from the esteemed Professor Dupré. "The smallest journal, dated 1922, reports his first sighting of the tiny moon. Of course, the math means nothing to me," said Audrey.

"The math means a great deal to us," said the younger man, pulling his mask below his chin and pushing his fingers through his long gray hair. "What a treasure. Do you mind if I photograph some of the pages?"

"You're welcome to take as many photographs as you want. I hope you don't mind if I play the piano while you work."

He pulled a small digital camera from his worn leather satchel as Audrey played Debussy's "Clair de Lune."

Both men suddenly looked up from the notebooks and stared, their mouths open as if to speak. "A most appropriate selection," said the old man, his eyes twinkling, "Light of the Moon," he whispered. He shuffled back to the chair near Audrey, lowered himself slowly, then recited the last stanza from the poem that inspired Debussy.

> *With the sad and beautiful moonlight,*
> *Which sets the birds in the trees dreaming,*
> *And makes the fountains sob with ecstasy,*
> *The slender water streams among the marble statues.*

Audrey's olive-brown eyes sparkled over her mask as her spotted, boney hands continued to play, "Papa's favorite music. Maman's favorite poem," she said quietly. Through the mask, no one heard.

"You play so beautifully..." said the younger man from across the room. A question seemed to float in the air. *How old are you?*

As if she'd heard the unasked question, she said, "I have played the piano for—let me see—it must be ninety-five years. I started when I was three. My mother bought this Blüthner for my fourth birthday. When the Germans occupied this building, they destroyed everything but my piano and my friend's harp." Warm tears soaked into Audrey's mask. "This year marks seventy-five years since the war ended. Let us leave thoughts of its horror in the past."

Moved by her music, the older man remained in the chair near Audrey while his son photographed the journals. The old scientist also carried unhealed scars from the war. "*Oui*, I agree. Living for today is all we really ever have."

Audrey felt quite comfortable with the old man, as if their memories of the war and their mutual fascination with both music and the stars made them old friends.

"Please stay for an early dinner," said Audrey. "It will not be fancy, but you can finish your work afterward."

Audrey's housekeeper lived in the room once occupied by Simone. Wearing a mask and gloves, she set the table and served their dinner: a cup of *soupe aux légumes, salade niçoise* and bruschetta bread.

Simone and Sergei joined them. The scientists sat facing the windows, while Audrey and her family faced the piano in the opposite direction. They enjoyed Pinot Noir and lively conversation with dinner.

"Tell me, Madame, what is your favorite opera?" the old man asked Audrey.

"That depends," she laughed a deep horse giggle. "Do you mean favorite to play or favorite to listen?"

He lifted his glass, "Tell us both."

"I love playing "*Martern aller Arten*," she said. "It brings to mind starlight playing on a crystal stream and fairy wings in moonlight."

"It is my favorite aria to sing," said Simone. "It's complex, complicated and a challenge. I love the challenge."

"And your favorite to watch?" asked the old man, looking into Audrey's olive-brown eyes.

"Bellini's 'Norma,' especially Act I, shortly after Norma's first entrance, when she sings "Casta Diva." I had the honor of accompanying Maria Callas when she sang for the Paris Opera in 1960. She was magnificent. Even after all these years, I can't get enough of it," smiled Audrey. "I cry every time."

"To Casta Diva," he said, lifting his sparkling crystal wine glass. The old man turned to Sergei. "And Monsieur, what do you like to play?"

Sergei stood by the piano, pausing for effect. "Boogie Woogie I think," he said with a straight face as he played a few bars of "Boogie Woogie Bugle Boy of Company B."

For a moment, no one moved, then Audrey broke into a deep laugh and soon laughter swept the room like a gust of sweet wind. "Oh, Sergei, I love your sense of humor!"

"Actually, I love performing anything Mozart wrote. Perhaps Audrey and I could play our favorite duet?"

"Splendid," said the old man.

They all replaced their masks, moved closer to the piano and Sergei pulled the piano bench next to Audrey's spindle-back swivel-chair. They played "Sonata for two pianos K.448" for their astonished Swiss guests.

"You are quite remarkable. It must take great stamina to play such a piece," said the younger scientist.

"That is a perfect segue for me to take my leave. I am quite tired, but you must stay and photograph the journals, please take your time... or...," Audrey turned in her swivel chair, "or you are welcome to stay the night in our AirB&B suite and resume your work tomorrow. We have not had guests of course since the pandemic but I think we will all be safe enough."

"That is most generous of you, Madame Dupré. Thank you," said the younger scientist.

Audrey turned to Simone. "Will you help them get settled?"

"Of course, Auntie, I'd be happy to." Simone turned to the scientists. "When you're ready, I'll show you the way."

Pulling the old red pashmina over her hunched shoulders, Audrey lifted herself from her spindle-back chair and moved toward her bedroom. She turned toward the small group, "When I leave the planet, I'd like for the journals to go to the university archives in Geneva. Until then, I need to keep Papa close to me." The old gentleman slowly raised himself from his chair, gathered his cane and shuffled toward Audrey. His stooped shoulders bent further to kiss Audrey's hand, more of a gesture than a kiss, considering the mask he wore. Then he pulled down his mask so she could hear. "What a lovely day we've had. *Merci beaucoup, Madame.*" As their faded eyes met, he added, "I only wish I could have met you when we were younger."

"Me too," she said through her mask. Her eyes smiling at him as she squeezed his hand. "Me too." Then she pulled down her mask and added, "I usually have a croissant and coffee at 8:00 a.m., please join me if you can. Good night, *Monsieur.*"

Audrey's 100ᵗʰ Birthday,
Sergei's 84ᵗʰ Birthday

Simone carefully carried the last dusty bottle of Musigny, Bouchard Père & Fils 1937 up the spiraling marble staircase to 3A. After gently dusting the bottle with a soft cloth, she placed it on a silver tray along with the Sommelier's knife and three Waterford, crystal, long-stemmed wine glasses.

As Sergei poured, sunlight from the tall windows refracted off the facets of cut glass. Burgundy shone like liquid rubies.

"Sergei and I have a birthday surprise for you," said Simone as her diminutive frame stood in the curve of the grand piano, her aquamarine eyes sparkling beneath her thick, white eyelashes. Sergei moved to the piano bench and pretended to toss the tales of an imaginary morning coat out of the way before seating himself.

As they performed *"Brindisi"* ("The Drinking Song") from *La Traviata*, Audrey treasured Simone's crystal-clear soprano and Sergei's exquisite technique while savoring the extraordinary Burgundy that had marked turning points throughout her long, music-filled life.

Tears of happiness flowed down Audrey's glowing, wrinkled cheeks, "The best birthday gift in the universe…, the music of my children."

The three crystal wine glasses tinged.

"To your health!"

"для вашего здоровья."

"Santé."

Recipes

Aimée's Recipes

Poule Au Pot
Coq Au Vin
Soupe À L'oignon
Niçoise Salad
Creme Brûlée
Soupe Aux Légumes
Bruschetta Bread
Cassoulet
Mornay Sauce
Chocolate Chunk Cookies

Trudy's Recipes

Duck à l'orange
Bûche de Noël
Thanksgiving Salad

Gertie's Recipes

Thanksgiving Dressing
Cranberry-Jell-O Salad
Cinnamon Rolls
Faux Mashed Potatoes
Gluten-free Brownies

Evelyn's Recipes

Cream Tuna on Toast
Fish and Chips

Recipes available at: marciabreece.com/recipes/

Music

Erik Satie - Gymnopédies,
www.youtube.com/watch?v=wnacdOIoTBQ

Rachmaninoff Piano Concerto no. 1 played by Valentina Lisitsa,
www.youtube.com/watch?v=7W

Mozart Sonata for Two Pianos, K.448 Barenboim & Argerich,
www.youtube.com/watch?v=9iePyP2HOr8

Mendelssohn Violin Concerto E Minor OP.64, Hilary Hahn,
www.youtube.com/watch?v=vzbC39utkTw

Casta Diva - Bellini (Norma, Act 1), Maria Callas,
www.youtube.com/watch?v=s-TwMfgaDC8

Chopin - Etude in G minor., Ingolf Wunder,
www.youtube.com/watch?v=fcRMSgVPsMw

Debussy plays Debussy,
www.youtube.com/watch?v=Yri2JNhyG4k

Mozart - Die Entfuhrung Aus Dem Serail K 384,
www.youtube.com/watch?v=6_qh-VaA-Zg

Boogie Woogie Bugle Boy of Company B,
Written by Don Raye and Hughie Prince
Played by Allen Dale,
www.youtube.com/watch?v=MK0k9Eetgmk

Brindisi - La Traviata - The Drinking Song, Saimir Pirgu,
Venera Gimadieva and The Royal Opera Chorus,
www.youtube.com/watch?v=SK-NUuTCras

Gratitude

The inspiration for this book began in 2018 when my brothers and sisters and I discovered, via DNA testing, that we had a sibling we didn't know about, born when I was about two years old and within days of my younger brother. I was particularly inspired by family members' various reactions to the startling news and by how many of my friends had discovered similar unknown relatives.

Additional inspiration came from Martin Schreiber's *My Two Elaines.* I highly recommend his book to anyone who faces caring for a loved one with Alzheimer's.

During the creative process, feedback and inspiration come from many directions. I appreciate the feedback I received from friends and colleagues. Jilly Eddy (founder and author of *Lipsology, The Art and Science of Lip Print Reading* and *Read My Lips)* gave my manuscript her full attention. Since we were in the middle of the Covid-19 pandemic, we met virtually and I can't thank her enough.

Joe Euro and his staff at The Wine Seller here in Port Townsend offered wine guidance. One day I asked for a bottle of Burgundy and my life changed! "Red or white?" Oh dear!

I also want to thank early readers who gave me valuable guidance and feedback, JoAnn Raines, Sonja Mathews, Rosemary Adang, Ruth Lytle, Anne Cameron, Tess Taft, Mara Lathrop, Betsy Barrow, Julie Anna Guy, Dick Lynn, Mike Neun (author of a very funny novel *Jail Time* and an equally entertaining memoir, *A Semi-Buddhist Ex-Comedian Golf Junkie Finds Joy in the Kingdom of Thailand)* and Rich Nevin, co-creator, writer, actor and producer of the fictional podcast series *String Theories.*

Julie Christine Johnson, (www.juliechristinejohnson.com) author of *The Crows of Beara* and *In Another Life*, provided comprehensive, rigorous writing guidance and editorial feedback. Her compassion and constructive evaluation made the process painless and actually, fun!

Thanks to all of you who made *The Last Bottle* possible.

The Author

Marcia Breece is an American author, memoirist, and self-publishing consultant based near Port Townsend, Washington. Her diverse life experiences—from corporate executive to llama farmer/inn—deeply inform her writing.

Breece began her professional life as a stay-at-home mother before transitioning into a high-powered corporate career in the telecommunications industry. She worked internationally in India, Hong Kong, and Taiwan, helping to establish wireless networks for AT&T Wireless and GTE in the 1990s. Despite the excitement of global travel, she eventually felt unfulfilled, prompting a significant lifestyle change.

In 2005, she left her corporate career to purchase a hobby farm on Washington's Kitsap Peninsula, where she opened a bed and breakfast and, in addition to her guests, cared for llamas, ducks, geese, rabbits, sheep, and chickens. While the experience was enriching, it left little time for writing. She later sold the farm and settled into a quieter life on Discovery Bay.

In addition to her writing, Breece runs Publishing Partners, a consulting service that assists authors with self-publishing, including editing, design, and distribution.

Marcia Breece currently resides in a rural cottage near Discovery Bay, Washington, accompanied by her two Havanese dogs, Dora and Ellie. She finds inspiration in the tranquility of her surroundings, which supports both her writing and her work with fellow authors.

To learn more, visit my website; www.marciabreece.com.

Book Club Discussion Questions

1. Which of the four Burgundy bottle moments in Audrey's life resonated with you most and why: The train ride, the furniture delivery, meeting Sergei, or Audrey's 100th birthday?

2. Did your perception of Audrey shift over the course of the novel? Did your feelings about her change after she reunited with Sergei?

3. DNA results play a major role in the story. Do you think uncovering the truth about one's ancestry brings closure—or chaos?

4. The novel blends historical and contemporary timelines. Did you connect more with the past or present storylines? Why?

5. Food, music and wine are central to this book. How do these elements define the identity of the characters?

6. What does the Stradivarius violin symbolize in the story? How does it link the characters across time?

7. What role does Gertrude Anna play? How do you feel about her DNA revelations?

8. How did the setting—especially Beaune and Paris—enhance the storytelling?

9. Who was your favorite character and which one surprised you the most?

10. The final scene brings several generations together. Did it offer a satisfying resolution? Why or why not?